Copyright:
All rights appertaining to the contents of this book remain the intellectual property of the Author.

A BEAR NAMED

Canadian

JOEY

by

SKIP EVANS

A bear named Canadian Joey is a work of fiction any similarities to actual people is purely coincidental.

Also by Skip Evans: Clive's Drive, Just an Ordinary Joe

Sketches by Skip

Cover design by Skip. Background: original painting by Philip Sandez

Acknowledgements:

With thanks to my own Joey without whose help I'd never have made it through childhood!

My heartfelt gratitude and thanks to all who've blessed me with their love and friendship through my good times and their support and understanding that enabled me make it through the tough ones.

To those I've hurt along my way let me with all my heart that I am truly and deeply sorry.

May you find peace, harmony, wisdom and forgiveness.

With my special thanks to Chris for proof reading for me

Prologue:

dateline: 2009

Stuart Wheeler stirred in his armchair and pressed the off button on his remote, his large flat-screen TV blinked and went black. He'd had enough of the output of the recorded nonsense stored-up in his Sky+ box for one day. He ambled through to the kitchen to make himself a cup of coffee, rummaging in one of the cupboards while the water boiled, for a Chorley cake to go with it. Coffee in hand he wandered through to his 'den' munching on the Chorley cake as he went and plonked himself down into his battered old leather armchair, it sagged welcomingly beneath his weight. He leant over, clicked the gas fire on and settled back in the chair, finishing off the nibbled-around centre bit of the Chorley cake and swilling its residue down with his coffee.

He rested the cup on the denim fabric of his jeans and let his head rest back onto the chair. Closing his eyes he listened to the slow and steady *tick-tock, tick-tock* of the round-faced old clock up on the wall above the fireplace. He felt quite sleepy. He was tired, he felt tired a lot lately or was he just jaded? He'd recently turned sixty, a month or so back and whether or not it was in the mind he really was beginning to feel his age.

Draining the remainder of his coffee he looked up at the clock, it was very special to him. It had been a gift from his mum many years ago, given to him when he'd first moved into his house.

She had acquired it from a family friend who'd worked for British Rail, he had come across it through his position at the time and knowing how Stuart had always been an avid railway enthusiast and in particular how fond he'd been of the local railway and 'his' station… well before Dr.Beeching's axe had fallen closing it all down…

Stuart rose from his chair discarding the empty coffee mug onto his desk as he went. He opened one of the glazed doors of the large bookcase that occupied a whole wall of the room, reached in then ever so gently and lovingly lifted out a very old, yet remarkably well preserved teddy bear from off the shelf. He returned to his chair and sat down with the bear facing him on his lap. It was wearing knitted garments that his mum had made for him half a century ago, the bear had two knitted eyes, a knitted nose and mouth and had patches on its face where its fabric appeared to have been restored... It was clearly a well-loved bear!

Stuart lifted the bear and sat it in the crook of his arm, "you remember the clock don't you Joey?" He pointed up at the round wooden clock, "from the waiting room at the station?" He wrapped his arm around the battered old bear, hugging it to himself and closed his eyes, of course Joey remembered the clock! His mind wandered back in time, to a place existing only in his memory now, a place where a young boy and his bear had lived in a world full of wonder and discovery, where each and every experience had been vivid and new... such adventures they'd had! What an imagination he'd possessed in those days... or so 'they' said...

This time he made no attempt to resist the rising warmth and darkness as it swept up over him and in moments he was fast asleep...

Chapter One

Burgulars

Stuart Wheeler   born: 21st January 1950

...go, the ...ear
...mouth and had patches on
...ared to have been ... . It w
...ear!

...ear and sa...
...lock don't ...
...n clock, "fro...
...d his arm arou...
...and closed his ...
...s mind wandered b...   ing
...is memory now, a...   and h
...d lived in a ...   ery, wh
...nd ever...   w... such
nture...

It wasn't that it was particularly unusual for Stuart to [wake] before the alarm, he'd often just have to go over to the window to take a look at the blackbird singing in the tree outside his bedroom window, even though it was only first light and the birds were still tuning-up for the day with their dawn chorus, the bird song always seemed wonderful, it was amazingly shrill and clear at this hour set as it was against the still quiet of the sleeping town, or sometimes he would get up in the night to watch the flashes of lightning light up the shiny wet roofs of the houses across the street and feel the thunder as it made the very ground shake and their own house tremble on its foundations. Pushing his nose against the glass he would lick at the rivulets of water streaming down the outside of the glass, before charging back across the bedroom and diving under the covers of his bed, snuggle around until he found the warm spot he had left, and with the soft sheets and comforting weight of his big eiderdown and candlewick bedspread over him he would soon drift off again to sleep, provided of course he was hugging Joey.

What was unusual on this particular morning was that there in the middle of the empty bed with the covers flung back, lying with his head in the dinged-in feather pillow, where Stuart's head had been was Joey. This might not seem unusual to anyone who did not know Stuart, I mean where else would you leave a Teddy bear?

The point was though that Stuart would never get out of bed and leave Joey behind, I mean, who would he show the lightning to or hug tightly when... one... two... three... four... CRASH!!!! The thunder came after the lightning, or who would he encourage to wave from behind the curtains to the milkman as his electric milk float came whirring along the

.reet with its milk bottles all clink-clinking? Who would he laugh with as the rag and bone man came along with his old cart rolling heavily along on its metal clad wooden wheels, pulled by his big old horse, lazily clip-clopping, with his crazy bellows of *Raaa-bnnn*...then the horse lifting its tail to nonchalantly let out a stream of steaming round poo-bombs! Although even funnier was the old man from across the road who'd scurry out afterwards with his shovel and a bucket and scoop them all up! Stuart would roll around laughing. Admittedly Joey didn't laugh much over the horse poo, but even so there'd be no point in bothering looking out would there without someone else to share it with?

Joey wasn't just someone though, he was one of the most beloved teddy bears there had ever been. He had befriended Stuart when he was a newborn baby after having travelled all the way from Canada, across The Atlantic Ocean along with Stuart's Uncle Arnold, who was his dad's older brother. Boy and bear had been inseparable ever since, he was the best friend a boy could ever have wished for. When he had arrived he had the most wonderful velvety soft, brown and golden fur all over his body, now eight years later he was getting a little worse for wear, patches of his skin were threadbare and Stuart's mum had to 'operate' on him at regular intervals. He had long ago lost his original eyes, his nose and mouth, but mum had set to with her darning needle and although Stuart wasn't totally convinced that Joey would still be able to see properly through eyes made from wool… he reluctantly had to agree that he would probably be able to see just as well with them as he had using the glass buttons he'd had sewn on previously!

So where was Stuart this morning? It was still only five forty-five according to the hands on the big round alarm clock ticking on the bedside cabinet that stood alongside Stuart's bed. The toy soldier (who stood to attention on top of the clock, poised as ever, ready for action with his two big shiny brass symbols to wake Stuart at ten-to-seven) was looking anxiously over at Joey, the significance of Stuart being out of bed alone was not lost on him. It was always obvious when he was getting anxious as his big moustache which curled up at each end would start to twitch as his mouth started working in sequence with his chin being pushed out and his neck stretching as if he was struggling with the top button of his bright red tunic being a tad too tight. It always happened for a few minutes before the alarm was due to go off and he was itching to start bashing his symbols, Stuart used to peep out from under the covers some mornings to catch him doing it and would laugh at him, which only made him even more anxious and the sides of his neck to go bright red with embarrassment as well.

He felt like bashing his symbols now to sound the alarm but his strict military training wouldn't allow it, orders were orders and his orders stated quite specifically that ten to seven was when he sounded the alarm, not eleven minutes to or nine minutes to… but ten to, precision was everything! Quite specific, no room for manoeuvre, not open to debate, damned orders! He could see Joey's eyes peering around desperately trying to see where Stuart was, and looking more frantic by the minute. "It's no good, you're going to have to go and look for him, I'd go myself, but I can't leave my post, orders is orders you see," he called over to the bear, who lay still for a moment agonising over what to do before rolling across the bed and sliding down the edge of the candlewick bedspread onto the floor. "I say, good show Joey old chap" encouraged the soldier up on the cabinet, "Best have a reconnoitre see if you can spot the little blighter," "Ssshush!" he responded turning to face the room… all was quiet. Turning back he crouched down to look under the bed, it wasn't that he expected to find anything under there, there never was, if he had a jar of honey for every time Stuart had begged him to look and see if the monster was under there, as he would hang him upside down over the side of the bed by his legs to look. Sometimes he would tease Stuart "Quick! quick! Pull me back up… its horrible, the green eyes, the giant sharp white teeth, the claws… it's coming for me… STUART QUICK!" the little lad would pull him back with a scream till he could feel Joey shaking with laughter and though he was annoyed for a second or two, he was soon laughing as well and tickling Joey till he begged him to stop, as he giggled inbetween saying "Big green eyes" and "giant sharp white teeth." Then they would lie together and invent more and more terrible attributes for the monster, until Stuart would start yawning and was soon fast asleep. Joey would smile to himself contentedly, before nodding off again himself, he had learnt a long, long time ago that laughing at your fears was often the best way of dealing with them.

This morning though when he looked under the bed all he could see there to his real horror were Stuart's chequered-brown carpet slippers, sat just where he had left them last night. Stuart's bedroom had polished floorboards as did most of the house, although he did have a nice rug at the side of his bed, at least on one side and as Joey said if you start the day by getting out of bed on the wrong side, well… the point was that it being February the floor was cold, Stuart wouldn't go off in bare feet, he'd leave that to Joey (bear feet! It was the sort of joke Stuart teased Joey with all the time). But Joey wasn't chuckling now, a deep furrow had formed in the soft brown velvety fur between his eyebrows as he frowned with concentration sidling his way around the side of the bed to the bottom where the wooden board now towered over him. He cautiously peeped his head around the corner. Nothing. The bedroom was empty and apart from the bluey white glow of the streetlight through the gaps around the curtains it was in darkness. Or was it? No… there… under the door onto the landing there was a flicker of light. Someone, maybe Stuart was going downstairs carrying a light. Throwing caution to the wind Joey ran across the open floor to the door and diving down to lie face down on the floor craned his neck to try and see underneath it. He caught a glimpse of a shadow as it moved along the wall at the side of the staircase and then nothing.

Back up on his feet once more he rubbed some dust from his chest, he had to get out onto the landing to find out what was going on. Suppose Stuart was in some kind of trouble. What if it wasn't Stuart he'd seen moving about? What if it was BURGULARS!? As Stuart had once referred to those rascals as, those wicked crooks that break into other people's homes… to steal things! More to the point he thought to himself… what if he couldn't get out of the bedroom! How was he going to open the door? It was firmly shut and the handle was way up above his head… he leant back so far looking up at it that he fell over and landed with a bump on his bottom! He sat there for a moment with his paws resting on the floor either side of his short little legs before he noticed Stuart's dressing gown hanging on the back of the door. "Oh my goodness, gracious me!" he mumbled, "He'll freeze to death with no slippers or dressing gown on." Then with a flash of inspiration he grasped the thick ropey cord of the dressing gown that was hanging just above his head and began to pull himself bodily up the door. 'Maybe this wasn't such a good idea!' He thought to himself as he looked down over his shoulder at the distance he was up above the floor already. He felt beads of sweat begin to break out on his forehead and gulped, which in turn made him realise just how empty his tummy was, it was a long time since he'd shared Stuart's Horlicks and shortbcake biscuits at bedtime! 'Nearly there, what a brave bear you are,' he told himself, only as a form of encouragement, as he was always doing so for Stuart. Suddenly to his horror the cord began to slide through the loops at the sides of Stuart's dressing gown. He scrabbled frantically with all his might up the belt as it slid faster and faster through his paws, then with a mighty effort he grabbed at the edge of the pocket... He swung there trembling with fear and exertion as the dressing gown swayed back and forth on the brass hook that was fixed halfway up the door, as the belt slid silently away into a neat coil on the floor. "My word sir! Jolly good show old boy!" called over the alarm clock soldier, who was still the only other one awake in the bedroom.

"What now?" Mused Joey as he noticed that although the handle to the door was out of his reach, it was nearer some of the time than others! Having pondered this phenomena for a moment or two trying to figure out why this was so, and then telling himself what a clever bear he was for eventually doing so, he proceeded to use his weight to make the dressing gown swing further and further across the door until in an act of sheer heroism, for which he could (even as he did it) envisage himself being given a medal by The Queen, at a garden party at Buckingham Palace, having honey butties and tea on the lawwwnnnnn... he nearly missed grabbing the handle of the door, the sweat that was now pumping out all over him had made the fur on his paws slippery, 'Concentrate Joey, concentrate!' he said shakily to himself. The next bit was easy. He shifted his weight along and pulled down on the end of the handle, the latch clicked and the door swung open an inch or two. Now what? The floor was a dizzyingly long way below him. He remembered how much it had hurt when Stuart had pushed him out of bed, by 'accident' of course and he'd landed on his head on the floor, especially as it was on the WRONG side of the bed with no rug to land on! Stuart had been very sorry and kissed his head better for him but... Stuart! That was what this was all about, without a second thought the little bear let go and landed with a soft bump on his head behind the door. 'Oh well, best place to land, it's got the most sawdust in it as Stuart would say,' he thought lazily as his world dissolved into a shower of spinning stars...

It was so hot in the Kasbah today, he hated living here, the sand seemed to cling to his sweaty fur, the heat of the sun made him dizzy, till his head swum. The strange exotic noise of a snake charmers flute resonated in his ears, ugh... snakes! Joey didn't care for them at all, horrible slithery things that they were, and always poking their horrible little tongues out at you too! He rubbed at his eyes to attempt to clear his vision as the music buzzed louder and louder in his ears. There before him to his horror coming through the mist of his gradually clearing vision was a giant snake. Most of its body was coiled up but the rest trailed across the dusty street towards him, its strange hairy head was almost upon him! "Aghhh!! a snake!" Exclaimed Joey, attempting to back away but unable to do so as he was still sat down. "Help! Somebody help me!" He called out with rising terror.

"I say down there, steady on, pull yourself together man!" Joey heard the reassuring voice of the soldier from the alarm clock, he turned confused to see him peering down over the edge of the bed side cabinet, "It's only the blinking cord of the dressing gown in front of you, have you gone stark-staring bonkers? Eh what? Speak up man!"

"For the record sergeant, I am a bear, I have always been a bear, and I shall always remain a bear. I have a nasty bump on my head and I feel really quite poorly." Nevertheless he could feel himself blushing with embarrassment, so he turned quickly away from the soldier, so he wouldn't notice.

He staggered up onto his shaky little legs and wobbled over to the gap between the door and the casing. He peered out onto the dark landing, which was still, quiet and cold. He listened intently to see if he could hear anything at all. Apart from a slight hissing in his ears there was nothing save for the rhythmical tick-tock of the big clock that hung on the wall downstairs in the hall, lost far off somewhere in the empty gloom that Joey now peered apprehensively out into from the landing through a gap inbetween the banisters.

'Oh Stuart, what are you up to?' He asked himself as he worked his way along to the big post at the top of the stairs. The stairs fell away before him into the darkness, he shuddered partly with the cold but also from his fear of the stairs. He normally went down them hugging onto Stuart, or being dangled by his paw from Stuart's hand. This in itself could be quite a scary way to go down as Stuart had a habit of hurling himself down the stairs in a whirlwind of flying legs, spinning himself around the corner halfway down from the corner post and then jumping down the last four steps into the hall. This seemed to agree with Stuart as he usually accompanied this procedure with long exuberant whoops, Spitfire noises or cries of G-e-r-o-n-i-m-o!! Meanwhile Joey would trail from his flailing free hand sometimes ricocheting off the banisters or the wall. He would always tell Stuart off about it afterwards, not that it made any difference, he also ignored his mum's comments of "Stuart! how many times do I have to tell you to WALK down the stairs, DON'T RUN, you'll hurt yourself" With the last part very rudely mimed along with by Stuart accompanied by one of the silliest faces he could contort his face into.

This was getting him nowhere, it was a well-known and acknowledged fact that Bears were prone to rambling thoughts and not staying to the point, prevaricating, or was it procrastinating he mused… "Stop it!" he said out loud to himself as he found himself doing it again! He pulled himself upright as if the sergeant had said "Attennnntion!" as he did to Stuart in the mornings, 'What we need is a plan' he told himself, rubbing ruefully at his little round and very empty tummy, which had just grumbled up at him again. Naturally enough this made him think of honey, jars of honey, on the shelf in the larder. Then it came to him in a flash of inspiration. "Paprika!" he exclaimed (using one of Stuart's favourite exclamations) as he spun around, yes the bathroom door was open. He scampered across the dimly lit landing and into the bathroom. Once inside he stopped, panting and checking out the room. Without further ado he grabbed hold of the towel hanging from the rail lost in the dark above him. Hanging onto both sides of it this time he climbed up the edge of the bath and clambered onto the wooden ledge at the end. Next he gingerly lifted the lid of the laundry chute, my but it was heavy. How on earth was he going to get into it and hold it open at the same time? More to the point did he really want to? What he had caught a glimpse of did not seem inviting at all, darkness, pitch black darkness and lots of it! 'Hmm… what would Stuart do?' he pondered… probably fling up the lid and make a mad dive for the opening, resulting in him ending-up trapped half-way in by the heavy lid, to be left dangling with his legs in the bathroom and his head and arms in that horrible black chasm! Ughh… he shuddered. He looked around the shelf for something he could use to wedge open the lid, aha! Stuart's tooth brush, as usual tossed down, covered in unused and wasted toothpaste and not put back in the cup on the shelf over the sink where it belonged. He shook his head, how untidy that boy could be. Nevermind he thought, his untidiness was fortunate for Joey on this occasion, 'this'll do just fine' he muttered to himself as he levered the lid open as far as he could, his arm was shaking violently with the exertion… then he stuck the toothbrush in the gap to act as a prop, just like the metal rod Stuart's dad used to prop open the bonnet of the car when he was doing 'his maintenance' on the engine. The toothbrush bent ominously and slipped a little, he shut his eyes, and cringed, waiting for the crash... nothing happened, he opened one eye and peeped, Stuart had taught him that it was always better to 'only risk one eye' in tricky situations like these. The toothbrush had held! He sighed with relief, but only for a moment as he peered once more into the seemingly bottomless black abyss.

Mum usually left the linen basket at the bottom of the shoot, didn't she? The linen basket usually had dirty washing in it didn't it, unless it was wash-day! Well, if it had dirty clothes in it, they would make for a soft landing he thought optimistically, but what if… oh why… why was there always *what ifs*? They were a mighty troublesome commodity *what ifs* were! Nevertheless, what if the linen basket wasn't there? The laundry room had a cold and very hard stone floor, or worse still what if he landed on Stuart's dirty under-pants, or dad's smelly socks? What if he was trapped in the linen basket surrounded by smelly socks and dirty underpants? "Yuk! Yuk! Yuk!!!" He muttered to himself shaking his head with his nose curled up in disgust. There must be a way, "Where there's a will there's a way" Stuart's mum always told Stuart, invariably to be followed by Stuart's dad saying "aye and where there's a will there's relations!" Which he thought was really funny but Stuart didn't get it at all.

Right let's analyse the situation he thought, sitting down on the edge of the shelf, leaning his head on his paw and putting on his most intelligent facial expression. His trusty thinking companion, who was now materialising before him looked up from the bathroom floor, "Well Professor Joseph, what do you advise as a suitable course of action?" Holmes was accustomed to turning to his mentor for advice when his wits had failed him so was glad to offer his help now, "Elementary my dear Sherlock" Joey replied in his best 'clipped, educated university voice,' "We analyse all aspects of the problem, then taking into account our experience and knowledge, whilst bearing in mind the resources we currently have available to us, we come up with a solution. So Sherlock, what is the problem before us? We wish to travel down a vertical shaft of indeterminate but quite considerable length without injury. Injury would be caused as a result of the speed at which we travel, or more precisely by the speed we accelerate up to and more pertinently by the momentum which we acquire, therefore we must slow down our rate of acceleration and therefore the rate of our descent. My solution to this problem therefore is to avail ourselves of the aid of a parachute!" Holmes removed the pipe from his mouth and looked up in admiration at his mentor, "Sir Joseph how will I manage when I no longer have you to advise me?" "Nonsense fellow, you'll do just fine" and to be fair he hadn't done too bad at all in his later years.

Joey jumped up to his feet and looked for a parachute. The flannel was big enough but far too heavy, besides it was damp, all that would happen if he tried to use that was that it would flop down on top of him! No he needed something much lighter. He fumbled around in the dark, fortunately there was a small amount of light filtering in from the street light coming through the bubbly glass of the bathroom window, the trouble was though it made lots of dark shapes and shadows around the room as well, shapes that looked suspiciously like monsters! Not deterred he searched on. Aha… just the job, one of dad's hankies that Stuart had borrowed and not put away, hmm… we'd better not concern ourselves too much about the damp bit! Joey quickly tied the two corners of each side together in two neat little knots. Stuart had been amazed how ambidextrous Joey was, with such stubby paws once before, when he had made a paper aeroplane for him. Joey had made him promise the Bear's sacred promise that he never tell anyone how he'd done it, and revealed to him the closely guarded secret of teddy bears paws, he also corrected Stuart pointing out that it was manual dexterity he was referring to not ambidexterity, which was the ability of being able to use both hands equally well, "Big head, big head, your head so full of saw-dust, you big head!" Stuart had sung contemptuously at him, oh the secret, well now…. I may tell you one day if you are really good!

Anyway Joey now grasped the two tiny knots as tightly as he could with his fingers, which in common with all teddy bears retract into their paws, very much in the way a cat's claws retract when not in use. Holding on very tightly and resisting the urge to shout "Geronimo!" (Stuart-style), he gingerly slid his chubby little body past the toothbrush and launched himself into the void.

Chapter Two

Happy Landings

Happy Landings

Joey cleared the edge of the laundry shoot and fell... The darkness...

WWwoooooshed!!!..... up at him...

as did his little heart, which he thought was just about to leap up from his throat where it appeared to now be stuck thankfully and it hadn't been able to fly right out of his mouth! Suddenly he felt as if he was tugged upwards by the hanky-parachute. The tug was so hard he nearly let it slip through his paws, but good old fashioned panic prevailed and his paws gripped at the cotton so hard they hurt. He realised that he was still falling but much more slowly now though. He looked down and could see a faintly lit square at the bottom of the shoot, "Oh my!" he exclaimed as he saw just how fast it was coming up at him, and sure enough there was the linen basket, he imagined he could almost smell the stench of dad's socks, no it was real! He COULD smell the stench! No time for indecision this, he was rotating slowly as he fell, and as he swung to one side he pushed deftly with one foot against the back of the shoot and bumped off the side lip of the linen basket to land reasonably softly on the laundry room floor alongside of it. "Phew! Elementary my dear Holmes!" he made a small bow to the imaginary miniature figure of Sherlock Holmes who had somehow already arrived at the bottom, he nodded slightly and made a silent gesture of clapping at his heroes latest triumphant exploit, then puffing on his pipe he turned away.... vanishing into his cloud of tobacco smoke.

Joey quickly crossed the laundry room floor to the back room, Stuart's mum and dad referred to it as the breakfast room. It was the small room previously used by the servants who had once lived in their house in Victorian days. High up on the wall in the corner by the door was an old fashioned wooden box with a glass front which had lots of little clear glass windows within the design that was painted on the inside of the glass. When you pressed a bell push in the other rooms of the house a bell rang alongside the box and a little marker swung about in one of the windows. Each window had a name underneath it, Lounge, Dining Room, etc. Stuart used to love pressing the buttons and then running as fast as he could to see the marker still swinging, his finest achievement had been running into every room that had a bell push, pushing it and running so fast that he could get to the breakfast room quickly enough so that he could see all the markers still swinging at once! "That'd give the servants a fine headache!" He laughed to Joey! "Indeed" was all the little bear could say as he felt like his eyes were swinging about in a similar fashion to the markers after flying around the house at the end of Stuart's flailing, trailing arm… Stuart would carry on doing this until his mother would become so exasperated with him that she would yell at him to… "STOP!"

The breakfast room was warmed by a coal fire which burned in a big black metal grate. In the winter mum would put a big shovel full of 'slack' onto it last thing at night, (this was all the dusty stuff that was at the bottom of the coal-hole). Stuart thought it was going to put the fire out but Joey explained to him how coal as all things required oxygen to burn, and by covering all the hot coals with the dusty slack it slowed down the fire's combustion till it could only smoulder. In the morning a brisk prodding with the big brass poker let the air get back into the glowing embers and away the fire went again. "Brain box!" had been Stuart's only response to Joey's careful and detailed explanation.

Well it wouldn't get going again this morning, for it already had… been got going! And there was Stuart sat on the hearth rug in front of the fire, illuminated by the warm rosy glow of a roaring fire!

"Stuart what on earth are you up to!" snapped Joey in a much less than friendly manner, "you just have no idea what I've had to do to..." his voice trailed off as he noticed that Stuart was completely oblivious to him, he just continued to sit stock still staring blankly into the flames. "Stuart are you alright?" he asked with mounting concern, a slight tremble creeping into his voice. He padded over to the little boy, feeling the welcome warmth of the fire, his fur turning a glowing red flickering colour to match the front of Stuart's striped pyjamas. He looked into Stuart's eyes, nothing. He waved a paw in front of his face, again nothing, not even a blink. "Oh my!" he exclaimed "sleepwalking! Well I never" and he hadn't, in all his years he had never seen anyone sleep-walking although he knew as well as anyone that you must 'never try and wake them up!'

So he sat down alongside his friend and lent his head on Stuart's arm. He was so tired after his exertion that before he knew it he felt that lovely warm glowing feeling as you slip off to sleep, 'Burgulars! Pah! Should have known it wasn't burgulars...' Joey was suddenly shocked in the most terrifying manner imaginable back to wakening by the deeply whispered voice of a man! "That cookie kid didn't have a teddy bear with him before did he?"

"Teddy bear? what the blummin 'eck are you goin'on about, I told yer to look for valuables, ignore the little brat and get looking!" Joey tried to look at the man without turning his head or moving his eye balls too much, the man was tall and thin, gangly you would call him, with a filthy flat hat on over his dirty grey looking hair that needed cutting badly (no it was already badly cut!!! How can you think flippant thoughts at a time like this Joey? He mentally reprimanded himself). Now he was peering down at Joey with his horrible little eyes that were way too close together, 'Oh no, he's seen my eyes move he's coming!' Joey thought! The man stooped down and stared point blank into Joey's face, his breath smelt awful, Joey felt his nose was going to twitch at any minute when the man roughly grabbed him and unceremoniously stuffed him inside his jacket. 'Oh the smell!' Joey muttered to himself. In common with the rest of his appearance the man's jacket was horribly dirty and smelt of something grimy and oily, Joey didn't know if he felt more sick or more terrified. He wanted to shout out to Stuart to help him but he mustn't, for one thing you must never wake sleepwalkers, for another the horrible man would also hear him and last but not least if he woke Stuart, the boy would then be in terrible danger himself. The burgulars didn't seem to care about him now as he was obviously asleep, but if he woke up it could be a different matter. So hard although it was he kept quiet.

"What'cher doin!" The first voice demanded angrily, "I just thought this bear'd be nice for my littel Alice, that's all I just ..." the first man cut him off short with "get the heck out of 'ere now!" He glanced up at the ceiling and gestured with his thumb, "I think somebody's up an' about up there" and they both scurried around like thieving rats picking up bags. Joey took the opportunity whilst the man bent down and his jacket went loose to quickly turn himself around so he could see out of the jacket. The man was climbing out through the breakfast room window. He turned around to take the bags off the other villain, Joey saw his face too now and what a face! If ever there was someone who looked like a villain this was the man. He'd thought his accomplice to be pretty evil looking but this man's face took the biscuit, and the mug of milky Horlicks with it thought Joey.

He had an enormous hooked nose with deeply etched lines either side of it going down to his thin-lipped mouth, which framed the most horrible broken and blackened teeth you could imagine, he looked as if he was just starting to grow a beard which was patchy with grey bits here and there. But it was his eyes that were the worst of all. Apart from the fact that he was boss-eyed, his one eye, the one that looked at you made you shiver and that was just what Joey was doing now as the man was looking right at him as he regaled his accomplice. "What the bloomin-eck yer got the kids bear for? You great steamin' nit..!" "I told yer I thought it would be nice for Alice" "it's a good job for you he didn't wake up, takin' a kids bear, didn't you think it might just wake 'im up, stupid? Eh? Didn't you think? No yer too blummin stupid to think, I 'as to do all the thinkin' 'round 'ere don'I" the evil looking man continued his tirade of whispered and muttered abuse all the while as they scurried down through the darkness at the side of the house till they reached the front garden, which was dimly lit by the street light in the road. They slipped quickly along the side of the privet hedge that grew between Stuart's home and Mr and Mrs Ramsbottom's next door and out of the open gate.

There an old van was parked facing up the street, Joey knew it was an old van because it had big headlamps fixed on top of its front mudguards. Stuart and Joey were experts on the motors that they saw in the streets. By now the men were throwing the bags in through the open back doors of the van. "Ere give me that blummin bear!" The evil man growled and snatched Joey so hard out of the man's jacket that he nearly squealed out loud, "Yer look like a flamin' big Nancy" and without any further thought he tossed Joey unceremoniously into the back of the van. He landed with a bump against something hard and metallic. He sat rubbing his sore head as the men slammed the back doors to the van no longer trying to be quiet and then ran around and jumped into the front. The evil man was sat in the driver's seat, Joey could hear him muttering and swearing as he struggled to start the ancient vehicle. The engine turned over once or twice groaning slowly and then gave up the ghost. "What'cher waitin' fer idiot, get out and crank it!" The evil man shouted at the other villain having already thrown all attempts at being quiet to the wind in his mounting panic. He shoved angrily at his shoulders as 'the idiot' struggled to get quickly out of the door. Joey could feel a giggle coming on as he thought to himself that this was getting to be like watching one of those silly Laurel and Hardy films that Stuart's dad liked to watch. The idiot was round the front of the car now swinging on the crank handle to turn the reluctant engine of the old van, "come on, come on, put some beef into it will ya!" the villain sat behind the wheel cursed at him. The van backfired and spun the crank-handle backwards in the idiot's hand. He let out a yelp of pain as the metal handle belted him on the funny-bone, he hopped up and down rubbing frantically at his arm, trying not to shout out loud in his agony. Uglyface, sat behind the wheel banged his fists against the steering wheel in frustration, cursing furiously. "Try again you blithering idiot!!" Joey was biting on his arm by now trying to stifle his laughter lest it gave him away.

The idiot came back to the front of the van and seemed to loom up over the bonnet, a terrible black rage was etched across his evil face, he rammed the handle into the slot and spun at it with such ferocity that the van's engine spluttered, coughed and then roared into life!

Now Joey was in a real panic, he was about to be driven away from home, from Stuart and what's more driven away with a pile of mum and dad's stuff that was here in the back of the van with him, stuff that the villainous thieves had purloined!! He had to do something, the idiot was already halfway back to the door brandishing the crank handle in the air with a hideous grin on his face as if he had just achieved some great victory with it, "gerra ruddy move on will ya!" snarled Uglymug as he revved at the engine furiously, creating great clouds of smoke from the exhaust at the back of the old banger of a van.

He told the tale later of how his mind cleared, time had seemed to slow down as destiny and bear came together in a moment of clarity, bravery and strategy! It really did seem that way to him as the man moved in what now seemed to be slow-motion for Joey as he scanned around the back of the van… there was a metal funnel sticking out from a wooden box of tools just behind the driver's seat and in a flash he had leapt across and had it in his paws even as the man made his next step, he lifted it up and placed the narrow end to his lips and even as the man's scrawny backside hit the seat and he was reaching across to pull the door shut behind him… Joey shouted down the funnel "STOP POLICE! You are surrounded! Turn off the engine and step out of the van!" The van leapt forward as Uglymug had grinded the gears in and had then let the clutch out roughly, then in sheer panic he had insanely hit the brakes when he heard 'stop Police!' The idiot had been flung forward so hard he'd belted his noggin slap-bang into the windscreen which had cracked right across like a spiders web and he'd then slumped back into the seat completely out for the count. Uglymug who had stalled the van with his incompetent driving and startled reaction, now leapt out of it in a blind funk and proceeded to run away pell-mell down the street but at the same time trying to look back to see where the police were coming from!

Joey had fallen backwards as the van jolted and had ended up sat in a heap with the funnel stuck on top of his head! He laughed out loud at the outcome of the villains response to his intervention, his master-plan, his heroics! He scrambled up over the mess in the back of the van into the front between the back of the seats and climbed onto the driver's seat where he proceeded to push at the horn button in the centre of the big old steering wheel, the old van had a lovely loud horn and it parped out a treat five or six times before the battery gave out completely. The idiot who was slumped in the passenger seat opened an eye and stared wide-eyed for a moment at the little bear who was stood up on the driver's seat, with a funnel on his head parping away at the horn, he tried to lift his hand to point and his mouth began to move as he tried to say something, but he passed into oblivion again before he'd managed either.

Typical! Joey thought of the idiots that were using the van not to maintain the vehicle properly, unlike Stuart's dad who did a thorough check over on their car every Sunday! Letting the battery run down like that, utter incompetence!

Meanwhile the thought also occurred to him of Stuart being woken-up by all this commotion as he sat on the floor of the breakfast room… and well… well… what was it that *actually* did happen if something woke up a sleep-walker?

It didn't matter it, wasn't going to be good, and if Joey had his way it wasn't going to happen either and with that he slid himself down onto his tummy and out of the driver's door which was still wide open after the villains flight from the van, he stood for a moment. He was trembling violently and feeling more than a little dizzy. When in the company of humans, especially children, Joey could move with ease and 'talk till the cows come home' as Stuart so rudely put it, to be technical it was called the 'energy of innocents,' or so they'd told him. Good children give off a pure energy, positive waves that in the right circumstances enable bears, and other toys to come to life, but as soon as a grown-up enters the room the energy changes. Joey used to marvel at the swirling mists of energy he could perceive, invisible to human eyes. He used to marvel from whatever position he happened to be in as he would freeze up in the energy void created when Stuart's energy was cut off from him. The trip downstairs had used up nearly all of his reserves, his close encounter of the smelly kind with the burgular and his mate's evil energies had almost made him black-out! Uglymug who had tried to dash so recklessly away from the van had collided almost immediately with a cast iron lamppost whilst looking backwards over his shoulder! He now lay half on the pavement, half in the road, dazed and with his head about only a yard or two from Joey as he stood leaning with one paw on the van. His eyes rolled and he groaned and muttered, "It was 'im there! It was the bear!" He tried to stir and Joey realised he could see him, he became more agitated, flailing his arms helplessly, "there 'e is, a tells yer, there 'e is." The tall Policeman who now stood over the prostrate man shook his head slowly, fortunately he had his back to Joey as he proceeded to put his handcuffs on the villain, taking no notice of the man's ramblings, despite him pointing directly at Joey as the shiny metal bracelets clicked tightly shut on his wrists… Joey in typically Stuartesque manner poked his tongue out at him and sticking his thumbs in his ears wiggled his fingers at him. Stuart would have been so proud of him… Stuart!

In an agonising and painfully slow movement Joey staggered back across the pavement into the cover of the shadow cast by the privet hedge. It seemed to take forever for him to get to the back door and to tumble in head first through the cat flap! He landed in a heap on the kitchen floor and sat dusting cat hairs off his fur as the flap clattered shut behind him and the funnel which had dislodged from off his head on his first attempt to gain access into the flap was now clanging away outside as it rolled away across the yard's stone flags! He wobbled across the kitchen to the breakfast room door, just as the door from the hall swung open and the light switch clicked on, he froze in mid-step and fell to the floor spinning around once in a neat little pirouette to end up just inches from where Stuart had been sat. Yes, <u>had</u> been sat, for there was no longer any sign at all of the sleepwalking boy!

"What on earth are you doing down here Joey?" dad asked as he bent down and scooped up the little bear. Joey was swooshed upwards from the breakfast room floor with such speed that he felt all the blood rush to his feet. In a moment of confusion he was just about to explain what he was doing there when he remembered he really shouldn't, then realised in dad's presence he probably couldn't anyway and he became the stuffed toy that he really was (well as far as the rest of the world was concerned!)

"This means that Stuart's been down here, the little monkey," dad frowned as he realised the implications of his little son being downstairs at the same time as the burglars, "My goodness if those rotter's have scared my little lad I'll, I'll..." Joey never got to find out what dad would do to them, although he thought it probably to be something terrible, punch them on the nose I'd say, he added to himself, and dad could do it too, he'd been a soldier in the war, but at that moment mum had come into the room as well, she was holding Lucy's hand, Lucy was rubbing her sleepy eyes with her free hand and forearm. "Look mummy Stuart's teddy has got a black mouth!" she laughed as she pointed at the bear. "Oh my! So he has!" Mum took the bear from dad's hand and stared at his face laughing. "What have you been up to Joey?" she asked looking at the little bear, who did in fact have a black oily ring around his mouth, and around his head too. "Just look at the state of his paws, they're covered in soil and dirt, and he's all wet, what on earth has Stuart been up to with him? He must have been outside with him!" Mum looked anxiously at dad and they both said at the same time "where is Stuart?" Lucy giggled to think Stuart was in trouble again, he was always in trouble, sometimes she even helped him to get there! Dad ran upstairs and looked into Stuart's bedroom. He closed the door quietly and came back down the stairs to meet mum and Lucy in the hall, "he's fast asleep, slept through the lot of it!" "Come on let's get you back to bed little Miss" he picked up Lucy and took her back up to bed.

Mum looked at Joey who she still was holding in her hands, "If only you could talk little bear, what a tale you'd tell!" Joey was getting quite fed up with being laughed at, fed up for having a black oily ring around his mouth from the funnel as well, especially as it was after his act of sheer unadulterated, unbridled heroism, why if it hadn't been for him the burglars would have taken all the stuff that the Policemen were even now bringing into the hall through the front door and got clean away with it all, Scott-free all their stuff never to be seen hide nor hair of again!

The Policemen were talking to themselves, "Can't figure out what happened, the van wouldn't start from what Mr Ramsbottom says, but why did the horn start peeping and wake up the householder?" "Don't know mate, and what's more you'll not get much sense out of the one we've caught as is conscious, that bump on the heads sent him a bit nutty, keeps taking about a teddy bear or something," "Oi!.. See mate," the other one nodded at mum, he noticed she was holding a teddy bear. "Oh I see! Well now this puts a different light on things, we might have to take the bear to the station for questioning!" he said laughing to mum! Joey could scarcely contain himself... the outrage, the indignity!

Mum said she'd put the kettle on and asked the coppers if she could she make them a cup of tea, "it must be cold being out there so early in the morning." They were more than happy to take the weight off their feet and have a brew so they took off their helmets, pulled up chairs and sat around the table. Mum had put Joey down on the chair at the end of the table and he felt like laughing, he wasn't quite sure why, something about being sat around a table with two policemen, their big helmets with their shiny badges on, right in front of him? It was all a bit surreal! He knew it was probably a touch of hysteria coming on after all he'd been through, he also knew that laughing just now would be a thoroughly bad idea as well!

Dad joined them at the table and they chatted while they drank their tea and ate the toast that mum had grilled for them. The sergeant was saying... "Terrible thing, all those lads and so young as well" the younger copper nodded, "Matt Busby was on-board wasn't he? He's okay though... wasn't he?" Dad nodded "quite a few were, Bobby Charlton too, about half survived I think." The Sergeant chomped on his toast and pointed with it as he added "bloody German's it was I've been told, not clearing the runway of snow properly, that Elizabethan's a cracking aeroplane and them lads flying her was raff boys too, so they'd know their stuff, they would, why one of them was a flippin' ace in the war. They'll try and blame it on them though I'll bet!" The men mumbled agreement as they ate, "hit a house after it came off the runway too, they had a lucky escape the family" "ended up burning didn't it?" "Yeah, terrible mess altogether it was" "what were they doing in Munich anyhow, thought Red Star were in Belgrade, Bulgaria that innit?" "Refuelling it was, they only landed there to fill her up, bloody shame, terrible thing..." So the conversation went and Joey's head was spinning, how he wanted a cup of tea himself and some of that toast... he felt himself drifting off as the men talked and talked...

Ten minutes later and the Policemen had gone. Mum and dad had cleared up and were sitting back at the kitchen table having another cup of tea. Dad lit a cigarette and chuckled to himself, "Lucky business for us all in all, a broken pane in the back door but nothing lost," "poor old Joey's got himself filthy somehow though!" Mum added. "You know" dad said, drawing on his cigarette and then pointing at him with it "that bear knows more than he's saying!" Mum laughed, "I'll give him a quick dip in the sink to get some of this dirt off him then he can dry by the fire… hey… did you get the fire going again?" She asked turning to dad, "no never touched it… the cheeky so and so's! You mean to say you think the burglars raked it up to keep warm?"

Mum sat Joey in the sink in some soapy water and sponged at the dirty marks, he was so wet that she couldn't see the tears that were running down his face. He'd had quite a night for a little bear, no quite a night for anyone, and the only thanks he'd got was to be laughed at! "There now Joey you look much better" she rubbed at him gently with a nice soft towel. "I think someone's going to be quite upset when he wakes up in the morning and you're not there with him little bear" and she kissed him gently on his mouth. A good job she set straight off for the breakfast room or she would have seen his little cheeks glowing bright red under his fur. She placed him on a seat next to the fire, "There you'll be all dry in the morning."

Dad opened the back door and as he went out into the back yard he caught his foot on the metal funnel and sent it off rolling noisily across the flags, he stooped down and picked it up, "where on earth has this come from?" He asked mum who had peered around the door to see what the racket was. "It's not ours is it?" she replied, dad who had stepped back into the light in the doorway peered at it, turning it in his hand, "no, never seen it before in my life!"

While dad had fixed a piece of wood over the broken pane in the back door and locked up, mum had put another shovel full of coal on the fire, after a last quick look around mum and dad kissed each other and with a flick of the light switch and a click of the door they were gone.

Joey sat in the warm glow of the breakfast room fire. "Didn't turn out too bad all things considered" he congratulated himself. Sherlock nodded as he leant on the hearth at the edge of the glow from the fire, "all in all, a jolly good show Joseph" he said before turning and disappearing into the shadows. Yes it had been he thought to himself feeling all warm and cosy. *He knelt onto the soft cushion in front of The Queen's throne as she dubbed him... "Arise Sir Joseph..."* and with a little snuffle he was sound asleep.

Stuart had been totally oblivious to any of the goings on in the night despite having been right in the midst of it all! It appears he had simply got up and sleep-walked himself back to bed in between the burglars leaving and dad raising the alarm.

He had of course been highly alarmed when there was no sign of Joey in bed with him when he woke up the following morning! At first he just thought that Joey was playing a prank on him, and had gone all around his bedroom playing hide and seek. After a little while he had started to get cross and had stomped around issuing terrible threats against Joey if he 'did not reveal himself...at once!' this was followed of course by panic and in turn by tears as his anger was replaced by a mounting and terrible sense of loss for his teddy bear companion and confidant. His wild charge into his mother's bedroom had ended well though and before he had chance to finish sobbing out "Mummy, mummy, Joey's g.....!" she had murmured sleepily from half under the bedcovers, "He's downstairs sat by the fire Stuart" and before she could add anything further, Stuart had spun around, propelled himself across the landing, launched himself from off the top step and was flying down the stairs to the despairing cry from his mother of "Stuart don't run on the st........" He was long gone, down the stairs, across the hall and half-way across the kitchen roaring "JOEYYY!!" by the time she had finished.

He exploded into the breakfast room spinning the chair that Joey was sat on around so fast that the poor bear was nearly flung off and would have been had he not been awakened by the charging, bellowing Stuart and he'd had the presence of mind to grab hold of one of the spindles at the back of the chair. Stuart had taken some convincing about Joey's tale, as he told him of the events of the night and he had been forced to say 'honestly' three times before Stuart completely believed him, and he had gone and checked to see the nailed up window in the backdoor for himself!

"Wow, me sleepwalking! I can't wait to tell Andy!" He had said, then he'd picked up Joey and charged back upstairs throwing himself onto his bed, where he lay on his back tossing Joey up into the air, until he squealed for mercy! Then hugged him again and agreed with him that he had indeed been a very brave bear, "and don't forget resourceful too," Joey had reminded him and "very tired too! It's alright for you feeling all chipper after a good night's kip, but I've been up nearly all night!"

Later on Andy had indeed been mightily impressed by Stuart's account of the 'goings on in the night,' it was just as well that the exhausted Joey was put back in bed before Stuart went out on his bike with Andy. Joey had been grumpy enough when Stuart had flung back the curtains in the living room and then had 'aeroplaned' him around the room! 'Aeroplaning' was being held by the hand, arm or paw and being spun around at such a great speed that your body 'flew' around the perpetrator!

After breakfast when he had taken him back upstairs, Joey had said that the thought of being shoved in Stuart's saddle-back and then bounced and shaken about all morning while Stuart raced around like Geoff Duke was just too much for him to contemplate after the night he'd had! So he was placed very carefully in the bed with his head on the pillow and the covers pulled tight and tucked-in, just like mum did! Had Joey been there to hear Stuart's account of the events of the night it would definitely have been more than he could bear... how with great bravery and without the slightest fear Stuart had thwarted the burgulars and got back all their stuff, single-handedly and all whilst he was sleepwalking as well!

Their plan for the morning included riding at top speed around the park, this had to include at least one full uninterrupted lap of the lake! This was the most daring part of the ride as the 'Parkies' would have their best chance of nabbing them then! There was of course a big 'NO CYCLING' sign at every entrance to the park, the notices had a whole lot of other nonsense on them too that nobody else took any notice of either, like not to let your dog run around everywhere pooing!

When he was on his bike, in his mind's eye Stuart was Geoff Duke riding in the TT or sometimes even George Formby, laughing and going 'ooh mother!' ha ha ha! He loved watching George Formby films on the telly with his dad. He loved the cinema even more, their trips to The Gaumont were a real treat, especially when he just took him and not Lucy and mum too. He had loved The Bridge on the River Kwai last year, those Japs were at least as bad as The Nazis! But despite his love of all things military, especially anything with war planes in, like The Dambusters that was super… his favourite movies of all were the cowboy films. He loved John Wayne, Gregory Peck, Gary Cooper but bestest of all his favourite was Jimmy Stewart! He reminded him of his dad and he loved the way the mild talking man always won through in the end.

To the boys the lap of the lake was the equivalent of a lap of the TT course on the Isle of Man. Andy had got caught one time, two of the buggers had waited for him on the bend by the waterfall, it was a tight right-hander leading into a long left handed U-bend across the front of the waterfall, Stuart was hot on his tail as they flew around the blind bend, they'd grabbed Andy before he could see them, grabbed him clean out of his saddle and off his bike they had, which had then skeetered, rider-less into the railings, he'd been very cross about all the scratches! Stuart'd had just enough time to veer off and just enough speed-up to get up the rise through the trees and pull up at the top, to watch as Alan was marched off as a P.O.W.! After a grilling and telling off at the Head Parkies office, having to give his name and address and a threat that it was 'the rozzers next time my boy!' He was allowed to go, he'd said he was Charlie Napier from number nineteen Fish Lane!

Today was okay though and they both did their laps setting new world records in the process. They also went all over the hills and through the trees, before they headed off away from the park and out towards the coast and along 'the bank,' which was a raised path set on an earth embankment some eight foot above the flat plains of the surrounding fields. The bank had been built as a coastal defence years back apparently they were told, but the sea was miles away? Anyhow it made a great track to tear along on your bike!

It was very peaceful out there too, when you stopped for a breather and took it all in, the sky was massive overhead, the open emptiness and flatness of the land unable to confine it in any way. You could lie on your back in the grass and look up into the clear blue yonder forever, with just the sound of the skylarks to listen to as they flew up and up until you could see but a tiny black speck when they got as high as they could go, their 'service ceiling', he smiled to himself. He wished he could fly up there with them and with that thought in his mind he jumped up and took off, arms stretched straight out diving off the embankment, engine roaring, before banking, turning and flying back at full throttle, all the guns of his Spitfire blazing as he tore in towards Herman in his inferior Messerschmitt 109…

On the way home they called in at The Post Office to get some sweets, they bought themselves a Jubbly each and sat on the low wall outside the shop enjoying the orange drinks. Andy got some Refreshers and Stuart got a tube of Spangles, a Penny Arrow and a tube of Horlicks sweets, he really loved them but he'd got them extra as he'd remembered that Joey did too. Most precious of all though, Stuart also bought himself a Street Plan of Worrell. He had seen it on a rack near the newspapers the last time he'd been in with mum when they'd gone in to pay the papers, and he knew right away that he had to have one. He'd asked her if she'd buy one, for the family of course, pleading his case about just how useful it would be for everyone to have a proper street plan of their town! "What for, I know my way around town already!" Was all she'd said adding "if you want one for yourself then you'll have to save-up some of your pocket money won't you?" It was $1/3_d$ and he had carefully counted out his money to make sure he had enough. He got 2/6$_d$ pocket money a week, in the form of a lovely big half-crown coin that his dad gave him on a Saturday, so it was half of a week's pocket money to buy the map, but it'd be well worth it even though it meant that he'd have to wait for ages longer to get enough to buy the Airfix Lancaster bomber kit that he kept looking at in the Hobby Shop window… he'd fished some coins out of his piggy bank too with a flat bladed butter knife when mum wasn't looking to put towards buying it, still the map would be all his this way!

Stuart receiving his pocket money had become a little ritual between father and son every Friday night of late when dad got home from work, of course officially he wasn't meant to have it till Saturday, according to mum but… and it was of course conditional on whether or not he'd incurred any penalties from mum… potential penalties ranged from not doing his chores, right through the spectrum of his misbehaviour including not keeping his room tidy, not cleaning his shoes, being cheeky…. There were lots of possible pitfalls, but usually just a look from his mum was enough to pull him up, get him to bite his lip!

The half-crown was Stuart's most favouritist coin of all, he did like the brassy thruppeny-bit too with all its little flat edges, but the half-crown was the best, first off it was just so big! It sat in the palm of his hand, all silver, shiny and heavy, with a special thicker edge with all those little grooves in all the way around… One week dad had given him a two-bob bit and a tanner! He looked down at them sat in his hand, his lip pouting out, "what?" Dad protested indignantly, "it's not half a crown!" He wailed back forlornly! "It's still two and six, you ungrateful little blighter and if you don't want it you can give it right back!" He peered down at the shocked little lad, who looked up at him as he pondered the situation, he looked back down at the coins in the palm of his hand and then back up at his dad… simultaneously they both began to smile, his dad's bottom lip trembled a little, Stuart felt the corner of his mouth twitch… then they both laughed with and at each other! Dad plucked his lad from the floor reaching under his armpits and held him in front of his face, he tickled him under the arms as he did, Stuart giggled and squealed as his dad *'told him off'* some more, "and it's a florin if you looked properly you grumpy little sod, a Queen Victoria one I got in my change and thought you'd like it!" Stuart had a proper look at the coin, it *was* an old florin, he should have spotted it straight away, it was a different colour to a normal two-bob, more silvery and smoother from all the years of wear it had experienced passing through thousands of hands for all those years, "thanks dad, it's great! Sorry for being a little sod!" He hugged his dad around his neck before he lowered him down to the ground, "now go on, be off with you, let a chap get into his home and take his coat off will you?"

Stuart was already wheeling around the bannister and flying up the stairs, he crossed the landing like a cannon ball fired from a pirate ship… blowing his bedroom door off its hinges in a shower of splintering wood, before bouncing off his bed, snatching Joey up with one hand as he did and finally landing on his stool by the chest of drawers… He pulled the flat cardboard box out which contained his coin collection, plucking out the lumps of cotton wool and folded tissue paper he used to 'keep them safe' "look Joey a Queen Victoria florin! He had everything in his collection, farthings, half-pennies, thruppences, sixpences… he even had an old fashioned <u>silver</u> three-penny bit! His dad had a sovereign that he kept in his wooden box on his dressing table. It was made of gold… real gold!

He had one or two ship ha'pennies too, normally they collected them all up for the collection at Sunday School for the missionary boats, they got put into the little boat when they passed it around, but Stuart had to have a couple to make his collection complete didn't he! He had some really old and very black pennies, they were so old that they had a little galleon on the back alongside Britannia, you could see it sailing on the water at her side on the blackened coppery sea…

But today it had been time to spend $1/3_d$ of his money and as he lovingly unfolded the map he knew it was money well spent! The two boys soaked in all of its wonderful detail, he quickly found their own street and then the corner where they were sitting just then, Andy teased him saying "why aren't we on the map?" ha ha ha! The park, the scene of their earlier Tourist Trophy race was there, even with the lake in the middle! The bank they'd ridden along was on too, everything was on, the railway lines, the stations, the sea, streams, everything! It was fabulous!

As soon as he got in, well once mum had made him take his shoes off and wash his hands and face! He raced upstairs to show the map to Joey, he was up and about and was sat looking out of the window, "hello Stuart, I saw you come tearing in on your bike just now, you never looked when you crossed the road, you could have been squashed flat under a coal lorry for all the care you took!" Stuart repeated… " nerr-nerr-ner-nerrr-*under a coal lorry*…! Never mind that! I didn't. I'da heard a big noisy coal lorry coming wouldna!? Look at my new map, it's fabulous!" Joey shook his head, "it might have been freewheeling…" "Our roads flat!" "It could have started off freewheeling up the road on the railway bridge!" "Oh yeah and come around the corner freewheeling too?" "Pah! If you'd been squished flat by the runaway coal truck your lovely map would have been covered in boy-juice!" Stuey plucked Joey up and dived rolling them onto the bed, "but it didn't and I'm here!" They laughed and rolled onto their tummies to look at Stuart's precious map.

"I had a wonderful idea on the way home Joey, I'm going to use my red biro to draw a circle on the map to show where every letter-box is located." Joey's sniggered remark of "ooh, where they are all *located*..." did not go down well with Stuart so he pushed him off the edge of the bed! Joey landed with a bump on his bum and sat waiting. Sure enough in a couple of seconds Stuart's face appeared over the edge of the bed, he frowned at him, he frowned back, he poked his tongue out at him, he returned the favour! Then he laughed and reached down catching his paw as he held it out and swung him up like a space rocket to land back on the bed.

They lay back on the pillow, "I thought it would be a good idea, after all that I know about letter boxes now!" Joey nodded, "It would and if that's what you want to do then it's something worthwhile just because of that!" He recalled the incident which had led to him explaining all about the history of the pillar-boxes. They had been posting a letter to grandma and grandpa with dad and Lucy, Stuart wrote at least once a month to them, well more to grandpa really. He'd pushed his envelope through the slot and then stood back to take in the details of the pillar-box, being observant, as Joey had taught him. They were a fine thing were pillar-boxes he decided, all lovely red coloured, with a big thick top stuck on, with little dints all around it. A big thicker bit at the bottom painted black and a list of the times when the GPO van would come and empty the box, with a little window that the postman could slot the number of the next collection into. All in all a fine and magnificent thing pillar-boxes were he thought.
"Come on Stuart, we haven't got all day, stop gawping at the

letter-box and get moving!" Dad called back as he and Lucy were heading off down the street. "Dad! Dad! Wait dad, I want to ask you something, why's this letterbox got different writing on it to the one by The Post Office?" Dad stopped, turned around for a moment and shrugged, "dunno, who cares? Come on!"

This had been a most unsatisfactory response and he had sulked all the way home as a result and gone up to play on his own when they got home. Joey had said not to mind dad and explained that as it was the Royal Mail, the letters on the boxes were to designate the monarch who was on the throne when the letter box was cast" *"What's cast?"* "Made then, they're made of iron and they are cast, that is the molten metal is poured into a mould with the shape of the pillar-box already in it." *"But its round…"*

"Nevermind that! The one at the end of the road is from the reign of King George the sixth, but they use Roman numeral so it's VI…" *"Why VI?"* "Well the Romans used…" There now followed a complicated and at times for Joey frustrating twenty minutes as he attempted to explain how the Romans wrote numbers down… "yes but why? Why didn't they just do it like us?"

Notwithstanding the debate about Roman logic, eventually they had written down in Stuart's Exercise Book, the one he wrote 'important facts and discoveries' in, all the different letters he could find on a pillar-box, from VR onwards. He had to go on then to explain why it was V**R** and not **Q**V and **K**G!! "Why isn't there one for HRVIII then?" Stuart had been learning about Henry the eighth in his history class at school, he was a bad king he was, nothing like our Queen Elizabeth II, he told Joey, our queen didn't go around having people's heads chopped off did she? Well not so as he knew of! "The

Royal Mail was only invented in Queen Victoria's reign" Joey had explained patiently to a response of "how did you get your letters delivered before that then?"

The whole discussion had definitely started something though and from that moment on wherever they went Stuart was an avid pillar-box spotter! The highlight of a trip to Ramsbottom that they had made on one of dad's famous 'ride-outs' in the car was to see his first Penfold design hexagonal VR pillar-box! It was wonderful! Unlike the 'normal' pillar-boxes which had a big ring-like thing on their top, this one had a beautiful, upward curved-shaped top with patterns of leaves all around it and a lovely oval shaped knob right on the very top, but most of all IT WASN'T ROUND!! "Look! Look! LOOK!! DAD! It's not round! It's all flat sided!"

So Joey thought all in all it wasn't that surprising really that he wanted to use his new map for this purpose, he just couldn't help himself saying "you could mark on the map which monarch's letters each one had on it!" "Oh WOW! YES! They'll have to be tiny letters, next to the red dot, or better still even, I could draw a little tiny pillar-box!!" Seeing how the lad had reacted he was glad he'd managed to hold back from saying 'of course there's all the wall mounted post boxes as well!'

Totally enthused Stuart ran downstairs to tell his dad all about his super idea, he found him sat by the fire, with his feet up on the pouffe, he was reading his paper, the radiogram was on and Michael Holliday was singing away out of the big brown cloth grille at the front… #*bu-bum-bum the story of my life…*# mum was leaning in the doorframe through to the kitchen listening, she loved Michael Holliday she said, 'this is his latest' she added as she wiped absent-mindedly at a plate with the tea towel… Stuart tutted at her, dad who was smoking a fag as usual chuckled, it was Saturday afternoon and he'd often flop down like that if he'd 'had a hard week at work,' *cluttering-up the place* mum called it 'and when there's a hundred-and-one jobs waiting to be done about the place as well!' Dad worked on a Saturday morning, but he had Tuesday afternoons off, so it wasn't that bad Stuart thought.

He showed dad the map and outlined his plan... but he'd just picked up his newspaper again, that he'd rested on his knees while he'd listened, had a draw on his fag and said "what for?" Slightly knocked back by this response he said more tentatively "so people can find where they are?" His dad's response was "what people? They're big and red, maybe that's why they painted them red? Did you think of that Stuart, perhaps it's so no one can miss them?" Now Stuart was just plain cross, dad was taking the mickey, "Well I think it's a really good idea, I'll ask mum what she thinks instead of you, you're just cluttering the place up anyway!" That did get a reaction from dad, "You watch it cheeky! It's my wages that puts this roof over our heads, I'll thank you to remember and if I want to sit under **my** roof cluttering the place up then I will!" Stuart flounced out of the room heading for the kitchen, what did he know anyhow? He hadn't even been interested in the letters on the pillar-boxes!

Mum was busy baking, her response of "ask your father, he's got nothing better to do apparently than sit around! I wish I had time to think up daft ideas like that!" DAFT IDEAS!! That was it, he stormed out of the kitchen and threw the map into the corner of the hall by the front door, behind the hat-stand and stomped up the stairs seething. "Blummin stupid map, cost me $1/3_d$ that did!" It took Joey quite some time to calm him down, explaining that other people often weren't as enthusiastic about our ideas as we were and if we wanted to do something, well why not just do it anyway, why worry what they thought if we thought it was a good idea, if it did no harm to anyone else and wasn't dangerous… then why on earth not? Accordingly Stuart crept back downstairs, not wanting to look foolish in front of either of what he now considered to be his uncaring, lazy and ignorant parents, (despite what Joey had said to try and defend them, to excuse their behaviour) and he retrieved his map, it was a bit creased and dusty. Huh! Dad could get off his lazy arse and help out with the house work he thought rudely, chuckling to himself as he ran up the stairs again.

Joey asked him when he came back into his bedroom, "did you apologise to dad?" "No!" He replied bluntly. "I just went down to get my map, like you said," although he was coming around to his idea again, it was clear he had still not forgiven his father, "dad still should have shown a bit more interest, miserable, lazy sod, he is!" Joey shook his head, disrespect was a bad thing and had to be discouraged. "Your dad works very hard to look after you all, he's out of the door way before eight every morning and its six before he gets back, six days a week. He really does get very tired, I don't think mum's always fair with him about it, so you at least should try to be. Anyway he's still your father and I won't hear you being disrespectful!" Stuart looked sideways at Joey, it was rare for him to be so direct with instructions, he was a bossy little sod for sure, but not like that! Dad did work hard and he did look really tired when he came in some nights, it was true, so he supposed he had been a bit unfair. I mean it wasn't that important his idea about the pillar-boxes, not really he thought. More particularly though he thought it was most unusual for Joey to criticise anyone like that, least of all mum.

Joey himself thought that he would try and get the lad to apologise later, he had to say he really did have considerable concerns about dad's health and welfare, he smoked way too many of those cigarettes for his liking, smoking was the most stupid thing that he'd ever come across! At least dad didn't waste all his money drinking down at the pub like a lot of men did, or at the bookies either...

Anyway Joey set to with Stuart marking the letterboxes on the map. They had half a dozen or so done and Stuart had plans to reconnoitre the entire town on his bike, with Andy if he wanted to help, when mum called up that it was teatime and the map was carefully folded up and put on his bookshelf between his Eagle Annuals and his very own copy of Swiss Family Robinson that grandpa had given him. So it was that the vitally important job of mapping the pillar-boxes of Worrell was abandoned… never to be resumed!

After tea Stuart sidled over to dad, "sorry I was rude before dad, I thought you really liked maps, that was all?" His dad pulled him onto his knee and put his arm around him, "it's okay sunshine, I'm sorry too for not showing more interest, I just get so tired sometimes I can't think straight. The maps I like are ones I use for going places really, finding your way somewhere new that you've never been before, you know? I guess I got used to doing it in the army, we had to find our way all over the blummin place then!" Joey smiled as he sat in Stuarts lap, he was a good hearted lad and so was his dad.

There was a mistle thrush singing in the tree outside Stuart's window when he and Joey went back up later, this prompted him to bounce over the bed to his bookshelf and pull down his Observer Book of British Birds. Bird watching was a fine hobby to have, everyone said so and he had put asterisk-stars with his red biro at the bottom of the pages of the birds he had spotted. Very much like the way he underlined, (with a ruler of course), the numbers of the steam engines that he spotted in his Ian Allen British Railway Locomotives book.

Of all his books Ian Allen was the most thumbed and looked at, it listed all the engines in use on the railway and told you all about each type, when they were made, the wheels layout and everything! His most prized under-linings were the engines with names, he had spotted seven of his favourites, the Coronation Scotts or 'semi's' as they called them.

He found 'mistle thrush' in his book, he'd seen them loads of times but he liked to see it in the book as well as out of the window. They had a lovely song he thought as he wished he had a pair of binoculars like grandpa had, they were army ones! He had a heavy duty khaki webbing box for them, that clipped onto his khaki webbing army belt, it was dead good, but was too big for his waist. Grandpa said that when it fitted him he would be grown-up enough to have it! He couldn't wait.

Chapter Three

Expedition to Bristol

Expedition to Bristol

At last the day had come, well nearly anyway, tomorrow they were going to drive down to see grandma and grandpa in Bristol. They were mum's mum and dad. It had come as a surprise when Stuart found out that his pal Andy had two of each, grandparents that is! It was confusing for him at first, then it seemed really unfair as he only had one set of grandparents, then there was the fact that his 'other' set, dad's mum and dad were 'dead'. This was a troublesome idea altogether, and had vexed him for a while, so he pestered his mother in an attempt to get to the bottom of it all. "They were very old" she'd said, he'd then pointed out… "but so are you and daddy, are you going to die too?" After being pestered for quite some time she started to get cross, "they've gone to Heaven!" she had said in the end… hmm… right Stuart thought, so that was ok then, wasn't it?

It was the best part of 200 miles to get to where they lived and would take four to five hours driving to get there. Stuart's dad had been in the army at the end of the war, although he hadn't been old enough to do any fighting, he had been there to help with the removal of all the equipment after it was all over. He had done his basic training after being called-up and then due to his poor eyesight, (he used to wear those Billy Bunter round glasses that Stuart used to snigger at in the old photos) he had been trained as a lorry driver. He had driven tank-transporters, which were mighty big lorries, Stuart was proud of this fact, that his dad could drive the biggest and the bestest of all lorries, the mighty Scammell!

The journey was always undertaken as almost a military manoeuvre, set watches, we leave at 04:00! Four in the morning was still the middle of the night at this time of year and it had an almost magical quality about it for Stuart. Lucy just flopped about all sleepy and was sometimes even carried to the car! Girls were such a waste of space, why couldn't he have had a brother like Andy, or have been an only child? You got so much more of everything if you were an only child!

Stuart didn't see why he should go to bed any earlier than usual, "I know that we're getting up early but it's not fair! Lucy's still up and ANYWAY I WON'T SLEEP! I'll be far too excited to go to sleep." "Off to bed now young man!" his father said quietly, he seldom had to raise his voice to Stuart, and since of course Stuart knew that it was sensible really, he gave in, but not too gracefully. He grabbed Joey roughly by his arm and marched out of the room without another word, shutting the door behind him. He stood in the hall waiting. Surely at least mum would come and say goodnight to him and ask him if he wanted a bedtime drink. But no, no-one came! "My arm hurts, you nearly pulled it right off!" Joey said in a pained little voice, "You know perfectly well that it's your own fault no-one's said goodnight to you, don't you?" he asked Stuart whose bottom lip was beginning to tremble. "No I DO NOT!" he replied and dropping Joey on the floor he stormed off up the stairs, only turning with a face as black as thunder to shout "and I suppose you don't want to come up to bed with me either!"

Joey shook his head sadly, and picked himself up off the floor. He brushed the dust off his brown velvety fur, and listened to see if anyone was moving in the living room. He could hear the television, with Lucy and mum chatting quietly in the background. He trotted across the hall to the bottom of the stairs. He looked up at the seemingly endless wall of red patterned stair carpet, held in place on each tread by a brass rod. With a deep sigh he began the laborious task of climbing the stairs. He was ready with a plan in case anyone other than Stuart of course, came out into the Hall, he would simply freeze wherever he was and wait for them to pick him up on their way up! He should be so lucky. "It would serve him right if I just didn't bother," he muttered crossly to himself, a vision of the little boy crying in his bed with no bear to hug came to mind, yes that would teach him a lesson! He then hurried as fast as he could to get to him so he could hug him and make him feel better. There were thirteen steps "unlucky for some" Stuart had said once, "nonsense, it's just a number Stuart" he had replied, he wasn't so sure now! It was certainly unlucky for him at the moment. "Never mind I am just climbing one step at a time" he told himself "and the exercise will do me good!" Ten minutes later he arrived on the landing, he was just having a breather when he heard Stuart's bedroom door open and saw his face peer around it. His eyes were all red and puffy where he had been crying, Joey's face lit up, "oh Stuart am I glad to see you, I'm worn out climbing up all these stairs," the little boy was distinctly not glad to see Joey though and he blurted out "I suppose you're going to blame me aren't you, you're ALL against me," he drew in a big breath and sobbed out "I HATE YOU!" with this he ran across to the little bear and pushed him with his foot, Joey tried to grab at the side of the staircase, but the big polished newel post didn't offer him anything to grip onto, he spun around and teetered on the top step of the stairs, "Stuaaaaaaaarttt... nooooo...." he exclaimed as he toppled off the top step and proceeded to bounce, one by one down the stairs he had just climbed, You.....*<bump>*... little....... *<bump>*........ rotter........*<bump>*.....I'm your....*<bump-bump>*......best..... *<bump-bump-bump>*....friend...*<bump-bump-bump-bump>*... <BUMP!!!!!>"

Joey bounced right across the hall with Stuart's shout ringing in his ears "JOEEEEEYYYY NOOOO"... it rose into an agonised scream at the end. Joey had landed with a bump up against the legs of the hat stand making it wobble slightly above him dislodging dad's trilby, which floated down and landed right on top of him. For a moment he sat with his head spinning wildly before trying to get up. "Sssffunny someone's sssturned d'lightss off" he burbled as he wobbled across the hall under dad's trilby. Just at that moment the living room door burst open and dad came bustling out into the hall, "just what is going on Stuart!" he demanded in a big loud voice, and looking down to see his trilby in the middle of the floor, he also demanded "and what have you been doing with my hat?" he turned so that he could look up onto the landing, where he beheld the tragedy struck face of his little son, with tears streaming down his cheeks, clasping onto the spindles of the banister rail looking with his faced pushed in between them, dad's heart melted at the sorry sight, "come here you silly little sausage" he called in a soft forgiving voice, Stuart leapt up and hurtled himself down the stairs with legs going like windmills and leapt off the third step flying through the air across the floor of the hall into the outstretched arms of his father, he hugged him for all he was worth "I'm sorry *SOB.. dad… SOB…* but Joey fell! *SOB… SOB...* off the landing" he informed his dad in a slightly modified version of the truth, what Joey would call 'a fib!' "Well where is he?" dad asked looking around the empty hall, "he's hiding under your hat!" Stuart replied, with the dawning realisation that this story wasn't actually going to hold water, "and how do we suppose he got hold of my hat then? Did he fly up and grab it or did the fairies flick it off the hook for him?" Dad asked kindly, placing the little lad back down on his feet. He looked up at him with a puzzled look on his face, "well erm..." he wiped his pyjama sleeve across his face where his nose was running, "come here" his dad said crouching down and pulling his handkerchief out of his pocket, he wiped his son's nose, "blow Stuart" he prompted, and looking into his sons eyes he decided to let it go, "never mind Stuart, you take Joey and run along off to bed. We've got a long drive in the morning, you should be fast asleep by now." "O.K. Dad," he snuggled into his dad and gave him a sloppy kiss on the cheek, picked the trilby off Joey, and handed it to his father, then hugging his teddy bear he ran up the stairs, "Goodnight dad!" he sang out as he turned at the halfway landing, "Sleep tight Stuart, and if the bugs bite… "KILL'EM" they both finished in unison this regular little saying of dad's. Stuart's father looked down at the trilby in his hand as he walked over to the hat stand, where he hung it back on the hook at the top, he stood for a moment with a puzzled look on his face as he pondered just how the little fella had reached his hat, "flicked it down with my brolley" he said to himself and nodding he turned back to the living room door. "Is he all right" Stuart heard his mother's voice from the living room, "oh yes he's just.." the door clicked shut and he lost the rest of the sentence to a muffled version of his father's voice, followed by his mother's laughter. Stuart turned away from the landings bannister rail and looked down at Joey, "I'm sorry Joey" he said in his saddest voice, the little bear looked back up and frowned at him "Stuart Wheeler, that was a horrible thing to do your friend, it would serve you right if I didn't talk to you for a week, or give you any hugs!" Stuart's face fell, he was used to Joey simply forgiving him whatever horrible things he did to him, he felt tears welling up in his eyes but caught the glimpse of a smirk on Joey's face and twigged that he was taking the mickey of him! "Well then *Canadian* Joey, if we're using our Sunday-best names, I might just boot you down the stairs again then…" Joey looked up and could see the silly look on Stuart's face and knew he was joking, "oh it's O.K. Stuey," the little bear replied, "I was only kidding!" "I know" he said hugging the bear to him and then planting a big sloppy kiss on his face, "ohh yuuckk!!!" Joey replied in mock disgust as he slid out of his grip and back down onto the floor, they walked across the landing to Stuart's bedroom, boy and bear best friends again, just the way it should be.

"I won't ever, ever-ever do anything bad to you again" Stuart promised Joey as they snuggled together in bed, "that's good" the little bear replied softly, trying not to sound patronising, "I'm sure you won't," but just to make it less likely he added, "because if you did, well, I might just have to pack my spotted hanky and go!!" "Your spotted hanky?" Stuart queried, "indeed, in the absence of a suitcase it is a method of conveying one's belongings, by wrapping them all up in a large handkerchief and tying it onto the end of a pole, which can then be carried over the shoulder." "Ooow is that what one can do is it?" the boy mocked in his silliest 'posh' voice, but then thinking a little further, an element of doubt, of fear creeping in, he snuggled even closer to the bear, "Oh, Joey! Don't say that! You'll never leave me will you?" Stuart asked, now quite alarmed, he sat up abruptly in bed and sat the bear on his lap so they were sitting face to face, Joey replied in his wisest voice, "to have a friend you have to be a friend and you should always treat your friends as you would like to be treated yourself." He sat looking sternly at the little boy for a few moments longer before standing up and reaching out his little paws, hugging him to him. Stuart hugged him back and snuggled them both back down under the covers and reaching over clicked off the light. They lay for a few minutes listening to the tick of the big round alarm clock, "I'll never get off to sleep!" Stuart yawned, "I'm simply far too excited," "of course you are" Joey replied, but Stuart didn't hear him as he was already fast asleep.

In the middle of the night, or so it seemed, Stuart felt a hand on his shoulder and he heard his dad's voice saying, "come on little chap time to be up and away," at the same time, he heard him click on his bedside light. Stuart looked up blinking, rubbing at his sleepy eyes, unable to comprehend for a moment what was going on. As he came around and his sleepy mind drifted back from his dreams he replied, at first calmly but growing in volume and enthusiasm… "we're going to grandma and grandpa's today… now! Whoopeee…" dad, ruffled his hair as the little lad threw back the covers and leapt headlong from his bed, "calm down lad, calm down…" but Stuart was already half way to the bedroom door still 'whooping,' as he shot through the doorway he nearly collided with Lucy who was already dressed, "Wha… why are you dressed already?" He queried as he slowed his hurtling trajectory through the door by grabbing the frame, swinging his legs up nearly into Lucy's face, she replied silently by merely poking her tongue out and turning and heading down the stairs. She turned her head at the half-landing and looked up at him, "Don't just stand there gawping all day, dummy, we're going in five minutes, don't want to be left behind do you?" She smirked to herself since exactly as she'd predicted he responded in sheer terror, the gleeful excitement draining away from his face to be replaced with abject terror, as he wailed "dad…. you won't go without me will you?" Dad was standing in Stuart's bedroom door by now looking down the stairs as Lucy just reached the bottom, she turned and smiled up angelically at him, "Morning dad!" Was all she said as she disappeared from view, but he saw the slightest hint of a smirk still lingering on her lips. "He ruffled Stuart's mop of hair again, and guessing what Lucy had said replied "Take no notice, how would I get there without my navigator? Come on then… scramble!" He nudged Stuart towards the bathroom, who now as instantly as he had been full of dread was once more full of energy and glee… he was now Wing Commander Stuart Wheeler VC, scrambling to his Spitfire for a sortie over enemy territory, "Aye, aye Sir," he stood to attention briefly and saluted, before spinning around and hurtling towards the bathroom, his arms straight out from his shoulders, engine at full pelt... rrrrrrRRRRRRRR! "Don't forget to clean your teeth, and have a proper wash not a cat-lick young fella!" Pah! Stuart thought, Jerry won't care if I've washed behind my ears when he's in my sights... he opened fire, the bullets streaming from the wings either side of him, "acc-acc-acc-acc-acc-acc..." he banked steeply as he rounded the corner of the landing, the port wing of his spitfire nearly touching the floorboards, but pulling up just in time to roar majestically through the door into the bathroom...

Ten minutes later and he was swooping downstairs, washed, dressed and ready to go. Joey was 'flying' down with him at the end of his flailing arm, gripping-on for grim death as the tortured V12 Merlin grappled to resist over-revving in the insane dive its young pilot had put the Spitfire into, just in time he pulled up "Rrrrrrrrrrrrrrrrrrrrrrrrrrrrrrrrr.........." she roared wildly as he banked around the bottom newel and shot along the hall to the kitchen. He burst through the door to take in the scene of activity as mum was packing bags on the table, dad was filling the big cream and red chequered Thermos at the stove and Lucy was clearing the dishes from the table. Feeling excluded and left out and left in bed when everyone else had been up, he now transformed from being a hurtling Spitfire into a major sulk and he flounced to the table, full of indignation, almost at the point of tears. He flopped himself down, deliberately dragging the chair noisily in with his legs wrapped around it while he lent on the table, exactly as he had been repeatedly told not to! "Stuart Wheeler! Don't start!" Was all mum said, but it was the look she gave him that said it all, there was not even a sixteenth of an inch, never mind an inch of give in that look, it had, 'or else' stamped all over it. "Eat!" It was a command. Pah! Was all he thought as he pulled the bowl towards him, in reality full of Cornflakes but to him now a bowl of the foulest gruel. They could keep him imprisoned here, force him to eat their filthy food but he was Wing Commander Stuart Wheeler, he would escape sooner rather than later and be back in his Spitfire before they could say Jack Robinson, or even Kurt or Herman Robinson, he smirked at his own joke, tucking into the cornflakes which mum had poured milk onto as he sprinkled sugar over them. She smiled down at him and all was well again.

"Don't make a racket out there, the neighbours are all still asleep" dad whispered, even though they were still in the kitchen. He opened the back door and the little family trooped out, each carrying a bag or a parcel or in Stuart's case a bear! Outside it was chilly and dark, but the air had excitement in it too though for Stuart, he soaked it all up, everything, the smell of the privet damp with rain from earlier, the crunch of the loose stones from the crumbly asphalt of the drive, the bright almost blue light from the street light that was still lit on the corner, the silence. He listened intently, nothing, then a clickety-clicking noise in the distance, he strained his ears, yes he could hear the engine too... chuff-chuffing along... "Come on!" His mother's voice in a loud whisper cut into his reverie, he realised everyone else was at the car, the doors open. He ran across and jumped into the front passenger seat, he leant right over and grabbed the strap to pull the door shut, it swung in and banged shut... "oops!" he exclaimed to the frosty look his dad shot at him.

Dad turned the key and the lovely little half-globe jewel of a red light came on, along with the orange one as well, "we have an ignition light Captain" he chirped-up, "roger that" his dad replied, he pushed the starter and the engine turned over, slowly at first then quicker and then she burst into life. Stuart smiled and shuffled back into his seat, watching as the red and orange lights went out, "we have good oil pressure Captain" he reported and he turned and beamed to his mum in the back, she smiled back, he then turned around the other way to look between the back of his seat and the window at Lucy, he could just get his head far enough, he poked his tongue out at her, she immediately kicked the back of his seat, "Lucy! Don't start." Mum reprimanded her, "we've not even started moving yet! It's going to be a long journey!" "He started it!" She wailed, "enough!" Now it was dad, he looked at Stuart, who just shrugged innocently, "I don't care who started it, I'm finishing it… and now!" With that he put the car into reverse and looking over his shoulder reversed the car down the drive and into the street. Stuart jumped out and shut the gates, he looked up at the empty house, the windows looked like sad eyes upstairs looking down at him, "don't worry we'll be back soon" he said to the house as he spun around and leapt back into the car. Dad had put the headlights on now and as the car slowly drove off, climbing up through the gears Stuart was full of the wonder of it all, the adventure. He looked up at his dad sat next to him, his hands on the steering wheel his eyes focussed out there in front on the road. He felt a wave of love for him, of pride that he was his dad. He loved it when they drove at night, the speedometer was all lit up, he could see the needle as it went up and down telling them how fast they were going.

Ten minutes later and they were leaving their town behind them, fields were opening up alongside the road, black empty places. The trees appeared to loom up as they were illuminated in the headlights. Banks of wispy mist would drift across from the fields every now and then in front of them, the beams of the headlights becoming solid as they found the mist, then it would swirl away as the car swept through it.

At first everyone had been chatty, talking about all sorts of things, grandma and grandpa, had dad cancelled the papers?

Mum had told the milkman when they would be back, chatter, chatter, chatter. Now an hour into the journey they had all shut up, thank goodness, Stuart thought. Lucy was fast asleep under a blanket her head leaning on mum. Mum was awake but seemed miles away. She barely noticed Stuart peering around to look at her. Grandma and grandpa were Stuart's mum's, mum and dad. It seemed really weird to him that she would want to live so far away from them, he thought he would never do that, move away from his town, his home. Going away was a great adventure for sure, but somehow if you didn't have your home to come back to after... it took on a much scarier feeling then.

On the way through Liverpool they had passed some areas that dad said were 'bombsites', war didn't seem as glamorous then when you saw the gaps in streets, where you knew houses had been, where people had once lived. What if it had been his home? What if dad had come home and found his house was a gap in the street? It was before I was born he comforted himself, but you'd have thought they would have built them up again by now. He'd asked dad, he said the Luftwaffe, which is what the Germans called their RAF had bombed Liverpool mercilessly, typical that, they were like that those Germans and that because so much had been destroyed it would be years and years yet before all the buildings were repaired. He said you could destroy the buildings and kill as many people as you liked but no one could destroy the spirit of the British. Stuart thought old Hitler had done a pretty good job trying nevertheless. He was a really angry man that Hitler was, he was always shouting, ranting, in German of course, whenever you saw him on old TV films. He'd looked really silly as well, he had a funny moustache, it had the sides shaved off, like Charlie Chaplin, which was funny too, well not funny ha-ha, but weird, because Charlie Chaplin was funny, he really was funny ha-ha, that was his job, he was a comic, he made people laugh but Hitler, who looked just like him was really bad and bombed Liverpool.

He'd had everyone marching up and down too, streets full of them, millions of them and they all had to be saluting back at him, they didn't salute properly, like our soldiers, like Stuart did, in a proper manner, but they did it by thrusting their arms out like loonies and he got them all to shout back at him when they were doing it…"seek hi-al" was what they said, over and over? They didn't march properly like our soldiers either, they marched as if they had wooden legs that didn't bend, maybe they didn't bend, or maybe they all had tin legs fitted when they had their square tin hats put on? Joey had just shook his head sadly and said "yes that'll be it Stuart!" Stuart decided that he was being a 'sarky sod!' He wasn't quite sure what that meant but it fitted the bill by comparison with when mum said it to dad when he said something silly in response to what had been a perfectly reasonable question mum might have asked, or indeed he had asked himself.

Like when he'd asked a perfectly reasonable question of dad himself, they'd been checking the car over one Sunday, like any proper car owner would. Stuart had been using the foot-pump to put some air in the front tyre, the 'near-side' wheel… it was called the nearside wheel because it was the side of the car nearest to the kerb, well when the car was on the right side of the road, which was the left… side of the road… anyway it was simple. Like the portside of an aeroplane, you couldn't say left side, like on a ship, 'cos if you turned around and looked back the other way say towards the stern instead of the bow, or the other way around… didn't matter, anyway then the left side would be on the other side wouldn't it? He'd had to tell Lucy to 'shut-up' because he'd tried to explain all this to her, but she couldn't understand any of it, well she wouldn't would she? After all she was just a stupid girl, girls were stupid weren't they, I mean all they could do when they grew up was be a nurse or a teacher and then get married and have babies wasn't it? They couldn't look forward to flying a Spitfire, driving a steam engine, being the captain of a battleship, or a sub! Or being a soldier, winning medals... anything like that ... could they? "Are you pumping that tyre up Stuart? or gawping up at the sky like one of Woolworth's?" "Stop day dreaming and put some umph into it!"

"Sorry dad!" Stuart had 'snapped-out of it' as Miss Hodgkinson his teacher at school would shout at him... 'Stuart Wheeler! Snap-out of it! Daydreaming again! Take a hundred lines, I must not daydream in class!' Old witch! That was what she was, bet she had a broomstick that she flew around on, she didn't need a Spitfire, she'd come banking and diving from around the church steeple and knock you clean off your bike, cackling as she went, bet she'd even have a big fat ugly cat sat on the back with her... like a pillion passenger on the back of a motorbike... he'd get her in his sights and let her have it given half the chance...*ack..ack..ack..ack!!* "Oi" dad shoved at his shoulder and jolted him away, off the foot pump, "shift you nincompoop! You're letting more air out of the damn tyre than you're putting in, pumping like a girl!" The pump flopped over on its side, dad knocked it back upright with his foot and started pumping, it was easy for him with his big fat long legs, he was a blummin giant compared to Stuart!

He was cross and felt silly been shoved like that and being called a nincompoop as well, all he'd asked dad was 'if you pumped too much would the tyre burst?' Half hoping it would now, serve him right pumping like he was, showing-off how hard he could pump, he'd pump harder than that when he was a grown-up, that'd show him. Then dad had said 'yeah and the tyre would explode and blow the car up in the air and right over the hedge and it'd end up sat on its roof in old man Ramsbottom's dahlia's!" That was sarcasm that was, as mum said 'no need to be sarky!' Dad could be a right sarky sod!

They were strange the Krouts, as dad called them, not like us at all he thought. He wondered what it must be like for Krout kids, awful he guessed. He had seen some dressed up a bit like boy scouts they were, on the telly once, they were marching around like their soldiers, dad said they were 'brain-washed' whatever that meant. Would your head be empty if it was brain-washed? All the thoughts washed out of it? He imagined, the Krouts, flipping open their kids heads and lifting out their brains, they looked like spongey things brains did and they'd have blood dripping off them as well, then they'd throw them all into a Servis twin-tub like mum had to do the washing, only a great big massive one, and a rotten German one too, probably made by Messerschmitt, then they'd throw in some Daz or Brain-Daz or Kraut-Daz and Bob's your uncle... only it'd be Fritz's your uncle wouldn'it? A quick spin and then they'd toss 'em back inside their bonces, they'd all be sat in a line with their uniforms on and their eyes looking upwards, or maybe cross-eyed with no brains in? Would they worry which brain went in which kid? Why bother they were all going to be little Natzi's so who'd care anyway? He loved the way that Winston Churchill had called them Nazi's, with no 't' that would show 'em! Then their eyes would spin around and they'd be off marching already... Would their parents notice though, that they had the wrong brains in? When they came home for tea? Hallo Fritz... I is not Fritz, I is Herman!! Ha-ha-ha... Heil Hitler!! They were just Krouts though so they probably wouldn't care anyhow? Stuart could speak some German, it was in the war books he spent some of his pocket money on sometimes, *Gott in Himmel!* they would say and *Achtung! Achtung*! They said that a lot, and it was like they couldn't spell properly, *feur*, they'd say instead of fire, but our boys'd let-em 'ave it and get 'em with a bren gun or a bazooka!

Joey had tried to explain that they were 'conditioned' or when he still didn't understand, that they were taught to think the wrong things, "not like our teachers who tell us the truth about things then?" he had asked, "well yes, Stuart, your teachers don't deliberately mislead you like they did in Germany, well probably not that much anyhow." "Do they mislead us though?" he had picked up on Joey's less than complete endorsement of his school. "Well let's just say that you should never take any information as true unless you totally trust the person who is telling you, well not even then… Let's just say that you should be able to test what you are being told by questioning it, by seeing if it fits with what you already know and believe to be true." "like Sherlock Holmes would do?" "Elementary my dear Stuart!" They had chuckled together.

Stuart was always excited when they came to the Mersey Tunnel, it went right down and under the river Mersey, which was a blummin big wide river, he'd been down on the docks with dad once and seen it himself. It was really wide and a horrible dirty brown colour and it went whizzing along past you at a fair old lick and it had great big boats that sailed up and down it and a ferry that went across to the other side for passengers. Dad said he'd take him on it one day, hmm… he'd thought along with all the other things that dad said he'd do with Stuart one day, they'd end up being mighty busy on that 'one day' if it ever came!

They had gone on the Overhead Railway that day, he'd only been six at the time but he remembered it quite clearly. That had been the reason for their trip, the Overhead Railway that ran right along the docks was closing soon and dad said he wanted to go on it one last time. It was a fine thing Stuart had thought even then, built up for a lot of its length on big iron pillars above the road so you looked down on everything and had a grand view of the docks and the ships.

Stuart had asked "why are they closing the railway down daddy?" He'd shook his head a little sadly and said it was progress, "everything must change Stuey, it's the way of the world. There's buses now that can carry people and there's no money to repair parts of it that need fixing. Everything's always moving forward, changing, just as well really else we'd all still be running round with spears and living in caves wouldn't we?" He had giggled at the thought, although it sounded like fun, a bit like their camping trips? Joey had said life had been anything but fun for people in those days, not that he'd been there himself he'd chuckled. Dad said when he was a boy and he'd ridden along on the Overhead Railway there'd been steam lorries working on the docks, they were much busier then he'd added, there were thousands of dockers in those days he said, in fact they used to call the railway 'the docker's umbrella he'd said! "Why?" Stuart had asked, "because they could walk under it without getting wet when it rained… like an umbrella!"

They stopped at the little booth and paid the man and then they were off descending down the shiny painted tube to the bottom of the tunnel, there was a turn off that took you out on the docks road that dad sometimes took on their way back and they soon passed that and were going down, down deeper and deeper…Stuart craned his head to look up, imagining all the rock and mud and water that was up above them! Millions and millions of tons there'd be wouldn't there? He'd asked dad, it won't flood will it dad, all that water come sloshing in and us all get drownded? His dad just laughed and said it wouldn't.

They hardly saw another car all the way through, early as it still was and soon they came out on the other side, Stuart breathed a big sigh of relief, it was dead good going through the tunnel but even better once you'd come out the other end all safe and sound! It had started to rain, at first a few spots now and then, dad turned on the wipers, they swish-swashed the water away. It was a lovely noise… swish-swash… swish-swash and it was hypnotic watching as the screen cleared momentarily in the arc of the blades and then as the rain filled it in again behind it. The tyres swished along now too and splashed through the puddles, the street lights twinkling through the watery windows. Then the rain came down heavier and heavier like cats and dogs. Dad had to slow to see where he was going. Stuart thought it was exciting. Dad turned the blower on to keep the windscreen from steaming up, but the side window was all misty and he had to keep wiping it with his hand. Lightening flashed, lighting up the whole sky, the big black clouds illuminated for a split second, then the crash of the thunder. Wow! This was great he thought peering out watching for the next flash. "Quite a night hey lad?" Dad asked without taking his eyes of the road, "It is yes, it's great" he laughed back looking across in admiration at the man who could carry on driving in all this. He caught the look on his dad's face, he was enjoying it too, he could see the excitement in his eyes, the look of thrill, the same look his son had now, the look of the boy he was once too and part of him always would be.

Two and a half hours later the rain had stopped, everywhere was still dripping wet, the dampness hanging in the air. The light was changing, over in the east the sky wasn't quite as dark anymore. It was a truly magical time for Stuart, by now mum was asleep as well, so he could share this time alone with his dad, just the two of them, and Joey of course who spent the journey sat with Stuart or held up to the window if there was something Stuart thought he really shouldn't miss! This morning though it was starting to go misty after all the rain and as dawn was coming. They were deep into the countryside, it was a good road lined with trees and fences that were whisking past, they had it all to themselves as well, they had hardly seen another vehicle other than the odd lumbering lorry or two awhile back. Dad was a great driver, he knew all about driving and what you needed to do from when he was in the army. He 'got his foot down' as he put it, which meant the accelerator, the pedal which made you go faster! Stuart had driven the car sat on his dad's knee on the beach at Southport. It was bloomin great, the big steering wheel was all smooth, but with bumpy bits at the back, and the way the car turned when you swung it to one side then the other. He had slid down so he could press the accelerator, but then he couldn't see out of the windscreen! Dad said when he grew a bit he'd let him have a proper go.

Today though the mist got thicker and thicker. Dad slowed down more and more, Stuart could see him, straining to see. "Huh! A real pea-souper!" He said as he reduced the car to a crawl, he turned the headlights off, they were just bouncing back off the fog and you could see more without them in the early morning light. Stuart sat right up on the edge of the seat and leant on the dashboard, his forehead resting on the windscreen, peering into the woolly grey blankness, the more you tried the less you could see. Suddenly the car jolted as dad braked really hard, the tyres squealed and the car skidded to a halt, "What's wrong?" Mum called out in a startled voice from the back, waking abruptly "nothing love, don't worry, just some cows on the road!" Stuart looked in amazement at the large rear end of a cow that had loomed up in front of them, its tail flicking casually a couple of feet in front of the bonnet, how had dad seen it in time to stop? He looked at his dad marvelling once more at his father's driving skills, he turned back to the cow which in turn looked back at him over its shoulder and mooed loudly at them! Stuart laughed and mooed back at it! "We passed a farm a bit back" dad said as he turned the car around, "I'll give the farmer a shout, there'll be an accident here if they don't get these cows rounded-up" Stuart chuckled as the thought of 'rounding-up them cows' conjured up images of John Wayne moseying on by on his hoss to round 'em up!

A little way back there was a turning off, which dad set off down, he slowed to a halt and peered across to the right. "Would you take a look at that!" He exclaimed, "it was probably struck by lightning!" Stuart peered across in awe and amazement, away to the right across a field, a barn was burning, the mist had thinned a bit now and the intensity of the flames shone through what was left. They were terrible, but fascinating at the same time, great plumes of yellow and red dancing up and away from the stricken building, the colours intensely bright in the half-light of dawn. Black smoke billowed up and away till it became lost in the fog. Stuart was mesmerised by it, so much so he had only just now realised that dad had reversed the car and was turning around again, he turned puzzled "there was a phone box a half a mile back on the main road, we need to dial 999!" His dad explained. This was turning into the best adventure ever!

Sure enough dad was right and pretty soon he was stood in the phone box alongside him. Normally you had to put your coins in the slot in the box, the big box fixed on the wall next to the phone. It was shiny black metal and there was a shiny chrome button with an 'A' next to it in a circle painted in white on it, oh and another button 'B' you pressed one of them to get through and your money would drop into the box, unless you pressed the other and it would tinkle down to the little silver tray you got it back from, that was if you didn't get through or you'd put too much in? Dad said you didn't need to worry about money if was a 999 and he listened in awe as his dad spoke to the Fire Brigade!

When it was nearly light dad pulled the car in off the road where there was a pull-in. It was surrounded by great big tall trees, which were pretty spooky in the half-light and the lingering mist that was floating around drifting off the river running along the far side of where they were parked. Mum had got out the big cream and red tartan Thermos and was pouring steaming hot coffee out into the Bakelite cups for everyone. Stuart and dad had blue ones, Lucy had a stupid yellow one, mum's was green, They were smashing mugs because you couldn't, smash them that was... ha-ha!! The handles were pointy at the end and a bit thin really and it felt funny against your lips, but the coffee was hot and sweet and they had a big chocolate digestive to go with it, all wrapped-up in a blue tin-foil wrapper, apart from dad's as his was in a red wrapper, yuk! They were dark chocolate mum said, which meant it tasted horrible!

Stuart wandered down to the bank of the river with his mug in one hand and the rapidly disappearing biscuit in the other. The water was fast flowing and looked deep and cold, across on the other side the water was flat though and he could see the trees reflected in it. He felt a hand on his shoulder and swivelled his head and looked up at his dad, he smiled down at him, "wouldn't fancy your chances if you fell in that!" he commented pointing with his mug. He nodded as he looked with a different take on the river as he turned back to look up at his dad "You'd get drownded for sure wouldn't you dad, sucked under the water and end up being eaten by fishes!" "Most definitely" dad concurred, "so don't get so near to the edge!" and with that he jolted Stuart towards the swirling water… his heart leapt up into his mouth as he saw the water looming at him, he felt he could feel the cold wetness of it, feel it pulling him under, the fish biting.. of course dad only pushed him a couple of inches towards the river and pulled him back mighty quick too, he had a firm grip on him so Stuart was never in any danger. That wasn't how he saw it though, not at all! He squealed in horror and then when he realised he wasn't actually going into the river he turned to face his father and throwing his mug, (which still had at least two mouthfuls of lovely sweet coffee in) onto the ground, placed his hands on his hips and shouted "you nearly drownded me dad! I hate you!" He took a wild swing at dad's leg with his foot but the big bully was too quick and he missed him completely and almost spun himself off his feet in the process! "Oi you!" Dad exclaimed, but Stuart wasn't listening anymore, he was too busy stamping his feet on his way back towards the car as he repeated over and over "I hate you!"

Mum was stood by the car and when he saw her the floodgates opened as tears started to streamed down his face, "what's the matter love?" she asked as he ran to her his arms reaching out for her long before he actually hurtled bodily into her and hugged himself to her sobbing "dad tried to kill me, to drown me! I hate him!" She ruffled his hair and said "don't be silly Stuey, I'm sure he was only playing" she crouched down and wiped his tears away with her handkerchief, she squeezed at his nose and he blew through it and cleared it out. She wiped his face and smiled at him, "see dad's here, go and say you're sorry to dad" "I won't! It was all *his* fault, he's a big fat bully and I hate him!" To make matters a million times worse dad just laughed at him! "Don't be such a baby Stuart!" Was all he said as he handed his mug back to mum, "that was just what the doctor ordered love, thanks" and he kissed her. Pah! Stuart thought and he turned his back on them and folded his arms across his chest, stamping his right foot on the ground at the same time. He stood there a little while but no one said anything? They were ignoring him! That was what they were doing! It was what they did at times like this! He turned his head a little and keeping it low peeped around to see what they were doing. Lucy was sat on the back bumper, laughing at him, she saw him peeping and pointed, pulling a 'boo-hoo' face and laughing even more. I hate her too, he thought, I'll show them, I won't go back till dad says he's sorry.

He heard the car doors shutting behind him, clunk, clunk, clunk… they'd all got in the car! I won't turn and look! I WON'T! He told himself even as he peeped. Dad wound his window down, "come on Stuart we're going!" With that he started the engine and revved it up! He spun on his heel and set off back towards the car only to be stopped by… "Oi! Go and get your mug" dad pointed over towards the river, "you're not getting in this car without it!" Stuart stopped dead in his tracks and stared at dad in disbelief, his mouth wide open as a consequence of his jaw dropping as it had done so abruptly. He took in the picture of his dad sat with one hand on the wheel of the little green A35, his other arm leaning out of the window, his thumb up gesturing back behind Stuart towards the river. Mum sat in the back seat looking forward deliberately ignoring him completely, but worse of all, way worstest of all… Lucy grinning all over her stupid face but not that in itself, but that **she** was sat in the **front** seat, in **his** seat!!

It felt like he was stood frozen, wide mouthed, wide eyed for ages till dad said "<u>now</u> Stuart, I haven't got all day!" With that he put the car in gear and moved it forward a little, sniggering as he did! "I **won't!** " He replied angrily to which dad responded "**Now!!**" much louder. Stuart was pretty flummoxed now with it all, he realised he'd got himself into a tight spot now, a humdinger of a pickle Joey would say, no doubt blaming him for getting himself into it! Where was that bear when you needed him? Slacking on the job, no doubt sleeping in the car, snoring, with his paws on his fat belly! How he wished he'd taken him with him to see the river, he'd have stopped him letting things go so far, escalatoring as he'd have put it!

He kicked his foot backwards and forwards in the dirt as he pondered what to do, he glanced back over his shoulder towards the river, there it was, the stupid mug! He would go and pick it up and lob it in the sodding river, that's what he'd do, that would show dad! He'd get a right walloping if he did though. Dad won't drive off and leave me, he tried to console himself, mum wouldn't let him, would she? Joey'd stop him, wouldn't he? No bet he's on dad's side too, bet they all are! "If I have to get out of this car mister…" "**I won't..**" he replied even as he was turning and he started to stomp theatrically back towards the mug, "I won't.." as he stamped so hard the trees shook and trembled thinking it was an earthquaker or a mighty ogre, a very angry ogre too, coming by, a mighty and horrible giant! He swept his hand down and picked the stupid, ugly, horrible, rotten-stinking stupid blummin mug up off the floor and stomped back towards the car, "I hope you're happy now?" He shouted in fury at his father as hot stinging tears burnt out of his eyes to stream down his face, "I hope you're happy, you big fat rotten bugger!" Dad pushed the car into bottom gear and slowly drove off, Stuart held his arms out in front of himself, fists clenched and screamed at the top his voice "NO!!" "You come back hear NOW!" Dad turned the car around in a large circle and drove straight towards him, switching the headlamps on as he did. Stuart shut his eyes and put both hands over his face and waited to have his bones all crunched up and be turned into a pile of mush... Peep-peep! He peered inbetween his fingers, dad was sat behind the wheel, drumming his fingers impatiently on the steering wheel, Lucy was sat next to him, still in *his* seat, smirking and mum was in the back, shaking her head as well and refusing to look at him.

It was all too much for him, he felt his head getting really hot, his cheeks were on fire, there was a loud hissing noise in his ears... he threw the trouble-making mug down and then fell to the ground lying on his back, his arms and legs thrashing and flailing about like someone having a fit, as he vented the most awful rage, a screaming, torrential release of anger and frustration with all the force his lungs could muster!

His tirade was cut short by the sharp stinging pain of having his legs slapped by his mother who then grabbed him by the arm and hauled him back to the car, but not before she had made him pick up the mug and carry it back with him. He sat in the back of the car sobbing and sniffling, with stinging legs and a smouldering hatred for all of them, it would serve them right if he pulled the big shiny chromium plated handle on the door and threw himself out of the car as it sped along the road again so that he'd be smashed-up and mangled and dead or end up wearing leg-irons and be a spaz, then they'd be sorry, his fingers felt the cold metal of the handle, he saw Joey who was jammed between the two front seats, there was a look of horror on his face, he mouthed 'no!' and went to move but stopped himself, he glanced over at his mother... her scowl had his hand back rubbing his red leg in a moment! That was it he thought, everything was spoilt now, the whole trip to Bristol was ruined, he wished they'd never come, they'd tell grandma and grandpa now and they'd all have a jolly good laugh at him again! Right! Well he'd show them once and for all, that was *it*! He'd teach them a lesson, his hand shot out and he pulled hard on the door handle, the door swung open and the noise of the road swooshing along beneath the tyres came roaring in, Stuart could see the tarmac whizzing by as he leant out of the car hanging onto the handle, big sharp lumps of it... he pulled forwards with his left hand against the frame to finish his exit but couldn't move as his mother clamped her hand onto his shoulder... shouting...

"Stuart!!"...the car swerved to the left as dad spun his head around... Lucy screamed... they all lurched forward as dad hit the brakes... the car slewed... the tyres squealed... the tyres crunched... the car stopped... silence... Lucy started crying, dad turned around and looked at mum, she was still leaning to her side her arm clamped around Stuart holding him to her... nothing was said? Mum leaned across him and pulled the door shut. Stuart looked up at each of his parents faces in turn, he was really going to get it now.... He cringed... waiting for the onslaught... nothing... he looked up again, his dad's face was as white as a sheet, what was going on? His mum was crying now, dad reached his arm around and held her hand. She rummaged for her hanky with her free hand and wiped her eyes, "drive on John, I'm alright, just drive on" dad looked down at Stuart for a moment, just a glance, but their eyes met momentarily as he turned forwards and set the car in motion once more. He reached across to Lucy and comforted her as she sobbed gently. Stuart sat with his eyes cast down at the back of the front seat unseeingly, feeling the comforting warmth of his mum's arm around him, she reached forward and picked Joey up placing him into Stuart's arm as he reached out in anticipation, he hugged the little bear close to his chest, he was trembling, he stroked his back to calm him as he realised in total horror what it was that he had seen in that fleeting contact with his dad's eyes… it was fear! He had seen his dad scared!

No one spoke for the rest of the journey. Stuart fell into an emotionally exhausted sleep. He stirred for a moment and peered around, they were coming into Bristol, he wanted to ask dad if they'd be going under the little iron bridge, the footbridge that went over the road where it went between two steep walls, with a park on either side. He went that way sometimes as he knew Stuart loved driving under it. He couldn't be bothered! To his chagrin he remembered how he'd 'ruined' the entire trip now, so he just let the warmth of sleepiness take him back away, away from all the unpleasantness that had occurred earlier.

He was awoken by the car coming to a halt and the handbrake being pulled-up, he lifted his head and peered around taking in the bleary image of his surroundings. They were parked just around the corner from his grandma and grandpa's house? He rubbed his eyes and looked again to check. Mum was getting out and so was Lucy? Dad looked around his seat into the back, "ah so you're awake are you? Come and sit in the front, I want a word with you before we go in to grandma's young man!"

Stuart dutifully opened the backdoor, pulling on the same lever that had nearly dispatched him onto the road a little earlier, he had a new reverence for it now! Clutching Joey he climbed into the front seat, 'now I'm for it!' he thought. He ducked as his dad reached across, "hey, I'm not going to hit you! Look Stuey I'm sorry, I shouldn't have scared you at the riverside, it was really silly of me, I wanted to make you realise how dangerous it was standing as close as you were to the edge, on slippery wet grass as well!" "I love you, you're my son, one day you'll understand how important that is to a chap, if you'd fallen in I'd have dived in after you in the blink of an eye you know?" Stuart looked up at his dad, frowning as he did as he grappled with this different interpretation of events, "would you dad?" "Of course I would, you mean everything to me you know?" "More than Lucy?" His dad chuckled and he hugged his son's shoulder, ruffling his hair with his other hand, "I love her just as much you, you silly sausage, but if you can keep a secret I'll tell you something… you're my favourite son!" Stuart grinned and leant across and hugged his dad round the neck, he patted the little lad on his back before placing him back in his seat and saying "come on lets drive around the corner and go and see grandma and grandpa!" Joey looked down as he felt Joey dig him in the ribs for nearly sitting on him, he digged him back and tickled him. Dad got out and shut his door, Joey giggled "favourite son! Ha-ha-ha! That was a good one!" "Shurrup you! I _am_ his favourite, he just said so, big-'ead!"

Grandma and grandpa were stood in the front garden by the front door, grandpa's face lit up as he saw Stuart opening the blue painted hollow tubed metal gate, the gate clinked as he knocked the latch down and it swung back against the spring that was wound around one side, it was a unique noise to Stuart and he loved hearing it knowing he was at the only place in the world where he could hear that exact sound… grandpa's!! He tore down the path and grabbed hold of his grandpa, who scooped him up and held him aloft in front of himself for a moment before hugging him to his chest and patting him fondly on his back, "oh Stuey-bach… my Stuey-bach…" Stuart hugged him tight with his free arm, the one that wasn't hanging on to Joey. Grandpa smelt of soap, not like the soap they had at home though, his face was prickly with white whiskery stubble which matched his snow white hair, well the bit he had at the sides of his head, the rest being bare skin, sun-tanned and weather-beaten brown skin. Grandpa set him down in front of him and examined him closely, "let me take a good look at you boy, my you've grown since I saw you haven't you?" Grandpa was Welsh, that meant he came from Wales, even though it should really have been Wales-sh or Walesish? It was a part of England like Lancashire was, or so Stuart had described it to Joey! He hadn't been convinced that Joey wasn't pulling his leg when he'd explained that Wales was actually a country and had counties all of its own, which is what Lancashire was. This had resulted in a lengthy debate in which Stuart had accused Joey of having a big fat head full of sawdust and up until just now when he had told him all about the subject he had really thought Wales was a whole lot of big fish swimming around in the sea, any one of which could sink a boat full of sailors when they were trying to stab one of them with their big spear! Joey shook his head, "that's wHales and whalers use *harpoons* not spears! You really can be the most silly of boys, just because you don't know something doesn't mean you're stupid, we all have to learn." Stuart poked him in the ear "Big fat head!" feeling very indignant Joey replied "Ignoramus!" "Hippopot*a*mus!" Stuart laughed back at him and as ever they ended up rolling about laughing and tickling each other. "Whales aren't fish either Stuart!" "They're mammals just like us" "they've got big fat head's like you and you're a bear not a mammal!" "Bears are mammals…" "*Shurrrr….up!*"

Grandpa really did have the most wonderful lilting accent though, it almost sounded like he was singing when he spoke. Stuart loved his grandpa dearly, he was the only person in the whole big wide world who called him Stuey-bach, it meant 'boy' he thought in Walesish? What was more his grandpa loved him too, there was no disguising it, he felt his love as surely as he felt the warmth from his hand through his jumper as he rested it on his shoulder.

Grandma was a different kettle of fish altogether, she had white hair too but it was all pinned up tightly onto her head. She was very kindly towards them, but she didn't go in for big hugs and the like, not even to his mum and she was her daughter, like Lucy was to mum? He wasn't bothered anyhow as there was lots to explore, everything was old fashioned at their house, like in the olden days before modern was invented.

Stuart had to help dad bring in their bags which was unfair because Lucy didn't have to help, and she was bigger than him, though not as strong, neither did mum they just swanned off into the house. It didn't help that Lucy poked her tongue out as she went in through the front door either. So he marched down the garden path like a Nazi with his legs dead stiff and his arms straight, he turned on his heel on the pavement and strutted up to the back of the car and then clicked his feet together, clanging his ankle bones into each other in the process, which really hurt but being a big brave soldier in Hitler's army he didn't let on and it didn't put him off giving the Nazi salute… and then getting a clip round the ear off his dad for his trouble! It was only a playful flick though and they laughed and then both goose-stepped back carrying the bags.

Inside the house at last Stuart soaked in all the detail as he recalled how everything looked and smelt. There was so much to remember that he'd seen from last time, so many exciting things, he ran around and around up and down the stairs in and out of the lounge which had a door into the hall and one into the kitchen as well so it allowed for circuits to be made or laps as Stuart called them. Eventually of course he had to be told to 'calm down' but not until Lucy had sent him flying and nearly killed him or at least put him in an iron-lung for weeks by sticking her foot out and tripping him up! He sat quietly for a while with grandpa as they waited in the front room for the little doors to open on grandpa's clock and the cuckoo to pop out and go cuck-oo, cuck-oo! How he wished they had a cuckoo clock at home.

 Grandpa helped him up, he'd seen what had happened and he waggled a finger at Lucy and told her she was a little monkey, huh! That was all the telling off she got! She was more like one of those naughty chimpanzees at the zoo, yeah one of them with a big fat red shiny bottom too! He poked his tongue out at her and pushed Joey's bottom in her face when grandpa's back was turned and made a farting noise! As you can imagine he was well and truly told off later for that when they were finally alone. Meantime grandpa had taken Stuart to the back of the room to let him play with his radio which sat atop a big tall dark wooden sideboard, Stuart loved the big brown shiny radio, grandpa put one of the dining chairs alongside the sideboard so he could kneel-up on it and reach the radio properly. It had a glass window on the front at the top with coloured strips and little tiny clear windows in it that the light inside shone through, one of the four big brown knobs at the bottom on the front moved a black line across the window and you could 'tune-in' to the radio station. There was a special little round window in the glass that looked like an eye, a green eye! It went wide and narrow as you turned the tuning knob. It was called 'a magic eye!' One knob was all clunky as you turned it and that one changed the wave-band, short wave was best as once it went dark you could get hundreds of different stations from all over the world, you'd get to hear foreigners jabbering away in their silly languages, they were so funny to listen to and there was strange exotic music as well. Every now and then you would hear a voice in English, or even a Yank *'this is the voice of America...'* but it would fade and hiss and go funny as well!

After twenty minutes or so though Stuart got bored with the radio and asked grandpa if they could go out in the shed? He said he would… but later. Huh! Typical that was and it was 'because we're all talking here, catching-up see.' Pah! That what was he thought, as grandpa steered him around to sit on one of the tuffet-like little boxes that were at either end of the brass fender that ran across the front of the fireplace, huh! and while Lucy was sat on the couch with grandma too. He scowled at her and started fiddling with the companion set of stuff for the fire, rattling the long brassy metal implements in the holder. Mum scowled at him and put her arm around his shoulder, "see listen to what's being said and join in. It's called conversation, you might learn something!" Huh! Fat chance Stuart thought, grown-up talk, bla, bla, flippin-bla!

He leant over and whispered in grandpa's ear, "can I turn the telly on grandpa?" He said he could as long as he kept the sound low. Stuart didn't waste a moment but leapt up to go to the telly knocking the companion set flying and clattering across the fireplace! So he had to pick them all up, the stupid things one by one up and put them back!

The telly was completely different to the one at The Wheelers, it stood in a highly polished wooden cabinet with two doors that folded when you opened them, they had little ball-bearings held in a plate that clicked into a slot to hold the doors shut. He loved to pull the doors and feel the click and listen to the lovely noise it made. Once opened the doors folded back out of the way to reveal the tiny little screen, you turned one of the knobs and it started humming, and a crackle came out of the speaker, then a man's voice came and then ages and ages later the screen began to come to life. Andy Pandy was on! He was a bit soft, more Lucy's cup of tea and she was sat on the floor next to him now watching. Stuart preferred Bill and Ben, girls!

He got up and wandered around with his hands shoved deep into his pockets, across the window behind the telly, round the back of the couch, examining the backs of everyone's heads and finally round to the fireplace again. The big wooden clock started its chiming, ding dong ding dong… like Big Ben did in London, then struck out the hour… Stuart took it as a signal and took hold of his grandpa's hand and tugged at the same time putting on his best 'pleading' face! The old man smiled and got up, "you'll have to excuse me for a while," he said to the rest of the room, " me and my Stuey-bach have important business in the shed!"

The shed… it was one of the best bits of going down to Bristol, it was full of grandpa's tools and a bench and a vice and jars of nails and screws and saws hung up on the wall and hammers too and of course bestest of all… grandpa's motorbike… 'Banty.'

Banty was a BSA motorbike, it was a 'Bantam' that was the name of the model you see and why grandpa called it Banty! It was pale green all over and it was simply smashing! Stuart used to love looking at it, taking in its splendour, letting his fingers touch it. He was in awe of it, it held him in a sort of spell… its thick pale green paint felt cool and smooth beneath the touch of his fingertips, the lovely curvy shape of the petrol tank fascinated him with its little colour picture of a cockerel on its sides and the letters B S A which meant British Small

Arms, which meant guns! They used to make guns at the same factory once upon a time grandpa had told him! He'd also told him that a bantam was a type of little chicken as well.

Banty was like his push bike in lots of ways, with its chrome handle bars and levers but it was so much bigger as well, with its dull silvery coloured metal engine with all its fins on the top and the shiny chrome exhaust pipe that came out of it… the big oily chain at the back, just like the one on his bike but much bigger. In the middle of the handle bars it had a black rubber honking-horn that you squeezed to make a parping noise, he always had to be told to stop parping it 'before it gets worn out!'

Stuart climbed up and sat on the big single seat, it was held up on two big springs which boinged when he bounced up and down on it as he gripped onto the handle bars and made roaring motorbike noises! He felt grandpa's hands around his waist as he was dismounted from Banty, "come on off there boy before you damage something!" "See come here and I'll show you how to use the tools."

Grandpa was dead patient not like dad and he showed Stuart everything you needed to know about how to make things with wood, "here hold the saw like this see… no not like that, like this… right now boy, what you do is push… no, not like that! See like this, nice and gentle and steady like, the saw only cuts as you push it forwards see… not on the way back, nice and steady not like that in a mad hurry, you should be able to saw nice and steady all day long, your arm'll be aching in no time going at it like a madman now! Keep it nice and straight, good lad, that's the ticket, we'll make a carpenter out of you yet!" Then he had shown him how to bang nails in, "use your arm not your wrist see, hold it tight not like a big

Jessie... whack it boy don't tickle it! Hit the nail not the wood, you'll put pennies on it!" "What?" "Look boy, see there where you whacked the wood..." and there was a big penny sized dent in the wood!

Hammering was great fun unless you got your thumb, then your nail went black, or if you got a nip off of the pliers and a 'black man's nip' it was really called a blood blister but grandpa said all sorts of silly things, he even pee'd (to Stuarts' immense amusement and naturally he had to do so as well)... in the big water bath thing by the shed which collected rain water, then he used the stirruppy pump to pump water out of it! Well he said it was good for the plants and he had lots of them too!.. He grew all sorts of stuff, blackcurrants, redcurrants, raspberries, apples, tomatoes, pears and then on the allotment at the back, cabbages, potatoes, peas, runner beans (yuk), butter beans (double-yuk), carrots, onions and millions of other things. They had to help preparing the vegetables too, shelling the peas, pulling the stringy bit of the beans, peeling... it wasn't that bad, in fact it was quite fun but the bad thing was that they made them eat them too! Yuk! Some were horrible... "waste not want not!" Grandma said, "yeah, yeah we know" Stuart would reply rudely "mum's always saying that!" He did a rude impersonation of his mum..." It's not that long since we were on rationing either! She says that too!" Grandpa had pointed his knife at him as he cut up his potatoes, "you show some respect for your mam young man, she's right you've no idea how hard it was for us all having to queue up for everything and coming away with nothing many a time and she's right it's only four years since it ended too!" Stuart'd shuffled in his seat and shovelled the disgusting butter beans in without further protest, trying to swallow them whole without chewing on them all the while feeling that he'd been put in his place! Didn't help that Joey was sniggering!

Grandma used to pluck the caterpillars off her plants on the allotment and then pull them in two! They were full of yellow yucky custardy stuff inside, YUK! Lucy squealed when she saw her do it and ran off to mum, but she was after all only a silly girl, he just laughed, he was tough and brave (and had to hide that it made him feel really queasy and sick!) The best place was inside his greenhouse where he grew his tomatoes, it had a wonderful smell in there like nowhere else Stuart had ever been, grandpa loved it in there too although he used to say wistfully "I do all this for my tomatoes and if I tried to eat one it would kill me!" He seemed to suffer a lot from indigestion and stomach pain Stuart was aware, he used to reckon fresh bread would kill him too! He did make the most delicious chutney out of the tomatoes and he used to manage to eat that with a hunk of cheese and some Jacobs Cream Crackers!

In what seemed like no time at all it was tea time and before he knew it bedtime and he was snuggled down in the funny bed with the funny smelling bed clothes and the scratchy sheets, it was all clean but it was different and strange, so unlike his own bed back at home. It was wonderful, it was an adventure wasn't it he asked Joey, he said it truly was and he seemed very happy to be there too. As soon as mum had shut the door Stuart sprang back out of bed, but quietly, like a cat, making no noise, slinking around the room looking at everything, exploring everywhere! The bed was a metal bedstead made of big pieces of iron that smelled really metally, it had a mesh under the mattress Stuart discovered as he skidded himself under it on his back on the shiny linoleum oil-cloth, it was like the chainmail that knights wore to stop their enemies swords from cutting out their gizzards! He bonged his head noisily into something and spun himself around by walking his legs sideways as he lay on his back, it was a great big blue and white potty, or *gazunder* as grandma called it! He sniggered at it and put his hand on the big pot handle, he called up to Joey "do you want a wee Joey? There's a potty under here!" before dissolving into a fit of giggling. He picked it up and stood next to the bed with it in his hands, "I could trap me a bear in this potty" he called out theatrically, Joey quick as a flash leapt up and swung himself around sliding down the post at the top corner of the bed, there then followed a game of 'catch me if you can' with Joey running around and under the bed with Stuart diving across the bed and even recklessly jumping up and down on it…if he bounced just a bit higher he'd be able to touch the ceiling…

The bedroom door swung open… "Stuart Wheeler! What on earth are you doing? That's a bed not a trampoline, you'll ruin grandma's bed, get into bed at once!" Mum was not in any mood for shenanigans Stuart could see and from mid bounce he shot straight back down under the bedclothes and pulled them right up to his chin. Mum picked Joey up off the floor and snuggled him in next to Stuart before she pulled at the sheets and blankets and tucked them in so tight that neither of them could breathe! She picked up the potty and slid it carefully back under the bed, this isn't a toy and it's only for doing a piddle in and only then if you really have to, go downstairs if you need to do a number two! She leant over and kissed him on the forehead and then with a very stern "go to sleep!" she was gone. Stuart kicked his legs like billy-o to loosen the sheets a bit and only just in time before they were both snuffocated! "Couldn't catch me" Joey whispered in Stuart's ear, adding "too slow to catch cold!" Stuart giggled and tickled Joey's tummy "you cheated 'cos you're such a short-arse, running under the bed like that!" "Well never mind that Stuart Wheeler… just you remember… no doing your plops in the potty!" At this Stuart set off giggling, adding "you can't either, no smelly bear's poo's in here thank you very much!"

It was so funny in grandpa's house they didn't have a toilet upstairs! You had to traipse all the way down the stairs and out of the back door, there you found a little covered bit that was open at one end to the back of the house and the garden and there was a door to the coal hole and one to the toilet. It was blummin freezing down there too in your jama's, the loo had a big water box high up on the wall and a chain with a big metal loop on the bottom and when you pulled on it the water came slooshing down a big long pipe into the bowl. It smelt funny in there, not pooey or anything bad but just funny and there was no proper toilet paper to wipe your bum with either, there was just a little white shiny pot thingamajig on the wall with a little cardboard box of tracing paper in it? That was all? It was pretty rubbish at wiping your bum with! Stuart had to go once when it was the middle of the night, his tummy was rumbling something awful, all those yukky butter beans them Jerry's had forced him to eat he reckoned, 'you vil eat them all or you vill be taken outside und shot!' "But they're 'orrible… and they're stone blummin cold!" "They ver hot ven they ver putten on your platten schveinhund!

Joey wouldn't wake up when he needed the loo and he'd had to poke him in the tummy two hundred times to get him to come with him, it was dead spooky and scary when he got down into the kitchen and then when he slid back the bolt and unlatched the back door and peeped out around it. He was shivering by the time he'd done and shot back up the stairs like a rocket. They chuckled together and inbetween yawning chatted for a little while about what fabulous adventures lay in store for them tomorrow and in no time at all they were both fast asleep.

Chapter Four: Abandoned!

As soon as Stuart woke up and had his dressing gown and slippers on he flung back the curtains and looked out into grandpa's garden, it was blummin fantastic to have a different view to look at from the one he had at home, the one he knew every single detail of. Here it was all new, well different, he remembered it from last time of course but not all of it!

Next job was to prop up the lid on grandpa's record player, or phonogram as it called itself on the lovely little faded coloured transfer that was on the inside, it had a picture too with flags on it! It was really, really old, probably antiquated in fact! It had a metal handle at the side, with a round wooden knob on the end which you used to wind it up! Yes you had to turn the handle and wind it up, no 'lectric, no plug to shove in a socket, one of those little brown Bakelite boxes on the skirting boards with the three little holes in, well two big ones and a little one… holes that were just exactly the right size for his finger… holes he'd been told sternly to 'never put your fingers in Stuart!' 'Why not?' 'Because you'll be electrocuted!' 'Is that bad?' 'Yes very bad, you'd be dead!' 'DEAD!' Now that was a bit blummin stupid wannit? Having holes that kids could put their fingers in and get deaded? Anyhow turned out you didn't get killed, it just bit you! True it was a nasty horrible bite and it tried to keep hold of you, grip onto your finger and you had to pull yourself away with your body as your arm wasn't for moving gripped as it was by them 'lectrics!

Once you'd wound up the clockwork you could put one of the big heavy records onto the soft green velvet of the turntable, with the little hole in the middle of the record over the shiny little knob in its middle, flick the little shiny lever and Bob's your uncle… the turntable would start whizzing around like mad, at a fair old lick too! Not like on dad's radiogram, which was 'lectric not clockwork and had a radio in it too, that went round much slower... anyhow there's your big heavy record spinning around like a whirling dervish and you picks up the thick hollow shiny silver arm with the needle stuck in the end and drop it down onto the record and dada-dada-da-da... the squeaky, tinny, scratchy, clicky music comes blaring out the front, you see the hollow metal arm echoes the sound of the needle scratching along in the groove on the record and sends it down... oops... quick open the two little doors to let it out! Shut the lid gently down too...

Joey dived under the pillow as the racket kicked off, he'd been having a nice lie-in after the long journey and the worry of Stuart's monster tantrum as well! Once he'd woken up a little he realised that it was anything but a racket it was a Gilbert and Sullivan piece from HMS Pinafore... he jumped up and bounced to the end of the bed and was hanging onto the metal rail singing along... (the part of Sir Joseph, naturalee...)
I polished up that handle so carefullee
That now I am the Ruler of the Queen's Navee!

To be joined in with by Stuart on the chorus...
He polished up that handle so carefullee,
That now he is the ruler of the Queen's Naveey!

At which point the bedroom door swung open and grandpa came in, he was wearing his stripey cotton pyjamas and was ruffling his hand through his hair over his ear... Joey dropped to the bed, Stuart froze, suddenly wondering if it was actually time to get up... whether he was *in for it* for waking the whole street up no doubt *at the crack of dawn* with his impromptu concert?

Grandpa smiled though, threw his arm forward theatrically and let rip with his wonderful tenor voice...
#*As office boy I made such a mark*

That they gave me the post of a junior clerk.
I served the writs with a smile so bland,
And I copied all the letters in a big round hand... #

The record was soon at the end, the needle clickety-clicking in the middle, mum who had also appeared gave a round of applause and grandpa put his arm around her as she came in the room, she brushed a tear aside as she kissed him on the cheek, "that was wonderful dad, it's been so long since I heard you sing!" She turned as they were leaving the room together telling Stuart 'to be careful and not to break any of grandpa's records!'

After breakfast Uncle Terry and Aunty Olive came round. Aunty Olive was mum's big sister, Stuart liked them. Aunty Olive was really, really clever, she had three sons, they were all really clever too, he wasn't that keen on them, they were just a bit too clever for his liking! Uncle Terry was a hero, not just a made-up pretend hero but a real-true-to-life RAF bomber pilot hero! He'd flown Lancaster bombers in the wartime, he'd been shot down and captured by Jerry! He'd got away and got home though, couldn't keep Uncle Terry locked up they couldn't!! Then he'd even gone back and flown more sorties!!! He was bit scary though, he was big and wide too, not a fatso or anything like that but dead strong! He talked loud and fast and with a funny, buzzy, warm accent, mum said it was a Somerset accent, which was down Bristol way somewhere, that Somerset was.

They were all going to go out for a ride with them, (except Lucy who went out for the day with Aunty Alice), to their house in the country, which was a super place to visit. Uncle Terry drove a Jaguar car, it was big and posh and went really fast. Stuart sat in the back but in the middle so he could see into the front, it was massive inside the Jag compared to dad's

Austin, the seats were made of soft leather and smelt lovely and the dashboard was a lovely grainy polished wood instead of painted metal. The Jag had lots more dials and switches too than the little A35 and at the end of the great long sweeping bonnet instead of a flying 'A' there was a fabulous leaping silver jaguar. He wished his dad had a Jaguar, he wondered if dad was feeling fed up now, seeing that he only had a little Austin A35 when other people had big posh swanky cars like Uncle Terry's. He had to admit that he did, well feel a little bit anyhow. Stuart decided though that dad was a better driver overall than Uncle Terry and that dad would be thinking, if he was here that he was a bit of a road hog!

Uncle Terry was saying to dad "do you remember when you tried to teach the old fella how to drive your car?" Dad laughed, by the 'old fella' he knew they meant grandpa, he'd pointed backwards with his thumb as he said it, he'd heard this story before, how grandpa had set off behind the wheel of the car and got to the green at the end of the road and dad had said go left and grandpa had leaned over in his seat and dad had said no turn the bloody wheel and he didn't and they'd bounced up the kerb onto the green and grandpa had said that was it, he'd had enough of cars and he'd stick to his motorbike in future! So Stuart sat back and leant his shoulder into grandpa's, it was a squeeze for them all in the back even in the Jag and he started talking to him so he wouldn't hear them two in the front taking the mickey out of him!

It started to rain as they got near to Uncle Terry's and by the time they pulled up at their house it was pouring down. On the way in Stuart admired Uncle Terry's motorbike that was leaning up under the covered bit between the garage and the house, it was covered in dust and rust and had bits missing and hanging off. He didn't look after it he thought, grandpa could fix it up for him he thought and looked up at his grandpa who was walking alongside him, he saw grandpa's eyes light up as he saw the motorbike then his face fell as he took in the condition of the bike, he shook his head and looked away. Stuart was going to say something but didn't get chance, as there was lots of chatter going on over his head, it was hard to get to say anything here, with all these grown-ups, they were always so very busy talking…and talking, yak yak, yak… He tried to listen, be interested as Joey had said he should, 'you might learn something!' He would chide him, 'why bother when you already know everything and can tell me anyway, it's all locked up in that big fat head of yours!'

The grown-ups were going on and on about something in London that had gone on recently, five thousand people had turned out for it apparently so it must have been something worth putting your hat and coat on for? Uncle Terry was saying it was 'bloody daft! Where would we be now if we'd had that attitude when old Hitler was on the march eh?' Grandpa joined in 'if he'd got his horrible Nazi hands on the bomb he'd have wiped us all out!' Dad said 'that was different, that was then and this is now and he thought forming the CND was a good idea, people having bombs that could destroy whole cities in one go was just plain evil, especially them Americans, who couldn't be trusted anyhow. Someone needed to say no to them and put a stop to the madness or we'd blow the whole flaming planet up!' He was getting hot under the collar now and Stuart saw mum put her hand on his arm to try and calm him down! It was way too late for that Stuart thought, he knew dad's fuse and he knew that it had already ignited his powder and that it was on slow-burn, he'd blow any minute… and he did… BOOM!!!
'…what's more what them Yanks did in Nagasaki was the biggest crime against humanity ever perpetrated, a city full of women and children! Not just a city, but the second one they

bombed, wasn't one a heinous enough bloody crime? Bastards!" That was it then… mum tried to calm him down, or just shut him up, even grandma joined in with 'there's no need for language like that…'

Stuart was terminally bored by it all despite what Joey'd said, he dug him in the tummy and asked "well then professor that was really educational eh?" Joey just made a dismissive little grunt and muttered "least dad tried to talk some sense…" Stuart scoffed, "yeah till he lost his rag?" "It's a very emotive subject Stuart and you'd do well to keep abreast of the developments and I hope for yours and everyone's sake that the CND can become a powerful voice in years to come, if it doesn't I have grave fears for you all!" Stuart brushed aside his remark with a sullen, dismissive and very bored 'huh!' and he plodded off leaving the grown-ups to their squabbling, he wandered around the rooms of the strange house, his hands thrust deep into his trouser pockets, Joey squeezed under his arm, dragging his feet and prodding at things with the toe of his shoe imagining what it must be like for his three cousins living here, two brothers each, no sister! It must be more fun for them? Surely?

They were all out, they were always doing something, two of them were much older than Stuart and the other one who was about his age was away at camp. Stuart wanted to join the scouts, but hadn't been able to yet.

Uncle Terry had a silver metal model of a Lancaster bomber on his desk, it was made of bright and shiny smooth metal and had four propellers that could be spun around, it was on a stand so it looked like it was flying, banking and climbing slightly. He was admiring it when Uncle Terry came in the room, he pulled his hand back sharply afraid that he might not have been meant to touch the plane, but Uncle Terry laughed, "you can pick it up if you like Stuey, its heavy though so watch out" Stuart shook his head, feeling a bit intimidated to be alone in the company of a bomber pilot hero, "s'alright thanks, I can just look. It's really super, is it like the one you flew sir?" Uncle Terry boomed out his big laugh again, "you don't have to call me sir! Uncle Terry or plain Terry if you like, I don't stand on ceremony!" "Can I call you Captain, or Squadron Leader?" Stuart asked, feeling a little more adventurous, he pushed Joey onto a chair behind him secretly, not wanting to look childish carrying a teddy! "My crew used to call me Skipper, or just plain Skip, you can call me that if you like!" "Wow! Thanks Skip!" "Is a Lancaster better than a Spitfire? I love Spitfires, I pretend I'm a Spitfire all the time!" Uncle Terry spun the propeller of the model around absent mindedly with his finger, "well they're different beasts aren't they Stuey, one drops bombs the others a fighter, ones slow and heavy the other light and fast. It's a shame it's raining so hard and you can't play outside..." he peered out of the window at the black clouds and driving rain, "I know what we can do! It's a game I used to play with my boys when we were stuck inside, we can make a Lancaster bomber in here and go for a sortie! Would you like that?" "Oh golly, wow! Yes please Skipper!" Stuart bounced up and down as he answered, "how? How do we do it?"

In ten minutes Flight Sergeant Wheeler was having his first lesson in flying the mighty Lancaster. Uncle Terry had rearranged the furniture and he was now sat in his cockpit, he had a piece of broom handle with a half-wheel screwed on it in his hand, he had two big books under his feet, wedged up at an angle, and various cooking utensils stuck in a plastic dish rack on the table next to him, which were the throttles, one each for the four mighty Merlin engines! The clock off the mantelpiece, a smaller clock off the desk, a plate with a fork balanced across it, and a plate with a teaspoon across it! A quick explanation of all the controls and they were off…

"Right Captain, check your controls, ailerons…port…starboard…" Uncle Terry had written 'port' and 'starboard' on two pieces of paper and had one on either side of the table for Stuart to help him remember. He said to help him remember which was which, say this 'Jack the sailor left port.' Stuart though that was a really clever way to remember and knew that he always would from no on! He turned the wheel to the left, "port aileron sir!" Uncle Terry lifted the cover of the book at the end of the left wing "check!" he had explained to Stuart using the model how the aileron lifted and keeping the explanation at eight year old level, he'd explained that it slowed the air down and pushed the wing down, which made the plane bank to the left, to port. They went through all the controls, the elevators, two encyclopaedias either side of the rudder, which was the fire-guard! You pushed the joystick forward and the elevators went up, just like the ailerons did this made the plane tip forward, or dive. By pulling the stick back it made them go down which lifted the nose. This was fabulous fun!! Then there was just the rudder, this worked just the same as it did on the motorboats in the boating lake, but you used your feet though in a plane, you pushed your left foot down and the plane would turn to port, right and it would turn to starboard. But you had to use the ailerons at the same time. Uncle Terry showed him again how the plane would try and rotate as the rudder moved and would then be flying at an angle but if you tilted the wings it could turn, or bank, it could climb or dive at the same time too. It was wonderful as he explained it to him and it made perfect intuitive sense to the boy who had loved to watch aircraft in action at every opportunity and studied how they flew in the movies. He had model aeroplanes too, a Spitfire naturally and a Mosquito, he flew them as he ran along with them, he flew himself as a Spitfire too. He surprised Uncle Terry by commenting, "it's just the same as the birds really, they move their wings like that don't they? I've watched them as they fly and come into land and take off, the ducks do it too and the swans are like the Lancaster, big and heavy!"

Grandma and grandpa and Aunty Olive all came through to see him flying his 'Lancaster' they complimented him on his skill. "Well done Captain Wheeler you have passed your test and earned your wings!" With that Uncle Terry placed a proper, real RAF cap on Stuart's head, it came right down over his eyes and they all laughed, Stuart was so happy he just pushed it back up onto his forehead and laughed with them, he knew they weren't laughing at him. He was a bit miffed though as blummin dinner being ready meant he never got his flying lesson!

After dinner Stuart wandered off back to the other room and sat in the cockpit of the Lancaster as it sat idly on the runway, Joey was sat with him too, now they were alone, he'd been a bit miffed himself at being shoved out of sight like that, but he understood the lad's motives so didn't say anything. He was explaining everything to Stuart again and had got to the part that Uncle Terry hadn't had chance to explain, what the clocks were for and the plates and cutlery! "This one is your artificial horizon Stuey, when you pull the stick back and the nose rises the little plane (or teaspoon) goes up above the line (drawn on the plate) the horizon," "wow!" "This one is your compass and tells you which way you're heading and this one is your altimeter which tells you how high you are…" Uncle Terry stepped out from behind the door where he'd been listening, "How the blue blazes did you know all that Stuey?"He asked incredulously, "and I love the voice you put on for your instructor!" Stuart blushed like a beetroot, "I err... I... saw it in a book sir!"

"Well you were spot on old chap, we really will make a pilot out of you! Would you like to be a pilot?" "Oh yes sir, I mean Skipper, I'd love to fly a Comet airliner when I grow up!" "Good show! Right let's start up those engines and take her up for a few circuits!"

Downstairs at breakfast the day after there had been a big shock in store for Stuart and Lucy, dad just casually announced like he was saying 'think I'll cut the grass' that him and mum were going back home in an hour or so and *they* (him and Lucy) were staying with grandma and grandpa... for a fortnight! Lucy had set off crying straight away, stupid girl and clinging to mum she really was a big soft nelly! Stuart however was in a turmoil of mixed emotions... there was sheer unbridled and utterly terrible, blind panic, tinged by the rosy glow of being out of reach of the Nazi's... the only power over him being vested in a kindly old gentleman who had never lifted a finger to him in his life! There was grandma of course who might well be a secret agent for the Gestapo of course? She *did* tell him off, frequently... hmm... There was lots to explore here, not just in the house but out in Bristol, well the bits around where grandpa lived, the park, the downs, the river and a little further afield the zoo even, a long bus ride away on one of the lovely green buses... So he just shrugged and said "oh righto" when mum said 'is that okay?' I mean it was just fine and dandy for them to swan off and leave him behind, they'd probably forget all about him and never come back for him, it was a really long drive wasn't it and after all he was a 'bloody pest' at times wasn't he? It was probably because of his tantrum wasn't it? With that he dropped his spoon into his half-eaten bowl of Weetabix and ran from the room, up the stairs and threw himself face-down on the bed crying his eyes out!

It was grandpa's voice that was connected to the person that came and sat on the bed next to him and rubbed his shoulders gently, "you'll be all right here with me Stuey-bach, I'll look after you just like your mam and da do, you know. I managed to bring up your mam and her two sisters didn't I now?" And knowing what a special place Joey had in his grandson's heart he added, "and see you'll have Joey with you here too as well won't you?" The little lad spun around and throwing his arms around the old man's neck sobbed out "I don't <sob> want them <sob> to go <sob> grandpa." He gently lifted the young lad away from him a little and looked at him eye to eye, face to face, "now you see here my Stuey-bach-a-soldier-boy, sometimes we just have to be brave see, it's what us big men have to do, when the women are all crying and a wailing and carrying on, like they do sometimes, us men, well we just have to stick out our chins, put our heads back, stand-up proud and tall and face-up to things we do!" Stuart looked deep into the old man's pale blue eyes, he was fascinated as he gazed into them, all his own family had brown eyes, his grandpa had the kindest of eyes, set in amidst the wrinkled and lined visage of his tanned ancient face, framed with his snow white hair and stubble. His face melted into a smile as they looked at each other, "I love you grandpa" Stuart exclaimed spontaneously as he hugged himself back around his grandpa's neck, "I love you too Stuey-bach, oh how I love you" he responded as he gently rubbed his little grandson's back and in that moment safely wrapped in the arms of his grandpa, Stuart knew he would be fine. Joey watching sat up against the pillow brushed away a tear and sniffled, grandpa looked up at him over Stuart's shoulder and winked.

There was a knock at the bedroom door, "can I come in?" Mum called. "Come in" Stuart and grandpa said as a chorus and then chuckled together. Mum sat and talked with Stuart after grandpa had gone downstairs. "This was my bedroom when I was a little girl, I lived here my whole life up till when I met daddy and moved up north. You'll be fine down here you know, I often wish we lived nearer so you could see mum and dad more, they love you being here and your cousins'll come over to see you too whilst you're here. Just remember that grandma and grandpa are old, they can't run around after you like me and dad do and if he seems grumpy sometimes it's only because he's old and has a lot of aches and pains" "is that why he walks funny?" Stuart asked, "yes my love, that's why, his legs hurt him too." Stuart looked closely at his mother, he could see her eyes were welling up with tears behind her glasses, he put his hand on her shoulders to comfort her but she bustled him up and off the bed with, "right come on now and be a big brave boy and wave me and daddy off."

There had been a few more tears as the car vanished around the corner and away but they soon dried up as they set off for a good long walk down along the 'reach', which was really along the river.

Back home later they busied themselves digging up some potatoes for tea, well Stuart, grandpa and Joey did, Lucy was *tired* and had to sit in a chair in the lounge and help grandma with her woolly-knittings or some such girlie nonsense or other! Stuart bombarded the old man with requests for him to take him for a ride on 'Banty' can we go along The Portway grandpa, right along and under the spension bridge?" "<u>Sus</u>pension bridge…" he corrected the lad kindly and agreed that they would, most definitely, before he went back, if he was a good helpful boy… take him for a ride on Banty!

A couple of days into the visit and grandpa decided it would be best to let the boy have his ride sooner rather than later, to give his ears a rest from the constant mithering! It was a considerable struggle for the old man to get the little BSA Bantam out of the shed and then through the gates at each end of the tunnel-cum-passage that ran between and under his house and next doors. There was another tight ninety degree bend at the front of the house to negotiate as well. Fortunately it was a lightweight little thing, nothing like the big AJS or the old side-valve BSA 500 he'd had in the past. He was old, plain and simple and things that hadn't been an issue for him in the past were major obstacles now. Still he'd promised the boy his ride and he wouldn't disappoint him.

Grandma fussed about strapping her old white pudding-basin helmet onto the lad's head and helping him to pull the big gloves on. Grandpa had a big long coat on and wore great big gauntlets that went half way up his arms, he had a silver helmet on too but his had leather sides to it. Grandpa kick-started Banty and she spluttered into life, phut-phut-phutting with little puffs of bluey-white smoke coming out of the exhaust. Grandpa settled himself on his seat and Stuart climbed up onto the rear seat, which was called 'the pillion' and was fixed atop the rear mudguard, "Put your arms around grandpa and hold on tight!" Grandma said, grandpa turned to ask if he was okay, then lifted his goggles down off his helmet and put them over his eyes… then he revved her up and they moved off down the street…

To Stuart it was the closest he'd ever been to flying, he hugged onto the old man piloting their green flying machine, his beloved grandpa, when they came to a bend they flew around it the bike leaning right over and the road coming up towards them, before they powered away and tilted upright again. As promised they followed the course of the River

Avon as it wound its way up along the deep gorge towards the docks. Stuart had to hold on really tight as he looked right up as they passed under the suspension bridge way up high above their heads. A little while later they rode over it, before parking the bike up and walking back across, looking down to the river way, way down below them.

How Stuart loved to ride on the motorbike with his grandpa, the feel of the road passing beneath them coming up through his seat and his feet resting on the foot pegs, the sense of the road surface with its different textures and undulations, he could feel the bumps come up through the wheels and the frame of the motorbike, feel the vibration of the little engine as it worked to power them along, hear the change in the revs as grandpa shifted through the gears, the forces that pulled him backwards as they accelerated, then sliding him forwards when grandpa braked. The air rushed past his face, pushing at his skin as they speeded up, there was so much to see as they were out in the open as they whizzed along the road not boxed up inside and behind the windscreen like they were in the car and with only the massive blue sky as a roof over their heads.

The sounds were wonderful too, the swish of the tyres, the whirring of the wind passing over his helmet, the noise of other vehicles, the sound of the bike echoing back of walls… it was pure bliss to Stuart as he soaked up all the amazing sensory input that assaulted his brain as a connoisseur would savour an exceptional vintage wine… when he grew up he was going to get a motorbike, all of his own, he would look after it with his spanners like grandpa did, clean it and polish it, fill the tank with petrol, put air in the tyres and he would ride it everywhere…

It was a week now since they'd been abandoned, as Stuart liked to think of it, he didn't care now, he was having a great time but sappy Lucy was pining for her mummy! Grandpa had three daughters, he'd always wanted a boy he told Stuart but he'd been given the three girls! Aunty Alice was his youngest daughter and she'd come round one day with her daughter Molly, she was about the same age as Lucy and it was awful then, as there was two of 'them' to gang up on him! Anyhow thankfully Aunty Alice took whining Lucy home with her this time to stay there for a few days. Which was great… well it seemed that way till they all drove off in their Morris 1000 and he was stood at the blue gate waving with grandma and grandpa.

Aunty Alice had a telephone so they could ring up mum and dad and let her talk to them so she'd not feel quite as homesick. Now that was blummin unfair, that was… "What's wrong my Stuey-bach? You goin' to miss your sister is it? We can have more fun with no silly girls around now can't we?" He nodded a little unconvinced, "well erm… yes.. but she'll get to talk to mum and dad and **I wont!**" Grandpa ruffled his grandson's hair, "well we can soon sort that out, my boyo! See we'll go right now to the telephone box down the street and we'll ring up your mam and da straight away pronto!" Stuart looked up at grandpa, "can we now? Will it be before Lucy?" "Oh yes, they'll be half-an-hour or more getting home they will!"

It was a very strange experience talking to mum and dad from two hundred miles away stood in a phone box when they were in the hall back at home, at *his* home! He chatted for a while then mum said dad wanted a word and then in next to no time dad said let me talk to grandpa and then they were saying goodbye… goodbye…. grandpa hung the big black heavy receiver hand-set onto the metal clip, the rest of the money dropped into the box, he reached over the top of Stuart and pushed the heavy red door open for him and as they left for home he slipped his hand into the boys. "That was lovely now wasn't it, to hear their voices sounding so near and all. Wonderful how progress marches on and we can do suchlike…" Stuart nodded, "s'pose so" was all he said. He fought back the tears that would make him into a coward and not let him be Stuart-bach-a-soldier-boy, soldiers didn't cry and he wouldn't… His granddad respected his little grandsons silence and they walked back home without a word.

It was bath night and Stuart was sent up with Lucy to light the geyser! It was funny how old-fangled so much of grandpa's house was, the way it was all joined up with the whole street for one thing, with only the little tunnels to go through to get to the back! Then there was things like the larder which had a window through to outside with a metal mesh over it, they didn't have a fridge. There was no hot water taps either like there was at home, just a white enamelled Ascot heater over the sink in the kitchen, which had gas in it that whumped into life when you ran the water and heated it up for you! At home the fire in the living room had a boiler built in to heat the water and you could turn the 'mersion-heater on to get a tank full of hot water as well and they had hot taps as well as cold ones too, on both sinks.

Anyway him and Lucy raced up the stairs with a box of Swan Vestas, grandma had given them, she said the geyser was filled up ready so Stuart was to turn on the gas tap and Lucy was to strike a match ready and poke it in to get the burner going. Lucy let Stuart do the match bit knowing how much he loved fire and matches and when he was ready with it poised burning she turned the tap and the smelly gas came hissing out, he poked the match in too fast and it went out! Panicked now he attempted to get another match out, fumbled pushed the slide right through the sleeve and tipped the whole box into the bath! Grabbing desperately at the box he scooped a match up, struck it and got within three inches of the opening in the geyser and WHUMP!! The gas that had been pouring out since Lucy opened the valve, building up steadily all the while… ignited in one mighty whump! Stuart reeled backwards, then realising that he was still alive burst into hysterical laughter, Lucy was laughing too and pointing, "look at your eyebrows!" She laughed, Stuart dived across to the bathroom cabinet and peered into the mirror at his reflected face, his eyebrows and the fringe of his hair had frizzled up with the heat of the exploding gas, he laughed and rubbed at the frizzy hair, "aw it stinks, all singed and burnt! Don't tell grandma!"

They left the geyser to do its work, it was nothing more than a big metal tank full of water fixed to the wall at the end of the bath with a built-in gas burner under it. They'd go back up later and it would be bubbling away, just like a big kettle Stuart thought, or a steam engine…

Grandma got a real telling off from an (*at his grumpiest*) grandpa 'letting the children light the geyser, you silly old woman, will you look at his hair, singed like it is, the whole house could have gone-up and the kids been blown to kingdom come!' She (as was her custom) totally ignored him, she was deaf, but not as deaf as she pretended to be some times!

The next day they went off on a walk down to the river Avon and along its bank. On the way down Stuart recalled the last time he'd walked those streets, it was back in November when they'd been down with mum and dad and grandpa had taken them on a mission to gather up fallen leaves! Stuart had been puzzled by this but grandpa had patiently explained that there were only a few trees in their own garden and that leaves rotted down to make lovely rich compost you see! He already used all the kitchen waste to go on the compost heap and the grass cuttings but said that the leaves made all the difference. So off they'd gone down the street with grandpa's big wooden barrow which he'd made himself using a pair of old pram wheels. It had two long handles and you pulled it like as if you were a horse, actually it was more like that, a smaller version of the carts that the big horses pulled. On the way Stuart rode in the cart, Lucy said she didn't want to, but he knew she did really, girls were so silly!

When they got down on the big road that had lots and lots of trees there were great big piles of leaves all along the pavement and they'd set to with a couple of wooden boards each picking them up and loading the barrow with them "watch out for any dirty dog-muck kids!" Grandpa had warned, "filthy animals it is that they are and filthy owners too them letting them dirty our pavements like that!"

The barrow had nearly been full when a tall man and an elegant lady walked past arm in arm, he had a hat on like dad's and a lovely brown coat and shiny shoes, she had a furry coat of some sort and matching hat, the woman looked down at them and turning to her husband said "oh aren't old people so funny darling?" He just made a dismissive humphing type noise as if they weren't even worth commenting on! Stuart remembered he'd been really angry, he stood with his hands on his hips and he'd wanted to shout after them, snooty beggars that they were, looking down on them picking up leaves, but worse of all on his grandpa! Grandpa saw his reaction and had put a hand gently on his grandsons shoulder and he'd told him, "you take no notice boy, they aren't worth it, the leaves are here for the taking and when we eat our lovely potatoes and veg that we've grown off our allotment in the compost they've made for us, it's us who'll have the last laugh then isn't it?" Stuart nodded and he'd turned away from watching the backs of the two tall people as they walked away from them and added as an aside, "bet you they have a dog!" Grandpa had looked up from where he was bent over with a pile of leaves between his boards, he'd tipped them in his barrow and stood up tall, stretching his shoulders and he laughed, "bet they have a dog he says!" he repeated Stuart's quip. He used to tip his head back and let his laugh come out from way down deep inside him, it was a wonderful laugh and in that moment without realising it at the time he'd created a double-stamped image in his mind, an image that would live with him for the rest of his days, the image of his grandpa, head tipped back laughing as he'd stood in the street collecting up fallen leaves, wearing his battered old brown sleeveless sheepskin over his old navy blue dungarees, his pale green flat hat perched on his head. His grandpa was a wonderful man Stuart had thought then and he confirmed it to himself again now, even though he was so very, very old! He squeezed grandpa's hand and looked up at him, he looked down and smiled as Stuart chirped "this is where we picked up all those lovely leaves last year isn't it grandpa?" He nodded, "and they're rotting down nicely they are now too!"

It was a good long walk, they saw a heron flying low over the water and along the exposed brown muddy banks, Stuart couldn't wait to tell grandma all about their walk but when they got home she was fast asleep in the chair, her knitting and her wool lying on her lap, some patterns and panels of neatly knitted blue wool on the table next to her. Her glasses had slipped a little down her nose, her head was lolled right back and her mouth was wide open… she was snoring too! Lucy and Stuart laughed so loudly that she was awakened, but not in a panic, she just opened one eye first, closed her mouth and smacked her lips together, pushing her false teeth back into place as she did before sitting up and smiling at them. "You were sat there with your gob wide open, you were you know, lovely sight it was too and snoring like a donkey too you were!" Grandpa informed her as he joined in laughing! Grandma laughed with them to, "oh that was a lovely little snooze! Was my mouth wide open?" Lucy nodded and chuckled, "yes grandma… like this…" she tipped her head back and opened her mouth as wide as she could and made an exaggerated snoring noise! Grandma shook her head, "and in front of my grandchildren too, well I never!" She bundled up her knitting and placed it on the table, then proceeded to struggle up out of the chair pushing herself up with her hands resting on its arms. "I'm sure you'll all be ready for a nice cup of tea, I'll go and put the kettle on and brew us a nice big pot full" she said as she hobbled through to the kitchen. Grandpa patted her shoulder as they passed in the doorway and kissed her cheek, "that was a struggle old girl!" He said fondly as they both went through to the kitchen. Stuart watched secretly around the doorframe as the two old people pottered about in their kitchen, working like a well-trained team, one getting the cups and saucers out, the other filling the kettle and turning the gas on, all the time chatting away to each other. His ears picked up as his grandma asked, "fancy them seeing me like that with my big gob wide open! Do you think it'll drop open like that when we go?" Grandpa laughed, "Well I would have thought so wouldn't it? Be the least of your worries by then perhaps? We can let each other know eh?" He nudged her elbow gently as he caught a glimpse of Stuart peeping, and nodded almost imperceptibly in the direction of the living room, "mind you my love, it will be a very long time before either of us pops off now won't it?" Grandma turned to face him and put a hand either side of his face and kissed him on the lips "you'd better believe it boyo!" She replied in a pretty decent impersonation of his own Welsh accent!

Suddenly and quite without warning there were only two more days left before mum and dad would be back for them! Before bed that night they all sat round the table with their mugs of Ovaltine and talked about what they would like to do before they went back home. Stuart was as quick as a flash in saying "the zoo, the zoo! Let's go to the zoo!" Lucy naturally wanted to go somewhere else, "I'd like to go to the museum, it was smashing there! Can we go there instead?" Grandpa scratched his head, well now I suppose if we got up early we could spend the morning at one and the afternoon at the other? How would that be then?" Stuart and Lucy both seemed pleased and went off up to bed, but as soon as the door to the living room closed though Stuart shoved Lucy to one side in the back on her shoulders and then darted to the foot of the stairs where he turned, "you and your stupid soddin' museum, that means we'll have less time at the zoo now dumb-cluck!" She rounded on him and shot at him… with "you little sod that hurt!" and she chased him up the stairs calling after him, "you always want your own way, you're a spoilt little brat you are!" He was too quick for her though and skidded into his room, slammed the door shut and leant against it as she barged into it and tried to get in! He leant hard, digging his feet in as hard as he could and pushing back with all his might, but she was too strong for him and the door was jerking further and further open with each of her shoves… until grandma shouted up the stairs "oi! You two, get to bed or I'll come up there and tan your hides!" Lucy stopped shoving and the door slammed back into its frame, Stuart laughed gloating, "ha-ha! Fat head, go to bed! I won!" To which she replied in a fierce whisper, "you just wait Stuart Wheeler, I'll get you…! When you're fast asleep I'll come into your room and put earwigs on your pillow and they'll crawl in down your lug-holes and eat out your brains! Mind you it won't take them long when they find out how few brains there are in that stupid fat head of yours!" He just laughed and shouted back "pah! No chance you wouldn't never go near an earwig in a month of Sundays!" Her reply of "oh no… well we'll see later won't we… ha ha ha?" made him look at the door with something approaching alarm though, so he tugged the chair around and pushed it up against the door, just in case!"

Joey was shaking his head as he got into bed, "best stuff something down into your ears then Stuey hadn't you eh? Don't want them earwigs chomping on your brains do you!"

Stuart was about to poke him when Joey added to save himself, "I suppose I could always watch out for her…"

Later on in bed Stuart protested indignantly to Joey "well anyway it really isn't fair though, we could have spent the whole day at the blummin zoo tomorrow if that rotten Lucy hadn't made a fuss about going to that smelly old museum!" Joey poked him, "don't be so selfish! It's Lucy's holiday too, why shouldn't she get to do something that she wants to do as well? Besides the museum's very educational!" He wasn't convinced, "pah! Educational is it, I get more than enough educational-ing at school, thank you very much, besides I don't need to go as you can tell me anything I need to know seeing as you already know everything, with it all stored-up in that big fat head of yours!" Joey shook his head, "there's no need to be rude Stuart! You know, you can be a very rude and peevish boy sometimes!"

Needless to say Stuart made it down to breakfast with his brains intact and the argument of the night before had been forgotten. So it was that at half-past-eight they were waiting at the bottom of the road to catch the bus into town.

Stuart was excited as the big green bus pulled up at their stop, it was the same type of bus as the ones that they had back home but somehow it being green and cream made it seem completely different to the brighter red and cream buses back at home. Stuart and Lucy jumped on board as grandma and grandpa struggled up the step. "Can we go upstairs?" Stuart chirruped as he swung on the silver chrome rail, already up two of the curved winding steps leading off the platform at the back of the bus. Grandpa looked at the stairs and replied "you can boyo, buy I'm certainly not! Lucy, you go up with your brother and keep an eye on him for me would you?" Lucy was glad to oblige as she too loved to ride up on the top deck of the bus looking down on the world as it passed by beneath them. They scampered up the steep metal stairs and Lucy followed on after her little brother as he charged down the aisle and swung himself into one of the seats at the very front of the bus where he was sat up leaning on the window with Joey pushed up against the glass when she caught up with him. The bus was swinging around a bend and descending down a steep hill as she moved to sit down and she cannoned into Stuart, he didn't even seem to notice and just bounced up and down on the seat asking her "isn't it great here sis? All the hills! Wish we had hills like this at home!"

It was a long ride into town and Stuart soaked up all the sights, reading out loud nearly every sign he saw, showing Joey and commenting on just about everything else, it was all so different from the bus rides at home, all the places were new and unknown to him, all the people that were milling around below them were too and would always remain so, total strangers to him, they were a bit like ants he thought all of them dashing around, about their business, here, there and everywhere!

They rode on the bus until they were right in the centre of the city, it was full of big and black, tall stone buildings and it was very crowded with people, cars and buses. The closest he had been to somewhere like this was in the centre of Liverpool and of course on their trip to London last year, but it seemed a bit nicer here than those, although there weren't any trams anymore like there were in Liverpool. Stuart loved the trams, they were like railways but running along the roads, right in the midst of all the traffic, their rails being set in the tarmac or cobbles. Dad said that you always had to give way to the trams when you were in your car, well as he said they couldn't steer round you, could they! There were wires all over the place above the roads in Liverpool, strung from tall poles or from the buildings either side of the streets and they had a pole type thingy on the tram that went up to get the 'lectric down to their motors. They had clanky bells that they rang at you to get out of their way, not horns like the buses and lorries had. They were proper old too some of the trams, right out of the olden days. Grandpa said that before the war Bristol did have its own trams but they were in the middle of getting rid of them all anyway and then the place was bombed to bits in the war as well…

The bus conductor stuck his head up the stairs and shouted down the bus to them, "your stop kids!" and they jumped up and charged back down the length of the bus, Stuart pushing in front of Lucy at the last minute to get down the stairs first and then slithering and sliding down them in his haste, grazing the backs of his legs. Lucy laughed as he pulled his face in pain, "serves you right, shoving like that, rude boy!" He naturally poked his tongue out and promptly kicked her on the shin!

Grandma caught sight of what he did out of the corner of her eye, or maybe through the eyes she seemed to have in the back of her head? And cuffed him across the head, damn! He thought as he winced, can see where mum gets her swing from!

He was told in no uncertain terms that he had to hold on tight to grandpa's hand as they walked across the big city to the museum along the crowded pavements. There were so many people, Stuart couldn't see that much until everything opened out and the people thinned out as they came to the big stone building they were looking for. It reminded Stuart of the family's trip to London the year before, it had been so exciting there, it was as if life ran at a faster speed in the big city. There was more of everything in London, people, cars, buses, lights! There was also a lot more smoke and fumes too! Lucy had trouble breathing some of the time and mum was quite worried about her.

The best bit of London though was The Underground! Not that Trafalgar Square with old Nelson stuck up there on top of his column wasn't fabulous, with the big black lions too… and Buckingham Palace where the Queen lives and Big Ben and Tower Bridge and the Tower of London… well there was lots and lots and lots to see in London! Oops… nearly forgot The Cutty Sark! Stuart had loved going around the old clipper, it was a ship that had sailed the oceans of the world and perfectly captured his imagination as he strode the decks as an adventurer travelling to far flung places in search of his fortune…

The Underground however was just magnificent! Well it was a railway for starters and you just went down from the busy, bustling and crowded mayhem of the streets wherever you saw the lovely round signs, down into the quiet, shiny tunnels, sometimes you went down steps, sometimes down great long escalators passing people who were gliding up past you the other way as they rose up from the depths of the labyrinth of railway tunnels that was represented on the wonderful coloured maps with all the different lines on it. You could follow where you wanted to go on the different coloured lines and work out how to get all over the massive city by changing lines here and there and you could pop up again anywhere you wanted! It was the cleverest of maps though as instead of drawing it like his Street Map, exactly as things were on the ground, like a birds-eye view sort of thing, this was all straight lines! Dad said it was a 'representation' of how it was because if it was drawn up as it really was it would look like a plate full of spaghetti! Stuart thought this was hilarious and Joey explained later at the boarding house that it was a topographical map! Joey had to stay in their rooms, mum said it was too busy to take him out in the city in case he got lost, they'd never find him! Stuart remembered he'd thought, 'pah, he wouldn't stay lost for long smart little Alec that he was!' But had agreed reluctantly to leave him tucked up in his bed. He told Joey all about what he'd seen every night though, for as long as he could that was until recalling all the excitement and sights of the day had him yawning and sent him off into a deep sleep. Apart that was from the night when he cried himself to sleep… he recounted to Joey how he had been stood on the platform with everyone and as always happened you felt the woosh of air in the tunnel that followed ahead of the tube train and then it had come gliding into the station, the brakes squealed and it came to a halt, then all the doors swished open and the man on the tannoy said 'mind the gap' and people poured off and then onto the train, although some people were in such a hurry they couldn't wait to get on and pushed past! Well this time the train had wooshed-in…. glided-doors swished open and all that and was sat there at the platform, panting waiting to be off again… so Stuart got on like they had every other time, suddenly though he realised was alone, he turned around, looked back…. There was mum and dad and Lucy stood on the platform!! He was on the tube train all alone!! The doors clicked, ready to swish shut… in a split second-blind-panic moment he hurled himself through the opening even as they snapped shut behind him like the jaws of a monster snake that would have swallowed him whole and then slithered off and away down its tunnels carrying him in its belly!! He had hurled himself into his father's arms and sobbed his heart out, his dad's response of 'what did you get on it for?' Had earned him a barrage of blows from the flying fists of the now outraged seven year old! Dad had to crouch down and grip his shoulders firmly and tell him in no uncertain terms that he had to behave!

"What would you have done if the doors had shut and you'd been carried off?" "Been lost forever and sold as a chimney sweep…" "Stuart! Be sensible! What would you have done?" Foot stamping and "I don't blummin know? Ask a bobby?" Dad wiped his eyes, "you silly little sausage! You could have just got off at the next station and waited for me to come after you? That might have worked might'nt it? Don't you think I'd've come for you?" He stood up tousling the little lad's hair, who looked up at his dad, "'spose so" He sulkily conceded, huh! It was alright for him, smart Alec, dad'd been in the war and found his way round Germany… he was only seven!

Joey said not to worry, all's well that ends well and let's face it he'd just been too fast for them doors! 'Yeah, I was like a leopard I was, I sprang out that train like a bat out of hell I did!' Nevertheless he woke several times in the night as his troubled mind tried to deal with the horror of the event!

Lucy'd had to hold onto grandma's hand all the way to the museum also and now they were there they set off to wander round the museum separately, grandpa showing Stuart the things he thought he'd find most interesting and grandma doing likewise for Lucy. Joey had to dig Stuart in the ribs after he'd asked grandpa for the third time 'can we go to the zoo now?' They all met up again later on for a cup of tea and a scone before setting off for the zoo.

The zoo was great and they had a fun afternoon looking at all the animals and laughing as Stuart proceeded to impersonate them! Lucy warned him that if he wasn't careful they'd round him up and put him in with the chimps thinking one of them had escaped and pinched some clothes, or had been dressed up for the tea party and escaped! He retorted that she'd get put in with the wart hogs then!

When they'd been to see just about everything else they went to see the snow tigers. They were very special as they were white and black stripey instead of the usual tigery colours. There they were strolling around in their cage minding their own business and Stuart, showing off naturally and being dead brave since he could see Lucy was really scared of them, climbed up on the small wall and stood right up to the wire. One of the tigers which was sat down across the cage, saw him and turned its great big head and looked directly at him, their eyes met and he felt the hair on the back of his neck pricking as the big cat peered right into him! Then it climbed up to its feet, turned and started to walk, well more of a slinking really but more importantly than that… right at him! He wanted to move, to jump down at once but those eyes seem to hold him, trapped and motionless, then in a split second the giant cat seemingly effortlessly sprang the remaining six or seven feet right up to the wire in a single bound and was there two inches from his face with what now suddenly only looked to be the very thin wire fencing separating him from it!

And it was huGE!!!!!!!!!!!!!!!!!!!

The tiger was so close to him that Stuart could feel his breath on his own face… he could also feel all of the blood draining down and out from his face as those great big eyes bore into him, the tigers face was the size of the moon as it rocked its head slowly from side to side, it's body was like the side of a stripy black and white house and it's legs were like tree trunks, with massive feet and claws to the terrified and transfixed boy! Then just when things couldn't possibly get any worse… they did! It opened its massive mouth and bared its enormous white, glistening, shining… fangs!! The two teeth at either side of its enormous gob were massive pointed tusks and it let out a the mightiest deepest throaty roar that seemed to resonate from deep within the depths of its cavernous chest. Stuart finally finding the ability to move as he felt as though the very force of the tiger's roar was driving him away from the wire, had forgotten he was standing on a wall and fell, tilting backwards… into his grandpa's arms!

He gripped tightly onto the old man, trembling. Grandpa patted the lads back and gently let him down onto the floor, slipping one of his hands into his and hugging the lads shoulder with his other. Stuart glanced back over his shoulder at the cage as they walked away, the giant cat was sat down now still at the wire, still watching him, it seemed almost somehow that it was smiling, as if it was amused! Lucy shoved his shoulder and chided him, "that's getting you back for when you shot a stone at next doors cat with your catapult, that is! Ha ha ha!" With that she poked her tongue out at him and then ran off ahead of them, with a very cross (and still utterly terrified) Stuart hot on her heels!
Stuart was very subdued the rest of the day, he even rode home on the bus with hardly a word. Grandpa asked if he was alright and surprisingly for Stuart he freely admitted 'that blummin tiger frightened the living daylights out of me!' Adding 'fair gave me the heebie-jeebies it did!' Grandpa nodded, "me too, it was too darn big for my liking it was! Mind you now, there was a big sign there saying '**DO NOT CLIMB ON THE WALL**' wasn't there?" "Eh?"

Joey could tell that Stuart was still shocked by what had happened at the zoo later when they went to bed, he asked him if he was still upset only to get "me upset, you soft nelly why would I be, stupid overgrown moggy couldn't get me, it was just a flippin big show off that's all!" Joey nodded solemnly, "oh right, well if you weren't bothered I could tell you about the tiger I came across when I was in India, I wasn't going to say in case it scared you too much…" Stuart scoffed, "pah like some silly tale you could ever tell me would upset me!" Joey smiled to himself, "oh well, okay then… it was just before the rainy season, the monsoons they call it and the temperature had soared, it was so damn humid, you sweated if you as much as lifted an eyebrow! We were camped close to the edge of the jungle, the night before the elephants had been restless, the elephants were used to carry the supplies on and we had one of course to carry the Memsahib. In the morning one of the goats was found to be missing, there was blood on the ground and its tether was torn in two, well more ripped apart…

That night after midnight, there was a terrible screaming from the servant's tent, it was so hot they had left the flap tied open and a young boy of eight had been snatched right out of his bunk by a giant man-eating tiger! It had just plucked him up off his bunk and then it had run off into the jungle carrying him in its mighty jaws… the men tried to follow it in the dark, but the jungle was impenetrable, his screams were terrible… but then they stopped…

The Sahib and some of the men went after the tiger in the morning at first light, they tracked it for days but never found it, the trackers called it the ghost-tiger… All they ever found of the boy was his left hand, still clutching the body of his bloody-furred little teddy bear…" "SHURRUP! You're making it up you little sod, trying to scare me!" Joey rolled about on the bed laughing till Stuart pushed him off onto the floor where he continued to laugh, shouting up "shall I stand watch Sahib lest ghost-tiger, him come in de night!"

The whole yarn telling backfired on Joey though when he was woken in the middle of the night by a screaming and terrified Stuart, who'd had the most terrible nightmare where the tiger had escaped the zoo, followed his scent across Bristol and prowled around outside grandpa's house. He'd looked out of the window, it had looked up and their eyes had locked once more… then it jumped clean through the living room window and it was on its way up the stairs… pad… pad … growl… pad… when he woke up screaming!

On their last day they went up on the downs and through Blaise Castle and walked over the bridge that Stuart loved to drive under. In the woods they came across a big burly man who had a small bonfire going, he was clearing-up, chopping and stacking-up the wood that had fallen off the trees. Stuart was greatly impressed when he saw how the big chap was able to snap branches across his leg before he tossed them either into his wheelbarrow or into a pile or onto the fire, "wow, he's really strong grandpa, look…" Grandpa nodded and acknowledged the big man with a friendly "good morning" however his face dropped and set into a black scowl when the man replied "Guten tag!" He almost spat his next accusative words out "you're a German?" The man stood up tall, from his leaning-over position, he really was a massive fellow for sure, he had great broad shoulders and his hair was yellowy blond and cut very short. He wiped his hands on his trousers and looked grandpa up and down, "you are not liking us Germans eh old man? Come now war is all over, ve are making friends now, yes?" He held out a massive shovel of a hand in grandpa's direction, Stuart was frightened by his grandpa's reaction to this man, he slipped his own hand into his grandpa's, he could feel it trembling, grandpa was shaking, Stuart looked up at him, was he frightened? No he was furious! He'd never seen his grandpa this angry before, yes he was 'a bit cantankerous' as mum put it and he did argue with grandma a lot, but now he was positively fuming! "I'll never shake the hand of a German as long as I live after what you lot did to us!" He growled out defiantly, oblivious to the fact that the man was at least twice his size and less than half his age! The man however just lowered his hand and sighed, he picked up another piece of wood, snapped it over his leg and tossed it into his pile. "Ah Tommy, ve haf to let go of da past, var is terrible, so many young men, German men and boys too don't be forgetting. You ver soldier in first war then mein herr?" Grandpa just huffed and made a humph-ing noise himself, similar to the noise the snobby sod had made at them, which Stuart thought was a bit rude really as the Jerry *was* trying to be friendly.

Grandpa turned to Stuart and ignoring the German said loudly enough for him to hear, "he's not that strong Stuey, the woods probably rotten anyway!" At this the big man laughed out loud! "Ha! You are bitter old man, but zis vood is gut, is strong, see…" He banged it on the path, "be picking one out yourself Tommy, for me to break and ve can see!" Grandpa looked at the pile of branches, Stuart tugged at his grandpa's hand, "come on lets go grandpa, I'm scared!" "yes come on, I am too, let's go!" Lucy added, who'd been hiding behind grandpa, but he would have none of it, he bent down and found a big stout piece of wood, he banged it on the path to test it, "like to see you break that one boyo!" He challenged, "more like break your leg that one will!" The German took the wood off him and tossed it around in his hands, "how much will you be betting me Tommy, that it will be too strong for me? Or is scared you are I vill break it eh? Be putting your money ver your bad old mouth is!"

"I don't make bets!" Grandpa blustered, but quickly realising that it would look cowardly to back down, rummaged in his pocket and rooted out a half a crown piece. "Half a crown, I'll bet you half a crown!" The German laughed again, "two and six of your pence! Pah! Not Five Pounds? You are as well a mean old man! But I am accepting your bet, if I break your piece of vood you vill be giving me your half-a-crown, yes?" "That's what I said!" Grandpa snarled back at him, "let's see what you can do with a proper piece of wood?"

Stuart watched, wide eyed and with his mouth half open as the German turned the wood over one last time in his hands and then quick as a flash he snapped it clean in half over his knee! Stuart's mouth fell wide open, Lucy was covering her eyes. The big man laughed and held out his hand into which grandpa placed his big shiny coin. "Not so cocky now eh Tommy?" Stuart was indignant now and he felt his angry

blood boiling up from his neck, rising up into his head, he let go of grandpa's hand and clenching his fists as tight as he could, he took a step towards the German and shouted out red-faced and furious... "you leave my grandpa alone, he was a brave soldier, he was gassed by you buggers, you should say sorry to him not laugh at him!" The German put his hands up and took a step back, "easy now little Tommy, is a joke, is no more, I am sorry is true zat your grandpa vas gassed, but var is terrible thing little Tommy, no one vins, everyone loses. It is vhy ve must learn to be friends. You little Tommy be friends with the children of Germany, let the old men be angry and hate if they must... here boy..." he flicked the half-crown

piece off his thumb, spinning up in the air towards Stuart…
"You are a good boy, brave boy too! You be buying old man and sister and you a good British cup of tea and biscuit, eh! Take as offering of peace from old foe, who vould be now a friend!" With that he turned his back on them and placing his hands on his now full wheelbarrow he tipped it forwards and headed off wheeling it away from them.

Grandpa took hold of Stuart's hand again and led him and Lucy off away along the path. Stuart looked back over his shoulder, the big coin still gripped fiercely in his free hand, the German had stopped and was leaning on the wheelbarrow, he was lighting-up a fag, he smiled when he saw the lad looking back and touching his forefinger to his forehead, made a little salute to him. Stuart smiled back and gave a little wave. Wow! He'd come across a real live Jerry! He'd seemed alright too? He looked up at grandpa, whose gaze was fixed forwards, he seemed to be looking way off into the distance, or at some remembered sight… or at nothing? He hardly spoke till they got home and then he just went out to his shed alone.

Grandma sat down at the table with the children as they had a drink and some biscuits, she asked what was the matter? They explained and grandma said not to take any notice. Grandpa would never forgive the Germans for what they did to him, Stuart feeling suddenly guilty fished in his pocket for grandpa's half a crown, "will you give this back to grandpa for me, after we've gone back home please grandma?" He handed her the large silver coin and asked "he was gassed wasn't he grandma?" She nodded as she put the coin in the pocket of her pinny, "what's gassed?" In reply she merely smiled and said "don't bother with that now, when you're a grown up I'll tell you all about it! Right let's play snakes and ladders, Lucy's our reigning champion let's see if we can beat her today Stuart!"

Stuart didn't wait to be grown up to find out what gassed meant, he waited till mum and Lucy were asleep on the way home, (they always went to sleep!) and he asked dad!

Dad said that grandpa had been in the Signals Regiment, which meant that he used to fix up the telephone wires and keep them working. He'd been called out as the wire was down again after a bombardment and he'd not been gone more than five minutes when Jerry dropped a load of shells full of gas on their position. It's heavy the gas is you see and it would run along the trenches and get into everywhere. The command centres were deep underground to be safe from the shelling, but the gas could go down... Half of the men in his platoon were killed or died from the effects of the poisoning. He was well away from the worst affected area but breathed some in and his lungs were damaged enough for him to be sent home.

Stuart sat quietly as he tried to imagine how terrible it must have been, he thought he knew now why grandpa was so angry with the Germans. "He really hates the Germans you know dad?" "I know Stuey, but they're not all bad, they suffered terribly too you know? I saw a lot of that when I was over there after the war, a lot of their country, their towns and cities were very badly damaged or destroyed" Stuart looked up accusingly at his dad as he drove the car, "they started it though!" He protested angrily. Dad smiled at his son's outrage, "the ordinary people English, French, Germans too never start wars Stuey, they just do the fighting, suffering and dying. It's the aristocrats and politicians that start wars, they cause all the bloody trouble they do!" Stuart wasn't used to hearing his dad swear like that, he had that faraway look in his eyes now too, the same one grandpa'd had that day in the park. He thought it was a funny thing, well not funny ha-ha but funny peculiar that if them Jerrys hadn't dropped that gas then, just when they did, well… when grandpa was away and he'd not got a bit gassed but not killed, like he had been, then, well he wouldn't have been sent home and he'd have had to stay there in the battle? If he'd been killed then mum would never have been born would she? So he wouldn't have been either? He was going to ask dad but didn't get around to it as uncharacteristically for him he fell asleep too.

Chapter Five: Back home

Back home again Stuart couldn't wait to tell Andy all about his adventures down in Bristol, especially about his ride on the back of the motorbike! He was up early and away straight after breakfast off on his bike pedalling furiously across the pavements of the few streets that separated their homes. It was Easter at the weekend and the schools were off now, him and Lucy had been lucky that mum and dad had taken them out of school early so they could go down to see grandma and grandpa. Dad had used the time while they were away and him and mum were alone at home to redecorate the hall and landing and they were all bright and shiny now with new wallpaper and in new brighter colours. Mum had given Stuart a stern warning that if he got his mucky hands on dad's lovely new wallpaper or scuffed the paintwork then there'd be hell to pay!

Andy was pleased his pal was home and they played with his train-set for a while until Andy's mum shooed them out of the house with 'it's too nice to be inside, get off out and get some fresh air in your lungs!' They set off on their bikes without much of a plan and ended up lying on the massive black stonework that topped the shiny red bricks of the railway bridge, watching the trains go past underneath. If it had been summer then they could have gone on the sandy wasteland and set fire to the dry grasses, but everything was still green yet. The dry grass made a lovely smell when it burned… Spurred on by the smell of the coal smoke from the engines, they decided instead to go to the chemist and see if they could buy some sulphur powder, it was great fun burning it as it gave off lovely yellowy smoke which stunk, you had to be careful not to sniff too much of it though or it made your eyes sore and made you cough!

They careered off round the streets to the crossroads where there were shops on all four corners, it was only a street away from Stuart's road so they had to watch out for people who knew them spotting them. On the block opposite the Post Office was Sidebottom's Chemists. It was a lovely little shop with a chemisty smell all of its own. It had tall wooden shelves that were stacked with all sorts of bottles of medicines and behind the counter were shelves that had big bottles of liquids. There were lots of little drawers behind there too and even more in the back where Mr.Sidebottom dispensed the medicines to make up your prescription that the Doctor gave you when you were poorly.

It was young Mr.Sidebottom who was behind the counter so they were snookered, he would ask awkward questions about what they wanted the sulphur powder for, then most likely would say 'no they couldn't have any' then he'd tell mum as well when she came in next, so they rummaged about until finally he asked what they wanted? They picked up a packet of Horlicks tablets, which was about the only thing they could find worth having but then fortune smiled on them as the big black phone in the back of the dispensary set off ringing its bells. "Just hang on a minute lads, I'll have to get that" he said and he called out up the stairs as he went through to the back "dad, can you come down and watch the shop for me?" They were in luck! Old Mr.Sidebottom wouldn't care less about what they wanted the sulphur powder for and sure enough he just weighed out a bit and wrapped it in a paper for them, he just smiled and said "experimenting are we?" They nodded and scarpered off quick out the door before his lad came back in the shop!

Andy told the lady in the Post Office that his mum had sent him out for a box of England's Glory to light the cooker and although she gave him a funny look, he just beamed his sweetest most innocent face at her and she ended up smiling back. He knew how to charm the old birds did his mate Andy!

So it was back to the bridge and make up little piles of the sulphur and set the alight, it was great fun, although Stuart burnt his finger on a gooey bit of hot sulphur and had to keep sucking it to stop it hurting.

Easter Sunday meant church of course as well as Sunday School, he was fed up with blummin Sunday School and having to wear his stupid suit and a shirt and tie! Him and Andy had bunked off instead of going the last Sunday before he went down to Bristol, there had been Holy Hell to pay when mum found out! If she knew what Andy had got up to as well at the newsagent round the corner from the church then she'd have blown a gasket, he had to say he felt bad about it himself but Andy had just laughed and said the shopkeeper was 'fair game' and anyhow he was an accomplice because he knew before they went in what he was going to do! Stuart was cross with him because he <u>did</u> <u>not</u> know at all, the only thing Andy had said with one of his cheeky grins was 'watch this, the old duffer won't know a thing!' He had told Stuart to ask for some cough candy, because it was on the top shelf of the big glass jars of sweets that were lined up behind the counter, when the old man was up his little ladder-thingy with his back to them Andy whizzed a couple of Mars bars straight off the counter and into his pocket! The old man was slow up and down the ladder and Andy had loads of time, Stuart had been shocked and hadn't known what to do, he'd blushed like a beetroot as he paid the old man for his quarter of cough candy and then left the shop with Andy without saying anything, but as soon as they were outside he kicked him on the shin and told him he was bloody robber and he was going to tell his mum on him! Andy looked surprised, but he just rubbed his shin and laughed and told him not to be a big soft Jessy and got on his bike and rode off pell-mell. Stuart followed him and they went to the fields and the den they'd been building in the thick tangle of the brambles. It was coming along great, they'd found an old door and some crates and had made a roof now. They dived inside and Andy offered him one of the Mars bars, he hesitated knowing it was wrong to take it, it had been stolen from that nice old chap at the shop… he was really hungry though…

Now back in the church again at Easter he still hadn't forgotten the stolen Mars bar he'd enjoyed eating. He looked around at the stained glass windows with all their holy saints looking down at him and the statue of Jesus who was also looking at him today! The vicar was droning on and on as usual, he kept looking at Stuart too or so he thought, he knew as well! He had a mark on him, the mark of the thief! Thou shall not steal! It was one of them commandaments wannit? Now everyone was singing again, he normally liked singing stood there next to his dad, he had a good voice did his dad unless he started with his coughing and Stuart'd sing along with him. Today though he felt like a sinner, a thief, he wished they were like them Catholics that mum didn't like as they could go and tell the priest that they had sinned and he would wave his wand and the sins would go away and you'd be fine, you had to do something good to make up for it but you were off the hook and no one any the wiser, except the old priest and he had to keep schtum as he was listening to you for his boss and not for himself. He couldn't understand why mum didn't think it was a darn good idea, he certainly did.

Eventually the service was over and other than having to try and dart past the vicar quick at the door without him seeing the mark of the thief on him he was away free, but still feeling terribly guilty. He asked mum if he could go to the shop and buy some sweets, she told him he could but not to eat them before his dinner and not to be long either.

The shop was open as it sold the Sunday papers and he went in and looked at the war comics until he was in the shop alone with the old man. He was blushing terribly again but he gritted his teeth and went over to the counter, jingling his coins from his pocket money nervously in his hands, "please mister, how much would two Mars bars cost, please." "Sixpence each, would you like them?" "No sir" he replied as he held out a shilling to him, "my friend took two without paying for them when we came in a few weeks ago, I'm sorry I didn't know he was going to…" The tears were welling-up now in his eyes as he held out his shilling piece. The old man smiled slightly and reaching out took the coin off the boy, "well you're a good honest boy and we'll let the matter rest then shall we?" Stuart nodded and held his head down, he glanced up at the old man as he pressed the till button and the drawer slid open, he tossed his shilling in and shut the drawer, it slid in with a clunk, "sorry mister!" He said as he turned and scuttled out of the shop.

It was a very long time before he would ever go back in that shop but as he walked home he felt as if a weight had been lifted from his shoulders, in fact just as Joey had said it would be when he'd told him all about the robbery he'd taken part in, he'd said "well Stuey you've got clean away with it so you could do like Andy and just laugh about it, think you were clever and think nothing more of it couldn't you? The thing is though you know better than that, you know it was wrong to steal even though you didn't do it yourself, you feel that you took part, which you did. When you make a choice like that you embark on a path, you set your course, you choose to accept that dishonesty is alright, it doesn't matter that much and a couple of Mars bars is hardly the crime of the century, but the next time is easier and you'll probably take a bit more too until one day you find yourself stood in the dock and then behind bars! It's a slippery slope Stuart and I'm worried that your friend Andy may be well onto it already!

If you want to feel better again about yourself then you have to put things right which means that you'll have to be very brave and do something that you really won't want to do!" He'd been right about that for sure, it had taken him days to come to terms with doing what his little friend said would make him feel better.

He found himself whistling as he came up the garden path at home and as he realised what he was doing, he knew it had been the right thing to do as he was happy and light-hearted once more, just the way he liked to be. Joey was a clever little sod for sure!

Back at school later in the week it soon became clear that Mrs Allington had not approved of his unscheduled absence from her class before the Easter break, she made him stay in at playtime and read, 'to catch up on some of the things you've missed!' Old bag she was! He didn't read the book she told him to anyway and he just sat drawing pictures instead, he loved drawing. They'd been reading a story in class that morning about some old man in the woods or something and it had stuck in his mind so he'd drawn a picture with wax crayons of an old gnome sat on a toadstool, he had a big pointy nose and a long chin and big ears, like Mrs Allington he chucked to himself as he put a big wart on her cheek for good measure! He was so engrossed though that he didn't hear her sneak up on him and stand looking over his shoulder at his handiwork! "I thought I told you to read your book Master Wheeler? Let me see that" and she held out her hand for his drawing, she took it off him sharply but then she stood peering at it, "have you copied this from somewhere Stuart? Have you seen this picture somewhere before?" He shook his head, "just made it up Mrs Allington, why is it no good?" "on the contrary, its exceptionally good! Why did you draw the legs like this?" She pointed to the gnomes thigh where it bent at the knee, "that's what a leg looks like isn't it?" She smiled, "it is indeed, you have a keen eye Stuart, you could well make an artist you could!"

When he got home he'd wanted to run up and tell Joey what Mrs Allington had said, Joey'd been showing him how to draw, how to 'see' properly and then how to put what he'd seen down accurately onto the paper, but he didn't get the chance to as mum was stood there when he exploded into the hall from the kitchen, with a suitcase and her coat on, she was putting her hat on while she looked at herself in the mirror, he skidded abruptly to a halt as his mind whirled as it grappled with what he was seeing, trying to make sense of it, for one horrible moment he thought she was leaving him, just like Johhny Marples mum had done, she'd packed her bags and upped and gone! Mr.Marples had hit the bottle and Johhny and his kid brother ended up in the children's home! He walked tentatively over to his mum and looked up at her, "you're not leaving us are you mum?" She looked down at him with a mixture of confusion and concern, then she smiled ruffled his hair and hugged him to her, he put his arms around her waist "no of course not, you silly sausage!"

She told him that he and Lucy had to be very grown up and stay in on their own till dad got home, she had to get the train down to Bristol to see her sister because she had been rushed into hospital, her taxi was coming any minute. Stuart listened wide eyed… Mum was taking a taxi! Was all he could think, blummin heck, that was something she would normally have called 'a terrible waste of money when you had two good legs to walk on!' Things must be serious! Mum had told them that they would get instructions off dad and that they had to be on their very best behaviour for him while she was away, they would be going to Mrs Sumner's house after school from tomorrow and dad would pick them up from there as soon as he could after work.

When dad came in he had to start making tea for them. He wasn't much good in the kitchen and Stuart laughed when he saw him frying bacon on the stove, with a fag in his gob of course! He'd just laughed and said "never mind standing there grinning bugger-lugs, slice some bread up and butter it and call Lucy down to lend a hand too!"

Lucy made a pot of tea while dad finished off by frying them an egg each and they sat down to a feast of fried bacon, fried egg and fried bread, with a big chunky slice of white bread smothered in Lurpak butter. It was just about the only thing dad could cook, but it was blumming great!

By the end of the week though dad's repertoire was wearing a bit thin, his grilled cheese on a tin plate which he thought was lovely hadn't gone down that well! Fish, chips and mushy peas from the chippy had been fine, but fried Spam and baked beans wasn't that great! Everyone was as pleased as punch when dad got a phone call to say mum was coming home and would be back Saturday afternoon. They all went down to the station and met her on the platform, Stuart was a bit jealous as she had gone on the mainline all that way, that would have been a fine trip he thought as he walked back up the platform with her enjoying feeling the warmth of her soft hand as it held his and basking in the glow of her presence.

In the morning mum was having a lie in, she was tired after her long journey dad said, her and dad had been up to something till late at night as well making a holy racket in their bedroom they'd been. Dad was making his own breakfast when Stuart came down, it was his speciality breakfast which consisted of two Shredded Wheat biscuits with a thick layer of Lurpak pasted on their top and then a whole load of sugar pushed in onto the butter, then some milk boiled up in the milk pan and poured all around them… it was scrumptious. Dad did one for him and Lucy as well and they all tucked into them with great gusto. Dad said they weren't bothering with church today, which was a bit of a surprise to everyone and they played cards, What and Sorry instead and generally larked about.

Later Stuart helped dad outside with the car maintenance and Lucy helped mum in the kitchen to make an apple pie once she'd got up. She said she was feeling fine now and she looked well too Stuart thought when he came in to wash his hands, once the car was all checked over and roadworthy again that was. Mum had the tin tray with the meat in it out of the oven basting it, the meat was steaming hot and the smell was wonderful, he asked her if he could have some dip-bread, Lucy ran over and said "oh me too! Me too!" and they both sat at the table with a chunk of bread each dripping with the yummy hot fat from the tray that had the strung-up beef joint cooking in it.

After dinner mum said it would be nice if Lucy and Stuart each wrote a letter to Aunty Alice, to help her feel better, she was home from hospital but had to rest for a few weeks so it would be lovely for her to get a letter from her niece and nephew wouldn't it? So they sat at the table and wrote a nice 'newsy' letter each as mum put it. Afterwards Stuart took the pad upstairs and wrote a letter to grandpa with help from

Joey. Joey said he didn't think that him and Lucy sitting there at the table slurping, chomping and dribbling all that nasty fat from the beef was a good idea really! Stuart just laughed, "yeah I saw you watching, you were just jealous 'cos you didn't get any!" he had just scoffed, "nothing could be further from the truth my friend!"

Chapter Six

Tea with Emily

Tea with Emily

"Why does he always have to bring that stupid bear with him mum?" Lucy whined agitatedly, "Everyone'll laugh at us!" By everyone Lucy meant Veronica Miley who they were going to meet with her mother in town, or 'Viley Miley' as Stuart rudely referred to her as, or as simply 'Your Majesty' which he did when she was there. To be honest though she was actually a rather obnoxious child, who was thoroughly spoilt by her doting mother. Mum would exclaim when hearing of her latest excess "She's more money than sense that Geraldine Miley!' Lucy however thought Veronica was wonderful, despite the condescending manner in which she treated her. Lucy would pout and protest that it was 'unfair' that Veronica had all the best dolls and toys when she didn't. Mum had explained painstakingly that Mr and Mrs Miley were very well off. Mr.Miley had been a Colonel in the army... 'and he behaves like he's still in the blummin' army!' Dad would complain as he wasn't that keen on the Mileys either, although for mum's sake he pretended that they *weren't so bad!*' Mum explained that as they only had the one child they had twice as much time and money to spend on her. This was not the best thing to say to an envious ten year old, who would then sit day dreaming how she could rid herself of her pest of a brother, the brother who was denying her everything Veronica Miley had?

The truth as it often is, was entirely different. Veronica was a miserable and unhappy child, bored with all the unnecessary toys that her mother and father bestowed upon her. All she really craved for was their attention, which came seldom and was superficial even when it did. They were always 'so busy'. Her mother's favourite saying was 'run along Darling and play.' Her mother was 'plagued' by headaches. Stuart asked mum once what a 'blummin' hangover' was as he had once heard dad say that Mrs Miley's headaches were more likely to be one!

"Don't be so horrible to your little brother Lucy!" Mum reprimanded Lucy as she buttoned up the toggles on Stuart's duffel coat. He promptly poked his tongue out at his sister as mum stood up. "Don't be so horrible to your *stupid* little brother" Lucy parroted back in a silly sing-song manner. "Just behave madam or you'll stay at home!" Lucy pushed her hands deep into her coat pockets and hunched up her shoulders scowling. "If the wind changes it'll stick like that!" Mum chided her. Stuart meanwhile was pulling the most grotesque face he could manage, using his fingers to pull the corners of his mouth at hideous angles to mimic how Lucy would have to spend the rest of her life if... as he ardently wished... the wind did in fact change!

"We'll tuck Joey into your coat Stuart to keep him warm" mum said as she pushed the little bear inside Stuart's duffel coat, "We don't want him getting a chill do we" Stuart wondered sometimes if mum knew more than she was letting on, I mean how could a stuffed toy get a chill? He let it go and followed his mum towards the front door, it was only the smirk on Lucy's face that made him realise he'd been out-flanked as Joey was now virtually invisible, thus letting Lucy have her way! "Mmmuum..." he started to whine but thought better of it as Joey tickled him under his arm and made him laugh. Joey smiled to himself too, sometimes mum was very wise, you needed to be when these two were together he thought to himself.

From home it was a five minutes' walk to the Mossleigh Park railway station and they set off along the tidy suburban street where their house was situated. It was a chilly morning for the end of April with a stiff breeze blowing in their faces. The still wet tarmac and pavements appeared shiny as the sun came out briefly through a break in the billowy white clouds. "There's enough blue sky to make a sailor a pair of trousers!" Mum said, she was always saying things like that although really that one was one of grandma's sayings. "Some of the clouds look quite dark, let's hope we don't get caught in an April shower!"

Stuart loved going into town on the train, the bus was O.K. well it was super, but the train was fantastic. Last summer he had gone with his friend Andy and sat on the railway embankment and watched the engines go past. The goods trains lumbered past clanking along on the outside tracks, the local trains were fun to watch, the side-tankers sometimes pulling their train of a few carriages backwards. The thundering monsters pulling the express trains were what they came to see though! With their great long boilers, tenders full of coal, their windshields and nameplates, with names on them like The Duchess of Sutherland, or The City of London! They made the ground tremble as they hurtled by, followed by the great long chain of dozens of clickety-clacking red carriages, with their blur of windows and faces and people sat reading the newspaper or having their dinner even! Then the monster tore away from them down along the tracks under its trailing plume of white steam and sooty smoke.

Sometimes the engine drivers would see the lads and wave out of the cab at them, their broad smiles made all the whiter by their blackened faces. Some would even let go a long hoot on the engines whistle, which let out another plume of steam. One driver had leaned on the window sill and stared impassively at their frantic waving as if he couldn't see them at all! Another wouldn't even turn his head from looking ahead up the track. "Moody sod!" Andy had shouted as he leapt up, poking out his tongue and sticking his thumbs in his ears and twiddling his fingers. Stuart had roared with laughter at his friends antics and lay back onto the grassy embankment, staring up at the vast expanse of blue sky, savouring the smell of the lingering coal smoke from the engine for a while before the smell of the warm grass filtered back to fill his nostrils once more and the chirping of the grasshoppers and buzzing of insects could be heard again amidst the returning peace of the countryside.

Those express trains only ran on the mainline, you had to catch the number three bus to the other side of town to see them. The line they travelled into town on was just a local one, with smaller engines pulling less carriages. The carriages were sometimes very old ones, with separate compartments which you got in and out of through a big heavy wooden door on either side. Some of the carriages had a blue sticker on the window saying 'first class' which meant they couldn't get in as they only had third class tickets. No-one ever explained to Stuart why there wasn't a second class. Others had corridors with little tunnels joining each carriage together, they were scary places to be as the floor was made-up out of metal plates, that moved around all over the place, sliding over each other so the carriages could go around corners. The sides were like a thick black dirty tent too, like a giant squeeze-box so that could bend as well and there were gaps that you could see the sleepers and rails whizzing past below, only they were a blur as your eyes couldn't see that fast, unless you blinked dead fast and it was mad noisy in there as well. All in all quite scary, it was blummin' great! Once you were on that type of train the compartments all had sliding doors, and seats facing each other, you could only get on and off from the corridor side too.

The five minute walk had passed quickly enough, they had dropped their letters to aunty Alice and grandpa in the post box on the corner as they headed down to the station, as they walked Stuart daydreamed about steam trains. Andy wanted to be an engine driver when he grew up and although Stuart wouldn't mind having a go at it, he had decided that he wanted to be a pilot. He could join the RAF like Uncle Terry had but he thought that would be a bit too much, a bit like being at school with all those orders and saluting all the time. He'd be a squadron leader if he did, join the RAF, soon enough of course but even so, you'd still have to go wherever you were told and although adventures were fine and dandy, it was nice to come home at teatime wasn't it? He did like the idea of flying a Lancaster, they were the best plane in the world of course, dad said so, that and the Spitfire which had won us the war, well pretty much so. He'd seen a picture of an American plane, a flying fortress, it did look good, all silver that one was, not camouflaged like ours, with a rude lady painted on the front as well! Still they didn't even fly Lancasters or Spitfires anymore anyhow!

He had a book at home all about B.O.A.C. which meant British Overseas Aeroplane Company, or something like that, anyway it had picture of a jetliner called a Comet and Stuart had decided that he was going to be the pilot of one of these beauties, just like the man in the picture, with the blue suit with a silver wings badge on it and wearing a peaked cap, although he wasn't sure if he'd have a moustache like he did. Dad said that only fancy-men and crooks wore a moustache and he shaved his face every single day to make sure he didn't become one!

He was rubbing his lip ruefully when he realised that mum and Lucy were stood looking at him. Lucy was rubbing her lip in mimicry with her mouth open and rocking her head about and with her eyes rolling upwards. Stuart let go with a flying kick at her leg, but missed by an inch as mum yanked him back by his woolly mittened hand which was still wrapped in hers, where it had been all the way to the station. "Stuart!" she reprimanded him "Don't be so horrible to your sister" "She was taking the mickey mum!" He retorted sulkily, "Sticks and stones can break my bones but mimicry can never hurt me!" Lucy chimed, "It's *names* not mimicry STUPID!" Stuart blurted back, "I KNOW dopey!" She blurted back. "That is quite enough from both of you, BEE-HAVE, or I'll bang your heads together!" Mum was really cross now and she tugged Stuart's hand as they headed towards the wooden steps that went up the bridge going over the railway line to the opposite platform where the ticket office was. He didn't like it when mum got cross and he could feel tears welling up in his eyes, "Come on now old chap" Joey comforted him from inside his coat "don't cry, try and help your mum by getting on with Lucy" "Oh, O.K." He looked up at Lucy from under his eyebrows without raising his head, she glared back at him, he poked his tongue out a little, but then quickly grinned at her as she opened her lips to complain to mum, her anger instantly defused by his cheeky but tearful grin, she grinned back at him as they started to climb up the wide wooden steps of the bridge.

From the top of the bridge you could look down onto the tracks, it was great when a train went underneath while you were up there. They would clank and chuff towards you as if they were going to bash into the bridge and send you flying to kingdom come, but they never did, they just passed underneath in a whole big cloud of steam and smoke. The smoke from the coal that the engine burnt was strong and could make you cough, but the steam was damp and misty. Mum used to say that it was full of lousy rotten 'smuts' and that when the wind was blowing the wrong way they'd get on her clean washing when it was out on the line. Stuart would wait till the engine went under then run to the other side to see it come out and look down into the cab and at the piles of big lumps of black shiny coal in the tender at the back. The big engines on the main lines had their own coal tender behind the engine, but the smaller ones on the local line just had the coal at the back of the engine. Sometimes you could see the fireman shovelling the coal into the firebox, the fire burning hot and glowing in the opening and see the driver stood in front of all the levers and dials.

Stuart who had slipped his hand out of mum's raced up the steps onto the top of the footbridge where he pushed his face into one of the diamond shaped openings that the metal strips formed all over the sides of the bridge. "Careful Stuart!" Joey cried out as he was provided with a dizzying view of the twin silvery parallel metal railway tracks shining up at him with rusty coloured wooden sleepers in between them. He'd had quite enough of falling from great heights down the stairs before their holiday!

The ticket office was inside the station building, down at one end of the waiting room, where a coal fire was burning merrily in the metal fireplace. Stuart ran over and held out his hands to warm them, Joey pushed his head a little further out from Stuart's coat to warm his nose which he feared 'may turn blue at any moment!' From the other end of the room they could hear mum's voice "One adult and two halves into town, returns please" From behind the window they heard the Station Masters voice and the clunking of the ticket machine. Stuart who now had lovely warm hands paced around the waiting room with his hands on his hips, looking up and down at the adverts pasted on the walls, taking in everything he could see, just as Joey had taught him, 'to be observant'. This meant looking carefully at things you saw not just glancing, but studying them properly, that way you not only didn't miss much but you also remembered what you had seen. "Most people wander around in a daze, it's no wonder they hardly learn anything at all!" Joey had said. Accordingly Stuart stood now beneath the station clock on the wall and watched its second hand tick, tick, ticking intently. If you looked very closely you could see that all around the little hole where you put the key in to wind the clock up, the yellow white face of the clock was covered in tiny little scratches where the Station Master had missed with the key.

Shortly Stuart started to feel cold again after the warm glow of the fire, so he decided he'd had enough of being observant, turned and 'Long John Silvered' his way back to the fire. "Is there something wrong with your leg Stuart?" Mum asked in a concerned voice, "Oh aye my lovely, 'tis in the belly of that accursed shark it is!" he replied in his best pirate voice. "It's his brain there's something wrong with mum, not his leg!" Lucy volunteered. Mum tousled Stuart's thick brown hair fondly, "He's just a young lad with a wild imagination," she said fondly "That's all."

Joey heard the bell ding-ding in the Station Masters office which let him know that a train was coming. Bears have excellent hearing and no-one else had noticed… 'not paying attention' he thought to himself. "Stuart, the trains coming-in" he whispered up towards Stuart's ear, which he immediately repeated at the top of his voice "mum! The train's coming in!" as he charged noisily across the wooden boarded room and out on to the platform, "Come on, come on," he shouted, "We've got to get back across the tracks!" Mum and Lucy were just coming through the doors as Stuart was already stomping up the steps of the footbridge. There was of course ample time as the train was not even in sight yet.

From the top of the footbridge he stared intently up along the track, "Here she comes" he shrieked gleefully as he saw the white smoke coming up over the trees just back from where the tracks curved away to the right and out of sight. Then sure enough the familiar shape of the black steam engine came into view. The driver shut-off and the steam stopped pumping out of the black chimney, "Hmm... 4-6-2 Stanier side tanker I think" Joey commented as he pulled against the edge of Stuart's coat to get a better view. Stuart placed the top of his hand on Joey's head as if he was going to stroke him but then rudely pushed him back into his coat. "Stua.." his protests were lost inside the muffling of the thick coat, "Clever clogs bear, can't just say look here's the train coming, like anyone else, oh no it's got to be 'oh look it's a 4-6-2 something or other with whirly-gig what-nots with bells on' He mimicked Joey's precise manner of speaking whilst at the same time making him sound silly. "It is what it is, Stuart. Remaining in ignorance is not an option I would choose" Joey retorted in a rather hurt little voice from inside the coat, through the little gap he had opened-up again with his paw. Having said what he wanted to he let it flap shut again and waited in silence. He only had to wait about thirty seconds before the gap was opened up again, this time by Stuart's fingers. He looked up to see Stuart peering down at him, a picture of consternation, "Sorry Joey, I just feel so thick sometimes with you being so clever" "Then I'm sorry too, it was never my intention to make you feel like that" Joey replied sincerely. It was hard sometimes to remember that his protégé was so young, and had so much to learn, Joey had already lived a long and full life before he came to the Wheeler household.

Mum and Lucy rounded the corner at the top of the flight of steps, "It's coming mum, see!" Stuart reminded them as he casually eased Joey back into his coat, to Joey he whispered "Friends again?" "Always" Joey whispered back.

Stood on the platform, but well back -of course- Stuart watched in awe as the giant black engine clanked into the station alongside the white paint-edged curve of the platform. Although freewheeling it still hissed and wheezed as it clanked towards them. Stuart watched intently as you could actually see the track sinking ever so slightly as it took the weight of the monster rolling over it. As it drew alongside of them the driver applied the brakes and the wheels let out their protests of squeals and shrieks. Stuart sniffed in deeply to savour the unique aroma of the hot metal of the steam engine as it passed him, the total smell being made up of a mixture of coal smoke, grease, oil and grime were like the finest perfume to him. The fireman who was leaning on the sill at the side of the cab lifted a hand in greeting to the wide eyed little lad, Stuart waved back energetically as he turned his head and craned to get a view into the cab. With a final groan the carriages shuddered to a halt, then seemed to rock back a little as all along its length doors opened here and there as people disembarked. The guard who had got out of the very last carriage with his rolled up flag under his arm, shouted along the platform "All aboard please, all aboard!" as he opened the guards van door for a man with a bicycle. Stuart surged forward and grasped the dull brass handle of the door to the compartment nearest to where they stood. They were strange handles, sort of like a figure of eight but not as pinched in the middle. They were fixed in the middle and you turned them to open the door. This was fine and dandy thought Stuart if you had hands the size of a docker and could grasp either side of the centre to turn, but for Stuart it required two hands and all his strength to turn it. Once unlatched the thick door swung back easily to bump heavily flat against the side of the carriage, prevented from doing so only by the thick leather strap fixed in the opening. Stuart clambered up the step into the carriage, and started bouncing on the sprung seats of the old upholstery, creating a cloud of dust in the process, until mum gave him *a look*! Naturally he had then occupied the window seat and was rubbing his hand on the varnished wood of the window sill, inbetween flicking up and down the heavy clunky metal ashtray that pivoted right upside down so it could be emptied and made a lovely metallic noise when you flicked it back. Mum who was now sat opposite looked sternly at Stuart and he shuffled about placing his hands under the backs of his thighs and rocked back and forth, "Mum can I watch out of the window please?" He asked enticingly, "pleeeaassse?" "Only till we start moving then" she replied only to howls of protest from Lucy, "Mum it's freezing outside, do we have to be frozen on the train as well?"

Stuart jumped from his seat and stood in the doorway, he thought better of poking his tongue out at Lucy, mainly as he knew Mum would see as well and might reconsider his request. He then pulled the thick leather strap that worked the window in the door and let it drop with a thunk into the heavy wooden door. He read out loud the sign on the door "do not lean out of the window" and promptly stuck his head out. The guard who was stood nearby winked at him and proceeded to walk back along the length of the train slamming shut the doors which were still left open. Stuart loved the heavy thunk, thunk noise they made as they shut. When the guard was back at the guards van he waved his green flag blowing his whistle at the same time. Stuart swivelled his head around to look forwards. The engine driver pipped his whistle and the engine leapt into life, with a mighty hissing and spinning of wheels, replaced shortly by the powerful chuff-chuff-chuff as it began to move. The carriages after a slight initial nudge began to glide out of the station, "get your head in now Stuart" Mum reminded him, "Before you get smuts in your eyes" but it was too late, at that very moment as if it was Mum that had willed it, he felt the stabbing pain in his eye.

"Muuummm!" he whined accusingly, as he rubbed at his sore eye. "Sit down Stuart, don't rub at it and I'll get it out, Lucy close the window please." Mum took out her handkerchief and licked its folded corner. She then gently pulled down Stuart's lower eye lid, "Keep still Stuart" she remonstrated with him as he squirmed about on the seat, "Pull the leather strap, stupid!" he rudely interfered as Lucy was trying to push the window up by the thick metal strip along its top, "Stuart! I won't tell you again," Mum this time very sternly admonished Stuart. Stuart felt the corner of the cotton hankie touch onto his eyeball and squirmed again, "It's done" Mum announced and Stuart sat blinking and staring just to make sure, then while she had him in her grasp she licked her hankie and wiped at his mucky cheek, much to his disgust as he tried to wipe away the smell of her spit!

The window clunked shut as Lucy pulled on the strap as instructed, sealing the carriage from much of the noise from outside. By now the train had picked up speed and was gently rocking from side to side as it clicked and clacked over the joints in the tracks. Every now and again it would cross over sets of points, the clickety-clacking becoming rapid and the rattling and swaying intensified for a short while. Stuart watched intently at the backs of the houses that slid past them, at the cars waiting at the closed whitely painted level crossing gates and at all the exciting paraphernalia associated with the railway. There was a whole world of it, strange signs and notices, little huts, piles of odd looking pieces of equipment and the signals. The signals were what told the drivers when it was safe to go and when they had to stop, Joey had explained to Stuart. They were worked by wires that ran all the way back to the signalman, who worked up in the tall signal boxes that stood alongside the tracks, way high up and with windows all around. Inside the boxes were rows of great big levers that operated the points and the signals associated with them Joey had told him "Wow!" was Stuart's wide eyed response, "if he pulled the wrong one there'd be a dogostrophe!" When he had enquired what Stuart had meant he explained that he did not consider a *cat*-astrophe to be a bad enough way to describe what would happen should some madman take over the signal box and pull all the wrong levers, so he had gone up to the next level of disaster from cat!

Some of the signals were small ones with just one arm on them but some nearer to the station where lots of lines joined together, were gigantic, going right across the tracks on gantries that looked like little footbridges. The arms of the signals were painted in all sorts of different colours, some had stripes on and some didn't and at one end they had little windows with coloured glass in that let a lamp shine through them, red for stop and green for go. Stuart had told Joey very seriously that it must be a very important job being a signal man.

It was only a short ride on the train into town and soon the train slackened its rocking ride a little. The beat of the tracks slowed as they approached the station. Stuart sat back savouring the sights of the carriage, from the curve of the roof and the luggage racks overhead the seats, to the adverts and controls for the heating. His most favourite of all was the 'communication cord' which was a little red chain that was visible in a small box-like opening over the door. Alongside it was a stern warning about 'Improper Use' and the penalty you would get if they caught you! Although of course he had never pulled it, it was nevertheless an almost irresistible magnet to his fingers. He could almost feel the touch of the chain as his fingers closed around it, feel the jolt of the train as the emergency brakes were applied. He chuckled to himself at the thought of someone on a mainline train in the first class dining car sat eating their soup when he pulled the cord! Joey who had seen where Stuart's gaze was held, gently nudged him in the ribs to remind him of the stern lecture he had given him on this subject.

The train glided into the station, the platforms appearing on either side, first the lampposts with their curved slender tops which bent right around so the big lamps hung down from them, swan-necks Joey had called them, then the sign with the name of the station painted in big white letters, WORRELL CENTRAL, then the mighty round metal pillars that supported the giant curved roof that covered the centre of the station, then the benches and advertising boards and people milling about, porters and men with little carts for carrying suitcases and parcels. Finally the jolt as the train came to a stop and the opening and banging back of the doors as people poured off the train, all streaming towards the ticket collector at the end of the platform by the metal gates. Stuart remembered that he hadn't seen his ticket and insisted on Mum giving it to him so he could examine it and get the man to clip it for him. They would need the ticket to get home and he collected all the old ones, he loved the thick chunky feel of the cardboard and the little shapes the ticket punch cut out of them. Once punched Mum took the ticket back off Stuart and crouched down in front of him, "Don't wander off when we're in the shops, if you get separated from us wait at the door to the shop, and what do you do if you get completely lost?" "Run away with the gypsies?" Stuart proffered with the most innocent look he could paint onto his face. "Yes that's right, ask a policeman" she replied. Stuart frowned as he puzzled over what had been said. He heard and felt Joey chuckling and felt silly when he realised what Mum had done, he poked at the bump in his duffel coat.

Shopping was boring, boring, boring. You had to stand around being quiet, not touching anything, not fidgeting, not pulling faces at people, at the same time you had to watch everyone else chatting, chit, chat, chat… all their boring, stupid old talk, while they were touching everything in sight, and pushing and shoving at you as if you weren't there or were the invisible boy!

"When can we go to the hobby shop Mum?" He kept asking as they entered yet another lousy boring shop, "You don't want to go to school in your bare feet, do you?" Mum enquired, "Don't really mind actually, Joey goes everywhere in his… (bear feet)!" Then there was the indignity of having to sit with the greasy haired shoe salesman, who was really a bald old coot, but thought he could line up his hairs all across his big fat head and grease them into place and no one would notice he was as bald as a badger! Badgers weren't bald at all so that saying made no sense either did it? Half the stuff the grown-ups told you made no sense, was it a way of confusing kids? Telling them all sorts of tomfoolery? Anyhow when it came to old baldy bonce… it wasn't working matey! He thought and smirked as he thought of flicking the long strands of hair out of place! That'd show 'im!

Baldy was telling madam this and telling madam that and then they were expecting him to walk up and down and say if they fitted or not only to be told that they didn't when he had just performed like a circus chimp prancing up and down and said that they did! "Wiggle your toes Stuart!" Mum said as she pushed down on the end of the shoe, "Ouch that hurt!" Stuart exaggerated, "I told you it didn't fit. Stuart! Will you try and be of some help? Please!"

Now he was expected to carry the blummin'bag with the blummin'shoes in Stuart thought sulkily. It was already hurting his fingers. "We can use the empty shoe box to make things" Joey volunteered as they sat on a chair 'out of the way' in yet another rotten shop while the whole process was repeated with Lucy. "Yeah I suppose so" he admitted grudgingly. Lucy loved it though and she just pranced about with her new shoes on like a flippin film star, well that's what she was thinking, more like a stupid goon, he thought! All he wanted to do was to look around the hobby shop. They had shelves in there that went right up to the ceiling, all of them crammed full of really fabulous toys and models and kits, but best of all they sold Hornby double-o train sets. They had a small layout in the window, with trains running round and around. It was complete with buildings, signals, stations, bridges and it even had little trees. True you could see they were made of wire but they had green bits on and well you had to use a bit of imagination.

Stuart and Joey were going to build a layout just like it, but much bigger of course and with better trees and tunnels. Inside the shop they had box after box of carriages, trucks, guards vans but best of all boxes with plastic windows in revealing the engines they held within. Some small ones like the little black engine that had pulled their train today, (although in real life it was still massive), but best of all they had models of the mainline engines, in green or red, or even blue! With the windshields at the front and double chimneys and best of all the names. Names on little name plates just like the real ones, the Duchess of Montrose, The City of London, Caernarvon Castle. Oh! how he longed to undo one of those boxes and place the engines wheels onto the tracks.

He caught his leg on the corner of the shoe box that had poked through a rip in the stiff green and white paper carrier bag. His leg was cold and it hurt, it really hurt, "Stupid shoebox!" he blurted out, at the same time throwing the box abruptly onto the floor, where he kicked it across the pavement to bounce into the shop window of the Victoria Tea Rooms that they happened to be passing. An elderly lady who had white whiskers growing on one side of her chin, pulled an expression of mock horror at the bang on the window. She had watched the little boy lose his temper and angrily kick at the bag.

Stuart blushed deep red, and became even more angry, poking his tongue out at her in the rudest fashion he could manage and mouthing the words in an accentuated fashion 'Old Witch!' The old lady shook her head slowly from side to side, but smiled slightly at the same time before looking away. Stuart's mother however was not smiling at all. In fact her face was nearly as red with anger as Stuart's was with embarrassment. She marched over to the fuming boy and cuffed him across the head with the palm of her hand, "you naughty bad tempered little devil!" she snapped at him, "pick up that bag at once, those shoes have just cost me a small fortune you ungrateful little beggar!" Stuart who was now in full sulk mode, put his hands in his pockets and turned away from his mother with a stamp of his feet and even though he knew this was not a good idea, even without Joey prodding frantically at him from inside his coat and shouting "No! Stuart, No!" He just couldn't help himself from blurting out "I WILL NOT!" as he spoke the words he knew he had not just overstepped the line but done a hop-skip-and-a-flying jump, okay a blummin' long flying jump then... right over it and he burst into tears. The red rag had exactly the effect he feared and the wrath of his mother descended upon him. But not in the way he expected.

His mother whose first instinct was to give Stuart a damn good hiding right there in the street, caught the eye of the old lady sat in the cafe. She recognised her as Miss Witherspoon, the retired postmistress who attended their church. Miss Witherspoon who was watching Mum, shook her head slightly from side to side and mouthed a polite 'no'. Now Mrs Wheeler was not one to be told what to do by anyone but there was something so compelling about the old lady that she stayed her hand and turned back from the café window to look at her little boy's back who was stood cringing waiting for the onslaught. She was so overcome by her love for her wayward son that she crouched down alongside him and put her hands on his shoulders. She felt him flinch as she touched him, a wave of revulsion swept through her as she thought of her intended response. "Stuart," she said, quietly and calmly, "I know you're very tired, and that you're bored with shopping. You've been really, well pretty good so far, don't go and spoil everything now by having a silly paddy. We're nearly at the hobby shop, you do want to go in the hobby shop don't you?" A deep frown formed on Stuart's face and he turned slowly to look at his mother. She smiled at him their faces level. His face turned from one of angry pouting, through puzzlement and confusion into sheer joy and love for his Mum. He leapt towards her putting his arms around her neck and hugging her. "I'm sorry Mum" he sobbed, "I'm sorry." "I know love" she said wiping his snotty face with her hanky, "I know, now there come on and be a brave little soldier." Stuart sniffed and wiped the back of his hand across his nose as Mum stood up again. He followed her face upwards till he was stood with his head tilted back looking up at her. "There's just one thing I'd like you to, after you've picked up your shoes that is..." she motioned her head towards the carrier bag lying on the pavement. Stuart shifted his weight from one leg to the other and his mouth twisted in concentration as he tried to weigh up what he should do. He had 'a stubborn streak a mile wide' Joey regularly told him and also that there was a time and place to 'give in gracefully.' Stuart decided this was one of those times, after all he thought as he picked up the carrier bag, sticking out now would be like 'cutting your nose off to spite your face' as Mum said and he really did want to visit the hobby shop, so he bent down and picked up the hateful bag. "Well done Stuart and the other thing is..." "Muumm..." Stuart started to protest, to be cut short by... "Hobby shop?" He stopped but started bristling again as he waited for his sentence to be passed. He'd picked up the blummin' bag, what more did she want, he was the one with the sore leg, he was the one who'd had to carry the bloomin' bag and had his fingers nearly cut off by the blummin' stupid handles. Why should he do anything else?

"I'd like you to go into the cafe now and apologise to Mrs Witherspoon for what you called her!" He turned, aghast at what his mother was suggesting, from looking at her face to look into the window. The old lady smiled angelically back at him. "I never <u>said</u> anything!" Stuart replied, with the emphasis on 'said'. "I know but if you look in the glass of the window you'll see me stood behind you!" He adjusted the focus of his gaze and sure enough became aware of the reflection of his mother in the glass. Damn! He thought to himself. "You've been rumbled lad!" Joey volunteered, "I know" he said under his breath to Joey and added out loud, mutteringly "Didn't think you'd seen me" he confessed as he lowered his head and kicked his feet together.

"Well?" His mother asked, "I'm waiting!" Lucy helpfully interjected "She'll probably eat you, I've heard she likes little boys with her afternoon tea!" "Lucy that's quite enough! Miss Witherspoon is a lovely old lady, and if either of you took the time to get to know her you would find that out for yourselves. Now Stuart Wheeler, get yourself through that door *at once* and apologise for your utterly reprehensible behaviour!" Mum's voice had got sterner and sterner as the sentence had unravelled itself until Stuart had almost felt he was being physically propelled towards the door by the sheer force of her words and the she sheer length of a word the likes of reprehensible! He'd ask Joey later what it meant, if he could remember it!

He turned and shuffled towards the shop door which was set back from the street at the rear of an open porch with lovely curved glass sides. He got to the door and reached up to the polished brass handle. He pressed down firmly on the spoon-shaped lever and the door swung open, to the tinkling accompaniment of a little bell fixed somewhere up at its top, he craned his head around to look up at it as he walked in turning and gently shutting the door, lifting the brass lever with the little curved handle. It clicked shut behind him.

Inside it was quiet with only a muffled reminder of the noise of the traffic from outside. In here there was only the clink of tea cups, the occasional tinkling of silver spoons on china and of course the murmur of polite conversation. There was however no conversation going on at Miss Witherspoon's table. She sat all alone at the table in the window. She had been watching Stuart's progress into the cafe with interest and guessing what was going on, having observed the exchanges between small boy and mother outside the café, albeit as a scene from a silent movie, she motioned for the boy to come over to her. She smiled warmly to reassure him. Stuart smiled back a little self-consciously and walked over to the table.

"Miss Witherspoon I'm very..." he started to blurt out at tremendous speed only to be halted by the old lady lifting her left hand in a stop sign. "Now then Stuart" she spoke in a thin high pitched voice, but very clearly and precisely, "Do you not think we should be properly introduced before we engage in conversation?" Stuart was puzzled, he could see her point, it would perhaps be the proper thing to do, not that he did know it but how did he answer her? Should he say 'Yes I do' (think it proper) or 'No I do not 'not think' it proper'? Instead he stood up to attention like dad had taught him and said in his boldest voice "My name is Stuart Wheeler madam, I am most pleased to meet you!" (word for word as Joey had whispered up to him while he was pondering what to say!). The old lady was clearly delighted by his response and replied, "Miss Emily Witherspoon sir, a pleasure to meet you also," she swept her right hand in the direction of the chair opposite her "pray do join me for a little while kind sir." Stuart who was completely taken aback by all this looked out of the window at Mum who was stood holding Lucy's hand looking back into the tearooms. "Lucy rolled her eyes as she wiped her hand across her mouth with a lip-smacking gesture and then rubbed her tummy, until Mum tugged her other hand to stop her. Mum nodded *'go on'* and pointed to the fashion shop next door, "We'll be in Slater's" she mouthed. Stuart nodded and pulled out the heavy wooden chair and perched himself on it. "Would you like a glass of milk and a cake Stuart?" She asked kindly, in response to his concerned expression and obvious uncertainty. She added playfully "I'll want to fatten you up a bit before I eat you!" Stuart's mouth fell open a little until he looked up and met her gaze. Miss Witherspoon had the most dazzling clear blue eyes he had ever seen. They twinkled with life and mischief and did not seem to belong there in the wrinkled and frail old lady's face in which they resided. She had fine silver-white hair and had it all pulled back and pinned up at the back of her head, just like grandma did, like old Queen Victoria too, like he'd seen her on the back of the old pennies he collected.

He laughed out loud at her joke. "In that case, yes please Miss Witherspoon, I'd love one." "You may call me Emily, I'm not one to stand on ceremony and Miss Witherspoon is such mouthful isn't it?" "It is a bit" he replied. "Emily, how did you know my name was Stuart?" He asked tilting his head a little, fascinated by the white whiskers on the side of her pale white face. "I've seen you at church Stuart, in fact I was there when you were Christened. I used to be a Sunday school teacher there before Mrs Bentham took over. I've known your mother since she was no bigger than your Lucy. She was such a pretty little thing, just like your sister. When ladies are as old as me they sometimes get the odd whisker or two on their chins my dear." She replied to his un-asked question. He was clearly startled. "I merely observed you looking at my chin," she explained. "You'll catch a fly if you sit there with your mouth wide open like that Stuart!" She said smiling at him.

Stuart was now seriously impressed with this old lady. First she was a really good sport, not being upset at being called a witch and all, but as well as that she was mighty observant too, just like him! Then he remembered he hadn't apologised properly yet. "Miss Wi… err… Emily… I mean, I really am sorry for being so rude to you." Emily nodded, "it was most unkind and hurtful Stuart, but I know you didn't really mean it. I can see that you are good boy at heart and if you try hard I can see a great future ahead for you." Stuart smiled, "one thing though Emily, you couldn't have known mum when she was Lucy's age as she lived in Bristol then!" Emily chuckled and put her hand to her chin, "am I getting confused in my old age?" She stared into space for a moment before smiling, "ah I know who I was thinking of and why I got confused, it was your aunty, your father's sister I was thinking of! I certainly didn't teach Sunday school in Bristol!"

They were both laughing together when the waitress came over and stood poised by their table, her pencil resting on her little pad of paper, "What can I get for you Madam?" "Some chocolate éclairs and a glass of milk for my young friend here please my dear" Emily replied. The girl marched purposefully away, returning very shortly with a plate with three éclairs on it and a large glass of milk. The girl smiled at Stuart as she placed the plate in front of him, she was very pretty and her face was so fresh and pink it almost looked scrubbed. He blushed uncomfortably not knowing why, but soon forgetting as he turned back and helped himself to one of the cream cakes. Emily sat quietly and watched whilst Stuart did battle with the éclair. She smiled slightly as he hesitated after finishing it, his hand about to reach for a second one, when his manners got the better of him and he stopped and looked up at her, "May I..." "Have another if you wish Stuart" she interjected to save him having to ask, "They do look delicious." "Mmm… they are!" He mumbled with his mouth full, Joey dug him for talking with his mouth full. He poked him back. He drained the glass of its remaining milk and wiped his mouth on the serviette. "That was delicious, thank you very much Emily" "You're most welcome Stuart, I'm glad you enjoyed it. What would you like to be when you grow up?" Old people were always asking that and Stuart had taken to coming up with silly answers lately, like a rag and bone man, just to relieve the boredom, but in Emily's case he simply replied "an airline pilot actually." "My word, that sounds an exciting job, you really will have to work very hard at school if you are to be able to do something like that" she paused for a moment her eyes looking into the distance. Stuart looked intently at the old ladies face, despite her age she had an elegant beauty that was timeless and so fascinating that even a young boy such as him could admire it, without really understanding why. She continued as though she had never stopped. "My fiancé was a pilot in the Air Corps during the war. The Great War that is of course." "What's a fiancé?" he interrupted, "The person to whom you are intended in marriage." "He was killed so we never married." She added starkly, before staring off in the distance again. This time she turned her head a little to look out of the window. She sniffed a little and dabbed at her thin nose with a lacy hanky. "Why look Stuart, here's your mother and Lucy back. You run along now."

Stuart pushed back the heavy wooden chair and stood up. He wasn't quite sure what he should do and in circumstances such as these he often would do the most bizarre things. Afterwards he would be quite convinced that Joey had put him up to it, "How? I never said a word" the little bear would protest, "Telepathy?" he proffered, yes, that must have been it… because after pushing the chair partly under the table he strode around to the other side and took Mrs Witherspoon's hand, which she lifted slightly as he approached, and kissed it gently on the back. "Why thank you Stuart!" She exclaimed, her eyes wide with delight, a bemused little smile on her lips. Releasing her hand he took half a step backwards and added "Thank you, it has been a pleasure Ma'am." He went to turn away but she called him back, "Err... a moment if you please young man!" She was unusually hesitant for the first time during their encounter, "Would you like to call on me some time? I could show you a photograph of my Henry by his aeroplane, and let you look at his medals." "Wow! Yes please

Emily, I'd love to. When should I come?" "I'll telephone your mother dear, you can bring your friend too." She looked in amusement at his puzzled face adding "The one inside your jacket!" His hand involuntarily moved to where Joey was beneath his coat. "We go everywhere together" he said. He opened his coat a little to reveal the bear. "I thought you might. Run along now." Stuart turned and as his attention shifted away from her Miss Witherspoon looked directly into Joey's eyes and smiled, he thought he caught something in her gaze, could she sense his presence? When she winked knowingly at him... he knew... Stuart oblivious to what had just transpired, marched away now over towards the door, he turned and looked back towards Miss Witherspoon to wave goodbye to her, but she was looking over towards the fireplace in a world of her own once again.

Outside Lucy set to on him about kissing Miss Witherspoon's hand. They had been stood outside and had witnessed his performance. 'I'll kill you Joey when we get home' he thought to himself, digging at his coat, as Lucy was in full spate "Oh I say old chap, weren't we just a little too formal! But then again it was your first date! Shocking! Shocking!" Stuart for once was non-plussed and ignoring his sister's chiding simply took hold of his mother's hand and allowed himself to be lead off down the street, she had patted him fondly on the head and although she said nothing he sensed despite Lucy's mocking ridicule that his performance had somehow gained her approval. He craned his head around for one last look at the old lady, but the table was empty now, she too must have left. "I hope you haven't eaten too much and spoilt your lunch Stuart, we're going for lunch now with the Mileys at the Strand Hotel." "No not really" he lied. He had, and he spent most of the interminably boring time in the hotel 'playing with his food' and 'being a nuisance'. Naturally this incurred a penalty. "... and if you think we're going to the hobby shop now..." Yes that was it, and although even Stuart could not quite figure out exactly why it was the little bears fault, he was definitely going to kill Joey when they got home!

Despite his best efforts at pouting and sulking for the next hour and a half, Stuart could not change his Mum's mind, and when they finally were sat on the train heading away from town he refused to speak and simply looked at the floor and would not lift his gaze even to the taunts of such remarks his mother made as "Look Stuart a goods train" or "Look Stuart a signal box." No that was it. The day was ruined. There was no longer any point. He finally snapped when Lucy volunteered "Oh Stuart look, a Jubilee class!" His head had turned before he could stop it "Where..." "Oh you've just missed it!" she lied. "Mum, she's picking on me!" "You're just being a silly little boy, cutting your nose off to spite your face, when you know you're dying to look out of the window. You love coming on the train" "I DO NOT! I HATE TRAINS! I NEVER WANT TO GO ON ANOTHER STUPID TRAIN EVER, EVER, EVER! AND I DIDN'T EVEN WANT TO GO TO THE STUPID HOBBY SHOP ANYWAY! NOT REALLY!" He shouted banging his heels in a frenzy of kicking against the front of the seat in a mad paddy. It was only the sharp slap, slap, slap, on his bare thighs that pulled him up. "I hate you!" he cried out at his mother through his tears, "I hate you!" He sat looking at the red hand prints emerging on his stinging legs, but would not rub them. He caught a glimpse from under his eyebrows as he looked without lifting his head, of Lucy looking out of the window, her smile showing clearly in the reflection. 'I hate you too!' He thought to himself.

Arriving home he threw his coat off, kicked off his shoes without unlacing them and stormed off upstairs Joey dangling perilously from his clenched and flailing fist. He slammed shut his bedroom door and stood inside fuming for a moment before flinging Joey across the room and then himself onto the bed. Joey bounced off the wall and landed by the toy box with a thud. This was one of the worst paddies Stuart had ever had, a real humdinger of a paddy and Joey sat for a moment or two wondering what he should do. Muffled sobs were coming thick and fast from the pillow into which he had buried his head as he lay face down on the bed. Occasionally he would beat his legs in a frenzy against the candlewick bedspread or punch frantically the bed either side of his pillow. After five minutes or so his rage subsided, although his sobs continued. The muffling effect of his pillow ceased as he lifted his head a little "I suppose you hate me as well now?" He spoke to the room, "I wouldn't blame you after being thrown across the room, I suppose you'll have a headache, have you? Are you alright? Speak to me please!" Joey sat impassively without replying. Stuart lifted himself up onto his elbows and twisted himself around to look in Joey's direction. He stared pleadingly at the bear with his sore red rimmed eyes. Joey almost weakened, but no he had decided, Stuart Wheeler was going to learn a lesson today, no matter how painful it might be to him, or to Joey himself. Without a word he walked across the room and went under the bed. He unbuckled the steamer trunk that he travelled with and took out a stick. It appeared to be a black walking stick with a silver handle. Stuart who was now hanging upside down over the edge of the bed, sniffling at his snotty nose had never seen the miniature steamer trunk before, or the cane that Joey had produced from it. He stared, fascinated as Joey held the stick out horizontally above his head, just in front of his face. He heard him speaking strange sounds, syllables he could not reproduce himself. Then descending from the cane, unrolling itself as a fabric blind would, was a door frame, with a thick panelled wooden door in it. The door descended till it touched the floor. He heard Joey mutter a further incantation and watched in utter disbelief as the little bear reached out and lifted the door's brass latch. With a metallic click the door swung open, creaking slightly as it did. Joey turned his head as if inspecting the creaking hinge and then stepped through the door. The door slammed shut behind him and simultaneously vanished in a puff of dust. The little strands of fluff that were under the bed wafting up a little in its wake. Joey was gone! Stuart stared in disbelief. The miniature steamer trunk stood there all alone amongst the now settling strands of dusty lint. His face though blotchy red and tear stained changed miraculously though when from nowhere the door reappeared. "Joey!" He called out "Come back, please! I'm sorry! I'm sorry!" The door creaked open and... Yes, yes it was him, but something was wrong, he wore a deep frown as he took one step back into the bedroom, bent slightly and took hold of one of the handles of the steamer trunk. Without further ado he lifted the end of the handle and dragged the trunk through the door. It caught on the frame as it went through, knocking a splinter of wood off the side, but with a mighty second tug it was through. The door slammed shut and vanished again. Now there was nothing left at all. He rubbed his eyes and looked again, still nothing. He swivelled around and dropped to the floor, crawling right under the bed. Nothing. Just the little strands of fluff. Wait... yes there was the tiny splinter of wood that had split off the door frame. He picked it up carefully between his thumb and first finger examining it closely, then in panic he turned full circle, banging his head on the metal frame of the bed. The springs in the bed boinged resonantly. He looked across the room to where he had thrown Joey and to his joy saw the little bear was still lying there! "Joey! Joey! How did you do that? That was REAL magic, wasn't it? I knew you could do magic all along!" He scrabbled madly to get out from under the bed, banging his head again as he went, but not caring. He skidded across the floor to where the bear lay and picked him up, gently, reverently. "Are you alright little friend?" He asked stroking his head, "I'm sorry, you know I never meant to hurt you." But something was wrong. Although outwardly there was no difference in Joey's appearance, it wasn't him. He lifted him up and shook him gently, nothing. Stuart's face went white as the blood drained from it. He lay the little bear down onto the floor as if it was made of eggshell and walked away backwards in slow motion till he collided with the bed. He sat down onto it as the awful truth came to him, what he had just seen was Joey's ghost! He sat slowly shaking his head from side to side, staring at the limp form of the teddy bear repeating over and over to himself in a hushed voice "I've killed Joey! I really have, I've killed him!"

Chapter Seven

Unbearable

The Portal

When Stuart never appeared downstairs, after repeated calls from his mother that his tea was ready, she knew something was wrong. No matter how much of a paddy he may have had, when it came to meal times Stuart always managed to find a way of saving enough face so as not to go hungry. He was a healthy little boy with a big healthy appetite! She knocked gently on his door, "Stuart are you all right dear?" there was no reply so she opened the door and came over to the bed where Stuart lay with his head buried in the pillow. She sat down on the edge of the bed and gently placed her hand on his shoulder. He flinched away from her. "Come on Stuey, let's just forget about this afternoon and start again, your tea's ready, it's your favourite, Shepherd's pie" "I'm not hungry, and I hate Shepherd's pie!" He blurted out angrily, before bursting into floods of tears again. Mum got up and walked around to the other side of the bed, kneeling down so that she could see her distraught son's face. "Whatever is the matter love, I've never seen you like this, come on now tell me, I'm not going to leave you here like this until you do." "You don't understand. You can't understand. You'll NEVER understand! It's **my** secret and I **can't** tell you!" Mum frowned her concern deepening. She gently lifted her son's shoulders off the bed and turned him so that with minimal co-operation from him he was sat on the edge of the bed, face to face with her. "Now listen to me Stuart Wheeler, you are going to tell me right now what's going on. Have you been bullied at school?" "No!" "Have you been in trouble with your teacher?" "No!" "Has someone bothered you on the way home from school?" "Nooo, no, no!" He whined at her. Nothing like that rubbish. It's far, far worse. I… I've... I've..." "Yes, yes, Stuart tell me, what have you done?" "I've killed Joey!" "Oh Stuart! You silly little boy, you've been worrying me sick like this about one of your made up silly nonsense games! I'm very angry Stuart. What have I told you about the boy who cried wolf?" She stopped as he erupted into a spasm of sobbing again, throwing himself back onto his pillow, where he mumbled into it "see I told you, you wouldn't understand, how could you?"

Mum got up and picked the little bear up off the floor next to the bed where he lay on his back. She brushed off the dusty lint that was clinging to his fur. He looked perfectly normal. A cute little furry teddy bear, a bit worn around the edges from years of Stuart's cuddles, but just as he always was. 'Killed Joey!' She mused to herself. Were there no bounds to her son's wild and vivid imagination? She had caught him several times embroiled in lengthy discussions with Joey. Boy sat facing bear talking to each other. She remembered what a nice voice Stuart had used for Joey's side of the conversation and how he had been flustered and would not continue when he became aware of her presence. Yet as she smoothed the fur gently away from Joey's little sewn on stiches of eye's, there was something strangely different about the teddy bear.

It was difficult to say what it was. There had always been something strangely odd about his eyes, although they were only bits of wool she had sewn on herself, after his original shiny button eyes had gone missing many years ago, they did seem to have a depth to them that they really shouldn't have had, they seemed however silly it seemed, almost alive. But today they weren't, they were simply bits of wool. Dismissing this as fanciful she placed the little bear gently next to Stuart. "I don't know what to make of all this Stuart, I really don't. If this is one of your silly games I suggest you stop it at once, it has got quite out of hand. You've made yourself quite hysterical over all this" She took hold of his hand gently. "Come on Stuey, let's go and have tea" He pulled his hand away, but less vigorously this time, "You just don't understand" was all he repeated. "Well we'll just have to see what dad makes of all this then when he gets home!" She expected some movement after this at least, but nothing was forthcoming. She stood up and walked over to the door, she rested her hand on the handle, pausing for a moment but for once she was at a loss about what to do. She started to frame another plea to Stuart but stopped, pushed the handle down and left the room.

Stuart did not come down for his tea at all that evening. Even his father could make no sense of his stricken son. In the end he was put into his pyjamas and tucked up in bed.

The cup of steaming Horlicks they'd left for him was still there in the morning, now stone cold, along with the biscuits when mum came into his bedroom. Stuart was kneeling up on his toy box looking out of the window his nose pressed against the window pane. It was raining again and he stared blankly out through the streaming glass. "Doesn't Joey want to look out as well?" Mum asked tentatively, observing the little bear sat on the bedside table. "He's dead. I told you. I killed him. I threw him across the room, he hit the wall and now he's dead" "Really Stuart, this is becoming most tiresome. Breakfast's nearly ready, do make an effort not to be such a grumble-puss!" She said good-humouredly. Hunger got the better of him and he put his dressing gown on and went down. He ate his breakfast without saying much to anyone. Lucy had been told in no uncertain terms to 'lay off' her little brother this morning, and by and large she did. Dad was cooking up bacon and eggs, his Sunday morning treat, "I need to have a full stomach to sit through one of the vicars sermons!" was his usual excuse. He would have eaten a cooked breakfast every morning if he'd the time, but during the week he was up and away at the crack of dawn. Stuart declined his usual 'special buttie' which included a bit of everything dad had, bacon, fried egg, fried bread, sausage and sometimes even a bit of black pudding or tomato. Dad let it go, he too had received instructions from mum not to fuss over Stuart and been told to 'leave him to it' and 'he'll come around in his own time.'

Washed and dressed in their Sunday best the Wheeler family set off to church. It had warmed up a bit after the unseasonably cold weather they'd been having but it was still drizzly so dad got the car out of the garage and they drove the half mile or so to the church. Stuart who had a good voice normally sang with great gusto, but this morning was silent. He noticed Emily sat on the other side of the aisle, she nodded slightly to him and he nodded back. He could hear her thin voice now amongst the others, a little shaky but still in key and vibrant. She tapped the underside of her chin with the back of her hand in response to Stuart's sullen demeanour. He could almost hear her saying 'keep your chin up lad.' But he didn't want to. He turned away and cast his eyes down again. It was fine and dandy for her to say 'keep your chin up' he accentuated the voice in his head to sound ridiculous, as ridiculous as the thought was to him presently. What did she know, Joey was dead and he'd killed him. He thought for a moment of what the old lady had told him in the tea rooms. Her *feeants* or something like that, had been killed too. So *she* did know what it was like! He turned again to look at her. She held her head high and sung out with all her heart. How could she sing so, sing to God? The same God who had let the Germans kill her, what was his name, Harry? No it was Henry wasn't it? Yes Henry. He had let her Henry get killed! I bet she had prayed and prayed and asked Him to look after him too, just like he and Lucy did every night about their family, but had He? No of course not. Just like He hadn't brought Joey back to him despite him praying himself to sleep and promising everything he could think of to cajole God into letting his little bear come back to him! Emily closed her hymn book and sat down. She smiled in amusement at something as she looked over towards him. He blushed crimson red when he realised that he was still standing after the entire congregation had sat down. "You may sit down now Master Wheeler!" The vicar spoke good humouredly to him from the pulpit. Lucy sniggered behind her hand, as did Veronica sat further along the pew. Mum put her arm around his shoulders and hugged him to her as he sat down. He was never, never, never, never, never coming to church again! God was a sod anyway, he just ignored you when you begged him for help, he'd let Henry die too. He reached into his suit jacket to find the comfort of his bear only to remember that this Sunday he was alone as he would always be from now on.

His heart ached, a real pain that tore at his innards. He felt the hot sting of his tears as they rolled down his cheeks, but he didn't care anymore. He let them fall as he stared, his eyes locked on the carved painted and gilt figure of Jesus who looked down at him watching his tears with his compassionate blue eyes set in his serene face. No one else was mourning his friend, no one else could. But his loss was real and he was not ashamed of his tears. Jesus was pointing. Stuart's eyes had drifted off the saintly face and along his arm, draped in folds of finely carved material from which his wrist protruded. His golden open hand had one straight golden finger. Pointing. Pointing upwards.

The rest of Sunday passed uneventfully. It was home for Sunday dinner, which Stuart had been told off for 'fiddling with more than eating,' by mum "after all the trouble I've gone to making it for you as well!" Followed by a visit to Aunty Eunice's. Aunty Eunice lived across town on a little cobbled street, one of many in Worrell which had rows and rows of the little joined-up houses facing each other. Dad said they were called terraces or back-to-backs, that was because when you went out of the back door there was only a tiny little flagged yard with a shed for the coal and the toilet! The toilet was actually outside, right down the yard! Stuart thought it was a rum idea. It was hard to believe really, it only had a shed door on it too with a great big gap at the bottom and the walls were rough and had 'white-wash' on them which came off on your clothes if you rubbed against it. He was blummin glad they didn't live in a house with an outside toilet, or 'privvie' as they sometimes called it or 'kasie' or one of a lot of much ruder names too! It would be horrible when it was cold and snowing if you wanted to go!

Next to the kasie was a gate in the wall which led to a narrow cobbled passageway, on the other side were the walls at the back of the next row of terraced houses, hence back-to-backs! None of the houses had front gardens either and you could look straight into the front room from off the pavement of the street, but most had lacey white curtains up to stop you beaking in. His friend Andy lived in a terrace too but theirs had a small front garden and they'd had a loo fitted inside as well as the one outside. When you went through their back gate though there was a big patch of waste ground where they played, some of it was overgrown with brambles but a lot was just uneven grass, it even had sandy patches in it.

Stuart was glad that they didn't live on one of the streets like that. Their house was much better than these. Joey had told him it was good to appreciate what they had but also not to look down on the people who lived here, people who had less than them. They were just as good as he was and just because you might have more money and possessions than someone else did not make you a better person. He had gone on and on about it, till Stuart had said it was like one of the vicars sermons, only worse. He winced as he remembered his loss as he thought of Joey again. He had dismissed Emily's suffering after further thought because it had been so long ago. How could she possibly still feel like he did? He was beginning to doubt that the pain ever subsided though now and even in the midst of his own grief he remembered her invitation to come and see 'her Henry's' medals. He would go, but he would go to see her, not the medals. He would go to see her because she had suffered terribly. He understood now.

Aunty Eunice lived alone. Her house was dark and dismal save for the rosy glow of the fire that always seemed to be lit in the big black metal 'range' that more or less filled one of the walls in the back room. They always sat in the back room. The 'parlour' which was what she called the front room was only used 'for best' which seemed to mean never. One of the few times Stuart had seen it was when Uncle Stanley, Aunty Eunice's brother had died. Uncle Stanley had been a coal miner, Stuart couldn't really remember much about him. One or two pictures would come to mind when he thought of him, pictures of a big man, with big hands and a deep booming voice which was punctuated by a thick, heavy cough. He remembered watching those great big hands of his as they delicately rolled his cigarettes into perfectly round thin little tubes, before licking them and sealing them off. He'd tapped the tube on the end on his tobacco tin before lighting the cigarette using one of the long spills lit from the ever present coal fire. Stuart could still see clearly the cigarette between those big coal stained fingers, the white paper starkly contrasted by his black and broken finger nails.

He had peeped around the door when no one was looking to see him in the coffin. All the grown-ups had been allowed in to 'pay their respects' to him, which was daft, I mean he was dead. He'd still looked like Uncle Stanley but he was white, his skin seemed so very white against the dark colour of his best suit he remembered from the glance he'd got. Stuart had thought it most unfair that he'd not been allowed to go to the funeral either. There was something strangely fascinating about the churchyard, with all its old gravestones covered in the names of the people who had lived in their town before they did. He had felt excluded, not permitted to share in the grown up's grief, he was after all as they said 'only a child!'

He'd been allowed to call round with his dad, there were sandwiches, he loved sandwiches. He'd eaten some finger rolls which had been cut in half and had thick beef paste on them, they were grand but the sandwich he bit into had tongue in it! It was vile, it had the same feel of his own tongue, but it wasn't, it was some smelly old cows! The same tongue that had probably licked its arse! He'd spat it out and slithered down under the dining table, beneath the table cloth and shoved the remainder of the butty and the spat-out-bit on a ledge under there. He'd had enough to eat then he'd decided.

The parlour was also home to Aunty Eunice's piano. It was a beautiful warm wooden colour, with wonderful polished white and black keys. He'd heard tales of how Aunty Eunice's family used to have sing-songs around the piano, but despite his fervent suggestions to have one now, they never would? She used to smile, her thin lips pulling right back over her long white teeth and complain about the arthritis in her gnarled and bony misshapen hands. If he had a piano like that he would play it every day he had exclaimed, half hoping that the old woman would say "Take it with you Johnny, let the lad have it, I've no use for it now!" She always called dad 'Johnny' but she never suggested parting with her beloved, (though never used) piano.

The only things of interest in that drab back room were the clocks. For some inexplicable reason there were three clocks. This might not seem particularly strange in its own right, until you saw how big they were. O.K. the one on the mantelpiece was reasonably sized, but the ones on the other walls were as tall as Stuart. One was long and thin with glass windows all around it and a big white face with roman numbers on it pointed to by large lacily woven black fingers. Its pendulum ended with a big silver disc that swung side to side ticking once every second. Behind the pendulum were big weights held by chains that made the clock work, and every hour it boomed out its brassy chime, which rapidly turned into pandemonium as the other clocks did likewise. The one on the mantelpiece ringing a bell and the other, bigger, wider clock clonging.

The big clock was Stuart's favourite. It had an intricate pendulum, and wires with pulley wheels on, the best bit of all was the top, for over the face of the clock was another window with shiny brass stars painted on it, and a picture of the moon which came out from one side and went right across till it slowly disappeared into the other. The sides of the opening were shaped so that the moon looked just like it really did up in the sky, its crescent shape accurately reflecting the real moons progress outside as it waxed and waned.

The clocks had been Uncle Stanley's but after he died Aunty Eunice had carried on looking after them keeping them wound and their shiny wooden cases beautifully polished. "I don't know why I bother!" She moaned every single time they went, "I never liked them... never liked them!" She was always doing that, repeating what she had just said. Stuart and Lucy used to imitate her on the way home. "Look a man on a bicycle... on a bicycle!" "Yes it's a red bicycle... a red bicycle!" They would laugh and run off as mum told them off for skitting, "It's not nice to skit… to skit!" she joined in their fun.

Today for once Stuart was content to sit staring into the coals of the fire, sat on the floor leaning on the front of the armchair that his dad was sat in. The room was so small there wasn't room for enough chairs for everyone. He sat listening to their talk of people, distant relatives, who was ill now, who had died, on and on it went. Today though he was fascinated by it all. "There's talk that we might be off rationing on the coal soon Aunty, a friend of mine who works for The Coal Board reckons stocks are mounting up now" his dad was saying, as he watched his ancient relative poking the coals with her long handled poker "Oh I do hope so Johnny, it's so hard to keep warm when you can't get all that you need. I've not heard anything about that on the wireless though, I like to keep up with events I do… keep up with events Johnny." He was glad to hear that the end to rationing might be in sight though, he thought it'd save his mother moaning on about being short of coal all the time and how *'that'* coal man was a pig because them next door's coal shed's full! His mood perfectly fitted the sombre surroundings and the resigned dejected way in which Aunty Eunice viewed life and the world and he looked anew at his ancient relative, through different eyes, for now he understood.

They left through the back gate as Stuart needed a piddle, as they shut the gate behind them and walked together along the narrow cobbled ginnel, he'd asked his dad why there wasn't an open space behind Aunty Eunice's like the wasteland behind Andy's house. "Some bombs fell there during the war, the only ones to fall on Worrell thankfully, they think the pilot must have got lost or couldn't find the docks at Liverpool so he just dropped them anywhere to save having to take them back with him!" Stuart had been wide eyed hearing this, "so there **were** houses there before? Where people lived?" "Yes Stuey, just the same, two rows, made a terrible mess it did. We're lucky really, because as it was the only bombsite in Worrell it got cleared-up fairly quickly, not like in Liverpool but there's never been the money to rebuild anything yet. Stuart had been quiet the rest of the way home as he tried to imagine the houses standing where they now played and made dens in amongst the brambles, he could be in someone's parlour sat there in their den, there could be skellingtons under the ground! "Dad will there be skellingtons underneath the wasteland then?" He looked up and asked his dad in a worried little voice as they turned the corner into their street, "oh yes and ghosts too, wailing for their lost children… whooo…" and he had chased after him all the way down their street to their gateposts!

Monday morning came and Stuart wasn't up again. Mum came into his room and put on the light. He shuffled further under the bed clothes still half asleep. She walked round to the side of his bed. "I'm glad to see you didn't waste all your Horlicks again!" She commented looking down at the half empty mug and half eaten biscuit. "I err... what?" he mumbled from under the covers. "Come on get up sleepy it's school this morning" "I'm not going. I'm in mourning for Joey. I'm too sad to bother with school today!" She pulled back the covers and he sat up all disgruntled. "Come on now don't be silly, he's not dead at all, in fact he was never alive, he's just a Teddy bear, a stuffed toy!" Stuart glared at her "you don't know anything. You're stupid!" He shouted angrily back.

"Stuart!" Mum exploded, "This has gone on quite long enough. Get yourself along to the bathroom. At once! I want to see you downstairs in your school uniform in five minutes, or else!" With a little shrug of his shoulders he dropped off the wrong side, the window side of the bed, "Right oh, I'm going." He walked around the end of the bed, as he passed her she saw the tears running down his cheeks. She stooped down and placed her hands on her sad little boy's shoulders, "What's wrong Stuey, please tell me" He looked away from her his eyes cast down, his lip trembling as he turned, walking resignedly across the landing towards the bathroom. Perplexed she shook her head and wiping away the tears that had started running down her own cheeks in sympathy with her sons, she headed off back downstairs. "Five minutes Stuart!" She called to him, forcing herself to sound stern.

Five minutes later he came through the breakfast room door, dressed, clean and tidy ready for school. He stood in the room waiting for further instructions. His sister greeted him with "what's up dopey? Forgotten how to eat?" "Lucy! Leave Stuart alone, he's not feeling well, be kind to him" Mum called ahead as she came through from the kitchen. "Well done Stuart, come on now, sit at the table and eat your Weetabix" He proceeded over to the table and sat staring at the bowl of breakfast cereal. "You are so weird!" Lucy whispered when Mum wasn't looking. She waited expecting to get Weetabix flicked at her or at least a wisecrack back, but nothing. Her brother just continued to sit staring at the Weetabix. "Weird!" she re-iterated shaking her head as she left the table, with her now empty dish and spoon.

Stuart was sent home from school at eleven o'clock. He had sat impassively at his desk and had been unwilling to go out to play at break time. It was unclear what exactly had happened in the playground, but the result was Stuart had ended up in the nurse's room with a bloody nose. This in itself was not unusual, Stuart was as boisterous a boy as you were likely to find anywhere. Good-natured and charming when he wanted to be, but with a penchant for getting into scrapes. What was unusual was that he was sat alone, his head tipped back holding a wad of cotton wool to his bloodied and streaming nose when Mr. Wilkinson the headmaster came in to find out what had gone on. He would have expected there to be at least one other wounded combatant with him! Stuart was again unusually unforthcoming. Normally it would be a case of trying to get a word in with Stuart, who although not disrespectful would be gushing in the defence of his actions. Now he just sat disconsolate barely speaking. It appeared from what could be pieced together that Stuart had refused to be drawn by some goading that had gone on, and had not lifted a finger to defend himself under a flurry of blows from one of the other boys. It was only the intervention of his friend and the teacher on duty in the playground that had prevented further injury. It was this uncharacteristic sullenness that prompted Mr. Wilkinson to telephone Mrs Wheeler and ask her to come and collect him.

Several hours later after a visit to the family doctor Stuart was tucked up in bed fast asleep. Even Lucy had popped in when she had come in from High School to see how he was.

"What's up Stu'?" She asked bouncing down on the bed to sit beside him "Nothing" Was the only response she got. "I heard mum talking to dad at work on the phone. Yes, she rang him *at work*! She said the doctor thought you'd have to see a psychiatrist if you didn't buck up! I always said you were weird, but come on Stu' they'll lock you up in the loony bin if you carry on like this!" "Don't really care" he muttered as he rolled over to face away from her. "You'd like that, then you could have mum and dad all to yourself again, like before I came along, you've always hated me anyway!"

Lucy climbed up and lay on top the bed clothes alongside the miserable little lad, she snuggled into him and put her arm around his shoulder, "I know I tease you Stu' but I do love you, you do know that? Don't you?" He nodded feebly in response. "Is there nothing we can do to fix Joey?" She asked as she leant up on her elbow and stroked his head, running her fingers through his hair.

At this he twisted himself around to face her, the realisation that she at least understood that there was something wrong with Joey was a first! "It's not that there's something wrong with him, it's that he's dead!" Lucy looked deeply into her little brother's troubled eyes, she was going to say *'stupid! He's a stuffed toy he's never been alive!'* But such was the depth of the misery she could see in his eyes, so deep and obvious was his pain, that uncharacteristically for her she burst into tears and hugged him around his neck and sobbed onto his shoulder. Stuart was a bit taken aback by this rare and spontaneous display of emotion by his big sister and patted her gently on the back. "Come on sis, don't carry-on" was all he could think of to say, something his dad might have said to his Mum when she was having one of her soppy-turns, girls were pretty much like women he guessed?

Lucy sat back and wiped her tears away, she reached over and gently took hold of Joey and sat him on her knee, "he looks the same as he always did to me" she said, but then peered deeply into his eyes, "although… I don't know what but… you know, he IS different in some way!" "See I told you! I knew you could tell!" Stuart exclaimed excitedly. "So when I overheard you talking to him, that voice, the other one I could hear, it wasn't just you putting a different voice on, it was really *his* voice?" Lucy asked incredulously. Stuart bounced clear out of the bed clothes and landed kneeling up on the bed next to her, "yes! Yes! YES! You mean you heard him?" Lucy nodded as a percolating thought dawned on Stuart and spread across his joyous face… as a thundercloud might do across the sun on a sunny day, "you mean when you were... SPYING on me!" He pouted-out angrily! Lucy ignored his outburst and just carried on, "so when did things change?" Stuart who was just so glad to have someone taking him seriously at last, forgot his outrage at being 'spied-upon' and instead related the whole Joey-throwing-across-the-room incident to her.

His account was meticulously detailed and accurate and when he had finished she asked him, "hang on a minute then Stu, if you say throwing him at the wall killed him, then how come after being 'killed' he walked under the bed?" Stuart sat looking at his sister with mixed and confusing emotions swirling and boiling around in his head, on the one hand it was blummin' incredible that she was taking him seriously in the first place, he half expected that she might actually be just teasing him and that any minute she would round on him and take the mickey again, but she had *hugged* him! She had cried... and *real* tears, she was listening to him now, taking him seriously when no one, not even Mum would and more importantly she had *heard* Joey's voice!

He puzzled with all this and her question for some time before shrugging, "I dunno... thing is when I looked back from under the bed, there he was still on the floor where I'd chucked him?" "So he couldn't have been on the floor and walking under the bed, unless there were two of him?" Lucy asked as she frowned trying to figure it all out. Stuart shrugged, "I figured it was his ghost?" Her face lit up as if a light had come on..."maybe it was his ghost, but what if there was always two of him, one living inside the other, don't you see? The alive one, the real one that was hiding inside the toy one, bringing him to life!" Stuart stared wide eyed at Lucy, she was suddenly someone quite different from that horrible girl he'd always been forced to share his home with, she was someone who he could talk to, someone who was good at figuring! She was like a boy! She carried on, "so the 'real' Joey was simply cross with you and went back wherever he came from in the first place!" "You say there was a door he opened?" Stuart nodded and rolled off the bed to 'swim' himself under the bed, Lucy had done likewise from the other side and they met half-way under the bed, "right here!" He said, "but there's nothing, I've looked and looked and looked…" He spun around and only missing his head by a gnat's whisker skidded across the floor ending up knelt on the floor by his bedside cabinet, he pulled the drawer open and rummaged about before diving back onto the bed with a small piece of ripped and folded-up newspaper. Lucy had joined him back on top of the bed and watched as he very carefully unfolded the scrap of newspaper, "see here it is, the piece of wood he knocked off the doorframe as he pulled his steamer trunk through it… clumsy little sod!" He laughed as for a moment as he felt connected to the little bear through the teasing and laughing at each other that they had shared together. His face fell once more as the terrible reality he now faced washed back into his consciousness.

Lucy was intrigued though and delicately picked up the tiny fragment of wood which was no more than three quarters of an inch long and barely a sixteenth wide. She held it close to her eyes and turned it around from side to side. "I know!" She exclaimed, "I'll run down and borrow Mum's eye-glass and we can see it close-up!" With that she delicately placed the sliver of wood back on the newspaper and jumped off the bed, "Stay put Stu' I'll be back in a mo!"

A few minutes later they were at Stuart's dressing table by the window examining the sliver of doorframe through Mum's eye glass. It made everything seem massive when you looked through it, your finger looked like it was a mountainside with great ridges in it and bits of skin looked like wedges of wood! The sliver of doorframe was a very dark coloured wood and polished black on what would have been the face side and all raggedy and split where it had been torn from the rest of the frame. Lucy looked first before giving the eye glass to Stuart so he could see, he struggled to get it to stay lodged in his eye socket as Mum did and Lucy had just done, as she said "thing is Stu, this is real, it's there in your fingers, now. So although the rest of the doorway's invisible now, gone, isn't here anymore, it WAS here when he went through it!" She thought for a moment or two before adding, "unless you just found it under the bed, it was there all along?" She went and looked under the bed, there was nothing else remotely like the splinter there. She then went and looked at all the furniture in the room as Stuart sat on the small stool by his dressing table and watched in awe as she was being a detective, like Sherlock Holmes! She examined all the edges of the furniture and came to the conclusion "well it's not come off any of the furniture in here!" She sat down on the end of the bed and looked across at Stuart, "the thing is though, why doesn't he just come back?"

Just then and before they had chance to ponder the problem any further Mum came into the room, "what's all the bouncing around going on up here about?" She asked sternly, but then seeing Stuart out of bed and obviously 'up to something' and more peculiarly with Lucy in cahoots with him… By the time he responded to his mother, Lucy's conclusion of 'why doesn't he just come back' had sunk in and the heavy blanket of doom and misery had descended back down upon him, "nothing Mum, Lucy was pestering me, make her leave me alone!" He peered under his eye-lids sideways at her imploring her to 'leave it alone' not to elaborate to Mum! She picked-up on his signals and flounced across the room "I was just trying to help the stupid boy to snap out of all of his stupid nonsense, but I can see there's no hope for him other than spending the rest of his sad and sorry days locked up in the loony-bin!"

"Lucy Wheeler! You just go to your room right now and don't you dare come out until I say so!" Mum angrily proclaimed as she pointed a finger Lucy's-roomwards! Lucy turned her head at the door and winked at Stuart as she left the room, "and you young man, get back into bed!" Stuart 'slouched' across to bed, dragging his feet, his head down and flopped disconsolately onto the bed. Mum came over and pulled the covers back over him, she ran her hand through his hair and shook her head in despair, before turning and brushing a tear away she left the room closing the door quietly behind her.

She returned a few minutes later having had second thoughts and stuck a thick glass thermometer under Stuart's tongue and gently stroked his head. She seemed to have decided that he must really be poorly to be behaving like this. Stuart had come to the conclusion that she too thought that he was on his way to 'the loony bin' and was just hoping to find something else wrong with him instead!

Later on he had a bowl of tomato soup sat up in bed and a piece of bread and butter, before snuggling back down. When dad got home he came up and sat on the bed, "what's up young feller," he asked attempting to be bright and breezy, but Stuart could see through his sleepy, bleary eyes that his dad looked tired and drawn, he ran his big fingers through the lad's thick hair, his hand felt cool against Stuart's hot and clammy skin, "my you're running a bit of a fever old chap!" There was a note of real worry in his voice, Stuart mustered as much cheerfulness as he could manage and told his dad,

"I'm okay dad, just a bit under the weather don'cha'know! I'll be tickety-boo again in no time!" His dad smiled appreciating his little lad's noble sentiment, "that's the spirit! Look Stuey I've brought you a present to cheer you up, something you can look forward to playing with when you're up and about again!" He showed him a bright yellow Corgi box, "look it's an AEC flatbed, it's got pillars and chains all around the back and little barrels too…" Stuart looked up at his dad and smiled, it was a weak little smile though and he made no attempt to reach out for what would normally be a much prized toy. His dad sighed, "I'll put it here by your bed so you can see it, give you something to look forward to when you're up and about again eh?" With that he left the poorly little lad and went downstairs.

Stuart rolled onto his side and looked across at the cardboard box on the table, it looked smashing he thought sleepily. But he was more struck by the significance of his dad's action in bringing it home for him, I mean he must have gone to the hobby shop on his way home specially to buy it, just for him. He felt a tear run down his cheek onto his pillow as the tears in his right eye pooled at the side of his nose. He sniffed and wiped at the little lake of tears with the corner of his pyjama's sleeve. He loved his dad so much he thought and his dad loved him too… he so wanted to reach out and pull the lovely lorry out of the box, feel the solid cool metal, look at it from every angle… but he felt so sleepy….

Mum looked in on him again at nine o'clock to see if he wanted a mug of Horlicks, "you had some last night after I left it for you" she went on to add, trying to sell him on the idea. "No thanks" He had mumbled back as he slid back into sleep, 'I never touched it last night' he said, or did he just think it? He was asleep before he could decide.

Stuart woke up late the following morning, very late, he could hear everyday life going on out in the street but not the early morning activity he would normally hear. He thought about getting out of bed to look out of the window, but couldn't be bothered and snuggled back down. What was the point, he looked at the lifeless teddy bear lying next to him, no point showing *that thing* what was going on outside was there? The clock said ten to nine! Mum must have turned the alarm off, the soldier was lifeless too, just a painted bit of tin now, Joey must have taken his magic away with him too. Wow! It really was late though, no school for him today, he thought sleepily, he marvelled at how he had slept so long, maybe he really was actually ill after all…

Mum came into his bedroom just after ten and asked him how he was feeling and then got him up and dressed anyway and got him to go downstairs and sit by the fire with her while she did the ironing. He had some breakfast and some beans on toast at lunchtime and then surprisingly at four o'clock dad came home! A whole two hours before he normally did!

The two of them mum and dad sat him in the lounge with them and said they wanted to talk to him, it was very serious and he needed to tell them everything that was bothering him. It was like being interrogated by The Gestapo he thought, he wouldn't tell them Nazi's anything he decided, they could prop him up and shoot him first before… "Stuart are you even listening?" Dad scowled at him! In response Stuart stamped his foot angrily, "just send me to the loony-bin now and have done with it!" He blurted out! Dad moved closer and sat next to him, putting his arm around his son's shoulder, "don't talk like that son, no one's sending you there" "Oh yes they are, that stupid fat old doctor with his slobbery lips said I need to see a si-trike-olist, oh you know what I mean, a nut doctor, they want me locked up in the loony-bin!"

Dad looked at mum and tousled his son's hair, "come on now Stuart the doctor and mum and me are just trying to find out what's wrong with you, that's all. The *psychiatrist,* the doctor spoke about is just a doctor that works with people's noggins, well what goes on inside of them, just like another doctor would fix your leg if you broke it, he straightens things out in your bonce if it goes a bit awry, do you understand?" Stuart nodded sulkily, "well I said what was wrong with me and no one believed me, so what do you want me to say?"

"That's just silly talk about Joey, there must be something real that's bothering you, were you upset by the break-in, the burglars getting in the house? You were downstairs with them after all!" Stuart looked at his dad, "I was asleep dad, I don't remember them at all!" "Yes but it could have affected your subconscious mind son, without you realising it, that's what they might find out, isn't it Mum?" Mum nodded.

Dad changed tack, "well if it's not that then, have you been talking to strangers, has any bad man done anything to you?" "Eh? What?" Stuart looked at his dad as if he was mad! He shook his head, "have any of the other boys at school done anything, or the teachers, have you been fighting again?" Stuart swung his legs agitatedly about and squirmed on the couch… their interrogation techniques were damn persistent he thought… he could hear mum and dad's voices as they asked him this and asked him that, he nodded and shook his head and said 'yes' or 'no' if it seemed a bit appropriate for quite a while, but in the end just said 'stop going on…' and finally in desperation 'SHURRUP!' For which his dad told him off… but all the time he was really just off somewhere else in his mind thinking about more important stuff, not all that tish-tosh they were prattling on about, I mean it was dead simple wannit? Joey was dead, they wouldn't believe him, or maybe he was not dead but gone away, somewhere, someplace and wouldn't or maybe *couldn't* get back to him, *bla...bla...bla...* they were going on and on, then Mum's voice in utter desperation… "is there anyone you think you *could* talk to? Clearly you don't want to or won't talk to us?" "What about grandpa?" She asked at the end of her tether! He heard his own voice saying "Miss Witherspoon. I want to talk to Miss Witherspoon!" He saw the confused look on the faces of The Nazi's, as they looked at each other questioningly, yes that had given them something to think about!

He smiled to himself at having confounded his parents so neatly, at the same time trying to catch up with his mouth which had announced without his assistance who he wanted to see! On this occasion he concluded that 'his mouth' which had on countless other occasions landed him in hot water with its spontaneous and outrageous take on life and with its unasked for, untimely and usually unwanted comments which had regularly had him 'stood-out' in the corridor at school, or with a cuff around the ear 'ole off his dad… well this time it had been pretty damn smart all-in-all hadn't it? Well Emily had lost her fella hadn't she? Killed by the Jerry's in The First World War, what the old 'uns like to call The 'Great' War? Hadn't been so blummin' *great* for Emily had it, flippin' daft thing to call it wannit? She'd understand how he felt wouldn't she… and what's more she was old and wise and her house looked spooky when you walked past and well without being overly rude she actually was a bit like an old witch too, she might know how to get to where Joey had gone, with spells or magic or suchlike or know someone else, another witch or wizard maybe who might, if she didn't know herself that was… "**Stuart,** are you listening to anything *at all*?" Dad sighed slumping back on the couch in despair, Stuart shrugged. Mum trying to be helpful asked in her nicest-most-kindest voice… "Would you <u>really</u> like to speak to Miss

Witherspoon Stuart? Do you think it might help you? You did have quite a conversation with her at the tea room." He nodded, hadn't he just said so? Grrr… "Yes I do! Can I play out on my bike now?" "**NO!**" {mum and dad, in unison!}

Chapter Eight: Beyond the Veil

Mum went out in the evening to visit Miss Witherspoon, dad said why not ring her, her number was in the book, but she was insistent that it was way too complicated and altogether a too peculiar thing to talk about over the telephone, besides she didn't like talking on the telephone, she could hear her own voice through the receiver and it was embarrassing! She also wanted to get some fresh air and have some time to think about it all away from the house and decide if she really was actually going to go and pester an old lady she hardly knew at all, about what ailed her eight year old son!

She was at the house where Miss Witherspoon lived in what seemed like no time at all, without anything any more resolved in her mind than it had been when she'd left home. She opened the small iron gate and walked up the path at the front of the house. The tall old building loomed large up over her in the gathering gloom of the evening, the school-kids scared each other silly that the house was haunted whenever they passed by there and even she felt a shiver run down her spine as she stood there at the top of the three worn down stone steps at the imposing doorway to the large Victorian house.

Miss Witherspoon had been living there since her husband John had been a lad. He said he'd known her all his life through the church and also from her time at the Post Office, he told June he could only ever remember her as being an old lady though, she had been his Sunday school teacher he'd added and she'd had white hair even then! The porch door opened when she pressed the handle down and she moved inside, it was tiled with beautiful shiny tiles on the walls and diamond shaped tiles on the floor, red, blue, green it was very posh she thought.

The front door was half glazed the top half being filled with leaded panes of coloured glass. Mum pulled the large metal handle down that was to one side of the door, she heard a ringing noise respond to her pulls, coming from somewhere deep within the house. A light came on in the hall, lighting up the colours in the glass of the door, it was still only early evening but it was starting to go dark, it wasn't too late Mum hoped to be calling round like this? Stuart really needed help though and just the thought of him being treated as if he was a nutcase was too much for her to bear.

The door opened and there was Emily, she smiled looking a little surprised, "why June, how lovely to see you, what a surprise to have a visitor..." she stopped abruptly as she realised that her visitor was a greatly distressed one and was only being partially successful in fighting back her tears. "Come in, my dear, come in, whatever is the matter?" June fought back her tears, "Emily I'm terribly sorry troubling you like this, I feel so stupid coming around here, but it's my little lad, my Stuart..." With the mention of his name she dissolved into floods of tears, despite this she still managed to sob out "I'm beside myself with worry about him, the doctor wants him to see a... *psychiatrist!*"

Emily ushered her unexpected visitor through to the back of the house explaining that in this big old draughty house that she lived in, the cosiest room was the little snug at the back next to the kitchen. She got June settled in a comfy chair by the fire and left her to calm down a little while she made them 'a nice cup of tea!'

Sat together with a cup of tea and some digestive biscuits June told Emily as much of the story as she had managed to extract from Stuart and everything she had witnessed herself. Emily sat patiently listening sipping her tea, nodding occasionally and asking for clarification of the odd point June raised.

June finally ran out of steam and sat quietly watching Emily to see what her response would be. Emily sat for a moment or two in silence before placing her teacup and saucer down on the little table that was between them. "Can I get you more tea June?" She proffered, June shook her head and thanked her. "Stuart did say he would like to come around and see my Henry's medals when I had tea with him, you know? So if he thinks I may be of help to him in his time of need then I would be delighted to offer any assistance I can. He seems to be a fine young lad, high-spirited for sure, but there's no harm in that if it's channelled in the right direction is there?"

June thanked her profusely and they arranged for them to meet back in the morning with young Master Wheeler.

In a change from his recent behaviour Stuart was up and ready without prompting the following morning, he ate his breakfast and was ready to leave by half past eight, as it had been agreed when mum had checked in on him at bedtime and told him Emily would be delighted to talk to him, to help in any way she could. "I think you made quite an impression on her Stuey!" She had added as she kissed him on the forehead and tucked him in.

So a little over a half an hour later Stuart was sat in one of Emily's comfy chairs in her 'snug' with a biscuit in one hand and a cup of steaming hot chocolate she had made for him in the other. Mum had asked him if he wanted her to stay with him while he talked to Emily, he'd shook his head and Emily had joked that she'd had her fill of boiled-schoolboys for the moment, so she promised she wouldn't eat him!

"So Stuart what is it that's troubling you? You certainly have got your mum in a fine old stew worrying over you" Emily started the conversation. Stuart squirmed in his chair a little, then remembering how Emily had lost her fella and how kind she was, decided to confide in her, I mean what did he have to lose, they were going to lock him up in the loony-bin if he didn't buck-up weren't they? He mumbled "err.. well..." and glanced up to check that it *really* was a good idea... his eyes met the kindly, inquiring gaze of the old lady, her pale blue eyes were so bright and alive, they seemed to look right into him, make a real connection with him... he leant back into his chair and felt himself relax a little, "well you see Emily, Joey is no ordinary teddy bear..." Emily nodded reassuringly, "I could see that the first time I laid eyes on him." "Well it's not just that he's special to *me*, it's... well... the thing is... he's alive! He can speak, he can move! He's alive!" Stuart was gazing into Emily's face pleading for her to accept his words, not to ridicule him, but then even before she had responded, his face fell into a look of utter despondency and despair as he added "well, he *was* alive, until I killed him!"

Emily comforted him and explained that she was a firm believer 'that there was way more to this world than meets the eye!' She went on to explain that she was convinced she had seen Joey move and that their eyes had met and she had felt a connection with him at the tearooms. At this Stuart grinned like a real loony and sat right forward on the edge of the chair, "you did? You saw him! Lucy heard him talking once too, she thought it was me, pretending like, 'doing' a voice for him, you know?" Emily nodded, "but it wasn't, it was him all along!" Stuart was in full flow, excited and animated, more like the boy he always had been prior to his bereavement "and he saved all mum and dad's stuff from being stolen by the burgulars as well, brave little fellow that he is... was." His face fell as his emotional rollercoaster hit the bottom once more, adding sadly "till I killed him!"

Emily sat back deep in thought, staring into the distance, she made a triangle-y shape with her hands as her elbows rested on the arms of her chair, Stuart marvelled at how wise she was and how old too! After a moment or two of thinking she looked back at Stuart and smiled, "I think there must be another explanation to this other than that he is dead, I think Lucy was on the right track when she said that there must have been two of him, a stuffed toy and a real entity, a living being of some sort, of which I am not quite sure, a spirit maybe? A pooka? A fairy? Who can tell, but whatever he may be, I think there is a different reason for him not coming back to you.

Everything you have told me about Joey suggests he is at the very least a benign entity, most likely far more than that, a caring and involved one who's mission is to help you and steer you in your progress through childhood. A most admirable mission if ever there was one and one from which it seems most unlikely that he would abruptly and permanently remove himself from. Yes I do think he went in order to make you sorry for your action of throwing him against the wall, for behaving in such a beastly manner, but it's my guess it was meant to be a short, sharp, shock and that he was being cruel to be kind and that he fully intended reappearing back through his magical door shortly afterwards, once you'd had time to consider your actions, letting your temper runaway with you like that! So the thing is, why? Why can't he come back?"

Stuart had sat listening intently as Emily reasoned her way through the facts she had assembled, he couldn't think of anything to say, he was still trying to catch up with everything she'd just said. Emily was still thinking "unless… oh what a pity you can't recall the incantation Joey used to open the portal." Portal? Eh? "What's a portal?" Emily smiled, "the doorway Joey passed through Stuart, I suspect it is a passageway, an opening, a gateway to another realm altogether…"

Emily shuffled herself painfully to the edge of her chair and rose, "I think this calls for a strong cup of tea, pass me you mug Stuart" he handed her his empty chocolate streaked mug, "come through to the kitchen and we can carry on our deliberations!" she declared as she headed out of the snug little room.

Sat back in the snug with their cups of tea Emily chatted easily with the young lad, she told him that when her Henry had first been taken from her how she had for quite some time visited mediums and spiritualists in a desperate attempt to be in touch with his departed soul. "The only thing that was departed was me from my money!" she scoffed, "they were all a bunch of charlatans!" "I'm sorry to say that I've come to believe that once we depart this life we are gone…" Emily caught the look of shock on Stuart's face, realising that she was talking out of turn in expressing such an adult view of death, she quickly covered her true thoughts by adding "well as you know I was a Sunday School teacher for many years and as it does say in the Good Book we should leave the dead alone and concern ourselves with the living! I know that one day I'll meet up again with Henry, when my time comes." Stuart's face had lightened somewhat and he added "when you go to heaven too?" "Yes Stuart, indeed when I go to heaven" she sighed heavily but quickly went on, "however one thing I did come across in my dabbling was hypnotism, they say that although we may not know it, we remember almost all the things that ever happen to us, deep down in our subconscious mind. If we were to hypnotise you Stuart there's just a chance that you may recall the incantation that Joey used to make the portal open!" "Could I? Remember it? WOW!" Stuart exclaimed wide-eyed, "but I'd never fit through such a tiny door though…" his face fell, Emily smiled "maybe we could post a letter addressed to him through though, couldn't we?"

Stuart perched on the edge of the chair, "go one then Emily hypnotiser me, I'm ready!" and he screwed his eyes tightly shut as if he was about to be shot! Emily chuckled, "why no, my dear boy, I can't possibly hypnotise you myself, for one thing I wouldn't know where to start but I do know someone who might. Besides we can't even contemplate such an undertaking without the permission of your mother."

The clock chimed out in the hallway and a few moments later the doorbell rang. "Your mum's right on time Stuart, an hour we said and an hour we got!" Stuart jumped to his feet, "shall I? Open the door, I mean Emily?" "Why thank you Stuart, you are quite the gentleman, please do."

Chapter Nine: Rescue Mission

Emily had explained to mum that she thought they had made good progress and that she thought it might help Stuart if she took him to see a friend of hers who was a hypnotist. Mum had said she didn't know about that, but anyway she'd have to discuss such a major thing like that with Stuart's father. Stuart was fidgeting around in the porch as the adults talked seemingly endlessly in the doorway, but all the time he had one ear flapping, (as dad would have rudely put it), to try and catch what Emily said. He had his fingers crossed so tightly that the blood couldn't get through to them and they were white and going pins-an-needley! His fingers were crossed to try and ensure that Emily kept schtum about Joey, the game would be up if she spilled the beans on him! Told mum what he'd confided to her. He shut his eyes and screwed up his face and said... 'Pleeaassseee' to himself... If Emily told on him... He could hear the door to his cell lock, feel his hands on the bars at the windows of... The Loony Bin!! He squinted one eye open a fraction to look back at them... They were both stood looking at him in silence, Emily smiled and gave a little wave, before stepping back inside and closing the door behind her, mum headed towards him shaking her head "what on earth are you doing pulling your face like that for Stuart? Sometimes I really do wonder..." she left her sentence hanging in the air as she slipped her hand into his and they headed off down the garden path. He looked up at her with a grin on his face and mouthed 'thank you' to whosoever it might have been that had heeded his fervent entreaties!

On the way back they'd called at the Post Office for mum to get her Family Allowance, Stuart fidgeted as they queued up at the counter, the old lady in front of them smelled of wee, he looked up at mum and held his nose and nodded at the old ladies well-filled and rounded brown coat, mum flicked his head in a light cuff and mouthed *'behave!'* but he saw her sniff and pull her face as well! Eventually after what seemed like weeks mum handed her book through the slot under the screen and the post-mistress stamped her book and counted out the money to her, Stuart liked the look of them stampers he thought, you inked it up on the pad and then really walloped it down on the book, it made a lovely clonking noise and made a print on your book which said **MOSSLEIGH POST OFFICE** and had the date on as well. He figured that they could change the numbers for the date just like he did on his John Bull printing set, he loved stamping with that, he'd got a proper walloping for stamping it on his bedroom wall one time!

Next they visited the greengrocers and once she'd done her shopping mum had asked Stuart to carry the shopping basket with the potatoes in, it looked as if it would be blummin heavy he thought and it was a girly *shopping basket* all made out of wicker, and she wanted *him* to carry it! "Why can't I carry the other bag?" He had demanded, stamping a foot on the floor, that one was dark grey and had two handles, not one stupid wicker handle, he wouldn't look like Little-Blummin-Red Riding Hood carrying that one! "It's far too heavy for you Stuart and you'll only drag it on the floor! Do as you're told, I'm already hours behind with my shopping and housework thanks to you!" "I WON'T! I'm big and strong, I'm not a girl!" "Right then, carry it!" Stuart watched in shock as mum complied with his demands, picked up the wicker shopping basket, rested it on her arm and strode off out of the shop. Leaving the large shopping bag on the floor next to him. He grasped at the handles and tried to lift the bag, it weighed a ton! What had she put in it, coal? Mr.Pament the greengrocer shook his head as the lad managed to get the bag off the floor by holding it to one side with both hands on the handles and twisting his body as he leant his hip into it... "Muuummm..." his lamenting cry trailed after the woman striding away from him down the pavement outside the shop!

Sat at the kitchen table ten minutes later Stuart's ear was red and sore where he'd got a clip off mum for scuffing the bag on the floor and then standing with his hands on his hips at the corner of their street and sulking. His mood hadn't improved when he'd been given a bowl full of potatoes to peel either. He wobbled his head and pulled a face mouthing *"and don't waste any of the potatoes..."* He finished the bowl and took it through thinking he was due the Victoria Cross at the very least for his heroic battle with the sodding potatoes, only to be told, "right start on the carrots next!"

He spent the rest of the day being treated like a skivvy, or a house-maid... doing house-work and even... of all things...dusting! I mean it was wrong, there had to be a clause or two in the Geneva Convention that dealt with punishment details like this? "If you're not at school and you're not ill enough to stay in bed you can earn your keep Master Wheeler!" His feigned response of weakness "I feel really tired, I think I can feel a headache coming on..." hadn't cut the mustard at all! By the end of the day when dad was due home at any minute he had come to the terrible conclusion that Mum was definitely a Nazi!! He'd thought about clicking his heels and doing the Nazi salute but remembered his sore ear earlier in the day and her later warning about him skating on very thin ice and he'd thought better of it!

Stuart ran to the hall when he heard the front door open and his dad coming in, he made a flying leap at the unsuspecting man as he turned around after closing the door, "hiya dad!" he yelled as he hugged his arms around him, smelling the unmistakable scent of his dad laced as it always was with the sweet sickly smell of tobacco smoke and nicotine. Dad plonked his trilby on the lad's head "hiya yerself!" he replied as he hung his coat on the hat stand. Stuart was in full flow "it's stew for tea, I made it and then it's pie for pudding, I made the pastry for that too! And I made us a jam tart each with the left over bits!" He flew ahead like a Lancaster bomber opened the door through to the kitchen and barged in ricocheting off the cupboard making everything in it rattle as he banked steeply round, the four Merlins roaring at full throttle… Mum snatched dad's hat off his head, snapping out "will you take *your* son out of here before I swing for him!"

Lucy was having tea at The Miley's with Veronica so it was just the three of them who sat down for their tea a little later. Mum told him what Emily had said about the hypnotist, he hadn't been keen at all at first, 'sounds like some circus act!' Was the general theme of his remarks! Mum said she was 'at the end of her tether' and something had to be done! Dad said that they'd discuss it later and had nodded in Stuart's direction, when he wasn't there that meant! They thought he was stupid, he scowled to himself, but not for long, it was a splendid stew he'd made and he set about mopping up what was left on his plate with a piece of bread just like his dad did. "At least he's got his appetite back" dad said as he mopped his own plate clean and winked at his son. Mum scoffed, but was smiling as she said "here give me your plates, you two'll have the blummin patterns off them!" They laughed merrily as dad reached into his pocket and then tapped a Senior Service on the box before sticking it inbetween his lips, "can't you wait till after pudding! Really!" Mum chastised him, he grimaced theatrically at his lad, pulling his mouth downwards into an inverted smile and laid the cigarette on top of the box, "sorry Mum!" He said pretending to sulk.

After pudding Stuart was banished upstairs to run himself a bath, he plodded sulkily out of the living room, dad was lighting his fag as he pulled the door shut and then he was out in the hall, he leant back on the door listening. He could hear mum in the kitchen, he could see dad in his mind's eye, sat back in the chair smoking away at his Senior Service! Dad was right though, he had got his appetite back, talking to Emily had been a cracking good idea, he was sure now that Joey was still alive and that he was probably wracking his little beary brains too trying to find a way to get back. If Emily's friend could get that spell out of his noggin then between them, him and Emily could get that door, that *portal* thingummy open again and... Stuart fell backwards as the door swung open... "I thought I told you to get up those stairs?" Mum towered over him scowling, he sat on his bum in the doorway and looked over his shoulder at dad who was sniggering. "I'm on my way! If you'd just've given me a blummin minute..." Indignantly he picked himself up and stomped across the hall to the stairs, dusting off his behind "don't see why I have to go upstairs straight after tea, anyway it'd serve you right if I didn't go..." he muttered with his hand resting on the bottom newel post. "STUART WHEELER..." mum growled as she made as if to leg-it across the hall at him and squealing in fright Stuart flew up the stairs more like a startled rabbit than a Spitfire this time!

He stomped across the landing fuming and into the bathroom, stuffed the plug in the bath and set the taps running, then he took off his slippers and slinked back down stairs like a Commando and across the hall to the living room door, he leant sideways and pressed his ear to the timber of the door... dad's voice "...well if Emily can vouch for her I suppose it'll be alright, but I want you to be there with him at all times June" mums voice, "I will, of course I'll be there! As if I'd just leave him, really John! But we've got to do something, the boy's two steps from Granville Manor at the moment <*the Looney Bin... Stuart shuddered*> I just wish I knew what he'd said to her... what's that noise John? I can hear the drain running from the bathroom, that idiot son of yours is running all the flamin' hot water down the bloody drain!" Stuart felt as if an electric shock had been applied to his entire body, he leapt upright from where he'd been leaning ear-wigging. Heavens to Betsy! Mum was on the warpath! He'd heard her push her chair back and knew she was flying towards the other side of the door he was stood at even as he panicked... frozen... Then he spun on his heel, took one look at the distance to the stairs... no chance, even if he made it to the bottom he'd never get up them before she burst through the door, the cupboard under the stairs was his only hope and he was just pulling the door to behind himself when she shot like a rat from a trap out of the living room and across the hall, screeching like a Banshee... "Stuart Wheeler I'll murder you...!" Stuart sat in the dark trembling, oh Joey! Where were you now? What would you say? Well after you'd scolded me for my bad behaviour... bla...bla...bla... lets skip all that eh? What to do?

Mum was in full battle-cry and on the warpath, she'd stampeded up the stairs like a buffalo and was stamping around like a rogue woolly mammoth upstairs now, bellowing "Stuart! Come out AT ONCE! Wherever you're hiding!" Dad must have come through into the hall, he heard him calling up "June, calm down, I'm sure he didn't mean it... have you found him yet?" Stuart peered around the crack, his dad was by the stairs, he was peering up them, he took a drag on his fag, looked skywards, shook his head, tutted and then headed up.

Curses to Murgatroyd! What was he to do? Then in a flash of inspiration that even Joey would have been proud of he snuck out of the cupboard and through to the backroom where the laundry chute came out! Joey's tale of the burgulars coming to mind! He could make it look like he'd fallen somehow down the laundry chute, explaining exactly why could be tricky but he'd think of something, anyway it would account for him being downstairs. Then they'd feel all sorry for him, wishing they hadn't been so horrible to him and he'd not get a larruping for (a) being downstairs when he'd been sent up and (b) for the crime of wasting hot water or for not putting the plug in properly! He sat on the floor and rubbed some dirt off the flags onto his forehead, this could work he thought then he decided to make it more convincing... this is the point where Joey might have been able to stop him... pull him up from his lack of thought... but in his absence though... Stuart decided it would look better if he had a bruise... on his head... so he banged his head on the wall, too hard... way too hard...

He staggered wobbling to the doorway into the living room, mum was just coming in from the hall, she was red-faced and furious, "**Stu**..." she began then stopped... the fury turning to panic, "your head! What the hell have you done now?" He lifted his hand up to his head, it was lovely and warm in here, he was floating, his head was all wet and sticky, he looked at his hand, it was bright red, it was covered in blood... his Spitfire was out of control, he fought the controls in vain, it banked and went into a slow spin... he was going to crash...his eyes rolled upwards in their sockets... mum crossed the living room in three strides and caught him as he fell into her arms... he smiled up at the concerned face of his mother "I say, well held!" was all he said!

Lucy told him later that there'd been a holy hell of a row next, she'd just been dropped off by Mr.Miley and mum was cleaning up his cut and wanting to put him to bed, but dad was insistent, in the end he told mum to 'just shut-up woman!' adding, "I'm taking the lad to hospital with or without you!"

Stuart at the time of course was totally oblivious to any of this. The first thing he remembered was opening his eyes and finding himself in bed on a hospital ward! He turned his head to one side and saw the worried face of his father, who was sat at his bedside, "was I shot down?" He asked, since his last memory had been one of fighting with the controls of his Spitfire, "I should say so old chap!" His dad said as a giant grin spread across his face, "that damned Jerry ack-ack outside Dusseldorf got you!"

He was let out after lunch the following day, but not until he'd spent a night on the ward. His head hurt horribly and he didn't like any of it at all, as adventures went, this was a lousy rotten, stinking one! If this is what it was like when you were injured in the war and you ended up in dock like this having to be mended... well all he could say was they blummin well earned those medals they gave to the brave lads!

He'd laid there awake for hours that night thinking such thoughts, listening to all the strange and mysterious hospital noises. His thoughts came around to Mrs Mellor's son who had worked for a time in the little sweet shop and the terrible tale about him that he would never forget as long as he lived. The tiny shop had big high glass-fronted displays on top of all of the counters, so you couldn't see who was stood behind them, there was only a narrow little gap where you got served. You'd ask for what you wanted from the jars stood in the glass displays and you'd hear him pour the sweets out from the jars into the metal scoop on the scales, then he would pass your bag of sweets around the shelving so you couldn't see him, but if you caught a glimpse of his face… it was like a candle that had been melted, it was lividly red, contorted and shiny, the skin drooped from beneath his eyes, showing all the whites below his irises, his hands were the same, red, shiny and bony like a chickens feet… Don't stare at him, he'd been told… why not? He looks funny, what's wrong with him? Why's he hiding? The explanation when it was given was so utterly terrible that he never tried to look at Alan Mellor again, he was forever full of reverence and respect for the man, for it turned out he was a real-life, living hero.

Dad told him when he'd asked him and on the strict understanding that it was man-to-man and he didn't let on to his mother what he'd told him, that it was thanks to lads like Alan that we were still British and weren't all talking German and having to say Heil-bloody-Hitler all the time, that Alan had been an RAF fighter pilot in the war, he'd been in a Hurricane squadron and had flown dozens of missions but he'd got badly shot-up and his plane had caught fire when he crash landed back at his base. He'd got it down okay but he couldn't get out, the ground crew had to smash the cockpit, it had jammed and they had to drag him from the burning aircraft. "That's why his hands are so badly burnt too," dad put his hands up, either side of his face, "he was trying to protect himself."

Stuart who was sat on his dad's knee spellbound, listening to him recount this terrible tale had looked at him in increasing horror as he told him more, when his dad put his own hands up to his face, he could take no more, he grabbed at his father's hands pulling them away from his face, "NO!" was all he cried out before he buried his head into his father's chest sobbing uncontrollably.

He'd recounted this tale to Joey who had shook his head sadly, "it is truly terrible what man can inflict upon his fellows" he said, "but it was war Joey, he was a hero, fighting to save us from the Nazi's!" Stuart protested indignantly, the tears flowing again as he clasped his own hands to his face feeling the intense heat of the flames and the horror of being trapped… "If only I could help him, do something for him?" Joey pondered for a moment, before making a suggestion.

The next time he bought sweets there he'd handed his coins over as he took the bag, "thank you" he said, "you're welcome" Alan had replied through his cruelly tortured lips. Stuart paused a moment, "thank you for everything, I mean, not just for the sweets" with that he put the bag of sweets into his left hand and as he had rehearsed earlier at home in the mirror with Joey, he stood as rigidly to attention as he could manage, then he saluted his best precision salute, "thank you *Sir*!" He wasn't quite sure what Alan's full reply was, since it was muffled, in later years he would identify it as a sob, but for now all he heard was the last part of it which was perfectly clear and was "God Bless you son."

Back from his mental wanderings, there had been a bit of a conflab at his bedside earlier on, just before lunch, he'd been dozing but had heard dad's voice and a doctor talking, it had been quite a heated exchange, words like negligence, carelessness, danger, protection of the child, even the police were mentioned. Dad had protested now and then with a hang-on a minute or a now see here, but Stuart could tell when dad was biting his lip, holding back, he was like a volcano then, with the pressure building up! '…referred to see a psychiatrist I believe? The mental health and well-being of my patient is paramount…' BOOM! The volcano blew… "He's my son and no bloody busy-body doctor or social worker or even the soddin police themselves will be taking him away from me. I'm taking him home with me, today and you'll have to get me locked up if you're going to stop me!" That was telling them, he turned his head on his pillow, away from the fracas and smiled, a proud smile, a smile for his dad.

Sat in the car with dad it had been a quiet ride home from the hospital. Stuart enjoyed the ride as ever watching all the sights and listening to all the sounds as they travelled across the town, but dad was distant, preoccupied concentrating intensely on the road and driving the car as he enjoyed a Senior Service. The wispy grey tobacco smoke curled around in the little car, it was a lovely smell, Stuart decided he would smoke Senior Service when he grew up, the white packet had a little colour picture of a jolly tar on it, inside a white lifebelt, when you pushed the bottom the inner sleeve slid up and there were your fags with lovely silver paper around them to keep them fresh, you could see all the little pieces of tobacco in the round ends, it smelt lovely. Dad had a shiny silver case he put his fags in sometimes, it was made of strong metal so your fags couldn't get crumpled in your pocket, it had a little slot with a tiny metal trigger thingy you pressed in and the case flipped open, it had a spring you see and a hinge and a piece of elastic too to hold the fags in! When he was grown up Stuart was going to have one like it, he'd use it all the time though. He'd have a flashy lighter though, one that you put petrol in and he'd use it to light ladies cigarettes for them, like they did in the movies, he'd probably meet his wife that way he thought maybe, he'd not use lousy matches like his dad did, he imagined Humphrey Bogart fiddling with his Swan Vestas while some posh lady was waiting with her cigarette in a long holder, rolling her eyes and tutting to herself!

Once he'd put one in his mouth imitating dad and seeing what his son was doing dad had lit it, he sucked on it and then fell about coughing as the vile smoke entered his lungs gripping at them as if it had claws, he hadn't been put off by that though, it was just that he wasn't grown up enough then!

Mum was the same, unusually quiet and not pestering him about everything when they got home, she gave him a little hug and he was sat down for a sandwich and a drink but very little was said. When he looked at himself in the bathroom mirror later he had an inkling why they were behaving in that way. His face and forehead were every colour of the rainbow, from red to black and he had the biggest shiner he'd ever seen! He pressed at the discoloured skin with his finger-tips, fascinated by his altered appearance, how he wished he could show Joey and all the boys at school! He shuddered a little as the realisation of what he'd done sank in, for he had done this to himself, it hadn't been an accident at all had it? Joey would have been furious with him, maybe he really did belong in the looney-bin?

He shrugged at his alien reflection, which in turn shrugged back at him, well he's not here is he and more's the point, he won't ever be here unless me and Emily do something about the situation!

Rose Lampeter was even older than Emily, she had thin bony hands with fingers that looked like spiders legs! They were icy cold too as she shook Stuart's hot sweaty little hand at the door to her house. Stuart had shuddered and pulled back against his mother's hand a little as they entered the gateway to the centre terrace house, it looked spooky! It was built out of yellowy coloured shiny bricks, with intricate patterns and shapes made into the brickwork, the tops of the windows were arches made out of bricks, like they made the railway stations out of, but unlike the buildings with blackened and sooty stonework these bricks looked like they washed clean every time it rained on them. Nevertheless the building still looked old, the one bit of blackened stonework high on a gable that was over the doorway said 'Melton Villas 1859' that really was in the olden days, Stuart had thought and now that he was stood with the old woman's hand in his he guessed she'd lived here since then too!

Mum and Emily bustled in behind him and shortly they were all sat in a dismal room at the front of the house. The walls were all dark and drab, the room full of dark wooden furniture, dull pictures hung down on the wall from the picture rail and dark dusty curtains were partly drawn at the windows. Rose turned on a small light, it shone out dully barely lighting up the dusty white glass shade, the light seeming to be swallowed-up by the general gloom of the room. "Sit down here Stuart and make yourself comfortable" she warbled in her shrill, shaky, bird-like voice. Like he could ever feel comfortable in this witches lair! He thought to himself as he settled fidgeting as the cold leather of the chair sucked the heat out from the backs of his bare legs.

Rose lit a candle and placed it on the table in front of him, "sit back in the chair my dear, this will be a most pleasant experience for you, nothing to be worried about at all" she twittered at him, huh! Easy for you to say he thought, shuffling himself back to rest his back against the chair, his legs now sticking straight out.

"Look at the candle Stuart, listen to my voice, you are feeling sleepy now, your eye-lids are getting heavy, so very heavy now, you can hardly keep them open…."

"…And wake up!" Stuart shook his head, "what… What happened?" "Where am I?" His mother's voice came reassuringly from the gloom and he felt her hand on his arm, "it's okay Stuey, it's all done, come on we can go home now." He didn't need any encouraging, in a single leap he was out of the chair and across the room, he darted a glance at the old witch who had tried to work her spell on him and scowled at her, she smiled angelically back, but he wasn't fooled for one second, nor was he hanging around and he left the room and was waiting by the front door when Emily got there a minute or two later. "Are you alright Stuart?" she asked resting a hand on his shoulder, he shrugged, "dunno, just wanna get out of here!" Emily opened the door, "come on then we can wait outside if you'd prefer." She tapped him on the shoulder as they left and he looked up at her, she smiled warmly and informed him "when you were hypnotised you did remember Joey's words, I know the incantation now!" When he was hypnotised? Eh? What?

Mum came out from the door, she was 'bristling' and Stuart could tell that she was cross, very cross. She was pushing her purse back into her handbag, she barely looked at either Emily or himself as she marched off down the path towards the gate, muttering just loud enough to ensure that they heard her "that was a waste of time and money, THAT was! Ten bloody shillings!!" The rest of her muttering was more to herself… she had no idea what John would make of wasting his hard earned money…

Emily made a little shrug and smiled like he did to Lucy when mum went 'off one on' "never mind Stuart, she'll calm down and I'll give her the ten shillings back, I'll tell her Rose gave it back to me when she found out she wasn't happy with the outcome. We are though, aren't we?" He nodded enthusiastically and didn't think it even remotely odd when Emily took his hand in hers and they walked on after the smouldering form of his mother.

When they got to the corner of the street mum was waiting, "I'm ever so sorry Emily, I didn't mean to get so cross, but really what was all that mumbo-jumbo she got Stuart to tell her, why did she even ask him about that? Encouraging his silly delusions was all that was! What was all that about 'the doorway' and the magic words? Did you put her up to it?" Emily shrugged, I fear she may be going a touch ga-ga in her old age! I'm so very sorry June, I'm sure she'll give me your ten shillings back and whatever the reason Stuart does seems a lot happier now?" Mum looked down at Stuart who beamed back up at her. "We have to go Emily, thank you anyway for trying to help, despite everything and if you could get my ten shillings back it'd save me having to try to explain why I've run out of house-keeping money to Stuart's father!"

They parted company as Emily headed off to her home and they to theirs. Mum had to say, however begrudgingly that Stuart did seem to be a lot more like his old self and as he opened the gate at their house for her and asked her if he could go back to school tomorrow her mood lifted a little more and after all Emily had said she'd get her ten bob note back for her!

Mum didn't think anything much of it when as he was leaving in the morning, Stuart asked her if he could call in and say a proper thank you to Emily on his way home from school, "maybe pick-up your ten bob? She really is a good egg isn't she mum? Even though the hypnotising was a load of rubbish?"

He hadn't arranged anything with Emily but he guessed that she would be expecting him when he rang her bell later that day. "My don't you look smart in your school uniform?" She had greeted him with as she let him in, adding "have you got it with you?" He nodded and patted his pocket.

Without further ado they set about their mission, Stuart painstakingly unwrapped the tiny splinter of doorframe and they sat at the table looking reverently at it. Emily unfolded a piece of writing paper and smoothed it flat on the table in front of them, it said *aperite mihi portas domus in mundo* "it's Latin Stuart, I think it means simply open the door to my world"

Stuart read the words as he held the splinter out over the table… nothing. He read them again, nothing… "Oh Stuart, I think maybe you should say *app-er-eye-tee* not *apper-right* ? Try it and see?" He nodded, "funny old language eh?" she nodded "quite so!" He screwed his face up in his bestest wizardiest face and solemnly incanted "aperite mihi portas domus in mundo!" nothing… again… but wait… there was a fizzling noise and tiny sparks appeared around the splinter in his fingers, he dropped it, startled by the sparks, it lay on the table, spat another spark out, spun around once and then stopped… they both sat staring at it open-mouthed, in silence for a moment "golly gee, WOW! Did you see that?" Stuart asked in wide-eyed disbelief! Emily nodded, she was clearly excited too as she said, "say it again Stuart and this time hang onto the splinter with all your might and don't let go of it whatever happens!"

He licked his lips and breathed in and out through pursed lips bracing himself, "aperite mihi portas domus in mundo!" this time he gripped as tight as he could as the sparks and hissing started-up, a shape of the doorway appeared momentarily, a transparent silhouette, it wavered, shimmered, vanished, re-formed, then stabilised, and finally became solid, but… it was tiny! It was only half an inch wide by an inch tall! Without thinking Stuart pushed at the tiny door with his finger… it opened a little in the frame, light poured around it but the harder he pushed the more it resisted until it shoved his whole hand back slamming the door so hard that it was dislodged from between his finger and thumb and fell from his grasp, even before it had landed on the table it was once more nothing but the tiny splinter it had been moments earlier. He turned and looked at Emily and then burst out laughing, she joined him placing her hands on his shoulders and then getting up from her chair she took his hands and they waltzed around the dining room as she sang out a lilting celebratory melody...

After a turn of the dance floor and when Emily's feet could bear being trod on no more, they stopped dancing. "I think we need a good strong cup of tea!" Emily pronounced as she hobbled off "while we think what to do next!" Stuart followed her through into the kitchen, he was a bit flummoxed really, he shook his head solemnly, "but Emily it's no blummin good to us, Joey could never get through that tiny door, a flippin mouse couldn't!" Emily smiled down at the lad, "oh Stuart my boy, to be so young! You miss the point my boy, totally! We just opened a magical door into another realm! It is the stuff of dreams!" She hummed to herself as she poured the water into the teapot, repeating "the stuff of dreams!"

They sat a while with their tea and a biscuit or two for Stuart and then Emily announced her plan, "I think we should write a note to Joey and roll it into as tiny a tube as we can and then post it through the portal!" Stuart exclaimed "Wow!" initially then added "what will we put? In the note I mean?" Emily nodded, "that, Stuart is the question, what indeed?" "How about come back Joey, please?" Stuart proffered enthusiastically. Emily smiled kindly, "if he could do that, I'm sure he already would have done wouldn't he? The thing is we have absolutely no idea where the portal emerges in Joey's world, on the other side, nor do we even have the slightest inkling of what his world may be like! It may well be that someone else, some other entity will receive the message, that is to say if we can even get the message to physically pass through, or if it is even transmitted to the other side."

Emily produced a piece of writing paper and scissors and cut it down to a an inch-and-a-half by three-quarters of an inch, she rolled it between her fingers until it was like the stub of a tiny cigarette, before carefully unrolling it again. "I think that will be as big as we dare try, not a lot of room to write on is it?" "We can write really small… and on both sides?" Stuart volunteered. "Indeed we can" Emily replied as she laid a full sized piece of the writing pad in front of herself, "we'll draught it out first on here" she said and set to writing with her fountain pen. After ten minutes of crossing-outs and re-writing they had it ready to transcribe to both sides of the fragment, it read…

> *Please pass this to Joey,*
> *the bear who has been*
> *with Stuart Wheeler*
> *for the last 8 years.*
> *He says he is sorry.*
>
> *Can we help in any way*
> *to get you back here Joey?*
> *Stuart says he NEEDS*
> *you. Xxx Will open door*
> *tomorrow at same time*

It all went according to plan and the tightly rolled-up message vanished through the tiny gap in the door! Emily smiled and watched as Stuart did a celebratory war dance, whooping around the room! "Stuart it's four-forty-five, remember that as that is the time we must open the portal again tomorrow.

Stuart barely slept that night, his mind just would not shut down, it raced with strange imaginings of what the other side might be like, how Joey was, if he could ever go there himself? He slept on and off, dozing fitfully, with wild dreams that melded with his conscious ruminating.

Mum had to shake him to get him to wake up when morning finally came, he was bleary eyed and struggled to stay awake during the day. Mrs Allington sent him to see the nurse halfway through the first lesson of the afternoon as he'd fallen asleep on his desk, much to the amusement of his classmates!

Emily fared no better, she however made no attempt to sleep, her many years of experience of occasions like this one told her it would be futile, besides she needed little sleep anyway these days. She simply stoked up her fire and wrapped a warm blanket around herself. She sat awake into the early hours, stirring occasionally to make herself a mug of cocoa and to thumb through the ancient and well-worn photo album of her youth and the precious images of her Henry, the last one she had was of him looking so smart in his uniform…

Morning crept through around the curtains at her window and Emily stretched stiffly in her chair, the fire was no more than a glow now and she stirred painfully to rise, she must have had a few hours shut-eye she thought smiling to herself. She stopped abruptly as she rose, her pain was back, she pressed her sternum with her deformed and arthritic hand and let herself settle back into her chair, her right hand scrabbling for her pills, she couldn't find them… Then a calmness came upon her, 'stop panicking you silly old woman!' she told herself, the pills are there, you will find them. She took a deep breath through the pain and turned, in her flailing she'd knocked the little glass bottle to the end of the table, she reached around and grasped it, unscrewed the cap and tipped one of the tiny tablets into her palm and put it under her tongue. The pain gradually eased and she sat back and closed her eyes. It was only a matter of time before her heart gave out one of these times she thought, she was well aware of that and she was resigned to it. It was just a fact, simple as that, there was no good to be had bemoaning it. She tried to think of what would come after as a new adventure, of meeting Henry once more… It was a lovely dream… she would rise as a shining body of translucent light, her form transparent as it left the decaying and redundant shell she had resided in for over eighty years… there stood in the clouds at the bottom of a brilliant white marble staircase was Henry, a young glowing ethereal Henry, smiling and reaching out a welcoming hand to her… she shook her head and scoffed!

The coal wasn't going to jump onto the fire on its own was it? She told herself and she was getting quite cold now! Come on Emily… once more into the breach! She stirred and unsteadily raised herself, leaning heavily on the arm of her chair, she then worked her way around to the fireplace leaning on whatever came to hand and shovelled some coal on the glowing embers… now a nice cup of tea I think…

The day eventually wound its way slowly to home-time for Stuart and he ran all the way to Emily's, he was sweating and panting as she opened the door and he pushed his way in as soon as he could squeeze past. His enthusiasm was stopped in its tracks though when he saw Emily, he reached out and touched her arm "are you alright Emily? You don't look well." She ran her bony fingers through his mop of unruly hair, "I'm a bit peaky, that's all Stuart, nothing to worry about, too much excitement for an old lady I think!"

They sat in the dining room at the table and watched as the clock's hand crept around to four-forty-four, Emily nodded to him, "now Stuart!" He repeated the ritual slowly and precisely with the splinter of doorframe gripped tightly inbetween his finger and thumb... the door sparked and spluttered into existence before their eyes, they sat transfixed watching... time seemed to have stopped, Emily tore her eyes from the glowing portal to check the time, it wasn't even four sixteen yet! Less than a minute had passed since the doorway had opened! The doorway fizzled and sputtered, flashed briefly but very brightly and was gone. Stuart and Emily sat blinking the shape of the flash burnt onto their retinas as a fading red stain, "damn it!" Stuart cursed, "nothing!" "No wait, look!" Emily reached out as her vision cleared a little, as it returned to normal, there on the table was a tiny piece of paper!

Stuart still blinking from the flash stared wide-eyed and wide-mouthed, he looked alternatively between the scrap of paper and Emily. The old lady smiled and reaching out scooped up the tiny scroll of paper, Stuart huddled right in next to her and between them they carefully unrolled it out on the table...

> *My name is Talis*
> *I'm a friend of Joey's*
> *he is back here safely*
> *but the programme has*
> *been shut-down so he*
>
> *can't get back to you!*
> *He has gone away and*
> *I will tell him when he*
> *gets back. Open portal*
> *again in 72 hours please*

"He's alright! He's alright! Whoopee!! He's alive!" Stuart could barely contain himself. Emily put her arm around the ecstatic boy's shoulder and hugged him too herself, kissing him on the top of his head, she felt tears of happiness running down her face.

Chapter Nine: Granville Manor

Stuart slept soundly that night, mum had said 'you seem cheerful this evening' as he came in from his visit to Emily's merrily whistling 'Pretty Baby' one of the many tunes he'd picked up off dad. When he came in Dad had said so too, 'glad you're feeling better son' Lucy had made a rude gesture spinning her finger by her forehead and rolling her eyes, when mum and dad weren't looking of course, but he had just smiled and winked at her which had totally flummoxed her and in the end she'd just smiled back!

When he woke up though it was still dark, he'd heard something outside, had it been a cat yowling or something falling over? He rolled over in bed, but then sat bolt upright as he remembered what he'd been dreaming. Him and Emily had hatched a plan, that old woman Rose was there too, somehow, most likely by witchcraft, they'd turned him into a little ladybird!

He could still feel how he'd marvelled at the sensation as he opened the shiny black-spotted, red carapace on his back and how he had opened out his wings, set them a buzzin' and how he'd then done a couple of circuits around the room, before landing back on the table in front of the two now-gigantic old women! Emily had opened the portal and at a suitable moment when the sparks weren't that big and too bright he'd taken off and flown straight through it!

When he passed through the doorway he'd found himself in a beautiful lush and verdant forest, like the one he'd visited once with mum and dad, only this one was massive. He flew around for a bit marvelling at it all then he came out of the edge of the trees and onto a mountainside, the sky was as blue as you could ever imagine it to be, with little puffs of white cotton wool clouds floating lazily across it… he dipped and soared, banked and turned, he was a pilot at last, he could fly… weeee…

This was fine and dandy until he sensed that he was no longer alone, he spun around and just in time as he saw a blummin enormous dragonfly set on a collision course with him! He flipped himself into a barrel-roll then dived to port, curses! This was bad, he was the blummin Dornier here in this dog-fight and the dragonfly was the Spitfire! He had no chance! He ducked and dived like a maniac, but it was hopeless, he'd had it… just as he realised he was about to die though there was a massive swooshing of air and a split second image of a large winged shape and the dragonfly was literally punched right out of existence before his eyes, he was in a spin now as a result of the turbulence, down and down he fell spinning round and round, over and over, tumbling until he was able somehow to correct his trajectory. He flew along wobbling now from side to side, still dizzy from all the spinning. Looking up he could see the shapes of a dozen or so birds sweeping across the sky plucking insects from the air above him, phew! He thought 'that was a close one!'

He realised just in time that he was back at ground level and he ducked from side to side between massive green circular structures, which he eventually realised were the tall stems of grasses, then he'd been brought to a juddering halt and found himself where he was now, sat up in bed!

It was completely dark though, why was there was no light from his streetlight creeping into his bedroom around the curtains? He rubbed at his eyes, but they were stuck shut with some sticky, stringy substance, he pulled frantically at it, brushing his hands repeatedly down each side of his face…

that was better, he could see now... **HELP!!!** He screamed at the top of his lungs... for now he could see again, he could see that it was broad daylight and far from being safe in his bed, he was trapped in a spiders web that was spread between the stems of the grass... and coming towards him was a ginormous blummin spider...

The light came on in his room as dad blundered in half asleep, his hair was stood-up and he was in the process of pushing his glasses onto his face as he bent over the screaming boy, "what's up lad?" He put his hands on his sons shoulders to still him as he was thrashing about frantically, Stuart stared wide-eyed and crazily back at him, screaming, squirming, kicking... he swiped at his father sending his specs flying across the room and smacking him full-on and hard in the face! "STUART! Calm down, calm down!" He called out, backing off as he'd instinctively tried to protect his face and to rub at the pain. Mum who had seen the kafuffle from the doorway arrived back with a cup full of cold water which she threw into Stuart's face. He stopped screaming abruptly and lay back on the pillow, groaning quietly. Mum approached him cautiously, but sensing he'd calmed down sat down gingerly on the edge of the bed and reached apprehensively out to feel his forehead. It was boiling, yet he was covered in a cold sweat as well as the water. "Stuart what's wrong? Can you hear me?" Mum pleaded, his eyes were staring but looked blank and empty, when she waved her palm in front of them they made no response, nor did he blink. "Is he asleep again, like when he sleepwalked downstairs?" Dad asked as he delicately replaced his specs onto the bridge of his sore nose. "I don't think so, I think he has a fever John. I'm worried, I think we should call the doctor!" Mum replied. "Are you sure? It's three thirty in the morning, you know?" Dad said as he paused in the doorway, where he met with Lucy who was peering anxiously around the frame which she was gripping with both hands as if she was clinging to a life raft!

Mum just nodded and dad put his arm around Lucy and let her accompany him downstairs. It was a while before the doctor answered but when he eventually did it was a swift response of 'take him to hospital at once!'

It had taken a couple of days at the hospital before any type of diagnosis had been made but eventually the sad and terrible cause of Stuart's illness became apparent and he was duly transferred by ambulance to Granville Manor. Stuart was totally oblivious to all of this, it seemed to mum and dad from what their own eyes told them and the doctors confirmed that their little son had completely lost his mind.

The doctors had little to offer in terms of any prognosis, of any idea when he might return to normal, if he ever did, or of the chances of this happening at all. They talked about the extreme fever he had been suffering from when he had been admitted and although they had done everything in their power to bring it down as fast as they could, it was still possible that irreparable damage had been done to his brain. They did however assure Stuart's despairing parents that Granville Manor had a reputation second to none and that they should still retain hope that the boy may yet recover, adding that the hospital had often achieved results with cases that other institutions had deemed hopeless.

It was a week later when Lucy was finally allowed to see her brother in the loony bin. She cried when she first saw him, but after a while she sat on the bed and held his hand, it was cool now but limp and lifeless. He was looking up at the window, but he didn't respond to anything she did, including pulling a face, poking her tongue out and even flicking and pinching him when no one was looking.

She talked to him about all sorts of nonsense, or more realistically talked to herself. When mum and dad left her alone with him to go and talk to the doctor though, she leant in closer and whispered "I've been round to see Emily, she sends her love and she says she's had more communications from Joey, that she's doing all she can to help!" Before she could elaborate, mum, dad and the doctor came over to the stricken lad's bed, they were talking, "so you think it's the best chance of helping him Doctor Lassiter?" Dad was asking. "Yes indeed, I've heard there has been a considerable success rate and to be honest, I don't know what else to suggest" the doctor replied. "What are they going to do to him?" Lucy asked, jumping up, grabbing her dad by the arm and looking pleadingly up into his face. "Come on now Lucy, time to go, let's leave it to the doctor, he knows best. He'll help him and bring him back to us, won't he mum?" Lucy looked pleadingly at her mum as she was ushered out of the ward away from her brother, mum was crying and didn't answer her dad.

Lucy was too shocked to go to school the following morning, even dad didn't want to go in to work! Mum had shooed him out of the house saying 'we've still got to keep the roof over our heads whatever else's going on!' When he returned from work he found Lucy asleep on Stuart's bed, he leant over and kissed her on the forehead, "are you okay my little princess?" He asked tenderly, she awoke and seeing her dad, reached up and hugged him round the neck sobbing, "he hasn't even got his bear with him…" She sobbed out, "hmm… I'm not sure it would help him in view of all that nonsense about killing him!" Dad said crossly. Lucy let go of her dad and sat up, "no that's not the case we know what happened to Joey now, can I go and see Emily, she can help bring him back…" She stopped abruptly realising what she'd said, she tried to cover it up, "well my silly little brother…" Dad held her by the shoulders and looked her right in the eyes, "Lucy Wheeler you tell me right now what crazy tomfoolery that old woman has been filling my son's head with?" "Nothing dad, nothing, she's a lovely old lady! I Want to go and see her, I must…" she trailed off her insistent demand as she could see one of dad's rages brewing, his neck was getting redder and his eyes were bulging… She flopped down with her head in the pillow and pretended to start crying again! Just in time as he stormed out of Stuart's bedroom with an angry threat left hanging in the air "you WILL NOT go to see that meddling old woman EVER again! DO YOU HEAR ME? NEVER!! And I mean it Lucy Wheeler!"

It was two days before Lucy was allowed to go and see Stuart again, she had to go back to school the day before as a condition. It was weird not having the little idiot around the house, she had an almost physical ache in her heart, she really missed him.

She desperately wanted to call around to see Emily but dad had repeated his warning adding, 'I'll go to the police and set them on her if I hear you've been to see her and woe betide you if you do!'

She was pleasantly surprised to find that her little brother was dressed and up and about, but her initial joy was dashed when she realised that although he was out of bed he was like an empty shell, a zombie. He could be led around but stared out blankly, his face an expressionless mask. Nevertheless she sat and talked to him, chattered really, held his hand, touched his cheek and horribly… had to wipe his mouth when saliva dribbled from it.

It was a horrible place to visit, the loony bin… or as she was repeatedly told not to call it that, but to say asylum or better still simply Granville Manor! It was still the loony bin though, whatever you dressed the name up as she thought and more to the point it was full of looneys! They were a very disturbing sight for a young girl and although the section that Stuart was living in was only inhabited by the relatively mild cases, they were bad enough to deeply upset Lucy.

Chapter Eleven: The Other Side

The door slammed shut behind Joey. He let go of the handle dropping down the end of the heavy steamer trunk. He leant back onto it, with a heavy heart. He *was* long overdue checking in with headquarters he told himself. He always left checking in with headquarters as long as he could, they were so, so… how could you put it politely? Rigid… yes that would suffice he thought to himself, rigid!

He checked that the label with his home address on was visible on top of the trunk, 'SE/3/2/4i', home sweet home, he thought, hardly though he'd barely seen the place in the last eight years. Apart from fleeting visits that was. The trunk would be delivered to his home after its contents had been no doubt scrutinised. It contained the few items that he could take with him to the other side, items he could refer to whilst in close proximity to the trunk should he need to. The trunk never truly existed in the other world they said, but could be summoned by him into solidity and remain there for short periods of time. It was all way too complicated for Joey to bother trying to understand anyway!

His long absences from home were his own fault they would tell him, "you get too involved," "you fail to remain objective." Pah! he thought, the O.S.Council didn't have a clue what it was like on the other side, most of the bears were so old they'd have forgotten, even if they ever knew in the first place! He reprimanded himself for thinking like this. He had to maintain a respectful attitude towards the O.S.Council whatever he may truly feel, after all they controlled the gateways, without their say-so he might never see Stuart again!

He had of course arrived at the very perimeter of Ursænia, the city that was home to him. He was at the end of West Street. Out here in the Eights, at The Institute's headquarters. West Street was a pleasant country lane, running between the fields of the large estates of the Eighth Level Bears and their families. West Street in common with all the radial streets (North, South, East, Northwest, Northeast, Southeast, and Northeast) ran perfectly straight towards the centre of Ursænia. From where he was he needed to walk the eight hundred yards to Eighth Street. Here he could catch the transport that ran every ten minutes into the centre. Eighth Street ran concentrically around the centre as did all the numbered streets, the transports running from the centre along their radial to their designated ring and then turning left or right to serve the properties on that segment of the circle.

The circular city was divided into eight sections, each being designated by its proximity to one of the four main radials, north, south, east and west; so there was Southeast district, Southwest district, Eastsouth district and so on. Joey's address therefore was Southeast octant, Third Street, number two, apartment four, oh yes the 'i' .This designated that Joey's house was on the inner side of the street. Needless to say there were eight street numbers in each section of street! The bears liked doing things in eights! It should by now be clear why it was eminently desirable to live on Eighth Street! Furthermore although there were eight blocks on First Street for every block there were sixteen apartments! This stepped down with each ring, Second street had eight, Third Street had four, Fifth Street had two, and the rest had one. This meant that the outer addresses were even more disproportionate in size to the inner ones. This created a circular city with 4,352 separate addresses of varying sizes, then there were the suburbs...we'll leave it there though shall we?

It should not be misinterpreted from this that this was a divisive city. Far from it, Ursænia was a meritocracy in the truest sense imaginable. The inner rings were mostly occupied by younger families, closer to the school, the university and amenities and was home to the key workers who chose to do the more menial tasks, the outer rings by bears who had worked long and hard for the benefit of bearkind, or ones who preferred the more rural lifestyle. Since everyone was paid the same wage for whatever job they did (all were considered to be of equal value to the community) there was not the clamour to push upwards as in the human world. It was unusual for the larger properties to be handed down from generation to generation as in the human world, for one thing bears incredibly long life span would make it tedious waiting to inherit and furthermore as the responsibility to maintain them could be quite onerous not everyone would thank you for them!

Besides life was not like in the human world, no one ever died, or at least no one could remember anyone dying. Yes bears seemed to age, there were indeed older bears and younger bears, but as it all took such an incredibly long time no one seemed to notice. They would tend to just decide to wander off, to go and tread the wild ways up north, or to go west to the forests for a spell, but never be heard of again. Then there were cubs, yes there were younger bears who had cubs, but they would just go to school one day and come home with one, no one ever really figured out how they came to be there, it wasn't important. Bears are like that they don't worry about things if they aren't important, why would you?

At the very heart of this web-like city was The Council. The Council was the name given to the building which housed, of course, the Council of Bears. Ursænia was after all the capital city of Ursa. Naturally enough the building was a massive circular structure, surrounded by eight hundred massive columns, their circular march being broken only by the massive porticos at the four points of the compass, and smaller ones at the four in between. The Council of Bears was split into three (that surprised you didn't it?) tiers. The Lower Council, the Upper Council and the Grand Council. The Lower and Upper council each had thirty two elected members. Out of these two would be elected from each chamber to serve on the Grand Council, which had in addition four permanent members. The mechanics behind the procedures for electing these four Grand Councillors was deliberately complicated, only the finest legal minds claiming to fully understand their intricacies! It was however sufficient for the populace to know that they were elected, even though few could remember the last change! Since there were four regularly elected members to balance them and most governance took place in the Lower or Upper Council no one seemed unduly worried. Accordingly each Councillor, whichever Council they served on, had sixty four constituent addresses. The people who lived at each address could contact their Councillor directly over any issue that concerned them. Although eminently simple at first glance this system meant that some councillors had far more individuals than others. This too was used to the advantage of the more senior members, who strangely seemed to get mostly outer addresses in their quota of sixty four! The members of the Grand Council delegated their addresses to other councillors, at their discretion! So it can be seen that in common with most political systems there was enough scope for Ursan error and nepotism, when they wished it! Furthermore since there were sixty eight councillors (as most lived at single unit addresses) it meant in practice that each only needed to represent sixty three addresses.

Joey boarded the transport and enjoyed the smooth ride as the tram-like vehicle glided silently into the city along West Street, Joey pondered on how different it was to the train in Stuart's world, for all this one's efficiency, quietness, smooth ride and lack of filthy black smoke, it was lacking in something. It had no character. It was coldly efficient and clinical. He felt strangely nostalgic for the other world he inhabited, for all its faults it was addictive. 'Never mind, won't be away for long' he comforted himself, but he shuffled in his immaculately clean upholstered seat, an uneasy disquiet stirring deep within him.

For a moment his mind wandered back to his steamer trunk, no problem, it would be collected by the evening pick-up service, (there were four per day to all sectors) and then delivered to his apartment within the hour, there was a certain comfort in the efficiency of Ursænia.

The transport was very rapid and it was soon passing Fifth Street. Here the properties were closer together and soon they began to crowd in more. There were shops beneath the properties up to Third Street either side of the radial streets, until First Street, which was entirely of shops and business premises on the ground floors. It may be noted from the description so far that in such a well-designed city that there seemed to be an absence of parks. This was not the case. Indeed this was a very green and pleasant city, although even calling it a city by human standards does not do it justice. The air in this pollution free place was clear and clean, filled with the song of spectacular birds who lived in the vast numbers of trees planted on the magnificently wide boulevards of First, Second and third Streets. The crowning glory of this horticultural city was the park at its middle out of the centre of which on a small hill rising above a ring of cedars several hundred years old, rose the magnificence of the Council. Joey could see the mighty white building standing in the distance as the transport pulled up in the West Plaza, an open area at the intersection of First Street, there were similar plazas at the ends of the other principle radials. He strolled across in the evening sunshine and boarded the central circular, from which he'd then take the Southeast radial transport. It set off in moments, the time tabling of the transports was as a work of art, some of the finest mathematicians had set themselves the task of making it so! It was only a few minutes before he boarded his final transport and shortly afterwards he was strolling along Third Street, he smiled to himself, only bears could be so clinical, this was the most spectacular of boulevards, rivalling anything in the human world, yet it was *Third* Street! He played around mentally with how he would rename the grand crescent avenues of Ursænia. Even a simple conversion to French: Boulevard Trois made it sound better, Bougainvillea Boulevard was his favourite, he decided as he arrived at the doorway to his apartments. Apartment four was on the fourth floor. He rode up in the vert (abbreviation for vertical transport... even the bears found this too much of a mouthful), he pushed open his door and made his way across the wide room to the window, the daylight visible between the slats of the wooden shutter that he now unfolded across the window. There was a wide veranda from which he gazed fondly up the curve of Third... no... Bougainvillea Boulevard, he corrected himself mentally chuckling! Leaning on the balustrade with the warm evening breeze combing through his fur, and the first brightest of stars turning up for work, his mind wandered back to Stuart. Ah! Stuart. He had been far more challenging than his first protégé Jessica. Jessica Urquhart had been the daughter of a British Colonel in India and though he had loved her deeply, Stuart was different. It was as if they were soul mates. Yes they were different in more ways than they were similar, yet still they felt as if they were part of each other. How could that be? Stuart was an eight year old human and he was, well how old was he now? Age was not the issue it is in the human world. When you could live to a thousand years or so who bothers counting? Joey was nowhere near as old as that, he had arrived at his precise age of two hundred and forty five years after a moment or two's mental arithmetic! True his years had taught him a deep wisdom and understanding but the passage of many years can also dull the exuberance of youth, the simple joi-de-vivre, that gushing energy with which Stuart was abundantly filled was a source of joy for Joey also.

He turned and ambled back into his living space. It was not uncommon to have a single room in Ursa, as large as an ordinary apartment but with no dividing walls. Since he lived alone he was happy with this, his room was simply furnished, bare really, (Stuart would have liked that, bear really!). He had very few ornaments and suchlike, 'tranklements' he referred to them derogatively, tranklements/entanglements he would say whenever he entered a room full of such clutter and he would tut-tut to himself. Still it was the individuals choice, he preferred the plain white walls and his uncluttered room, it helped he thought to keep one's mind likewise.

There were a few notable exceptions to his general rule however in the form of three items he had 'brought back' from his travels. The first was a beautifully carved figure of Buddha, who sat cross legged on a small table against one wall. He was half as tall as Joey in his seated pose and had he been able to rise from his meditation he would have easily have been as tall! His arms were outstretched with his open hands palm upwards ready to receive blessings. The fingers were incredibly delicately carved, the first fingers curved slightly to touch, but only just, the thumbs. He had an expression of utter serenity on his dark mahogany face, and though his eyes were shut, still you felt he was watching you. Next to him sat an identical figure but small enough to sit on the palm of his paw, the prototype the carver had made for his approval before he carved the full size one. In many ways it was more beautiful than the large one, it was so small that the intricacy of the detail was all the more amazing and Joey had nearly said 'don't bother with the full size one!"

The second separate item was a crucifix, that hung on the wall alongside his bed. He never failed to be inspired by the talent of the artist who had carved and painted the figure. Maybe some of what he saw was from his own emotions but to Joey the artist had captured the very essence of the suffering that Christ had apparently endured on behalf of Mankind. His pale blue eyes pierced into you, challengingly, yet not accusingly, you felt unable to break the contact of your eyes with his, to turn away from him, from his call?

There was total religious freedom observed in Ursænia as there was throughout the Ursan world. The theme in the state church was very similar to that repeated throughout all worlds, the sign of the cross appeared over and over again in the worlds the bears had visited. No one doubted the existence of God, but there were endless discussions about the minutiae of beliefs etcetera, bears love to discuss things, some may say argue! To stand in the church which was on a massive scale, occupying a circular area in the centre of the Council, you could easily mistake yourself to be in a great cathedral on earth, although of course approximately eight times smaller! The ceiling which was several hundred feet high, was covered by a monumental dome, containing coloured glass panels of incredible beauty, the top sixty feet or so of the circular walls which were punctuated by windows, rose above the rest of the Council, the distinctive shape clearly visible from miles away.

His third keepsake was entirely different. It was one of Stuart's railway tickets from Mossleigh Park to Worrell Central-Child-Return and best of all it had an odd shaped piece cut out of one side where the ticket collector had clipped it! But even 'bester' (as Stuey would have put it) of all though, was the fact that it was bent and grubby. Grubby and bent from the hot little hand of his friend, the very hand that hugged him close every night whilst he slept and whilst Joey watched over him, protecting him, guiding him in the Land of Dreams. It was also different in one very important detail, it was the only one of the three items that he had actually 'brought back' with him. They were told that it was impossible for physical matter to make the crossing, or if it did it could damage the separation between worlds. Joey had never questioned this and had meticulously drawn out the details of his Buddha and the crucifix from memory and had them made by a craftsman back home in Ursa. The ticket was different though, one of the other bears he'd chatted to one time in the arrivals room at the O.C.C. had shown him a tiny silver charm he'd brought back with him, smuggled back Joey had said! He'd just laughed and said, "well it's impossible isn't it? Will cause damage won't it? So how come they didn't even notice?" He though had felt terribly guilty when he had done as instructed and held the ticket fast and close to his heart as he traversed dimensions. He'd expected to find the ticket on the floor under Stuey's bed when he returned, dropped to the floor as he'd vanished from that world, but no, much to his surprise it was still clasped to him when he emerged back home!

It was the fact that it was a 'real' part of Stuey's world that made it so precious to him, he was also a little scared that simply by having it in his possession he could get into trouble.

He was tired so decided he would have an early night. He rummaged in the cupboard for something for his supper, 'mmm! Honey, can't say fairer than that' he chimed out to himself as he scanned the shelf full of jars of every imaginable type of honey! He settled for his favourite, high mountain clover, and set to on it with his spoon, toast would have required bread and he was too tired to bother going out, 'should have called at the shop' he mumbled as he pulled the big fluffy cover over himself, and licking his lips, savouring the sticky sweet honey, he could hear Stuart reprimanding him for not washing his face and cleaning his teeth. "Not tonight Stuey," he murmured, "Not tonight," and in moments he was fast asleep.

Chapter Twelve: Trapped

The following morning Joey woke around seven. It was so peaceful, Ursænia had a special feeling of calmness and serenity. True there was the odd noise floating through his open window now and again, bears calling out good morning, the paper cub whistling as he went past, but they were unobtrusive, welcome. He had a quick wash and pottered down to the corner shop for some fresh crusty bread rolls. It was one of the real pleasures of life in Ursænia for him, fresh crusty bread. It was baked three or even four times a day by most of the bakers, the aroma hung temptingly in the streets as you passed. He headed for home with his bread and a few other essentials, 'I don't need much I won't be here long' he thought to himself, but yet again he felt uneasy. This time he stopped in mid-step and turned as if to see who or what was following him, but he knew that what was dogging him now was a premonition, and not a good one. Something was wrong, he could sense it. For some reason the vague feeling of unease was solidifying into a sense of impending doom! He sat and ate his breakfast without any real enjoyment.

It was too early yet to report to the O.S.Council, he could be there in minutes and although the offices were manned twenty four hours a day, his Control Officer only started at nine. Unable to settle he decided to walk to the Council, by the time he had got there it should be getting on for nine o'clock and the walk will do me good he thought, he poked fondly at the round tummy that was a feature of most bears physique, too much honey he thought!

He walked at a brisk pace, smiling at passing faces and returning the odd '*morning*' that acquaintances greeted him with. He had few friends left in Ursænia, he had been working on the other side for twenty one years now and as most of the pals who he'd gone through university with had also joined the O.S.S. he had lost touch by and large. It was part of the price of O.S. work, he had always thought that he would spend up to a century on it before coming home for good.

There were many places in the mountains to the north of Ursænia that he wanted to visit and he had read of the many splendid sights that were to be seen in the other cities of his world, although it had to be said none were thought to be as beautiful as Ursænia itself. Of course he had relatives here, but he had little in common with them. His father Randolph had married young whilst still in his first century, they had a son Milton but had not had Joseph for another century and a half. When Joseph went to university his father had decided to fulfil a lifelong ambition of sailing around the world. He had not been seen or heard of since.

It was unusual for bears to have more than one or two cubs in this period of Ursine culture, back in the far distant history of Ursa (the name they gave to their planet) there had been over population and wars, diseases and famines had ravaged civilisation for centuries. In this more enlightened time with lifespans sixteen times what they had been there had to be a balance and after the last pandemic a World Council had been set up with the aim of creating a better future for all. It had been staggering in its success and had flourished now for eight thousand years. There were eighty cities across the face of the planet, each one autonomous with the others, each sending eight representatives to the World Council.

In keeping with the policy of 'bridled' technology, the cities were interlinked by deep level tunnels along which the most advanced transports ever conceived hurtled at phenomenal speeds. Production of goods was shared between the cities, each trading with the others rather than competing. His mother had left Ursænia on a spiritual journey the previous century and had also never returned. This left his brother Milton and one or two cousins he knew of but probably wouldn't have recognised now and his uncle, the very grand Eustace Surein of the Grand Council. Uncle Eustace was in his seventh century and he clearly saw Joey as a cub of little consequence! Milton was a lawyer for the Council, the law was taken very seriously in Ursænia and Milton took himself equally seriously. He was to be blunt a pompous ass, thought Joey. He had been against Joey joining the O.S.S. in fact he was against all aspects of contact with Other Sides in general, particularly with earth which was considered the only other world to represent any form of a threat to Ursa.

He was not alone in this. There had been a constitutional uproar when Professor Cornell Eunson had 'breached the veil' creating an opening, a corridor into the parallel existence of the human world. The rush to visit this other world took the authorities by surprise and it was only the near destruction of society by a wave of criminal activity inspired by the lawless and unruly example of the humans that resulted in an emergency session of the World Council setting up the Other Side Service (O.S.S.). This was a global organisation with total power over all other side matters. Overnight other side travel was made illegal, all portal equipment was confiscated, most being destroyed, and a bureau was set up to study life on the other side, well exclusively earth. Professor Eunson was set to work trying to ensure that the voracious humans never found a way of coming the other way and invading their own world! The Eunson Veil Field was duly created to patch the tear in the fabric of existence that he had created. It was however at best papering over the cracks and the best minds on the W.C. (unfortunate abbreviation isn't it!) were convinced that it was only a matter of time before the humans became aware of Ursa. The great sociologist Bruno Bearson who had laid the foundations of Ursan culture had also left behind the Bearson Institute which he had founded. This organ of society was a guiding light in all things relating to cultural and social matters. They came up with a plan of sending emissaries into this fledgling human civilisation to steer it away from its path to self-destruction. The question was exactly how to achieve this.

There was a faction who wanted to simply create an army to invade and conquer this other world but it could not stand the Test of Morality applied to all legislation, the fact that for all their science and ingenuity they wouldn't have stood a chance of winning such a battle seemed never to have even occurred to them! In the end the answer was brilliantly simple, although there were many who had grave reservations about the whole scheme, armies would be trained, but armies disguised as toys, toys who would train the human young, the young who would one day inherit this troubled world from their misguided parents.

In time it was said they could civilise the entire planet. So this brave, if somewhat insane scheme was implemented, the first steps of creating a fashion for what became known as 'Teddy Bears' were the most difficult, but once under way the humans took the toys created in the image of the bears to their hearts and with their crude manufacturing capabilities produced the bears in their millions. The transfer over to the human dimension it was said could not permit the possession of a truly corporeal body, so the Ursan agents were able using advanced meditative training to possess the inanimate bodies of the toys. This Joey had figured out for himself and from his own experiences was only a partial truth. Over a period this became a natural sensation for the host, and the human created toy became to all intents and purposes their real body.

The other bi-product of Professor Eunson's reckless act of experimentation was the strangely named T.S.S. (This Side Service). Crime had been hitherto a very minor problem on Ursa, there were no real reasons for criminality in this enlightened culture, but the wave of violence and mayhem imported from the human world demanded draconian measures. The T.S.S. was formed as a twin to the O.S.S. as the information each had was vital to the other. Its effectiveness was frightening. It ruthlessly carried out its mandate with the ursine efficiency they applied to everything. True there were few actual casualties but there were fears in high places that society had created by its formation what might in time become the agent of its own destruction.

There was great concern about the T.S.S. at all levels of society, stories of bears who'd had a brush with the service were alarming, although generally dismissed as exaggerated and unbelievable. Joey shared this opinion, at least up until now.

Joey had arrived at O.S.S. HQ and having signed in had gone straight to debriefing with his Control Officer. He had arrived at the outer office to be greeted by two large bears in uniform. Now this may not seem strange to an inhabitant of Earth, from most eras of its history, but to Joey it was extremely odd. He has never seen a bear in uniform in his life, nor a picture of one either, since other than for special occasions when dress uniforms may be worn, bears do not wear clothes in the first place, this should help to enable you to understand his consternation!

His consternation deepened in big sinking slumps as they brusquely escorted him into the office and stood intimidatingly either side of him as he was sat down in front of the desk.

Neither was it his C.O. Talis sat at the other side of the desk, Talis who was an amiable bear of similar age to Joey, he was one of the team of scientists who operated the portals as well as his C.O. and support, but according to the name plate sat on the desk this was Kovak-Brunson, an altogether less amenable looking character and one who was quite clearly no scientist either!

"So Joseph, you've returned to Ursænia" he paused almost theatrically, "eventually!" "I'm sorry? where is Talis my CO? Who are you? Have I done something wrong?" The replies came back like bullets, quick-fire and staccato, "accepted, he has been moved, I am your new CO!" Joey retorted "I was unaware that any set timescales were specified for my visits home and my reports" Kovak scowled at him "It appears your protracted absence has led to more than a few unawareness's on your part!" "Am I in some kind of trouble? I mean just who are these two?" he motioned at the two large bears looming over him "are they really necessary? Do you consider me to be a threat?" "Should we consider you to be a threat, Joseph?" "What...." Now completely exasperated by the proceedings Joey stood up abruptly, only to be forced back into his seat even more abruptly by the very strong and large paws of the two bears, who he now acknowledged as guards.

More disconcerting was the way Kovak had pushed his chair back with lightning speed and had levelled what looked like a revolver at him. What he had expected to be an informal chat of a de-briefing, with tea and biscuits and good humour was turning into a total nightmare. Add to this the fact that no firearms existed on Ursa, yes wars had been fought but no mechanisation of slaughter to speak of had occurred as it had on Earth.

Joey sat in stunned silence. Kovak placed the heavy metal weapon on the desk, its presence no longer a secret. "Good, I see you are now becoming aware of the seriousness of your situation!"

Indeed he was, the very presence of that horrible instrument of death, here in <u>his</u> world meant that The O.S.S. had deemed it necessary to start bringing things back from the human world, no it was even worse, they had commenced the fabrication of scaled-down copies of their own. Either way it meant that there were horrible things in store for Ursa. His concern spilt out into words, "what is that wicked thing doing, here in Ursa? Have all the protocols been abandoned? Is nothing sacred anymore?" Kovak picked up the revolver and toyed with it, "yes things have changed Joseph during your absence haven't they? You see the thing is, criminal elements have acquired the technology to move between worlds as well and to put it simply, one must fight fire with fire!"

It was several hours later that Joey emerged from the O.S.S. building into the late morning sunshine. Everything appeared to be normal, the same as always, life was continuing as it always did in Ursænia, smoothly and happily. Bears were strolling around oblivious to the knowledge that had just been imparted to him. He found a seat and slumped despondently down onto it. His entire construct of the peacefulness and tranquillity of Ursænia lay in pieces at his feet. He stared down at the pavement, wondering how this could be.

What had been unfolded before him was a tale the likes of which he could not comprehend happening here in Ursænia, or anywhere on Ursa. After the horrors he had encountered on Earth and read about in their histories, he was more prepared than most bears, but here at home, it was unthinkable. It appeared that some of Cornell Eunson's students had been so fascinated by his breakthrough that they had not destroyed some of his equipment in the initial purge. There were suggestions, though unproven as yet that Cornell himself had been helping them, and encouraging them and far from destroying all the equipment, they had carried on working in secret, refining and developing the original designs. Their work unfettered by the watchful scrutiny of The Bearson Institute had already progressed parallel to the official programme, but without the constraints of responsibility and a proper respect for the appalling danger of their work, they had since raced ahead unchecked and they were in fact vastly more advanced now than the O.S.S. itself! The constant use of the illegal portals had caused more damage to the veil than had been imaginable, and it had led to a total suspension of all Other Side travel by OSS agents, other than for vital operations. All returning operatives had to be suspected of involvement with the illegals and were rigorously interrogated until it was proved they were innocent, or they simply weren't released at all!

Eventually Joey had been allowed to leave, so he guessed that at least they didn't suspect him of anything more serious than flouting a few 'so called' rules, rules that Talis hadn't been even remotely bothered about anyway. He wandered through the park, stunned and bewildered by all that he had heard, unaware of his surroundings or where he was walking.

The terrible truth that was still sinking in to Joey was that he was trapped. The lesson he had set out to teach Stuart was going to be a much harder lesson than he had ever intended, or would ever have exposed him to in a million years if he'd had any choice in the matter. Oh Stuart, my poor dear boy. He murmured to himself. Whatever will become of you now?

He plonked himself down dejectedly on a wooden bench and sighed deeply, as the surrounding world gradually poured itself back into his consciousness, colouring in the green of the grass, the reds and browns of the leaves and the wonderful blue of the sky. He wiped away a tear that was rolling down his cheek and sniffed as he marvelled at the beauty around him, but shivered as he thought of the threat he was now aware of that threatened it all.

What to do about it all he asked himself as if he was discussing it with Stuey. Look at all the facts, from every angle, consider all the options and select the best solution... hmm... it was much easier with a child of Stuey's age to convince him that there was always a way, *where there's a will*... If only it was really that simple! He just drew a blank whatever he thought, there was simply no way to get back to Stuart's world without the O.S.S.

Once home he decided to meditate on the matter and rummaged around to find some candles which he set up at his little shrine. He'd made a considerable study of Buddhism during his first assignment and now he sat in front of his statue of Buddha trying to empty his tortured mind. He found the practice of meditation and the teachings of The Buddha to have a real resonance within him. Religion was different on Ursa, there was the church of course but it was more of an institution for ceremonies than a solely religious thing, there was a culture of bearism, what you would equate as humanism. There was a respect and reverence for nature and the elements, also for the ancestors, but by and large bears just lived in the moment and enjoyed life. In many ways there was a ready match to Buddhism, Joey felt somehow that his little ceremonies added something extra for him by making a focus of his little Buddha and sitting in front of it allowing his mind to connect with whatever may come along.

The bell chimed on the small timer he had fabricated to strike the little bell after twenty minutes had elapsed. He found himself in a state of deep relaxation and gradually brought himself back to the reality of his living room. He had been in a state of emptiness, floating it seemed, without conscious thoughts, it seemed that only seconds had elapsed. Had he dropped off as bears were so prone to? He laughed a little disconsolately to himself at his folly, then realised that somewhere in the process he had decided that he really had to go and see his Uncle, the very distinguished Eustace Surein, Grand Council Member. Exactly why this was what he should do was completely beyond him, but such was the strength of his feeling that he set out to go to see him without a second thought.

Uncle Eustace had risen up to high office through the ranks of the military, Joey couldn't recall which branch of The Service he'd been in, merely seeing pictures of him in a dress white uniform jacket sometime. Unlike the norm on earth there was only The Service, with two branches that dealt with land or sea deployment. There was no air force as such, the airships that they had being looked on as ships and crewed accordingly.

He now lived well outside the city in a large rambling house near a vast lake, the house was lost in a tangled woodland and could not been seen other than from on the lake. Joey trudged along a small track that wound its way through the thickening woodland. He had been dropped off by the bus at the end of the lane ten minutes earlier. The bus ride out from the city would normally have been joyous for him as the countryside sped past his window, but preoccupied as he was he had barely noticed it. Neither had he thought much about why he was going all this way to see someone he hardly knew and from what he could remember, didn't even like that much anyway!

Now walking in the gathering shadows of the thick woods he wondered if Uncle Eustace would even be in, or would even see him if he was? He was such a pompous ass from what little he could remember and from what he knew of him, that he would probably send him away with a flea in his ear anyway, wouldn't he!

Nevertheless he carried on until he was stood at a large wooden door, without further ado or thought he lifted the heavy knocker and let it boom out the announcement of his presence into the echoey interior. No one came, what had he expected? He asked himself, the foolishness of his impulsive journey began to seem very clear to him now. Should he knock again, would it seem rude? Rudeness was considered very bad form in Ursan culture, had he picked up more than his share of rudeness from living in the human world he wondered? They were certainly very rude creatures at times! Just as he reached his uncertain paw out to lift the knocker again there was the loud clicking noise of a heavy metal latch lifting on the inside and the door swung slowly open before him.

Uncle Eustace was a shadow of his former self, he seemed to have shrunk in on himself, his fur was nearly white and was long and straggly around his muzzle. Bears don't grow beards like humans of course as they have still got all their fur, not had it all mostly rubbed off by wearing those clothes that they have! Nevertheless as they become ancient their fur can change colour to white and grow in a way that gives the appearance of a beard. In addition to all this he was stooped and leaning heavily on a silver walking cane. He peered at Joey over the top of small half-moon glasses that were perched precariously on the end of his snout, "who is it? Who's there?" He demanded in a weak, trembling and somewhat shrill voice. Joey fidgeted awkwardly, feeling stupid having come all this way to see this relic of a bear, I mean how could he be of any help him in his quest? Yet it had been the result of his meditation that had brought him to this door so he announced himself, albeit a little stumblingly "it's me Joseph, Uncle Eustace… your nephew? Son of your brother Randolph?" The old bear peered intensely at him, "Joey… Joey? Is that you Joey? Oh my so it is, why come here my cub and shake an old bear's paw won't you." His face had lit up as he recognised his visitor and any fears that Joey might have had that he would not be welcomed vanished as he felt the weak grip of his Uncle's paw and then a welcoming pat on his shoulder as he ushered him in, "come in my cub, come in, what a wonderful surprise you have given me."

Sat in comfy chairs in Uncle Eustace's lounge they drank tea and ate toasted buttered muffins that his house-keeper brought in for them. They had a spectacular view out across the still, greeny-blue surface of the vast lake, the white peaked mountains appearing to rise up from its waters away in the misty distance.

Joey related his tale and how devastated he was on discovering the news about the shutdown, and of his predicament over Stuart and not being able to return to the human's earth to carry on with his mission. His uncle nodded sadly as he listened patiently until Joey paused wiping a tear from his eye. Uncle Eustace took off his glasses and leant back wearily into his chair, "I'm sorry to have to tell you this Joey, but things are far worse than you imagine!" He shook his head gravely as he rose and collected a cut-glass bottle of aged mead from on top of a sideboard, he poured a glass for both of them "I think you'll need this!" He took a sip, "for what I have to tell you is a long and terrible tale…"

"You will know as does every bear of *Professor* Cornel Eunson and his *wonderful* works?" He said the words 'professor' and 'wonderful' as if they were slurs, insults! "Well what you won't know is that his discoveries were not his alone, in the beginning it was known as The Surein-Eunson Field when we discovered the connection between the two realities. He was *my* student, he accompanied me on *my* expedition to The Barren Continent, some seventy years ago, when we sailed that first time to its terrible shores. You will know there has been folklore and terrible tales for generations of what lies on and around that continent. My first love of the sea and then my second of science put me in the perfect position to wish to go there to explore it and to uncover its secrets.

Also we had received a strange report about a very large object that had been seen in the sky by three separate vessels, it was way off in the distance admittedly, but each report was very similar and the sources were totally unconnected. It was definitely not an airship from its configuration so we were left with a real puzzle.

First we circumnavigated the entire continent, it took many months, we were mapping the coast as we travelled and monitoring the strange magnetic fluxes that have been known to pervade in the area of since the first compass was used.

When we came upon the most remote part of the coastline we were stunned to find a structure close to the shore. No settlement has ever been established there, the waters around the coast have no sea life worth eating for several hundred miles out for some unknown reason and there is no water or vegetation to speak of that has been discovered there. What was most astonishing of all though was the size of this structure and most particularly the size of the two skeletons we found lying inside it. They were our first encounter with humans!

There were ten graves nearby and metal posts had been driven into the sand leading away through the dunes. We followed them for half a mile or so till we came upon a vast plain, an expanse further than the eye could see, so flat it looked like a mirror as the sky was reflected in the layer of hot air over it. In amongst the shimmering light we could see a massive shining silver object, it fitted perfectly the description of the flying object from the reports. It was sat on the ground resting on two giant wheels with a smaller one at the back, it had two vast and mighty wings and two giant engines with propellers, like those we power our airships with but the likes of these was staggering, they were so enormous." He held his arms wide apart as he talked of the objects size, with tremendous gusto and vigour for one so frail.

"It was clear that this was the flying machine, what we now know to be a human aeroplane, a Douglas DC3 to be precise, or a 'Dakota' as they referred to it. But then we had no idea where it was from, or who the giants were. We returned with ladders from our ship and eventually managed to get inside the flying machine. We discovered a log book and learnt a great deal about the giants and where they were from and how they came to be on The Barren Continent. It seems they had taken off from a place called Miami en-route to a place called Bermuda. On the way they encountered a disturbance, a storm of some sort and when it cleared the flying machine was above our very own and very vast desert continent. They recorded seeing an expanse of wreckage beneath them, aircraft, boats, ships of all sizes scattered across the plain far and wide. They landed and explored but found nothing but wreckage, and the bleached bones of many of their fellows.

Joey interjected saying almost to himself "the Bermuda Triangle? Now it all makes sense!" Uncle Eustace had nodded wisely as he listened, merely saying "indeed so!"

Uncle Eustace resumed his narrative, the captain it seemed had attempted to fly out across the land beneath him but it became apparent that his compass was forever spiralling his course back towards the centre of the wreckage field. He wrote of observing wreckage of the same aircraft he'd spotted earlier around the field and attempted what he described as dead-reckoning to fly constantly outwards. It was a vast continent he was flying over though and he recorded sighting several other aircraft on the ground below him who must have tried the same thing he was attempting, but had run out of fuel. He had decided quickly to attempt his flight outwards and he'd had a good quantity of fuel on board when he'd been sucked through to our world and he eventually made it to the coast, but only just. He estimated that he could barely make another 100km by then and there was no other land in sight from several thousand feet up."

Joey had sat in stunned silence as his uncle had talked, "and they all just died there?" Eustace merely nodded.

"Of course we couldn't journey to this wreckage field then but we knew we had to come back and find it nevertheless! So it was that the following year we returned travelling in the very latest airship! We landed at the structure and studied everything again and then did the same at the aircraft. We had calculated from the log book that the wreckage field, the centre of the conduit from the other world was almost in the centre of the continent so we set off to find it.

It was exactly as it had been described in the captains log book. We spent several weeks exploring the wreckages, but we could have spent years. We learnt a tremendous amount about this other world, this land of giants, but most importantly we conducted a great many experiments and made measurements of the vast energy fields and energy flows in that strange and terrible place. At night sometimes the swirling patterns became visible in the skies above us, it was both a magical but at the same time truly terrible place to be. We could spend no longer owing to the limited supply of water we had been able to carry with us and we had to depart."

"To this day there are only four bears who have been to this awful place, Eunson, Talis, Morson and myself. We were all sworn to secrecy on our return and we set to work on processing the data we had collected. Eunson was like a bear possessed, almost a maniac! He had this wild plan to manufacture artificially the same forces that created the conduit, the bridge between realities. His physics were almost inspired, a work of pure genius... or utter madness! I begged him not to pursue his research, it was plain to me what the consequences of tampering with our limited knowledge of such forces could be. These are forces so utterly beyond our comprehension I said, trying to get him to see how it was at best foolish but at worst recklessly irresponsible and so incredibly dangerous, that it was inconceivable in its scope for destruction, that it could even trigger the total annihilation of both worlds or even of all of reality!"

Joey interrupted, "but why did the authorities go along with him, why wouldn't they listen to you?" Eustace nodded, "indeed, why not? The thing is Eunson instilled fear in them. Fear is a most terrible thing Joey, he painted a picture of armies of these giants coming through what we too learnt they call The Bermuda Triangle, the rift, in their great aircraft by the thousand. Laying waste to Ursa and plundering its wealth!"

Again Joey interrupted, "but how would they take back all this plunder? Isn't it a one way portal?" "Excellent Joey, why oh why couldn't **they** see that, why were they so easily persuaded by that… that scoundrel? I pleaded with him, I even begged him in the end to see sense…

Of course he would hear none of it, he was as clever and skilled at scheming and manipulating as he was at theoretical physics, bit by bit he manoeuvred me, side-lined me, shared less and less information with me, until finally he set me up in the most scandalous fashion to appear to be a fool, and an incompetent but most appalling of all a criminal! If it hadn't been for my friends in *very* high places I could have been disgraced, as it was I was allowed to retain my rank as Admiral but I was banished from the project, that thief Eunson claimed all the work, all the research as his own and he even had my name struck from all the records!"

Joey watched as the old bear poured himself another glass of mead, his paw shaking noticeably as he did. The treachery that had befallen him had clearly broken his spirit and Joey's heart went out to him.

"It's all so hard to believe uncle, but tell me is there anything you can think of that could help me to get back there, to earth, to Stuart my protégé?" He watched pleadingly as the old bear slowly shook his head, after all his rambling tale his reply was brutally short…"haven't a clue my cub, not the faintest, foggiest idea!"

Joey stayed the night at his uncle's house and set off home the following morning. The only thing Eustace added over breakfast was that the only person who could possibly help him was Eunson himself or someone in cahoots with the criminal gangs he operated smuggling from the human world. Joey had asked him if he really believed the high and mighty Eunson was truly involved in the illegal travelling, his reply of 'no doubt in my mind whatsoever' had been deeply disturbing. He added as Joey departed "the one thing criminals understand is money and this new greed for it that the humans have infected us with. I've none to give you my cub I'm sorry or I would, but be very careful the T.S.S. have sweeping powers and getting on their wrong side nowadays is to be avoided at all costs!" I know that already! Joey thought glumly.

The thought of trying to contact such despicable criminals in order to travel back was horrific, what could he offer as inducement, he was by no means a wealthy bear either, his knowledge of the human world? Was that marketable? He shuddered at the very thought, it would have been a betrayal of everything he held dear, it was unthinkable.

Everything changed for the better though as he glumly pushed his front door shut behind him, with his foot (Stuart fashion) and saw the folded sheet of paper lying on the floor. He picked it up, half expecting it to be a summons to the TSS for his immediate internment on Devils Island, not that Ursa had such a place! Well not that he knew of, although the way things were going… He fancied that Stuart's wild imagination might be contagious! However as he read the note his spirits lifted, it was from Talis and it read, *must speak to you urgently about message received from Emily!*

In less time than he would have imagined possible Joey had trotted around to the address Talis had written on the paper along with his message. He listened as Talis told him of the message he had intercepted when the portal opened unexpectedly and how he had concealed it from the authorities. He informed him that he'd had more news since and it was bad news, very bad. His protégé had been taken seriously ill and was in a mental institution! Joey paced up and down as he listened, becoming more and more agitated, shaking his head and muttering. Talis however was upbeat and enthusiastic…"But don't you see Joey, it's a two way communication, we may not be able to open a portal from our side without The Institute but all we have to do is pass your cane through the little gap that they can open from their side! It'll just fit through I think and once they have it there they can use it to open the portal using the energy from their universe, just like you would have done, creating the same flow and effect of a mini Bermuda Triangle but what they never let you know was that this is a two way conduit and you can go back!" Joey who had been barely listening by this stage snapped to a standstill from his pacing as what he had half-heard percolated down to his consciousness… "what???" was all he said!

Chapter Fourteen: Rescue Mission

Emily and Lucy were sat on the top deck of the number 10 bus as it headed out of town into the suburbs. To any observer they appeared to be nothing more than a grandma and her granddaughter sat chatting, they could never in their wildest fantasies have imagined the true nature of the conversation!

The old lady was asking "do you have him with you?" Lucy nodded and patted her more-full-than-usual school bag, "safe and sound, tucked up in here, but why do you want it, he's not there, inside it!" The old lady smiled, she'd looked incredibly frail, when she had been waiting outside the school the previous evening, Lucy had spotted her and had run over, "are you alright Emily, you don't look very well?" Emily had just smiled and assured her that she was 'fine' however Lucy could see that this was far from the case as her face had a ghastly pallor, it was pale beyond white and she could see her veins as dark lines beneath her thin skin and her lips had a bluish tinge to them. Lucy had instinctively taken her arm as they walked side by side and Emily had formally introduced herself, Lucy had smiled as she informed the old lady "oh Stuey's told me loads about you, he really likes you. Dad said I'm not to go and see you though, he's mad at you!" Emily had seemed concerned about that for a moment, but patted Lucy on her arm, the welcome arm that was steadying her a little as they walked "well you didn't come to me, did you? So you haven't disobeyed your father, well not exactly! We will have to be very careful though! I'm sure it's only that he's so worried about his little lad."

Emily had sought Lucy out as she had been worried about Stuart, he hadn't called around as he had promised the last time they'd met, her subsequent phone call to his mother had brought the terrible news of his predicament.

Lucy put her hand on Emily's arm to steady her as the bus swayed a little as it went around the bend in the road as it followed the long curve of the parks wall, "you look a lot better today Emily, how do you feel?" The old lady turned and looked down at the shiny bright young face of her companion, she had the same eyes as her brother, eyes that danced with life and had that same enquiring vitality. "I feel a lot better, thank you Lucy, I've had company the last two days you see…" She opened her thick woollen coat a little and a strange little face peered cautiously out through the gap! Lucy's eyes went as wide as saucers as the battered little doll put a finger to its lips and said "shh... Lucy, keep it down!" Instantly recognising the voice she whispered incredulously leaning in towards him "is that you Joey?" She was mentally grappling with the possibility as she asked, her hand instinctively feeling the bulge in her bag where her brothers teddy bear was still concealed. "Yes Lucy, it's a long story, but it's so very good to see you" the ancient dolly replied!

Emily explained during the remainder of their ride out to Granville Manor that she had been in communication with a friend of Joey's called Talis, 'on the other side' and that between them they had managed to get Joey back. It had only been when he reappeared that they had realised a flaw in the plan, he had no corporeal existence on this side! "Where's my body?" Joey had quizzed somewhat desperately! "Oh my goodness!" Emily had exclaimed in shock at the realisation, she'd grabbed at her ancient dolly from where it sat on the end of a bookshelf, "will this do?" Joey had looked at it for a moment in shocked disbelief before simply muttering "it'll have to!" and then he had coalesced with the doll.

Emily had wondered if she hadn't in reality simply lost her mind as she sat talking with her childhood dolly way into the wee small hours, she was old she thought, your mind can go peculiar as you come to the end of your time, maybe that was what all this was about? I mean… she thought to herself… I'm sat here at two thirty in the morning talking to my Polly! Polly the dolly that she'd had when she was a girl!

Lucy warned Emily and Joey that Stuart was in a really bad way "he sits there dribbling like he's not in there anymore" she bit her lip fighting back the tears, " I don't like it there in The Loony Bin, it's really scary!" Emily put an arm around her young friend's shoulder, "be brave Lucy, we'll bring him back won't we Joey?" The little doll nodded, Emily went on, "It's not so bad at Granville Manor really, I served there as a doctor towards the end of World War One, there were so many troops with shell shock, there wasn't a lot we could do to help them but just being somewhere so peaceful seemed to help a lot of them. It was a stately home once you know Lucy. It has a story to of an angel that visited the first Lord Granville when his young son was dying, he probably had some form of epilepsy from what can be made out it was the end of the eighteenth century so they had no treatments as such then. Anyway he was sat at his son's death bed when the angel appeared and held up his hand the boy was cured! Lord Granville devoted the rest of his life and a considerable amount of his wealth to helping the mentally ill, he had two new wings built added to the original Hall which are still in use today." Lucy had sat wide eyed as she listened, "do you think the angel will come and help Stuart Emily?" Emily smiled and hugged her, "it's only a story, but who knows. I seem to recall there was a picture on the wall depicting the scene, maybe we'll be able to see it?"

The staff at Granville Manor knew Lucy and she was allowed to come in to see her ailing brother without any real difficulty, a simple if untruthful explanation that Emily was Mrs Wheeler, their grandma was accepted without question by the nurse on the reception desk! Stuart when they found him was sat in what by now was his usual chair by the window, he sat there staring apparently sightlessly out at the beautiful gardens of lush green lawns and wonderful mature conifers that surrounded the building.

Lucy wiped away a dribble of saliva that was drooling from the corner of her brother's mouth "hi Stu, look who I've brought to see you!" Emily sat on the chair Lucy had dragged over for her and reached out and took the lad's hand and held it inbetween hers, she leant across to place her face right up in front of his and peered into his vacant eyes, "Stuart can you hear me? I think you can. I think you are still in there but that you can't reach me." She peered deeply trying to see the faintest of flickers in his eyes, but there was nothing, no response at all. His hands were cool and clammy inbetween hers, she squeezed one gently but the boys hand remained limp and lifeless. She muttered half to herself "oh dear…" as she turned to Lucy, who was crying again, despite seeing him like this for days now she still could not bear it any better.

Emily released the lad's hands from her grip placing them gently in his lap, she rested her hand on Lucy's arm, "there, there my girl, be strong! We will bring him back to us too, have faith, we'll do it just like we did with Joey!" With that she unbuttoned her coat as she looked around to make sure that they were not being observed, "it's lovely and warm in here!" She explained to no one in particular.

Now she sat with her old dolly on her knee, she nodded to Lucy in the direction of her school bag and the girl obediently produced the form of Joey, her brother's teddy bear. She handed him to Emily who sat him on her knee alongside Polly. "Look whose come to see you Stuart" she said as she took his hand in hers again, "it's Joey!"

Polly looked up at Emily, Lucy smiled as she listened to Joey's voice, "oh my goodness! Heavens to Betsy he **is** in a bad way isn't he? No time to lose, it's now or never then!" He had already explained to Emily as they'd talked till the sun had come up, that he felt that the only chance he had of separating himself from the form of Polly and returning to his more familiar form was to attempt it in the presence of his protégé, his ward and friend Stuart. He had only a superficial understanding of all the metaphysics and mumbo-jumbo that Talis had tried so hard to explain to him about co-existence, coalescing, trans-dimensional disparities… he just felt instinctively, in his heart that this was their one and only chance.

"Place *him*" he pointed at the lifeless stuffed form of the teddy bear, onto Stuey's lap, then take both of his hands in yours and look into his eyes… Emily did as she was bid as Lucy made the best effort she could to stand screening the old lady and her brother from any prying eyes. Nothing was happening, Lucy wondered just what might happen anyway? Then she heard Joey's voice, quite loudly too, she looked over her shoulder anxiously and laughed self-consciously, to try and conceal it, a silly forced laugh and a little too loud! He was saying "come on Stuart, I need your presence here, snap out of it boy! Do you want to stay stuck like this for the rest of your life locked up here in the looney bin? FIGHT IT!! That's an ORDER! Do you hear me Squadron Leader Wheeler? I'm giving you a direct order! Obey your orders! Call yourself a fighter-pilot? SCRAMBLE!!" Emily was getting a little anxious now as she listened to her dolly barking out orders from her lap, she laughed, a shrill little laugh which she tried to stifle, the laugh of a crazy old mad woman she wondered? As she felt a rising tide of panic, panic and fear that all was lost, that none of this would work, ever could have worked! Lucy was guffawing louder than ever trying desperately to cover Joey's barked orders… Emily squeezed the lifeless fingers she was grasping onto and added her own plea "oh Stuart my lovely boy, please, please come back to us… Oh Henry if you're out there somewhere help me now my love, please help us…."

Chapter Fourteen: Bedlam

As the spider closed in on Stuart he could see its mouth, its sharp teeth, it was much hairier than he'd ever imagined they were… fear gripped him in an icy frozen terror, he screamed out for help, but none came… surely he was dreaming? Why couldn't he wake up then? "Help me grandpa!" He called out instinctively and he felt the welcoming arm of his grandpa around his shoulder, he turned him gently away from the vision of horror, he was a boy again, it was dark again, "you're safe boy, you're with me now, come on see its still night, go back to sleep Stuey-bach…"

When he woke he was somewhat startled, but not nearly as startled as one might reasonably expect to be if you found yourself sat on the top of the ridge of your house's roof, looking across the neat rows of roofs of the town and watching the sun climbing slowly up into the sky! The birds were singing out their chorus of welcome as night gently faded into the dawn.

Stuart looked around himself and without further ado launched himself off the end of the gable… He fell for a moment until he acquired airspeed then spread his wings and felt the pull of lift as his descent curved upwards, he banked and turned away over the gardens, he pulled downwards and backwards against the air lifting himself with each thrust, it was the most joyful experience imaginable!

He saw down below him the familiar curve of parallel lines of shining steel and banked across to a signal gantry alongside the railway, he curved his wings as a brake and deftly slowed himself feeling the air filter between the tips of his feathers as he intricately manipulated the air flowing between them to land himself precisely onto it.

The early morning goods shuffled past below him, clanking, wheezing, chuffing, its trucks clickety-clacking, groaning and complaining metallically behind the engine as it slowed on its approach into the goods yard, he sniffed the air's aroma as it became flavoured by the steam engine's passing.

Then he was soaring upwards again, higher and higher up into the far blue yonder... the land was tiny below him, then he could no longer see it, he was in a white colourless void, he reached out clawing at nothing, he was falling... falling...

There was noise now, clanking of crockery, cutlery... voices, hands on him, a face peering into his eye? Bright light, a sharp pain in his arm! Quiet... peace... rest...

The noises started again, it was strange he wasn't really thinking anymore, just experiencing... noises, a strange mixed sound of incoherent noise which was echoing around inside his empty head. Then the sound had changed, it was less confined, the sound was freer more able to move around outside around his head. The weight of his body was no longer on his back, it was bright here too, strange patterns danced and swam in his visual cortex, swirling colours blending and interacting with the sounds...

There was another sound now, in the distance... was it a voice... it sounded familiar... he knew that voice? It was insistent, hectoring... but far away, so very far away.......... Squadron Leader Wheeler?..............

...............all yourself a fighter-pilot? SCRAMB**LE!!**"

He blinked... the swirling miasma crystallised for a moment...then another voice, frail and trembling... "oh Stuart my lovely boy, please, please come back to us ..." he blinked again and saw Emily's eyes, those wonderful clear blue eyes looking straight into his…

Emily gasped as she saw Stuart blink, she squeezed his hands hard and called "Stuart!" but it was only momentary and although she thought she felt a slight movement in his fingers she was unsure if she'd imagined it. She let go of his hands and laid them gently down on his legs, she sat back and closed her eyes fighting back the tears, "I fear this is hopeless" she murmured sadly.

"No! No! Didn't you see?!" It was Lucy's youthful voice full of excitement that startled her back to alertness. Lucy who had been observing, who had seen her brother blink too, had also sensed his fleeting presence, but more spectacularly had witnessed that in that fleeting moment of consciousness that he had achieved, the other transformation that had occurred! A glowing light had expanded from Polly as she sat on Emily's lap and passed from her across into Joey! Emily looked down in amazement as she watched Stuart's arm move to hug Joey to himself, Joey looked up at the old lady and fighting back his own tears congratulated her "I say… well done old girl! Well done! We've reached the lad!"

By now the kafuffle that they'd caused had drawn attention and it was Doctor Lassiter that was ushered through by the concerned orderlies, "is everything alright here?" He asked sternly as he scanned the faces of his patient and his visitors in turn. "Oh yes Doctor! Nothing to worry about, I think we made a breakthrough, look…" She pointed to Joey, "he's hugging his bear." The doctor looked and leaning across gently put his hand on the boys arm, he pulled slightly to move it but felt resistance, he was startled and repeated his pull only this time a little harder only to be met by more resistance. "This is indeed interesting! This is the boy's teddy bear I have heard referred to, the one in his delusions?" He asked turning to Emily, before adding "and you are the boy's grandmother?" Side-stepping the issue of who she was, Emily replied "yes it his teddy bear, he has a very strong bond with it as you can see, I would strongly advise doctor that you do not separate him from him... err... I mean... it!

The doctor stood upright at this and bristled, "Madam! I would ask you to kindly leave matters of the boy's treatment in my hands, the hands of the expert! You did not answer my question, are you in actual fact this boy's grandmother, you look remarkably well for a woman I was informed has been dead for many years!"

Lucy was taken aback by what followed and the information she learnt in the process, Emily quietly rose from her chair and stood right up in front of the doctor, old and frail she may well have been but nevertheless she was quite a tall woman and she was eye to eye with the somewhat startled doctor when she gave him the dressing down of the century! "I may indeed not be Stuart's grandmother, Stuart by the way is the name of your patient, who you continually refer to as 'the boy' but nevertheless I am his friend and someone who has nothing but his wellbeing as my sole interest. I have lived considerably longer than you have my man, I have seen things and had experiences that you cannot even imagine during my service as a medical officer in a career that ended when you were still in nappies! And I am telling you, if you have the slightest interest in his recovery, do not separate him from his bear!"

The doctor seemed to deflate a little, "I erm... well... erm... of course I wouldn't do that! He is obviously very attached to it!" Then in an attempt at humour he made a silly little laugh and added "besides I think it would be somewhat difficult to do so?" Emily however scowled even more darkly at him and seemed to grow taller than him, "don't you think for one moment that I won't find out if you do! You know as well as I do that a quick shot of sedative and you could do anything you wanted with him! I still have friends in high places doctor, *very* high places and you would do well not to cross me!"

They were nevertheless still escorted from the ward and out of the hospital by one of the orderlies. On the way out though Emily launched a charm offensive on the large, burly and unsuspecting man! "You know my fine fellow, I used to work here at Granville Manor as a doctor way back in 1917, it's a wonderful building to work in don't you think and those magnificent gardens too?" At first he had remained surly, merely muttering something like "might be if weren't for all the nutters...!" Emily had been unperturbed and had carried on chatting to him, by the time they were halfway to the door she'd found out his name and had gone on to recount her tale of the angel, ending , "... I don't suppose you know if the painting is still here do you Alan?" By now he had thawed a little as she added, "my young friend here would love to see it if it is, wouldn't you Lucy?" Lucy beamed her most angelic smile as she nodded enthusiastically and Alan finally weakened, "well yes it is still here, but it's in the old wing, I shouldn't really show you, especially after you riled up Doc. Lassiter like that..." Emily smiled and nudged his shoulder, "he's such a stuffed shirt though isn't he, go one, he'll never know!" Alan laughed, "stuffed shirt! I like that one, although I can think of few other things I'd call him... not that I could say any of them in front of two ladies such as yourselves!"

They made their way along a long corridor through to what had been the original house, it seemed to be used as a residence nowadays and in the large entrance hall hung on the half-landing at the top of a short flight of stairs, where they went up again to the left and right to either side, was a very large painting of a sick child lying in bed, his worried father sat holding his hand and an angel stood by the bed with his right hand held up. The angel was glowing and the boy was looking up into his eyes.

Alan stood with his hands on his hips looking up at the painting, "that's the one innit, knew straight away when you was telling your story. Grand innit? Though looks as if it could do with a darn good clean to me!" Emily smiled, "it always was a dark painting, I think it was done that way to show the light of the angel better, but I do agree it looks duller than I remember."

Walking back to the bus stop Lucy had beamed up at Emily, "you were magnificent in there Emily!" The old lady smiled back at her and put her arm around her shoulders, "bit of life in the old dragon yet eh Lucy?" "Oh yes! You were positively scary in there! Was it true you have friends in high places?" Emily chuckled, "well they're all up there" she motioned skywards, "can't get much higher than that!" Lucy laughed and took Emily's hand as they walked, "and the way you charmed 'Alan' had him eating out of your hand like that! I was terrified of him, great oaf that he was!" Emily laughed, you learn a few tricks to keep up your sleeve Lucy by the time you get to my age. Did you like the painting?" Lucy nodded, it was amazing, though it was a bit scary too somehow. I've never seen an angel with a black face before though Emily" Emily smiled, no I expect you won't have, your Sunday School books have Jesus and everyone looking very white and British don't they? Thing is though Lucy Jesus was an Aramaic Jew in reality, what we'd probably call an Arab nowadays and he wouldn't have looked like us at all!" Lucy looked up at her old companion a little perplexed but said nothing, Emily left her to ponder the thought for herself.

When he was led back to his bed that evening Stuart clung onto Joey at all times. He showed signs of real distress when he was separated from him even for a moment so the nurse snuggled the little bear in bed beside him when they finally had him settled down for the night.

When the ward was settled and quiet Joey gave Stuart a dig in the ribs, there was no response so more than a little impatient to get on with saving the boy, he poked him in the eye! Stuart stirred and blinked, he saw Joey, at least through the eye that wasn't sore and he could open properly

It was exceedingly difficult to keep Stuart with him, the slightest pause and his eyes would glaze over, his expression would set blankly once more as the spark that transformed him into a person vanished to goodness only knew where, some dark recess of his damaged mind where it could hide itself away? Protect itself from more damage? The mind was indeed an incredible instrument he mused as he tugged hard at Stuart's earlobe!

His task was made all the more difficult since he had to keep his voice down, barking orders at him had seemed particularly effective earlier but was no longer an option anymore.

By two o'clock when he decided he would just have to leave it at that and let the lad rest, get some rest himself too, he had managed to teach Stuart how to reach the physical part of his being, it was a similar technique to that he'd been trained to use to coalesce with and control the body he was currently within. It was very hard for the boy, he had to concentrate intensely and he found it difficult to maintain it for very long. Hopefully he would find it easier the more he did it, Joey thought sleepily as he drifted off to sleep, snuggled up with his friend once more, it seemed so long since he had done so.

The nurses were full of praise and encouragement for Stuart in the morning as he was able to exhibit some control over his limbs as they got him up and as he had his breakfast. When they were settled in the chair in the day room Joey went over the plan with Stuart one more time. "Tell me you understand, no not just by nodding, I want to hear you Stuey!" Joey requested kindly, "a…a…. ah undstan…" Stuart fought out the sounds through his uncooperative lips, Joey hugged him, "that's my lad! Well done, fight hard Stuey, fight hard!"

Later on he was led by an orderly to Doctor Lassiter's office, where he was sat on a comfy chair while the doctor talked to him. "I see you have your bear with you today Stuart. Does he have a name?" Stuart nodded as his eyes rolled and then went blank again. "Try and stay with me Stuart, does the bear have a name? Can you tell me the bears name Stuart?" The doctor quizzed him. Stuart smiled, he remembered Joey's plan, try and annoy the puffed-up, stuffed-shirt fool of a doctor! "John!" he said patting Joey, "called John!"

"Eh? What?" The doctor flipped irritatedly through a leaf of papers, "ah yes, here it is, no Stuart, your father is called John, the bear is called Joey!" He got up and came around the desk to crouch down next to the boy, he touched Joey, "he *is* called Joey, yes?" Stuart rolled his eyes upwards, this time deliberately though, "no John, my bear called John!"

"Right give me the bear now!" The doctor got hold of Joey and tried to take it from Stuart, who in turn kicked the doctor's arm and set to screaming at the top of his voice. The door opened and the orderly came rushing in. By now Stuart was lying on the floor with Joey underneath him, kicking his legs and bellowing at the top of his voice, "help! Help! Help!"

Eventually Doctor Mawdsley the senior psychiatrist came through, he told his colleague to leave to see if that would settle the boy, funnily enough it did, instantly and Stuart returned to being the model patient. Doctor Mawdsley unaware of anything that had occurred thought nothing of it when the little lad carefully sat his bear on the leather couch next to Doctor Lassiter's desk before leaving the room with him. As soon as the door clicked shut Joey climbed off the couch and hid underneath the doctor's desk.

He didn't have long to wait before the doctor returned and sat at his desk, he seemed agitated as he rustled papers around on his desk. Joey slid under the desks centre panel at the front and stood leaning against the front of the desk, Lassiter was muttering to himself, 'never seen anything like it... one minute coherent, then violent, then good as gold as soon as that old fool comes in?" Joey thought with a smile, 'the fellows barking mad, talking to himself like that, this should be easy!"

With that he pulled himself up onto the chair in front of the desk... "Erm.. excuse me Lassiter, sorry to interrupt your conversation... *with yourself...* but..." The doctor sat bolt upright in his chair in shock and panic... all he could manage to say was... "YOU!" Joey pushed home his advantage, he placed his paws down on the desk and leant towards the doctor, "I'd close my mouth if I was you Lassiter, you might catch a fly!" The doctor closed his mouth, dumfounded. "Call yourself a doctor, you're little short of a quack sir! You will listen to me and do exactly as I say, do I make myself clear?" The doctor nodded, a mixture of fear and bemusement on his wide-eyed face.

"You will seek out from Emily, that kindly old lady you treated like an outright bounder yesterday and acquire the name and address of the incompetent meddler of a hypnotist that has caused Stuart's present predicament. You will bring them here and under the supervision of Doctor Mawdsley, who I can only hope is more competent than yourself, you will have her undo the harm that this amateur hypnotism has caused to the boy"

The doctor nodded mumbling, "yes, yes, Emily, lady I was rude to, hypnotist… bring them here…" Then he seemed to regain some composure, "you mean that he was hypnotised by some amateur and this has caused his illness?" "Penny dropped has it? Well done Lassiter, now get off your stupid fat arse and open the door for me!" The doctor was startled back into his stupor and got up and crossed the room, Joey was trotting along across the floor following him. He put his hand on the door handle, "but they'll see you outside if I open the door?" He mumbled, clearly confused. "Yes indeed, now how can that be? Clearly I am a manifestation of your own mind, your poor tired over-worked and clearly unbalanced mind, teddy bears can't walk, talk and in my case have a far greater intelligence than you can they? Although in your case, I'm not so sure… ha ha ha! But there we have a dilemma don't we doctor, if I am in fact a real talking, walking bear then you should just open the door, yes?" The doctor nodded like a complete imbecile, "so by inference not opening the door would have to be an admission that I am a figment of your imagination?" Completely confused, the doctor opened the door and Joey sauntered out, tapping his head with his forefinger in a hatless hat-doffing gesture.

Once he had closed the door, doctor Lassiter staggered back to his desk and reaching into the cupboard under one side of his desk produced a bottle and a glass, he slumped down into his chair and with trembling hands poured himself out a very large whisky and knocked it back in one, he was just refilling his glass when Doctor Mawdsley came in through the door, he had Joey in his hand, "isn't this our patient's teddy bear I've just found on the floor outside…" he started to say before beholding his junior colleague pouring whisky out whilst on duty… Doctor Lassiter put the bottle down and necked the whisky that was in his glass, "D-d-doctor Mawdsley… I-I-I need your help!"

Notwithstanding being suspended Doctor Lassiter did convince Doctor Mawdsley of the urgency of checking out the badly managed hypnotism hypothesis as the catalyst for Stuart Wheelers predicament. The woman was contacted, brought to the hospital, given a severe reprimand and the damage she had inflicted on Stuart's mind was undone.

The very same night it was in a bedroom of a vastly relieved and grateful Wheeler household that a bear and boy snuggled down after Horlicks and shortbread to go to sleep. Stuart was feeling restful and happy, nay joyous, his best pal Joey was back with him. Joey lay shedding silent tears, a mixture of joy at being re-united with Stuart but also of a terrible sorrow over what simply had to be done in the morning.

Chapter Fifteen: Forbidden

In the morning after pacing up and down most of the night Joey told Stuart his terrible news. "Stuart, there's no way I can make this any easier for you, I've just got to tell you straight out, no beating about the bush, no prevaricating, no trying to make it easy, no trying to soften the blow…" "WHAT?" Stuart demanded, laughing at the little bear's nonsense, "I have to go back to Ursa, possibly forever…and I have to go now!" Stuart, flopped down on the floor next to him, pole-axed by his words, all he could manage to say was a flat "why?"

Over the course of the next hour Joey tried to recount what had happened to him in Ursa, making it all simple enough for Stuart to comprehend, though he barely understood a lot of it himself. He'd had such little time to spend with Talis before he came back, he hadn't wanted to waste any time at all but Talis had insisted he was made aware of just how bad things had become.

The main problem was that whether it was due to a natural phenomenon or not, who could tell, they had only been studying the veil for decades there was no way of knowing if its present state was temporary, normal, unusual… the thing was it could be the effect of Eunson and his cronies, what? Joey had demanded! Well there has developed a time distortion between the two worlds, a disparity between Ursa and Earth, most worryingly it seems to be accelerating!

Do you recall when you returned and I wasn't allowed to debrief you? I spotted it then, when I went over the file, it didn't really register at the time, you were criticised for the length of time you'd left between check-ins? How long do you think it had been, Joey had said it was only about seven months, making him only a month late Talis had laughed. Two years Joey, two years had elapsed here!

But it's far worse than that, Eunson has set up an insane program, the man is a megalomaniac, he has agents that are infiltrating the governments of the world, more specifically America and The USSR... they... oh I should explain other things too... so much information... so little time... they have a device now that they wear, it looks like a medallion but it is a stabiliser, it can do several things, it can create or maintain, sustain if you like the wearers physical form across the barrier, so you could just be you here and there, no need for a host? You see? Not that it has always been as cut and dried as that anyway, you may have experienced it for yourself that all is not as they teach you at OSS training school? But worse still this device can be used to allow them to exist without a body at all, to retain their integrity as a non-corporeal entity, then they can then coalesce, meld with an actual human, any human and fairly quickly they can influence them, even take complete control of their mind...

They plan to destroy the Earth, mankind, the threat they perceive the humans to be... by using their own hands! Joey had been horrified, he had just asked dumbly, how? Talis ranted on, imagine if they took over the President of The United States and of The USSR! Add some key military personnel and hey presto WW3?

"So you see I have to go back, and I have to go right now!" Stuart hugged Joey tearfully, "it's the only way? I'm so sorry Stuey, but you are a very brave boy, you will be okay, I know I can rely on you, I expect great things of you Mr.Wheeler! I'll always be with you, in your heart and in your mind you know and I will never forget you either. There's just one thing you have to promise to do for me, for everyone's safety's sake… give me the splinter of wood from the portal's doorframe!" He held out his paw, "it HAS to be returned to my world!" "I can't! Emily's still got it!" Stuart explained. Joey shook his head and frowned, "in that case you must promise me that at the first chance you will get Emily to throw it into her fire! Promise me!" Stuart nodded and mumbled sadly "I promise."

Joey gave him a last hug and then tapped his chest, explaining that Talis had given him a talisman portal device. The portal opened and he took a stride towards it, "I love you Stuart, goodbye!" and even as Stuart cried out "I love you too" he stepped into the portal…

What happened next is hard to explain, even Talis was uncertain, it should have been impossible for so many reasons, it was so unthinkable… well at least no one had thought of it anyway! Whatever else, it should never have been attempted as it was utterly forbidden!

Stuart not ready to be separated from his companion again so soon, dived for him to try and prevent him from leaving, he grabbed his paw just at the moment that he entered the portal, thus connecting himself with Joey. Talis's best attempt to explain what happened was that as Joey was by then effectively 'in transit' already, Stuart was carried across with him… The relative size of the boy and the opening whilst at first seeming to be an unsurmountable issue were apparently largely irrelevant, our bodies are mostly empty space, he'd brushed that aside with! Why his consciousness ended up residing in the teddy bear that had been in his arms was a total mystery, he had no theory whatsoever for that one!

So it was then that moments after Joey thought he'd be back in Ursa, and back alone, he was sat in a heap on the floor, looking at himself! Well the form he had inhabited during his time on Earth! How was this possible? Stuart had been holding the teddy bear when he left, then he remembered feeling the tug on his hand, oh no! He prodded the lifeless form of the bear, to his amazement and confirming his worst fears, it stirred! "Uh... where am I?" It said. "Stuart, is that you!?" Stuart leapt to his feet, which were now more like his back-paws and let out a holler "What!!!" He patted at his body with his stubby paws and at his big round head... "What's happened? Where's a mirror? I want to see myself!!!..." Joey stood in front of the startled boy, "effectively my little friend you are looking into a mirror right now! Welcome to my world! Welcome to Ursa!"

Talis, opened the door to the chamber they had found themselves in and stealthily crept in around it along with another bear, before shutting it quietly behind himself. "We should be safe I was able to set your remote to use this old experimental portal. I'm afraid we have a few hours to wait before we can attempt to get away, things have changed a lot since you went, how long do you think you've been away this time, how long does it seem to you?" Joey thought for a moment, "it's been two days I've been gone. Why how long is it for you since I left?" "Three months Joey, the disparity is accelerating almost exponentially now! It may start to slow, to reverse, we simply don't know!"

At that moment Stuart who had instinctively hidden behind Joey when the door opened, was revealed as Joey stepped sideward. To Talis and the other bear it must have looked really funny as she tittered as Joey appeared to duplicate himself, well at least make a tatty copy of himself. Talis however stood frozen as his jaw dropped, "oh it gets worse!" Joey said, "say hello to Talis Stuart!" Stuart took a faltering step on his unusually short legs in the direction of Talis, who backed away in horror muttering… "this isn't happening… this can't be happening…WHAT HAVE YOU DONE!"

Over the course of the next few hours, Talis brought Joey up to speed, inbetween trying to explain what had happened with Stuart every now and then. The other bear who was with him was his sister Mazsla, she was working for the TSS, she had spearheaded an investigation of the OSS when several of the agents who had been travelling to Earth decided they could no longer be a part of Eunson's crazy plan, two more had attempted to whistle blow but had been trapped before they could get away by his hench-bears!

Eunson was routed though, his secret bases were stormed, there had been fighting and casualties, one facility had been completely destroyed, it was at first believed Eunson was still inside, many more were injured in the blast, no trace of him was found, so there were fears that he'd sacrificed the entire base just to cover his escape! The facility they captured was taken over by Talis and a group of leading scientists from the OSS and they set to trying to unravel what Eunson had been up to. The achievements and the progress he'd made was both staggering and horrifying in their scope and consequences. Everything was shut down but his agents were already in-situ on Earth and with no way of recalling them would remain so, to carry out whatever orders Eunson had given them!

All travel between worlds had been banned, with the severest of penalties for anyone having any part in travel, attempted travel or any ancillary role in facilitating travel in any way shape or form! All the equipment had been destroyed except one heavily guarded chamber at the OSS, which had been totally deactivated.

Eunson had reappeared a week later with an army of the finest legal team of bears that money could buy. He was to go on trial but was attempting to justify all that he had done in the name of patriotism! Talis went on, that's why we need you here to testify, to speak for the human race, to defend them! Expose him for the madman he is!

Talis broke from his dialogue for a moment to examine Stuart, who had groaned that he was hungry. Maszla had found a bar of flapjack in her backpack and given it to the lad, who'd set upon it with gusto! Talis held a detector over Stuart's body and muttered as it hummed and whirred, "look at these readings" he said to Maszla, who shook her head and concurred, "this isn't good, what about one of Eunson's stabilisers? The Z2?" Talis agreed, "think you can get one out of the lab? Without being compromised?" "A bear with my charms? Really, don't be insulting! Of course I can!" With that she opened the door a fraction and peered around through the crack, before slipping out through it.

Under the cover of darkness the small party made their way to Joey's apartment. Maszla had found some bandages to cover the darning on Stuart's face and to hide the resemblance to Joey! He looked like a blummin mummy he had whined!

Talis had calibrated and then hung a medallion looking thingamajig around his neck and said he felt much happier about the lower readings on the dial of his measuring box. Joey had looked as he watched anxiously as Talis passed the device over the boys altered body, "What could happen to him?" he asked, Talis shrugged, "wish I knew, he could explode like an inter-dimensional bomb, destroying all of reality?" Everyone looked at him horrified! "Sorry I was joking... I think! But I suppose he could simply readopt his normal form?" Joey shook his head continuing for Talis...

"which would be bad, as he would be approximately four times the size of the largest bear ever seen on Ursa!" Stuart's response of "wow I'd be a giant!" Was ignored!

The others left Joey and Stuart to try and get some sleep, it was weird because Stuart was the same size as Joey now, so they slept together but apart from each other in his bed. Not that either of them was able to sleep that much.

Joey was making some porridge for them in the morning when he heard Stuart call out from the bathroom, he took the pan off the heat and went through to see what was the matter. He found Stuart with the bandages Maszla had wrapped around his head lying in a heap on the floor and the boy, well alright the bear, examining his face in the mirror. "Look, my fur's growing back already!" Joey moved in a bit closer and sure enough the patches on his face where the stuffed toy version of him's fur had been rubbed away down to the fabric were peeling off, showing new skin underneath, with new fur beginning to grow! It was a slightly different colour though, "we'll look like brothers! I always wanted a brother!" Stuart gleefully exclaimed, more like twins he thought, although the different coloured fur did distinguish them and for some strange reason his eyes were a much darker brown than his, the same colour as Stuart the boys in fact! Maybe he could pass him off as a cousin? He looked over the rest of his doppelganger's body and could see quite clearly that his fur was improving all over!

After breakfast they made their way over to Talis's house. Stuart was in total awe of the strange and wonderful land he found himself in, everything was so different, everywhere was so clean! There were no soot blackened buildings here, no bombsites, no traffic, no poor people, well okay poor bears! There weren't any steam engines though which was a shame, he pointed that out to Joey, he said that was why there were no blackened buildings! Joey wasn't himself at all since they'd come here, Stuart thought, well in more ways than one! The thing was he actually was himself now, the real him and not the bear he'd known back at home. It was an amazing feeling being in someone else's body too, so to speak, he looked at his strange reflection in every shop window as they passed and wobbled his big fat head!

He thought Joey was angry with him at first, because he'd jumped through after him, but he began to realise as he listened to him and Talis talking and he was getting bored by it, that it was simply that he was worried sick that they wouldn't be able to find a way to get him back home ever again! He wasn't that bothered he thought, at least at first, why would he be it was great here? Then he thought about mum and dad and home, and grandpa and grandma and Emily, even Lucy and he knew he would soon begin to miss them terribly, in fact as he thought more about it, he realised that he was beginning to miss them already.

Maszla agreed to take him out to occupy him, give him a tour of Ursænia, take him for a ride on the transit. He jumped at the idea and in no time at all he was in the park with her eating a sticky bun from one of the bakers they'd passed on the way.

Joey and Talis sat with a big pot of tea, a loaf of bread and a pot of honey, trying to think of a way to get the boy home. Joey recounted his tale of going out to see his uncle and how he'd heard from him all about the expeditions to the Barren Continent. Joey had asked about the Talismans, couldn't they use one of them to send him back? Like the one he'd given to him on his last trip to get him home, Talis explained that although it could open a portal back it was only one way, he had after all gone back to Earth through his own portal opened by Emily from her side! If only they could have contacted her somehow to get her to open the portal from her side. They wondered why she hadn't tried herself already.

Joey sat quiet for a moment and tried to clear his head, he reasoned that if there was only one portal left at the OSS and it was shut-down and heavily guarded then surely the only possibility left to them was to return to the barren Continent and try somehow to use the natural portal? He said he understood that it was a one way passage into Ursa from Earth but wondered if there wasn't something in the new research that Eunson had carried out, some way however desperate that might somehow allow them to sneak through it somehow the other way? Talis shook his head, he said he simply couldn't see how, but he would go back and scour the files and try to see what he could glean in the hope of something turning up.

A couple of days passed and Joey could see how uncomfortable Stuart was becoming. He'd been full of his trip out with Maszla for a short while and had a list of all the places she'd told him about that he'd like to visit. But his enthusiasm didn't last. He kept saying he wasn't hungry and the novelty of being in another world was clearly wearing off fast, he was succumbing to a severe bout of homesickness.

Talis arrived just after they had eaten their evening meal, well after Joey had. Stuart had pushed his around his plate mostly. Talis was excited and said he had a plan that might just work. Joey's idea although it had seemed barmy to him at first had led him onto something. He had been out to see Joey's uncle Eustace and had even sought help from Eunson himself! Joey was staggered, wasn't that unwise? He'd asked, "no, no don't you see, he has nothing to lose, he can't repeat what I told him, he has no evidence anyway, besides what I said was put as hypothetical cases, it's not a worry, trust me."

It seemed that from what he had learnt from Eunson that the portal from earth was a type of vortex, it was only possible for passage to be made at all at certain times, at phases of its cycles. He likened it to a tornado that comes spiralling down from a storm cloud, most of the time the vortex is way above Ursa or more precisely not in contact with our universe and travel is only possible when it reaches down trans-dimensionally into our reality and as we know even then travel is only possible into our universe and not from it as it sucks things one way like a plughole draining from one into the other once it connects!

However what he postulated was that it may be possible to follow it back as it moves away from us, sneak through by flying up the vortex in the opposite direction and at its periphery and if we used one of Eunson's devices to shift the phase of the craft it could be that it would cease to have mass in that space. "It's incredibly difficult to explain, Eunson is the only one who has even the slightest idea of what the reality of the phenomena truly is, if even he actually has, but he has provided me with this" he pulled out a thick cardboard folder from his bag and dropped it onto the table "these are the calculations and instructions he has carried out for us, well not specifically for us, it seems he had already been working on this as an alternative way of travelling to Earth himself! It came with a price though I'm afraid to say." Joey prodded at the folder suspiciously with his paw, as if it was in some way toxic, not to be touched "what price, what does that scoundrel want in exchange?" Talis shook his head, "I'm sorry Joey but I had no choice, I've promised him that you will not give evidence against him at his trial, or try and defend humanity in any way!"

After Stuart had gone to bed, the bears sat and drank mead. Maszla had come round as well and they sat talking in a dark and sombre mood. "How would it work anyhow?" Joey asked, "would we be able to use an airship to do this insane flying up the vortex malarkey?" Talis laughed and emptied his glass, pouring another one out straight away, he was getting tipsy. "No chance Joey old bear, the currents would toss it about like a feather in a hurricane! That's the beautiful part of the plan and the most insane part of it too, we fly the humans own aircraft back to earth! That bloody great big flying machine thing that's been sat there waiting to go back home for years!"

Chapter: Seventeen

The U.A.S. Intrepid

The U.A.S.Intrepid

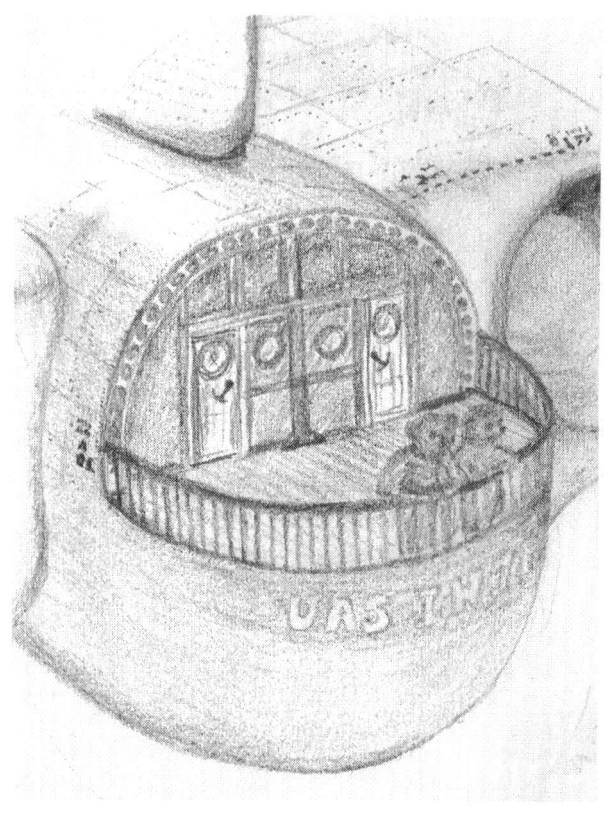

Talis had gone on to say that he was pretty well convinced that by now Stuart would resort to his normal form and size once the talisman was removed from around his neck, he'd added that in his opinion they should not delay a moment longer than they had to in leaving either, for he feared that it may fail to contain his form indefinitely and if it did fail it could be without any warning. He had acquired a further device to use on their venture which as he explained further he said Joey would appreciate the necessity for!

The point he eventually got around to was that the boy would be large enough, well more or less and probably with some adjustments, that he was sure they would be able to make on the scene at the aircraft as and when, indeed if even, they found them to be necessary… to man the controls of the aeroplane. Joey would have to familiarise himself with the technical side of flying the machine from using the cockpit manual and instructions that he would give to him himself based upon his comprehensive reading and interpretation of how the device most likely operated.

Joey had sat looking at Talis, his eyes growing wider and his jaw dropping further as he listened to *the plan*. Eventually once Talis had finally stopped gabbling he recapped, "So this is *the plan*, you expect me to supervise an eight year old boy without any previous experience of doing so, to fly a ten ton or more aeroplane off the ground without crashing it, then to fly it up a trans dimensional one way vortex… the wrong way, I must point out, then if by some inexplicable miracle we aren't killed, atomised, transported to the ninth dimension or God only knows where or what else could happen… and we do actually in fact emerge somewhere back in Stuart's world over the Caribbean… the <u>ocean</u> that is I must again point out! The <u>middle</u> of it! Well then, after that all we'd have to do is just fly to land, if we can find it, find an aerodrome and then simply land the same ten-ton-odd flaming thing… without crashing again, of course!" Talis nodded, "so no problem with any of it so far then?" They laughed, there seemed little point in doing anything else really, for however barmy this plan was… what else was there to do?

Within a week they were boarding the UAS Intrepid (Ursan Air Ship) at the airship docks. She was as close to a military craft as the bears had and was a Manta Class, named for the similarity of her overall appearance had to a manta ray. She was one of the latest, fastest and most sophisticated designs of airship they had ever built. She differed drastically in shape from the more conventional cigar shaped airships common to both Earth and Ursa, in that she was more like a flattened doughnut shape. From above she appeared almost circular, but blunted on the front edge and with a small projection in the centre of the flatter bit, but looking from the front she was more like a flattened rugby ball shape, with two massive holes through the airship structure either side of the centre, where the central superstructure was a monocoque which was integral to the airship frame, with the cockpit protruding at the front and the passenger space bulging out below the main superstructure and above it along the centre line to accommodate viewing windows. The outer edges of the airship curved downwards to be slightly below the bottom of the central fuselage, enabling the airship to settle down even onto water. The entire shape of the ship viewed from the side showed how it was one massive aerofoil capable of generating additional lift once it attained forward airspeed.

Mounted inside each of the openings through the airship was the latest technology in engines, mounted on gimbals to allow them to rotate and vector thrust in virtually any direction, even through the openings above and below, as well as in front and behind them. The motors had multi-propellers, two at the front and two at the back and were electrically powered and the vast surface areas on the top of the airship were coated in solar cells to harvest the suns energy. To complement this the ship had conventionally fuelled engines that could power generators to supply additional electricity when needed.

Rising from the top of the superstructure was a massive fin, which could be used for lateral stability and even rotated for use as a sail if the wind was in the right direction. To control the airship in flight it utilised conventional aircraft control surfaces on the trailing edges of the wing shape and with a tail-plane, rudder and elevators to the rear.

Speed was not a major consideration on Ursa as a rule, what did it really matter how long a journey took? It was the quality of the travel and the experience it provided that was most important after all. These airships however were the fastest that had ever been built by the bears and it had been a remarkable feat that Uncle Eustace had been able to wangle one of their number for the mission!

Talis had pulled as many strings as he could as well to facilitate the mission, which he had presented as one of 'vital scientific importance in establishing the present danger and exploring the future risks faced from the result of the meddling with the other side by Eunson and his associates.' Such was the state of alarm over the whole fiasco that it had been relatively easy to procure he'd said modestly.

Talis leaned on the rail of the open deck that ran the full width of the rear of the superstructure of the Intrepid as they sailed majestically up and away from the dock and back over the Capital buildings in the centre of Ursænia. They were already at a fifteen hundred feet and climbing all the time into the clear blue sky ahead of them. He turned to Joey who was absent mindedly wondering if he'd be able to see his house as they passed over Ursænia… well more if he'd ever see it again at all! Talis spoke disturbing his reverie, "one thing that's till concerns me is the time disparity, it's been ten days now since we last tried to calibrate the differential," Joey shrugged disdainfully "what difference does it make, it's not as if we're going to just drop Stuart back into his bedroom as if nothing's happened is it? I mean if… and let's face it is in an enormous 'if,' but if by some miracle, every single impossible step of the madcap plan goes exactly as we hope it will… then I'm going to be sat there on a runway, in *Florida* probably?" Talis nodded as Joey looked up quizzically at him, "sat there with an eight year old boy who was last seen in Lancashire, England and has been missing for… well we'll have no idea if it will be hours days or what it will be will we?" Talis nodded, then added helpfully "I erm... suppose it's even possible if the divergence has overtaken itself, that he may even still be there in his bedroom?" Joey looked daggers at Talis, "thanks for that! Nevertheless there we will be sat… oh yes, nearly forgot we'll just have landed in a plane that vanished God knows how many years ago… oh and also none of the crew or passengers are on it now!" Talis nodded, "He's an eight year old boy, you're a stuffed toy, what they gonna do?"

Joey shook his head, "I'm really bothered by all this Talis, I love Stuart dearly and I want nothing more than to get the lad home, but I can't help wondering if we're making a terrible mistake. I mean, just suppose that we do get him back, what are they going to make of what he tells them? What is he going to say to them? We can't try and brief him, give him a story to stick to, he's only eight! I know he has a vivid imagination but he may be questioned by all sorts of army, intelligence, FBI even? I shudder to think by whom? But I'm darned sure that they'll get everything he knows out of him, sooner or later, one way or another. If only it had been an airport in England I wouldn't have been nearly as worried, the English are so much more civilised about everything than the Americans!"

"I've read about The Bermuda Triangle in my time on Earth and I know it's all veiled in mystery and folklore so that's a plus but if they piece together more from what he says, well who's to say what they might do? I tell you Talis these are a wonderful race of people, capable of magnificent achievements but they are capable of the most appalling atrocities also. What if Eunson's right God forbid and they do decide to send their aircraft through the vortex, that old thing we're hoping to use to fly him back home in is nothing compared to the stuff they have now, they can fly faster than sound, they have a bomb that could destroy every single building in Ursænia and miles of countryside beyond it in one single explosion! What if time has moved so fast there that they are now a race of people we have even less ways of assessing?"

Talis shrugged, "what's the alternative? Let the boy return to his true form here and live like a freak, penned up somewhere out of harm's way? What if the authorities decide that he's too dangerous to even do that with, decide that he should be killed? Things are not what they once were my friend, fear and paranoia have exacted a terrible cost on the values and standards that we, you and me and bears like us have held dear our entire lives."

The two bears fell silent, an unusual spectacle in itself to see two bears stood together and both silent! They watched as the Intrepid slid virtually silently over the outskirts of Ursænia and then out over the open countryside. Presently they were joined by one of the crew. She stood next to Joey, "may I?" She asked indicating her desire to share their view. Joey a little startled by what to him lost once more deep in his reverie was a sudden appearance, nodded his approval. "You were miles away then Mr.Ursein, Joseph. Will you allow me to introduce myself?" He nodded, the formal etiquette of Ursan culture seeming somewhat alien to him now after so long living with humans. "Lieutenant Suraied,Yasil at your service!" Joey decided he couldn't be bothered with etiquette and stuck his paw out, somewhat surprised she tentatively held hers out, he gripped it and responded by merely saying "pleased to meet you Yasil, I'm Joey, this is Talis!"

She stood there for a moment and then turned and placed her forearms on the rail assuming the same posture as the other two, leaning on it and looking back where the ship had passed overhead.

Joey pulled himself back from his thoughts and realising he had been a bit rude, turned to look at the bear. She was probably about his age, give or take fifty years and was in good shape. She wore what he now realised was the norm onboard, a white jacket of the Airship Service and had a cap on her head. All in all she was pretty foxy he thought to himself! Then he did a double take on her and what he had just thought! "I'm sorry, Yasil, I was indeed lost in thought then, I have a lot on my mind, way too much for someone like me to cope with. I'm feeling so completely out of my depth to be honest with all this…" He spread his arms out over the railing to encompass the ship and their passage through the air and everything!

Yasil nodded, misunderstanding what he meant, or so he thought, she said "yes she's a fine ship The Intrepid, I've served on her since her launch. I should explain… err… Joey that the entire crew have been fully briefed on our mission, Admiral Surein, you uncle is the most revered bear in The Service. He has the trust of this crew and we the crew in return have complete faith in his judgement and true loyalty to all we hold to be Ursan!"

Joey spun around to face her "what you know *everything?* Even about my nephew? Err… I mean Stuart?" She smiled and what a smile Joey thought, even in the midst of the chaos his mind was in! "That he's a shape-shifted human?" Joey simply shook his head and placing his arms on the handrail he let his head fall into his paws as they covered his eyes and he groaned. She went on, "and that he's currently compressed down to the size of a bear?" She looked over at Talis "and that all of this is being stabilised by one of Eunson's clandestine gadgets? Oh and that it could fail at any moment?"

Talis stood up straight and walked around the back of Joey to be next to Yasil, "no, no there's no need for concern over that, I've doubled the strength of the dampener, he has two of Eunson's talismans now, I'm sure he'll remain stable at least till we get to the Barren Continent."

She smiled again, "I've every confidence in you Talis… how did he just do it? Oh yes… pleased to meet you!" She held her paw out and shook Talis's! Joey lifted his head from his paws and looked up to watch, he laughed as she mimicked his 'human' way of meeting someone, they all laughed together. Yasil nodded to the door, "they're serving up some food about now, would you like to come and join us?" The two bears nodded and turned from their view of Ursa, now vanishing over the horizon behind them. The land below turning to yellow and green sandy dunes as they neared the coast and the vast ocean that they must cross.

They sat and ate their meal with the Captain who was a somewhat brusque old bear, Stuart joined them but as was now usual for him ate very little and asked if he could go to bed early. It was so unlike him Joey thought, here he was on an airship flying over a strange land, in another universe! Why it was the stuff of dreams for the boy he loved and nurtured back in his home. Talis had warned Joey that the second talisman might make him feel unwell, he'd added that the whole process of his compression and possession of the bear could be an enormous strain on his essence, his aura, his whatever we and humans truly are, well what our essence really is!

Joey was finding it difficult remembering who Stuart was, insofar that he was only an eight year old boy, a human boy. The fact that Stuart now looked pretty much like everyone else, especially himself and more to the point that he was the same size as everyone else, as in grown-ups, meant he was finding he himself was treating Stuart differently. To say it was different for Stuart himself is an understatement too! He was used to being small, having to look up to see adults, the adults accordingly looking down on him both physically and metaphorically and consequently making allowances for him since he was so obviously a child. The fact that he and everyone knew who and what he truly was made no difference, unless they made a conscious effort to remember. It was a profound adjustment for Stuart to effectively have 'grown-up' overnight!

The Captain informed Joey that The Admiral wanted to see him after he'd eaten, he had his own executive cabins on the upper levels. 'Your uncle prefers to eat alone' the Captain had said. After he'd eaten Joey excused himself and rose from the table, he headed in the direction the Captain had indicated to a staircase in the centre bulkhead, Yasil looked up and smiled from where she was sat with her crewmates having her meal, he smiled back, she really was the most alluring creature he thought and his step felt a little lighter as he padded up the stairs to the Admiral's quarters.

He knocked on the ornate wooden door, which was out of keeping with the ultra-modern design of the rest of the ship, his uncle's voice sounded out "enter!" He sounded altogether much more vigorous and alive than when he had last met him. When he entered the Admiral's quarters Joey had to stop himself gasping, it was as if the room was part of a different vessel, a sea going ship and an old one at that! Eustace noticed the bear's reaction, "like my quarters do you cub? Well she is the flagship you know, and rank does have some privileges! I'm old school, love tradition! Love it!" He got up from where he'd been seated at his dining table, "come, sit over here Joseph" he poured out two glasses of golden liquid, "here, vintage mead, warm your cockles it will!" He laughed a wheezy asthmatic laugh as he handed the glass to Joey before slumping himself into a chair opposite him. "Lot happened since you came to see me cub, eh? Some predicament we find ourselves facing!"

Joey sipped the mead, it was magnificent, he had never tasted the like of it before, his face gave away his pleasure, "good stuff eh?" His uncle nodded, clearly pleased by his mead's reception. "Uncle may I speak candidly?" The old bear raised his mightily bushy eyebrows right up his forehead, almost scarily! "I'd hope to blue-blazes you'd do nothing else!" He took a mighty swig of mead and motioned with his glass "get on with it cub!"

"I've been worrying about it since we decided we'd do our darndest to get poor Stuey home, I've tried thrashing it out with Talis but I simply can't convince myself that we're not risking making a terrible mistake just letting him go like this, that the risk of the humans finding out about us is too great?" Eustace nodded, "I know, I know. But surely Joseph you must have realised that we'd have come up with some sort of plan to deal with this? Do you think we're nothing but a bunch of senile old blithering nincompoops?" He was by this stage leant right forward in his chair, glaring with his big wide watery eyes and scarily raised eyebrows at Joey!
"Err…err…err…" The old bear sat back "pah! Err…err… err! He says! There's only one nincompoop in this room and it's not me!"

Joey hadn't been able to prevent himself laughing and the old bear had laughed too, he beckoned Joey to get up and pour more mead and by the time he wobbled down the stairs back to the crews mess he was a far happier bear in more ways than one for Uncle Eustace had explained that he had brought the very best psychologist in the land with them, that he was also an expert hypnotist and that he was going to commence working with Stuart tomorrow to begin to build a blockage in his mind, a blockage that would be so permanent that even any manner of future hypnotism would be unable to unlock it.

He'd then raised his concerns for the lad's wellbeing, for his mental health after all that, but he had been reassured as his uncle had pointed out, just consider the lengths we are going to in order to return this child to his family? Have you any idea of the cost of this mission? He'd asked Joey, waving his hand away to dismiss it as nothing even as he spoke, 'it is how we are, who we are! I will have no truck with the new ideas, the polluted thinking that Eunson is espousing, the man has danced with The Devil in my book!'

Yasil was sat at one of the side tables playing cards with a couple of the crew and Talis and Maszla, she motioned for him to join them. Joey hadn't realised Maszla had come with them on their mission and he gave her a big bear-hug. Talis could see his friend was more relaxed and smiled at him pouring him a drink, it was some sort of dark sugar derived alcohol, what he would have called rum back home… back home? What had he just thought? He had thought about his life on earth and called it home! He drained the glass in one and pushed it back at Talis for more with a hearty laugh! What the hell, home was where the heart is he'd heard someplace! It was a lively gathering as Joey caught up with Maszla and chatted more with Yasil…

In the morning he bumped into Talis as he was sneaking out of Yasil's cabin, his friend patted his back gently and just smiled as he passed down the narrow corridor, he called back over his shoulder "come and find me later. I've something else to show you, a new idea I've come up with to help you with what you were worried about!"

Joey scuttled back to his cabin and once inside stood leaning with his back on the door. He was still blushing, but he was also grinning like a fool. It was all too much he thought, he was flying over the ocean in an airship on what had to be the maddest mission ever conceived by any mad bears in the history of time?!? Then he was laughing at his reflection as he splashed water on his face, the same face as his ward Stuart now had!?! His laughing became hysterical now as he flopped onto his bunk face down as the laughter turned to sobs… he was utterly exhausted, mentally, emotionally and physically… In moments he was asleep.

It was early evening when he awoke, someone was knocking on the cabin door, he stirred painfully his body still in the same position it had been when he had flopped down many hours previously, "who is it? Come in, come in!" Talis stuck his head round the door, "awake now sleepy-head? You had a good night... in more ways than one!" He raised his eyebrows, "you old dog you!" Joey swung his legs round off the bunk and sat up. This movement did not agree with his brain which complained vigorously by trying to beat its way out through his skull with its fists!

"Thought you should know that the ship surgeon has had to sedate Stuart." Joey tried to focus his foggy mind, he tried to get up to rush to his young ward's side but wobbled and sat back down on the bunk heavily, "why, what's wrong with him? Is it the talisman?" "He's not sure, he thinks it might be or a combination of that and the motion of the airship, not eating, being homesick, being in someone else's body, another creatures body, being in a parallel universe... take your pick? It's a lot for the little fella to deal with isn't it?" Joey stood up more slowly this time and steadied himself, "well we'd best try and help him, in a few days he's going to need to be at his very best if we've even the remotest chance of this bonkers scheme working! He was meant to be seeing the hypnotist today as well, maybe he can help him to deal with this as well as the other thing he has to do!" Talis nodded, "yeah, I'm up to date with that part of the plan myself now. You know that's a jolly good idea Joey, kill two birds with one stone, he can make a start with Stuey and at the same time talk him around and make him feel better! Talking of which, I think you'd better sit yourself down before you fall over and I'll get someone in the galley to bring you something to eat and drink! We'd best say that you've not got quite your sky-legs just yet eh?"

Talis had set himself up with a small bench in the corner of the engineering workshop. Workshop was a bit grand a title though for despite its considerable overall size space on the airship was at a premium. Joey had indeed felt better for something to eat and a strong cup of coffee and he was now stood with Talis at his bench. They were surrounded in the confined space by crates of equipment that he had brought with them from Eunson's labs. "I honestly can't say what the effect will be of activating this device, I asked Eunson but he won't elaborate, to be honest I think it was what he was working on when he was shut down, so it could well be that he's not sure himself. The thing is we can't test it, here on our side, it's not set up for our reality and even if we did know how it performed here, it might not be an indication of what it will do over there!" Joey who was finding that his exasperation level was reached in shorter and shorter time when Talis was trying to explain something, snapped "just tell me what you think it *might* do that could be of some use to me!" A little taken aback the scientist coughed, a throat clearing, awkward little cough, "I think it's a phase-shifter. It could put you out of phase with the human's reality, effectively making you invisible to them!" Quick as a flash Joey saw where he was coming from, "so we could just sit in the plane somewhere after we've landed it and they'd never find us?" Talis nodded, "well not by merely looking, you'd need to get off at the first opportunity before they started sweeping the plane with whatever equipment they might have, something they have might detect you, how can I know? I have to add though that I have no idea how you may interact with your environment, whether you will pass through things or even be able to move at all!" Joey just grunted "great!"

They went up along to the Mess together and had another coffee and as they discussed the device they came to the conclusion that since the whole thing was such a long shot anyway, if it came down to it, being on the aeroplane and being invisible was going to be a hell of a lot easier than trying to explain how they got there. It would be a mighty fine puzzle for the authorities, a ghost plane apparently returning empty after vanishing years ago! They agreed that if it ever came to it that Stuart would need to make sure he couldn't be recognised through the cockpit window should they send up other planes to fly alongside them and to bring them in. If somehow they got away from the Dakota, how the hell he was to get Stuart back home to Lancashire was another thing altogether! He was sure he'd think of something!

Yasil was passing through the Mess and asked if she could join them? They nodded and she fetched a coffee for herself. Talis excused himself and Joey was left alone with her. She sensed his discomfort and put her paw on his and smiled, he was about to speak but she shushed him kindly, "I don't want you to feel embarrassed about last night. I find you very attractive and it's pretty obvious you reciprocate!" He laughed a little nervously and nodded, "thing is we're going to be together for quite some time on this mission, everyone knows everyone else's business anyway on a ship like this so there's no point in trying to pretend nothing's happened and the thing is no one will think anything of it either, so there's no need for you to worry. In fact it will boost your credibility with the guys most likely!" Joey laughed, freely this time and visibly relaxed, she smiled back at him, it was a wonderful smile that seemed to make him melt... Melt? Had he the time for any of this mushy nonsense at the moment? I think not! His sterner side curtly informed him! She was wonderful though, she had such lovely eyes... he realised she was talking to him! "...really quite a stud in fact! How long had it been since the last time you had a proper cuddle?" Now he was flustered again, the truth was he'd never really had much time for that nonsense, bears were nothing like humans with their

obsession with forming inter-gender bonds with each other! He'd had a romp or two in the fields as a youngster when he was in his sixties but since he signed up with the OSS and went on his first mission there'd never been time, he'd never really given it a thought! It had come so out of the blue when he had fallen into Yasil's arms, he had been taken totally by surprise. He realised he was sat looking gormless, as dad would say to Stuart when his internal thought processes were such that he failed to respond as Joey was doing now!
"…erm… erm… a very long time, a very long time indeed! I've been on the other side for so long I sometimes forget I'm a bear!" She finished her coffee and got up from the table, bending slightly to kiss him on the lips, "I'm off duty in an hour, see you back here, or just come to my cabin at bedtime if you like." She smiled and gave him a cheeky wink before turning and walking away, did she wiggle her behind like that when she walked all the time, he wondered?

It took just under three days for the Intrepid to reach the shores of The Barren Continent. The plan was to fly right across it to the human's camp and the aeroplane. It would take a full twenty four hours to cross, the ship being loaded to its absolute maximum weight capacity such was the estimated fuel requirement for the DC3. Of course there was very little information available to the scientists to calculate the fuel consumption as they had such little experience of aviation in terms that humans would understand it to be. The whole concept of powered flight such as that appeared to be way too wasteful of resources the only trade off being speed and speed was so unimportant to them. The plan was to load all their fuel onto the aircraft, they had determined that it would be compatible with the piston engine internal combustion principles the DC3 employed by analysing some of the samples taken from its fuel tanks on earlier missions. The

Intrepid would then wait for several weeks for a supply ship to rendezvous and refuel her for the return trip which was to include a further visit to the centre of the island to install new monitoring equipment. The supply ship was also loaded with a mass of equipment to be used in the setting-up of a two permanently manned bases, one on the shore where they had eventually landed, at the human camp and another at the centre of the continent to study and catalogue in depth the vessels that had come through and to constantly monitor any activity of the phenomena.

Yasil along with Maszla were amongst those who would become basecamp personnel for the first rotation so they were away off the ship now and Joey saw little of Yasil. Indeed with only the airship crew left it seemed empty around The Intrepid. Stuart had been spending as much time as was considered possible with Doctor Treyde the psychologist. Since they had landed and he had been working with him he had at least returned to being much more like his old self, in his behaviour anyway if not his appearance. Indeed it was very difficult now he was up and about with everyone to remember he was a very young cub, well boy in fact, for despite knowing this the evidence of the eyes fooled you. Bears would be having a drink in the evenings and Joey would have to dive in to prevent Stuart being poured a glass of neat spirit! He was constantly having to interrupt conversations as well as the subject strayed into areas his ears should not be listening in!

Such was Joey's concern that he sought out Doctor Treyde and raised the issue with him, he concurred that it was a problem and suggested that from now on Joey stayed in constant company with the boy, as he would have been back in his home. He added that it was also causing considerable changes in the boy's own behaviour since he was no longer smaller than all the adults and since his appearance did not differ either and because no one was looking down on him either in a physical or metaphorical sense he was becoming far more adult in his own behaviour and in how he saw himself in relation to his environment. He laughed then as he went on to say he was even more concerned when the boy was released from his shape-shifted confinement tomorrow and suddenly became a giant to everyone else on the ship and at the base, "I mean he won't even be able to get on board The Intrepid then!" Joey looked startled as he realised that he'd never even thought that far ahead, "where will he be accommodated then?" The Doctor smiled "Don't be concerned work is being done on the human shelter that was left here for him to use, it should only be for one night though anyhow!"

For that was the plan, even as Stuart was seeing the therapist the ground crew were hard at work on the DC3, cleaning the engines out and checking all its systems. Racks of batteries had been carried on The Intrepid adding to her payload and these were being ferried to the aircraft and a small quantity of fuel in barrels. The bulk fuel was to be loaded that evening when the Intrepid would land alongside the DC3 leaving only a small quantity on board for her return to the beach after escorting the DC3 to the edge of the vortex and for any emergencies.

As the Captain of The Intrepid, Admiral Surein and the officers in charge of each task assembled on that final evening, all the reports were positive. The ground crew were delighted with the state of the DC3, it was they said the perfect place to have stored such a machine, it was perfectly dry and there was seldom any wind beyond the slightest of breezes so the mechanics were as good as when it had landed. There was still even a fair amount of air in the tyres which themselves were in good condition and had taken being fully inflated again perfectly well. They had started both engines successfully, the chief engineer had grinned like a fool as he said how sweet they ran and how amazing the raw power of the rotary piston engines was! They had even found it was not necessary to use the replacement lubricating oils they had brought with them for the engines such was there preserved condition, merely to top up the levels in one of the engines a little. They had managed to recondition and refill the batteries on the plane as they had dried out but remained serviceable now. She was ready to fly they reported beaming!

Talis and his team were a lot less confident, they had installed the equipment on board the DC3 and run as many tests as possible. In theory to the best of the available knowledge that they possessed and if the aircraft was able to position itself in the right area of the rising vortex, travelling against its rotation then… it just might work!" The faces of the gathered ensemble fell a little at his report. He shrugged, "what can I say, this has never before been attempted, it should work, there is simply no more that I can say! One thing that will impact on our chances enormously is the radio, have you been able to get that working?" The wireless operator of The Intrepid took his turn now, they had encountered difficulties with the radio set on board the DC3, but having stripped the set down and rebuilt it had returned it to operating condition with some adaptations to use their much smaller replacement components. He had established from the various manuals from the plane that another team had been studying that there was a frequency used by the humans for emergency use. Accordingly he had set the radio on the plane to this and had adapted the radio on The Intrepid to receive and broadcast on this frequency also. He had taken the second headset from the DC3 and made it smaller to enable Joey to use it as well as the one that Stuart would use. Finally he said that having spoken at length with Talis he had made ready a tethered balloon to carry a cable up to several thousand feet to try and keep communication as long as possible as it was well known that the phenomena interfered with radio transmissions.

The scientists from the Eunson labs reported that their monitoring was showing that the vortex was travelling down to Ursa and would reach its lowest point around dawn tomorrow and if it behaved as predicted would only dwell in contact with Ursa for an hour at the most and that it would start to withdraw shortly afterwards.

Admiral Surein, brought the meeting to order as general chatter broke out and a positive buzz filled the Mess, "so it just remains Talis, Doctor" (he faced them each in turn) "for your updates on our guest. How is Stuart? Will he regain his true form when you remove your devices and has his memory been suitably arranged that he will present no threat to us if by some miracle he and Joseph traverse that vortex nightmare?"

Talis spoke first "I am as certain as I am of anything that he will regain his true form almost instantaneously on removal of the dampening field devices. I have no idea how it will affect him physically or mentally, we have no experience to draw on?" He looked to Doctor Treyde and then to the Eunson men. Doctor Treyde took it up "I have worked with the subject for as much as I dared, during this time I have created compartments within his memory that will become locked from his consciousness when a trigger is used. This is a sequence of words which will act as a key turned in the lock to the compartment. The first and deepest compartment contains all of his memories acquired whilst he has been here on Ursa, once locked he will have no knowledge of any of this," he swept his hands widely, "or any of us. The second lock will block every memory of his interaction with Joseph as a living person, this is a real cost as we can have no way of knowing how much of the positive conditioning will remain with him afterwards. His new memory will be that he had a toy bear, which he has imagined that he has had a real relationship with. There are of course dangers with this amount of tampering with the mind, he is however very young, this is an advantage, the mind grows and adapts as a matter of course and I am relatively confident that he will suffer no harm nor will he ever be able to access the locked memories, even if attempts were made to hypnotise him to. I have embedded positive thoughts and attitudes as well which will hopefully aid him in his development."

Admiral Surein thanked the Doctor, "when will these locks be deployed sir? I understand that it has been deemed most unwise to do so until after the boy has carried out his mammoth task of flying the aircraft?" The doctor nodded, "indeed Admiral, he will need all of his knowledge from every source if he is to succeed. Joseph has memorised the keys to lock away the boys memory, when exactly he uses them must be at his discretion. They are just two words, as soon as Stuart hears them the effect will be instantaneous, even should he have to use the words in front of someone and they were to hear and remember the words they are of no value in unlocking his mind. There is an unlocking keyword, I have embedded just in case we have need of Master Wheeler in some unforeseen future! I have provided this key to yourself Admiral for inclusion in the Top Secret File."

The Admiral rose to his feet now, "bears, one and all, I thank you all for your dedication and hard work, what we do here tomorrow could well shape the future of our entire world and even that of the humans in time! I would ask you all to go about your final duties now, and then get some sleep, we have a big day tomorrow. Joseph will you bring the boy to the human shelter please. Talis, Doctor will you join us there please.

Chapter Eighteen

The Miami Belle

The 'Miami Belle'

Stuart was nowhere to be found when Joey went to fetch him from his cabin on The Intrepid, he was supposed to be resting after his last session with the doctor, 'where can the boy be?' He muttered as he almost ran through the Mess and then down the gangplank and away towards the new encampment. It seemed they were having something of an impromptu party there in the centre of the camp where a roaring fire was going and a dozen or so bears were sat around chatting, someone had managed to get some music on as well, 'quite a party!' Joey thought as he scowled, 'probably me and Stuart's wake if the truth be told! Where is that boy!' Curses! He realised that he was looking for an eight year old human, drat! He sighed, it was a very deep sigh, he really was more exhausted than he dared admit even to himself. Then he saw Stuart sat leaning on a table, with an arm around Maszla chatting very intimately with her! He scurried over and demanded "what the blue blazes are you doing Stuart! Can't I turn my back for a minute… Oh no! What have you given him?" He knocked a glass of liquid flying off the table with his paw as Maszla leapt startled to her feet, Stuart just raised a paw, smiled at Joey and then fell slowly backwards off his stool to land in the sand laughing hysterically! Maszla stammered out "it was only the one Joey, I'm so sorry, I forgot!" Joey was beside himself now and he yelled "he's eight years old Maszla! Oh my goodness! What will we do now?"

He staggered back to The Intrepid with Stuart stumbling and leaning heavily on him, somehow maybe in an attempt to stave off a complete mental breakdown, he mused on how funny they must look, virtually identical twins staggering back to camp! He was brought abruptly back to reality as he neared The Intrepid by the doctor rushing to his aid from the large human-sized building. They got Stuart laid down on the large bed inside and the doctor rummaged through his bag for something suitable to give to the now snoring boy.

He made up a drink to give him which would help balance his system and sent out for lots of black coffee! A quick test revealed that the lad had not consumed very much alcohol, his general health and state of mind, not to mention his atoms being squeezed down into his present body were probably a contributory factor for his apparent intoxication the doctor assured what was by now the worried gathering.

So it was that two hours later than originally planned Talis prepared to remove the talisman dampening devices from the boy. Stuart was given a sedative so that he was quite drowsy and calm. Talis unclipped the two devices, flipped them open with a small screwdriver and deactivated them. Nothing happened. They all stood there looking at one another. After half an hour still nothing had happened, Stuart had gone back to sleep, as a bear and was snoring. Joey looked across at Uncle Eustace who was now sat on a chair that had been brought in for him, Joey asked "if he's stuck like this then it's all over?" The elderly bear just pulled his mouth down and raised his eyebrows as he shrugged dejectedly. Talis shrugged as well and pushed his hands even deeper into his white lab-coats pockets, "what would be the point of returning him in his present form? That is if it wasn't impossible for any of us to fly the plane anyway!" Everyone turned to the doctor, in response he went and took Stuart's pulse and looked into his eyes, "this is way beyond my field of expertise, he's quite normal… for a bear that is, I suggest we leave him to sleep and hope for the best?"

Uncle Eustace struggled to get up out of his chair, he growled under his breath and Joey jumped forward offering a paw to his elderly relative. He thanked his nephew, adding "I for one am off to my bed, nothing I can do here. He either will or won't return to his normal form. We will deal with either consequence tomorrow. We have other work to do regardless of what happens to this boy." With that he shuffled out, for the first time since the start of the mission looking old and frail once more.

Joey agreed he would stay with Stuart and the others left, he went outside with Talis and stood for a while marvelling at the spectacle of the stars overhead the barren land, the crystal clear, cleanest of air seeming to make them feel close enough to reach out and touch. Talis patted his shoulder "see you in the morning old friend, I can stay with the boy if you have somewhere else you'd rather be?" He smiled his wide cubbish grin and winked. Joey smiled weakly in response, "no I feel this is my place tonight, but thank you my friend." He reached out a paw in friendship only to have it brushed aside as Talis put his arms around him and hugged him. With a final grim smile they parted company.

Joey pushed the big door over and crawled under the covers that they'd put over the sleeping boy as the night's coolness began to replace the dry heat of the daytime inside the cabin. He pondered over what tomorrow would bring, if Stuart was stuck then that was it, he would have to remain in Ursa. Would there always be that risk of him returning to his true size? If time went on for, well months, for years? He could almost hear Talis's reply, most likely of how could he know? In some ways he thought it would be a hell of a lot safer for him personally if the boy didn't return to his full size, 'my life expectancy would improve dramatically!' He thought wryly.

Despite his exhaustion Joey couldn't get to sleep, he rolled about on the big human sized bed, his mind unable to release him to the rest he so badly needed. Eventually he succumbed without being aware, to him he was fighting with the controls of the DC3 along with Stuart as it dived out of control screaming downwards, hurtling straight towards the Wheelers house… He awoke startled and breathless. He sat up on the bed, reaching for some water which he gulped down clumsily, before settling back down into the bed. He tried to shut out the images and feelings from his dream, it was as a real to him as any other experience at that moment though, the sensations, the sounds but most of all the fear! However he tried to rationalise, to reason things through, at his core he was scared, no that wasn't adequate, he was terrified!

In the morning there was no change. They assembled for a meeting to discuss the situation, which went around in circles between allowing more time for things to happen to the boy, through to setting off at once on the second part of the mission. The scientists provided their latest readings on the situation of the vortex, it was progressing as they expected through its cycle but was moving somewhat more slowly than predicted. They gave a deadline of noon the following day before it would be beyond reach and any attempt would be pointless to try to fly the aircraft back through until the next occurrence, which could be weeks or even months. The doctor suggested that it may be the boy's mind that was somehow holding him in his present form and agreed to have a session with him to explore this possibility.

At lunchtime the doctor came with Stuart to see Joey, he suggested that they go and run through everything in the DC3 in the hope that by tomorrow Stuart would be back to normal size and able to operate the controls. He said he felt that it might help reinforce the suggestions he had tried to implant into the boys mind to try and aid his metamorphosis!

The two friends walked the quarter of a mile through the dunes to the vast flat plain and there in the shimmering heat stood the colossal, shining silver aircraft. Stuart stopped in his tracks as it came into view and he beheld it for the first time, "wow! Golly! WOW! She's blummin enormous!" With that he ran ahead at full tilt to stand beneath the nose of the giant aircraft. When Joey caught him up he was stood with his hands on his hips, same Stuart as ever he thought as he recognised the stance, he was leaning back looking up at the image of a scantily clad lady that was painted beneath the cockpit, in the style of pictures the American bombers had been adorned with. In further homage to them she was named 'The Miami Belle.' Joey's guess that the skeletons they had buried would have been ex-airforce men seemed even more likely now as he looked up at the plane, he put his hand on his young friends shoulder. "Come on Stuey, we can climb up the ladder and go aboard her."

Stuart didn't need any encouragement as he ran around, skipping up and down to the door at the rear where a bear-sized ladder was leaning. He was up the ladder, along the fuselage and climbing into the pilot's seat in no time. Joey puffed his way up to the front of the aircraft behind him to find Stuart sat there in the pilot's seat, a little teddy bear, hopelessly small, with no chance whatsoever of reaching, never mind operating any of the controls! He was staring dejectedly at the array of dials, with all of his enthusiasm drained out of him. "Don't suppose I'll ever get to fly her, or any plane ever now, or see home again, or mum or dad, or Lucy, or grandpa, or grandma. I'll just be stuck here, like this... forever!" His last cry of *forever* was part shout, part cry as he threw himself off the seat, stumbling and falling roughly, he picked himself up and hurtled back down the plane to the door with Joey running after him calling out, "wait, wait Stuart, we can still make it yet, we've got until tomorrow…" But the boy was already in the doorway, he tried to go down the ladder front first, lost his grip, tried to spin around to grip the ladder facing it, lost his footing and fell. He landed brutally hard, face down in the sand and lay there motionless. Some of the ground crew had seen and ran to his aid, they gently rolled him over and were brushing sand away off the fur on his face and from round his mouth by the time Joey joined them. One of them looked up at him "I think he's just winded, he's breathing okay, nothing feels like it's broken."

They sat him up and he opened his eyes, tears welled up as he looked around, taking in the bears faces and the giant aeroplane looming up above them. The tears streaked through the remaining sand on his fur as he leapt up, shrugging off the hands that were trying to assist him. Joey put his hands on Stuart's shoulders, he looked into his young friends eyes, they were wide and blazing, but there was something else, he seemed to be literally seething with rage, no it was more that, he was shimmering? He started to say "It'll be okay St…" but Stuart shoved him in a furious outburst of anger, shoved him so hard that he was sent sprawling backwards onto the sand! One of the ground crew, reached out to him to try and calm him but he rounded on him and knocked him flying with a right-hook before running away from them back in the direction of the beach. The other ground crew bear helped Joey up, "shall we go after him?" Joey shook his head, "leave him be, are you okay?" He asked the bear sat on the sand next to them, who was rubbing his jaw.

Joey strolled aimlessly back towards the camp, they were in a fine pickle and no mistaking, he thought to himself. He found the 'boy in a bear's body' sat despondently near the edge of the sea on a slightly raised hump of sand. He was staring sightlessly out at the vastness of the ocean which was flat, dead calm and still, it lapped gently at the wasteland's shore. He sat down beside him and looked sideways at him, at his own image, the form he had occupied in his time on his second mission to earth. The boy's tears had stopped but there was an emptiness about him now, that spark of the Stuart of old that had burned so bright when the lad beheld the DC3 had burnt itself out again as he'd sat there in the cockpit and cold, harsh reality had wrapped its dampening blanket of doom around him once more.

He pondered on what he thought he'd seen in the boy's face as his anger burnt brightly earlier, was it the face of the boy he'd seen, that face of a devil that the little blighter had when he was in one of his full blown paddy's? Had his anger been able to trigger something, act as a catalyst? What if he could make him really angry, would it cause him to flip back? What could he do to him? Hmm… a bloody good hiding would be a start he thought, for all the times he treated me so badly! He smirked to himself at the thought. Stuart caught the expression on his face, "so you think this is funny do you?" With that he shoved at Joey, but he wasn't quick enough as he dodged the shove and having put all his spite into it Stuart now fell into the sand… "why you little sod…" he started but Joey had spun around and put his boot on Stuart's backside and gave him an almighty shove-cum-kick which sent him sprawling and rolling off the little sandbank right down and splashing face first into the sea! He was furious, as he rolled around flailing in the water trying to get up, spitting water and sand and uttering terrible curses. Joey scampered down to the water's edge and reached out a paw to help, Stuart grabbed it fiercely and pulled himself upright only to be met with a beautifully timed right-cross which connected with his chin and sent him flying backwards into the deeper water where he went right under. He came up coughing, spluttering and fighting, he flew at Joey and caught him at the edge of the water and sent him sprawling onto his back as he landed on top of him at the water's edge, he started to rain blows down onto him only to be met with a solid punch to the side of his head which sent him rolling off Joey to his side. Joey leapt up and put his foot on the boy's chest and pushed down hard, "how do you like it you lousy rotten little sod? Getting a taste of your own medicine eh?" He panted the words out a the boy, who fumed and spat vile words back at him, words he'd never heard, words that made no sense… Joey released his foot from the boy's chest, Stuart was foaming at the mouth, his eyes were rolling and his body was convulsing as he went into some sort of fit! His body seemed to be shimmering again, swelling… Joey stood back, he was terrified now that he had miscalculated, that his attempt to make the lad angry had caused him to have a fit, that he would die here, now in front of him on this truly God forsaken beach, on an alien world… but no, he had been right, he stood in awe and with tears of relief streaming down his face as he watched the familiar form of Master Stuart Wheeler re-materialise before his very eyes.

The boy lay perfectly still for a while, Joey edged forward and peered anxiously at him, he was breathing thank goodness! Presently he stirred and leaned up on his elbow, he rubbed sand away from around his eyes and looked blinking at his once more *little* friend, he rubbed his jaw ruefully and smiled at him, "nice punch matey!" And with that he prodded Joey in the chest with his finger so that he fell back to land sat on his bum on the sand! Joey laughed with him "I'd better go and get you some under-crackers lad!" With that he got up and left the boy, who suddenly realised he was sat stark naked on the beach, to gather his wits!

He returned a few minutes later carrying the large bundle of material that was the pair of underpants that the bears had made up ready for him. Stuart quickly pulled them on as he furtively looked around to see if anyone could see them! "Sorry I couldn't carry the rest but they've made you some pants and a Tee-shirt as well, all guesswork of course size-wise! Shoes we couldn't manage I'm afraid so you'll have to go bear-foot!" He laughed, "you've had plenty of practice lately!"

Stuart nimbly skirted around the back of the Intrepid and into the human size shack, where he quickly dressed. Joey in the meantime organised for Stuart's 'teddy-bear' which was now lying on the beach where it had been shed like a shell, to be carried up to the workshop on The Intrepid as he knew that Talis had work to do on it from their lengthy discussion and planning meetings with his Uncle. He would be needing it himself if they made it back to Stuart's world and once Talis was finished with it, it was to be carried to the DC3 to accompany them.

Stuart had of course been spotted as he tried to creep back, giants are difficult to miss! Soon the team of bears were all there with them, there was a tremendous buzz of excitement now as the mission was definitely back on! After the hubbub died down Talis suggested that they go at once to the DC3 and spend the rest of the day going over the controls, the operation of them and the methodology of flying the enormous contraption! Stuart couldn't wait and they were very soon sat back in the cockpit along with Talis and two of his technicians.

There was a major problem, one they had anticipated in that because he was only eight, even though he was a tall lad for his age, there was no way that he could sit up enough to see anything out of the windscreen and even touch the rudder pedals! Now they had the boy sat in the seat they set to with the bits and pieces they had ready to fabricate the necessary extensions and padding to lift the boy up high enough to see and still be able to operate the pedals. It quickly became obvious that he was not going to manage in his bare feet! Talis said that there were some human boots that they'd found that they could perhaps alter, cut down to Stuarts size and he dispatched one of the technicians to attend to it at once with a template he had drawn up from the lads feet, to take with the boots to the workshop on The Intrepid. He thought it better not to mention that the boots were found on the bony feet of the pilot in the cabin!

The training went well, Stuart was a very willing pupil and Joey had been studying the flight manual for some time now with the technicians help. It was decided that they should go through the entire sequence up to the point of taking off as a practice run. Stuart was beside himself with excitement as they went through the start-up drill for the engines and step by step from the manual they proceeded until… 'contact!' Stuart held down the starter… The starboard engine started to whine as the giant propeller began to spin… slowly at first then quicker and with a splutter and a bang the engine fired up into life, Stuart under Joey and Talis's watchful eyes, set the throttle and mixture controls to let the engine idle as they repeated the procedure with the port engine. There they sat with the two giant rotary engines ticking over, the DC3 brought back to life once more, poised ready to take the air beneath her wings and lift herself off the sandy ground into the skies…

They proceeded to test the controls, turn the wheel and watch the ailerons move, pull the stick and watch the elevators… check! The rudder pedals also steered the jockey wheel that the plane 'rested her butt on the ground with' as Talis put it, so she could be steered whilst the plane was in contact with the ground until take-off. That was the hardest part of the training they were trying to impart to Stuart... the configuration of the undercarriage in common with aircraft of the DC3's era sat with their noses up resting on the big wheels beneath each wing and the single wheel beneath the tail-plane. This meant that to take off the pilot had to gain enough speed for the tail to lift up off the runway so the plane was running just on its two main wheels, sounds easy but... to do this he has let the stick forwards as the plane's nose pitches downwards, which is counterintuitive when all you want to do is go up off the ground! Pulling the stick back hard whilst the rear wheel was on the ground would be a seriously bad idea as the aircraft could become unstable if it pivoted about on that one small wheel.

Everything was tested and all the indicators for the engines were showing normal so Talis shouted down 'chocks away!' From the little opening window, as it said to do in the manual! Now the aircraft was free and without the brakes applied which Stuart was having difficulty reaching with his bare feet and the parking brake off, she started to roll forwards slowly. They were ready though and Stuart felt how she turned as he pushed his feet down one or the other, it was straightforward too, left foot down she turns left, right foot she turns right. They taxied her up and down on the vast open expanse until everyone was happy with things, Talis and Joey pushed the brakes as hard as they could from the co-pilots seat and they throttled her right back to bring her to a halt.

Talis went and rummaged around at the back of the cockpit before emerging with a blue and white peaked pilot's cap. He handed it with both paws to Stuart, who excitedly placed it on his head. Naturally it came right down over his eyes, but with help from the tech, and some wadding in no time it was sat up on his head! He sat in the pilot's seat beaming like a simpleton, Joey sat in the co-pilot's seat grinning back at him, although it was just as well Stuart had no idea what his little pal was thinking, for it was 'this time tomorrow we'll both be dead! I only hope it happens quickly when it comes!'

There was only one thing left to check now and with his hat now resting in a reasonably stable manner on his head, Stuart placed the headphones over the top of it. Talis nodded to Joey, "perfect, they will hold his hat on nicely and help to obscure his features a little, erm… maybe these will help as well?" He clambered up to reach a pair of Ray Ban sunglasses, which he passed over to Stuart, they were too big for his head of course, but with the arms pushed inside the headset they were steady enough on his nose. "Excellent!" Joey exclaimed, "he looks the part of a pilot, all we have to do is pray to whatever Gods we can dream up that he can fly it like one!"

The radio worked perfectly although it was decided that Joey would use the microphone, held in both paws, leaving Stuart free to concentrate on flying. Talis had re-jigged the co-pilots headset to enable Joey to use it, as he was unable to support its weight on his head he had fixed it to the seat so the earpieces were either side of his head!

They switched off everything and shut down the DC3, Stuart slid down the full size ladder that they had put back in place and patted the side of the aircraft lovingly, "I can do this Joey, I know I can. If they've fixed up the boots for me, we'll be fine. Don't worry little pal, I'll get us home!" Joey smiled, it was great to have Stuart back, the real lad he knew so well. He just wished that his confidence had some basis in reality, which he feared it did not.

He was quite content to travel back to base camp in Stuart's arms, to save his legs! 'I suppose there's a chance we might make it?' He allowed himself to think. It was a tragedy he thought that if by some miracle they actually did make it, that he would at the very first opportunity he could do so, have to take it all away from him, the memory of it anyhow and not just the memory of the flight either, first the memory of Ursa and his time there, but then and most terrible of all his memories of him, of his 'little pal.' He would be replaced with the implanted memory version of him, Joey the stuffed toy that Uncle Arnold had given him as a baby, that he had imagined having all sorts of adventures with as he grew up… It was terrible, it was a truly horrible thing that he had to do and do it to the person that he loved more than any soul in either world.

The Mess of The Intrepid had to be forsaken for the farewell dinner that night, the guest of honour simply was unable to fit on board her now! So they all dined out under the stars to the side of the airship. Although there was no alcohol consumed, for obvious reasons, there were toasts made with fruit juice and water! Uncle Eustace had to make a grand speech of course, congratulating everyone on all their efforts and hard work and saying how he had every confidence that everything would go well and that our valiant young aviator would earn his wings on the morrow! "There remains just one thing left for me to do… Would you come forward *Captain* Wheeler?" Stuart who was sat on the ground, there being no chair big enough for him, got up and went round to the head of the bears table, Talis was stood next to a large sheet-covered object which he then swept the sheet off to reveal the flying boots that his tech's had cut down! Uncle Eustace went on, "We present you with these fine boots!" To the accompanying applause of the party Stuart gingerly went round to the boots which were just about as tall as Talis, he had to watch where he trod as the sand was quite soft here and he could cause chaos for his much smaller companions if he wasn't careful!

He pulled the boots onto his feet and grinned, "why thank you! They fit fine! And I'd like to thank you all myself, for doing so much to get me home, I'll never forget you all and your kindness to me. I just wish that everyone back home was as nice to each other as you are my lovely little friends." Joey sighed deeply as he watched Talis and Maszla also exchange knowing looks, even Admiral Surein held his chin in his hand and shook his head sadly. Stuart was unaware though as everyone else was busy singing *'for he's a jolly good fellow!'*

Joey took some time after the meal to seek out Yasil, she was looking for him too and soon they were sat holding hands talking together. They could only manage half an hour or so before they had to part, as she said she would have to be at her station early in the morning, she added sadly that she most likely wouldn't be able to see him tomorrow before he went, so this was goodbye… They kissed in each other's arms, beneath what was by now an unbelievably bright canopy of stars, she wished him luck and they parted, vowing that they **would** soon be together again, both choking back the tears and far from certain that they would in reality ever see each other again.

Lastly before turning in Joey reported to Talis, as he'd agreed to do earlier. Talis was still working on the teddy bear when Joey arrived at the workshop, "what are you doing to the thing?" He asked somewhat alarmed as he found Talis up to his elbows inside the opened-up body of the bear. "Don't worry I'll have him all sewn up in another half an hour, be as good as new! We've decided to put a remote recall portal device in 'him' it has a SW receiver built in and the plan is that we fly a drone up into the centre of a vortex disturbance as high as we can then signal it if we need to!" Joey looked sceptical, "would that have any chance of actually working?" Talis laughed, "probably about as much chance as flying a human sized aeroplane up through it the wrong way has?" They laughed, Joey somewhat less heartily than Talis, who caught the apprehension in his friend, "we've got one up now at twenty thousand feet and its picked-up radio transmissions from The USA intermittently, so it stands a good chance of working. We'll need it up there tomorrow to try and keep in communication with you as you fly around it and cross over." Joey just responded with "humph! If we don't disintegrate or crash first!"

Talis shrugged, "we've tried to allow for everything we know of…" he said trying to be positive. He pulled his hands from out of the bear's torso and went over to his bench and returned with one of the talisman devices, "here, this is your own recall device and I've incorporated Eunson's latest bit of jiggery-pokery into it as well!" Joey peered at the device he now held in his paws, "the invisibility, phase-shifting gadget?" "Precisely my friend, you just press it hard in the centre to activate… there's two settings, with the dial like so, downwards…" he took the device back off Joey and turned the centre of the talisman, "you operate the phase shifter, like this, upwards and you will open a recall portal! Put it round your neck now and never take it off, it will pass with you when you merge with your little friend over there on the other side! If my guesswork is good… it won't be visible! If it is you'll have to keep it up your jumper!"

Joey was about to say goodnight to Talis when he remembered something, he was wearing a small bag on a strap across his shoulder, "will this be okay to take with me? I won't be bringing it back through the portal or anything…"

Talis shrugged intrigued "it's as much chance as anything else has of being invisible when you're wearing it if that what's you mean, nothing I need to know about is it?" Joey just laughed but didn't elaborate and the friends parted company and he made his way back to the human shack, it was quiet now and deserted everyone was turning-in early. Stuart was already there getting ready for bed, the doctor was just leaving having left them each with a little help to make sure they got at least some sleep, Joey with two small sleeping tablets, Stuart with a small bottle full of bear size pills!

The two friends climbed into bed, back to their normal relative sizes once more, it was on the surface the same as any of the other nights they had snuggled down together to sleep so many times before over the last eight years. What happened in the morning would determine whether or not they did so ever again.

The Worrell Gazette

Chapter Nineteen: In the Newspaper   Dateline: 18th June 1958

Eight year old local boy discovered on flight bound for America ten minutes before take-off!

Worrell schoolboy Stuart Wheeler was found by cabin-crew on board a B.O.A.C. Comet Four bound for Idlewild Airport, New York as it sat on the apron at Manchester's Ringway Airport yesterday. He was unaccompanied when he was found asleep on a seat at the rear of the passenger compartment apart from by his teddy bear 'Canadian Joey.' When asked where he was going he was reported to have told Captain Matthew Riley 'to see my Uncle Arnold in America Sir!' It is believed that the boy had travelled from his parent's house in Worrell by foot, train and bus to the airport and had somehow managed to gain access to the flight-side tarmac without a ticket or any other documentation. He was re-united at the airport with his frantic parents after being missing for some thirty-six hours from his Stirling Street home. A Police spokesman said that they were just delighted that the story had a happy ending and that they had been informed by the boy's parents that he had recently recovered from a spell in hospital suffering the effects of a head injury and they believed this to be responsible for his out-of-character behaviour. The boy reportedly had no memory of how he had come to be asleep on the aircraft.

Vancouver Bridge Collapse

A bridge being constructed to span the Burrard inlet connecting eastern and northern sections of Vancouver collapsed yesterday killing 59 worker who fell 175 feet at 3.40pm.

Mum had told Stuart that Emily would like to see him, so would he call around on his way home from school, the old lady had been very worried finding out that he was missing when his mum had called at her door the other day frantically trying to find him. She had asked Stuart's dad when he'd telephoned her to let her know that the boy had been found safe and sound if he'd call round when he had chance.

So there he was stood at the door when Emily opened it, she stooped down and gave the boy a hug, "it's so good to see you Stuart, are you alright? I was so worried about you." He just nodded and smiled "I'm fine thanks, can't think what got into me! Must've been that bang on the noggin that did it, like the doc said!" They sat in the snug and had a cup of tea, Emily sensing a change in the boy asked "how's Joey, what did he make of your little adventure?" She wondered why he'd let Stuart get so far from home without intervening. "Oh he's fine, he's in my bag." Emily was more puzzled still now, "would you mind if I had a word with him Stuart?" Stuart laughed, she was a queer old bird he thought to himself as he unbuckled his bag, what the heck though eh? He handed his teddy bear over to Emily, "here you are Emily. Can I have another biscuit please?" She smiled, pleased that he was remembering his manners, "of course you may." She turned to Joey as she sat him on her knee, "and what have you to say for yourself Mr.Bear letting Stuart get all that way from home and onto an aeroplane like that, why he could have ended up in America if he hadn't been spotted before the passengers got on! Why ever didn't you stop him?"

Stuart laughed as he dunked his biscuit, "you're really funny Emily, you're such a good sport! Talking to him like I do. He *is* only a teddy bear though, he's not really alive or anything, you do know that?" Emily nodded, wondering just what exactly had taken place. Stuart swilled down the last of his tea. "Stuart, would you do me a great favour and sweep up the leaves that have collected around the back door and put them on the compost heap? You'll find a barrow and shovel and a brush in the shed. It would be a tremendous help for me if you did. Your mum said you wouldn't mind!" Emily smiled sweetly, as if butter wouldn't melt in her mouth, even though the last bit was a complete fib! Although she mitigated her conscience by telling herself that she was sure June would be more than happy for the boy to lend a helping-hand to an old lady! He was indeed more than willing, he was a helpful lad and he was ever so fond of his elderly friend.

Once he was outside, Emily went quickly back into the snug, closing the door behind her and then picked Joey up off her chair where she'd left him. "What's happened?" She asked him urgently. The little bear shrugged and sighed deeply, "you'd better sit down Emily I have some tale to tell you!"

Joey realised that he had insufficient time to give Emily all the details, so much had happened! So he sketched quickly through the events, following Stuart being sucked through back to Ursa with him and the desperate gamble they had undertaken to return him home and how it had been conditional on all his memories of Ursa being locked away and worst of all… that he would have to forget that Joey had ever been alive! "You see Emily I should already have returned by now, I activated the mental blocks the hypnotist had established in his mind once I'd got him safely back to Manchester, oh the tale I could tell you of how I got him there! If only I had the time. He thinks of me now as just his teddy bear, he believes that everything we ever did together was just something he made up in his head a game, merely his own imagination at work and it has to remain that way. I didn't tell anyone back home that you and Lucy know as much as you do, well anything really, the only other person who knew was Talis and he'll keep quiet too but the authorities are running scared so I had no idea what they might try to do." Emily looked a little shocked on hearing this! Joey continued quickly "oh no…really Emily you're both completely safe, they'd never do you any real harm, at least I don't think so…hmm… anyway I kept it all from them. I would ask you to talk to Lucy please though, try and impress on her how vitally important it is that she never tells a living soul what she witnessed, the safety of my entire world could rest on her silence!" Joey paused a moment as Emily nodded taking in the gravity of what she had been told.

He smiled and added, "besides I just had to see you, one last time, you have been such a good friend to me and to my world, I wanted to thank you and for you to know for sure that it had all been real! One other thing I have to ask is that you look out for the lad." He brushed away a tear as he looked pleadingly up at the old lady, he hesitated a moment then added, "I really shouldn't do this, but..." he put his hand inside his jumper and produced a small locket, instinctively Emily's hand went to her lapel… where the brooch had resided for many years… "I'm sorry Emily I purloined this last time I saw you, on the bus in fact! Sorry! I had Talis install a mini-portal activator inside it, he was careful not to damage it, you need to press a point into the little hole he has made in the back and it will activate. It will only be big enough for a message…" Emily took the brooch and examined it, it was a fine piece of Victorian craftsmanship, she turned it in her fingers, it was undamaged as Joey had said, in fact it looked brighter and cleaner than she had ever seen it! "It was my mothers, I was so upset as I thought I'd lost it! I should be very cross with you!" She poked him playfully with her thin finger, he chuckled, "you will let me know if the boy's ever in trouble won't you Emily?" She smiled, "of course I will, in fact I'll keep you up to date with his progress for just as long as I can."

She sat back in her chair and breathed out a deep sigh, she stared blankly into the distance for a moment or two as she assimilated all this new information, she looked down as she returned to the moment at the little bear who was watching her intently… "it must be heart-breaking for you Joey" she gave him a little squeeze, "but you have someone waiting for you now you say? A lady friend? She will help you to carry on my little friend and you can rest assured that for however many years God spares me I will do all I can for our Stuart." Joey sighed in relief that he had accomplished his goals, he smiled up at her then rested his paw on her chest and following some crazy impulsive notion, without really knowing why… he willed some of his energy to flow out into her, he had absolutely no idea if such a thing was feasible, or if it could possibly have any beneficial effect on Emily but somehow he felt that he wanted to do something, anything he could to see that she was there for Stuart as long as possible, surely it was worth a go? After the multitude of other impossible things he had witnessed that he didn't understand why shouldn't it work? Emily watched him somewhat startled as she felt a warm tingling glow spread out from her chest throughout her body, she looked down at him and he smiled back up at her. She was about to say something to him about it when out of the blue he asked her "we often wondered why you never used the splinter of doorframe to re-open the portal when Stuart disappeared?" he chuckled, "it would have made things so much easier for me to get him back here!" Forgetting what she had been about to say Emily replied instead "oh did I never say that it burnt up the last time I received a message from Talis?"

The little bear was rummaging in the bag he'd had over his shoulder as he replied distractedly "oh right…" he sighed and shrugged as he produced a small intricately carved wooden statue of The Buddha from his bag, "would you give this to Stuart for me, of course he can never know it came from me but I would like him to have it anyway." He passed it to her quite reverently and with such great care that she could tell how precious it was to him.

"There's just one more thing Emily…" he hesitated and looked around the room, "this sounds silly really, but can I whisper it to you?" The old lady smiled, "been a long time since a fella whispered in my ear!" She chuckled as she leant her head down to make it easier for him to do so.

She started to say something in response to Joey's whispered request… "so I should put this in a letter and leave it with my solicitor and…" when they both looked up sharply as they heard the back door bang shut and the sound of Stuart whistling away as he came into the kitchen. Joey sprang up and hopped down onto the floor, he looked up at Emily one last time his hand hovering over his chest. He seemed to be thinking as he frowned momentarily, then he drew himself up to his full height and bowed formally, blew her a kiss and called "farewell Emily!" Then he banged his fist into his chest and in a flash of energy was gone, the empty form of the teddy bear falling lifelessly to the floor.

It had been just in time as Stuart had tapped a little knock on the door and then entered Emily's snug a moment or two later. Emily apologised saying that she had just dropped Joey accidentally, he just shrugged and said he'd have to get home, he'd done the leaves, weren't that many, wrong time of year really for that! He'd then picked the bear up and was on his way. She watched the little lad as he strolled off down her garden path, he didn't seem as little as she remembered him, he seemed to have grown up somehow. She felt tears rolling down her face so she pushed the door shut so he wouldn't see her crying and wonder why. She leant for a moment against the closed door and sighed, it had been a wonderful adventure, an amazing, incredible, impossible adventure! Somehow it made absolutely anything seem possible now! After what she had witnessed anything *must* be a possibility surely? She returned to her snug and lifted down her silver framed picture of Henry, "who knows my love, maybe we will be together in the end after all?" She ran her finger down the side of the face in the photograph, before kissing the glass. She sat down heavily into her chair holding the frame to her heart and cried herself to sleep.

Epilogue

dateline: 2014

Oliver Wheeler bounced up and down on the seat of his granddad's van, he held his teddy bear up to the side window to let him look out at the countryside that was gently floating past them. They were out for a leisurely drive together in his granddad's much cherished dark green, little 1967 Austin A35 van. Stuart Wheeler looked over at his joyful little grandson and smiled, he felt happy. Oliver's arrival five years ago had changed Stuart's life completely, then he was becoming jaded, he'd been recently retired from a hectic and exciting career as a foreign correspondent and journalist, he'd been kicking his heels unable to find direction or meaning to his life any longer. Oliver's arrival had galvanised him, he'd joined the local gym (at O.A.P. rates too!), reverted to being a vegetarian and had generally started to look after himself better, or as Yvette had succinctly put it "maintenant 'e wants to leeve forever!!"

Yvette was nevertheless delighted at the turnaround in Stuart's demeanour, his descent into becoming a grumpy old curmudgeon had started to become wearisome. Yvette was the love of his life, he'd courted her when he was with the BBC, working in Paris, she was working at *Libération* at that time and they'd had a whirlwind romance, although it was a number of years on before their worlds were synchronised enough to facilitate any thoughts of marriage. Somehow they'd managed to find the time to have a baby, although only the once and their son Gregoire grew up being a very well-travelled young fellow! Stuart had readily agreed to the choice of name as he could shorten it to Greg! Naturally Yvette was less inclined to do so.

Oliver loved to hear his grandma say his name, for to her he was Oliverre... 'say it again grandma, say it again...' for although she had lived continuously now in England for over twenty years she had never lost her accent, she was actually perfectly capable of sounding as British as Stuart if she felt like it, but as she put it… 'mais porquoi?'

Stuart blipped the throttle a little and eased the long gear stick across to select third as they entered a bend, then he powered the tiny old van around the bend to the burble of the diminutive 848cc 'A' series engine. He loved driving the old van, it was the van derivative of the car his dad had driven all those years ago when he wasn't much bigger than Olly! Now it was he himself that would be experiencing pretty much the same view his dad would have enjoyed, looking down the beautiful curve of the short, bulbous bonnet and wings, the centre of the bonnet complete with its wonderful chrome 'flying A' sign. He still vividly remembered the view his grandson was now experiencing from the passenger seat, as Olly looked up at him now in the driver's seat, where his dad had sat, although he'd no doubt have been most likely smoking one of his bloody Senior Services, those deadly white sticks that had eventually robbed him of that wonderful, jovial man a few months after his fifty-third birthday…

He found himself whistling…'Pretty Baby' the old Al Jolson song, it was something he'd picked up when riding in the car with his dad, he'd often have whistled it or sang a few bars of it or some other tune from his youth. Sometimes his mum would've joined in too and they'd have sung together… *'California here I come, right back where I started from, there's bowers of flowers that bloom in the spring…'* or any other one of the dozens of tunes they both knew.

Olly was trying to whistle along with him, he laughed with him as he struggled, "keep trying, you'll get the hang of it Olly!" He encouraged him, wondering if he'd get infected with the tune too and pass it on again himself one day? He wiped away a tear that had welled up as he thought about his dad, he was never far from his thoughts even after all those years and he was always present in his heart. He made himself smile and be happy to be thinking of his dad instead of maudlin and spontaneously burst into song…

Everybody loves a baby, that's why I'm in love with you…
Pretty baby… pretty baby,
And I'd like to meet your sister, brother, dad and mother too
Pretty baby… pretty baby,
Oh I want a lovin' baby and it might as well be you…
Pretty baby of mine… #

Olly chuckled and laughed as he sang and he spent the next ten minutes of the journey trying to learn the words!

They were on their way back from visiting 'nana-June' as Olly called her, of course she was really his great-grandmother but for a five year old the distinction was largely irrelevant. His mum was eight-five now and still lived at number twenty-three Stirling Street, where he had grown up. It was wonderful to return there, for whenever he called around the house was full of happy memories for him. Of course it was also sad that his dad wasn't there anymore but he felt almost as if he was or at least that he should be as not much had changed over the years of his absence, his mum stubbornly resisting any suggestions of modernising the place, all she would say was that it had served her well just the way it was all those years and there was no reason why it wouldn't 'see her out!'

She had been out on the front drive washing her little dark green Toyota Starlet when they'd arrived earlier on, she had replaced the car since his dad had died, twice in fact but always they had to be dark green! She was always glad to see him and of course delighted to see one of her four great-grandkids, for all his love for her though he had never felt the close bond with her that he'd felt with his dad or his grandpa or even (although he felt guilty admitting it even to himself) with Emily.

His mum had never had another relationship after his dad had died, she had married for life, 'that was how it was in my day' she'd say and to all intents and purposes she still considered herself to be married. She still wore her wedding and engagement rings, she had once declared to him that 'your dad was the only man I ever went with, or ever will!' She often went to his grave and sat talking to him, in a way he'd never left her he supposed, his persona surviving within her own mind and personality. It obviously worked for her as she had never really changed, she seemed to just get on with life, just accepting it as it was and not wishing it away on things that could never be.

She obviously was aware of his dad's absence though as a few years back she had commented that it was thirty years since he had died, longer than they had been married, their silver anniversary had been as far as they got on the major marriage milestones front.

Stuart wasn't at all surprised that his thoughts kept creeping back to his dad, visiting his old home always had that effect comforting though being there was, he caressed the black plastic steering wheel, absent mindedly running his fingers over the indented ridges on its back, remembering sitting on his dad's knee doing the same thing when they were on Southport beach. His fingers ran across the centre spoke and returning from his reverie to the present moment, his thumb couldn't resist pressing the Austin emblem in the centre…

peep-peep!! Olly chuckled, then demanded… "again!" *peep-peep!!*

Stuart's eyes were drawn to the tiny carved figure of Buddha that was Blu-tacked onto the centre of the green metal dashboard, he had put it there as a reminder to himself of the person he should strive to be. It was barely a couple of centimetres tall but the carving was so incredibly intricate you could almost believe it was a real person that had been miniaturised. Both he and Yvette had found some resonance with Buddhism having seen the tragic consequences of religious fanaticism and dogma all around the world in their jobs. They both felt that the simple and pure teaching of The Buddha had a lot to say about how we should try to live and treat each other.

He turned on the radio as it was approaching eleven o'clock, he still liked to keep abreast of the news and in moments the ever so familiar sound of 'the pips' on Radio 4 sounded out. It was the usual roundup of woe and disaster, in fact he was giving it scant attention, lost as he was in the moment… driving with his grandson, but one item caught his attention, it was the announcement of the death of an elder stateswoman, Lady Jessica Urquhart who had been an Ambassador and U.N. delegate. There was a long list of her achievements and some accolades from a few of her former colleagues. He had met her himself once on an assignment in New York, she had made a lasting impression on him he recalled, there had been something special about her which he had never quite been able to put his finger on… what was it that she had said to him? They had sat and had a drink after his interview, she was the most engaging of people… that was it, she'd said something along the lines of 'we all have gifts and it is our duty to do what we can to use those gifts to make the world a better place.' He remembered he'd quipped 'we can't all be

U.N. Ambassadors!' She'd smile patiently before adding "No that's very true Stuart, but even our everyday actions can affect the course of history, each little act of kindness, each time we hold out our hand to offer support or friendship, why even a single smile can change an outcome, create a singular event, just as a flake of snow drifting down a mountainside might land in just the right place to start an avalanche? For what is an avalanche but a very large number of snowflakes combined together? Yet look at its force once they do combine…"

She had been a very wise woman for sure and he felt a real sorrow now for her demise. It also had the effect of making him want to do something, something he'd been pondering for a while but hadn't been able to reach activation energy over. He'd increasingly become involved over the last few years with the local Green party and had also become an activist in local environmental groups, well Oliver needed a decent world to grow up in didn't he?

He felt that for all his investigative work and seeking of truth in his long career as a journalist, that he hadn't done anything particularly significant to aid this… his new cause. True no one could ever know what might have been if he hadn't exposed the things he had, whether history would have moved in a different direction? Another journalist may well have done it anyway? It was imponderable and largely irrelevant, he was here now and what he'd done was done, it was what he did now that mattered.

On that note he decided that on Monday morning he would ring Angela at the Green Party office and tell her that he had decided he would stand as their candidate in the forthcoming elections as they had been trying to persuade him to do. There was a real change in the air he felt, his reporter's instinct told him as much, it was almost palpable, people were fed up with the present system, the waste, the greed, the corruption. There was a growing realisation that we only had one planet and just how tiny and fragile it truly was in real terms, in terms of the cosmos and most importantly of all just how infinitely precious it was.

There was talk of a Green Alliance being formed right across the political spectrum to work together to start to tackle the problems we faced in a united fashion, sweeping away party political dogma and prejudice. In all modesty, he was a pretty well-known public figure he admitted to himself, through his work in the media and at the B.B.C., maybe this was his moment, his chance to shape the future? Stuart Wheeler M.P. or maybe even… P.M. one day?… he quite liked the sound of that… Too ambitious?

He pulled up in a queue of traffic and looked at the little Buddha and smiled, try as could and he often had, he couldn't recall exactly how he had come by it… he seemed to remember Emily giving it to him yet still he felt somehow it was something to do with his teddy bear Joey, which didn't make any sense at all, Joey… ah… Joey! He smiled as he remembered all the attributes he had imagined onto him! *He*'d always had *'high hopes'* for him hadn't he? His little alter-ego, Joey!

They were nearly back to Greg's house and the road ran alongside what had once been a grand stately house within its own grounds, it had a tall stone wall along the edge of the pavement all along the road they were now queuing-up on. As he moved a little nearer to the traffic lights, he smiled to himself as he saw the familiar red shape of the letter-box mounted in the wall, with its elaborate swirling VR set in the casting on its front. He still wasn't able to pass a letter box without looking to see who was on the throne when it was cast!

Half an hour later after he'd dropped Olly off and he was back home sat at his desk in his den, the desk from which he'd written so many of his articles, the desk that'd been given to him… along with the entire house! He leant back in his chair and looked at the two small picture frames on the beautiful Victorian mahogany mantelpiece. One was of a man in uniform standing formally, he looked a little stern, but was nevertheless a handsome fellow, it was after all a pose of its day. It was an old photograph in sepia tones which fitted perfectly with the beautifully shaped and tooled frame, which was made of old and well-polished solid silver. Alongside it stood a more modern version of the frame, it held the image of a frail old lady, with pinned-back white hair and piercing blue eyes, she was smiling out at him, it was a wonderful smile, a smile he could still see even now when he closed his eyes.

It was she who had left him the house, her home, in her Will. He'd been away at university at the time of her death and had rushed home when his dad had rung him with the sad news. Despite what his parents had told him by way of advice, he had insisted on going and seeing her body at the undertakers, to say goodbye to her… for the final time. He felt she would have wanted that for him and he felt he owed it to himself in light of the way the death of his beloved grandpa had been handled when he was eleven.

His mum and dad had gone off to Bristol for the funeral and 'to sort things out' leaving him and Lucy behind, apparently 'it was for the best' Mrs Sumner had been installed at home to look after them! They had seemed utterly insensitive to the devastating grief he had suffered on merely being told that grandpa 'was gone now!" He had also realised looking back many years later how angry and resentful he also was for their seemingly cavalier attitude. He also realised having lost his own dad by then how his mum had been too consumed with her own grief for her daddy and that she was simply incapable of imaging his own. Sadly at the same time she was also too inhibited to attempt to share it with him anyway.

Emily had looked so peacefully calm, serene and at rest. Her face actually had more colour in it than when she was alive! He smiled to himself remembering her ever so pale white skin. No doubt the undertaker had thought she'd look better that way, he'd also put a tiny stitch between her lips he noted as he craned his neck to look more closely at her face, closer than he had ever looked, he felt he was invading her space somehow, however ridiculous a notion that may have been! He couldn't shake off the feeling that she would at any second open her eyelids and those wonderful pale blue eyes would turn and look at him… and she would smile at him, one more time… He leant back and laughed, a silly self-conscious, almost embarrassed laugh.

He remembered listening to his grandma and grandpa talking one time when he was a child, 'looks like it was right grandma' he thought, noting the stitch, 'your mouth probably would drop open!' He shed a few tears as he sat quietly alongside the recumbent body, the empty husk that Emily Witherspoon had left behind, but was nevertheless glad he'd seen her, as he left he rested his hand tentatively onto hers, it was as cold as ice, he let it linger a short while allowing some of his warmth to pass into the lifeless hand of his oldest and dearest friend.

The undertaker asked him if everything had been alright for him, he thanked him and said there was one small thing he could do for him, well more for Emily really for it had been the only time in all the years he'd known her that he had ever seen her with her hair combed straight, down and flowing, it was so strange to see it like that, long and framing her face, it seemed to hint at the girl she had once been he'd thought, nevertheless he told the undertaker that he was absolutely certain that it would have been her wish to have her hair pinned back and off her face, before she was laid to rest, in the style of Queen Victoria he added for guidance. The undertaker thanked him and insisted that he wait a few minutes whilst it was attended to 'at once' he had been a very conscientious chap and ten minutes or so later he said his final goodbye to the more familiar visage of his friend, mentor and guiding light.

She had no family other than a great-nephew, it was he who after the funeral had rather tersely handed him the business card of a local solicitor, saying 'I don't know what you did to deserve this young man but the mad old bat has left almost everything to you!" He'd been utterly startled and confused, but when he'd gone with his dad to the solicitor all had been confirmed.

His dad had taken him for a drink afterwards at the pub on the corner of the street where the solicitor's offices were located, he said they both needed a stiff one! He'd said it was a wonderful gesture the old lady had made but what could they do with a house of that size? A nineteen year old student could hardly run it, even he and Mum would rattle around in it now Lucy was married and in a home of her own, plus they couldn't afford to run it anyway! There was all her furniture too… Stuart had knocked his whisky back in one and bought them another, then he'd pointed out to his bemused and somewhat flummoxed dad that she had also left him a substantial sum of money to go with the house!

Help had come in the form of the Rev. Simon Appleton who they'd also met at the funeral, it had been a surprisingly well attended service and as several other people had wanted to say something about Emily, Stuart also had stood up and spoken of how he'd come to love the old lady as if she were his own grandma. Reverend Appleton knew of an elderly couple who were his parishioners and well known to him, who had fallen on hard times, they had known Emily well and he was sure she would have approved of his idea… The old couple were indeed charming and they lived in Emily's old home until their deaths four and five years later whereupon Stuart had made it his own home and it had been ever since.

Emily's funeral had been the last time he'd seen Andy too, he had taken leave in order to attend, to be there for his friend. He had looked so smart in his Marines uniform. When the war in The Falklands came he had thought to himself how lucky he'd been when he was turned down by The RAF otherwise he'd have been at the height of his career and could have seen action there. Andy did though and was so badly scarred by it that he was never the same afterwards. He went downhill after a medical discharge and had died at the age of fifty-eight a shadow of the man he had once been. Stuart had felt terribly guilty that he had never made the time to look him up, to see how he was doing, who knows he may even had been able to help him? They'd drifted apart after Stuart passed his eleven plus and went to Worrell Grammar School, Andy failed and went to the Secondary Modern. It created a rift between them somehow as if Andy felt second best now in some way?

He'd called round to see Andy's mum when he first heard of his old school chum's demise, she'd been polite enough but had remained distant, maybe he imagined that there was an accusation in her manner? He could sense how much she had suffered watching the demise of her eldest lad. She didn't impart much information to him other than saying that he had seen and done things *'over there'* that he couldn't cope with. He had turned to drinking heavily and had drifted away from his wife and kids, he'd moved back home she'd told him, 'good job his dad was dead by then!' He'd got in with a crowd of heavy drinkers, 'bloody n'er-do-wells they were!' She'd said with venom in her voice.

Stuart hadn't been surprised really when he was turned down by The RAF, his heart had never truly been in it, all he wanted was to fly really, there'd been no training going on for civilian aircrew at the time when he was at Uni as there were so many pilots leaving the RAF after the war, so his dream of flying a Comet remained a dream. Besides what would Emily have said? He remembered he could almost feel her disapproval riding alongside him as he'd driven down south to Biggin Hill for the selection procedure!

He often put flowers on Emily's grave, on days such as his dad's birthday when he would be there at the cemetery visiting his grave… Before he'd gone back to Uni he'd gone with his dad and insisted that he let him (and indirectly let Emily) buy him a new car, it was a 'Goodwood' green Ford Zodiac mark three! It had been sat there on the forecourt of their local Ford dealership as they walked past from the pub after the solicitors that day, it had only had one owner, an elderly man who had barely used it and it was pristine!

They'd both walked around it taking it all in, father and son, each with their hands thrust deep in their pockets, sharing so many characteristics as they did of build, stature and mannerisms, they admired its American influence styled front with its four headlamps and how it was smothered in chrome plating, the sweep of the flat bonnet and the gorgeous 'supercar' fins atop the rear wings! His dad's face had been utterly priceless when his son had quietly said "let me buy it for you dad with some of Emily's money!"

His dad's little A35 had been getting decidedly tatty by then despite his best attempts to maintain it. His dad had initially point blank refused to accept such a gift and off his son as well! He said it just seemed wrong somehow? In the end though he capitulated, but only after considerable persuasion from Stuart on the way home and then from mum too!

He could still see his dad's face as the salesman handed him the keys when they'd gone to pick the car up, he'd turned to mum looking a little sheepish and asked her, 'you don't think it's a bit too flashy for us do you?" She'd just laughed, squeezed his arm and kissed him on the cheek, "it's fabulous!" was all she said!

They took her out for a spin that evening for a ride up the motorway to Forton Services and they had a meal in the elevated restaurant along with Lucy and her husband Geoff. Dad had laughed as he recalled how they had driven the stretch from Bamber Bridge to Broughton in the A35 when it first opened back in '58, 'was it in December? I remember it was after Stuart's first little brush with fame wasn't it?' Mum had confirmed his recollection, 'Stuart's little jaunt to Manchester was in the summer though I think,' then adding 'yes the Prime Minister, that lovely man Harold Macmillan opened it didn't he? That was before that awful Harold Wilson got in!'

His dad loved the big Ford and he'd travelled the length and breadth of the country in it on his holidays with mum. Stuart wished he'd kept it now… when his dad had died…

Emily had left him the little framed photo of her Henry along with her brooch and a note in a large envelope the solicitor had handed to him. The note had said for him to try and see in Henry what the real cost of war was, not in terms of the millions, but in terms of the pain for each single life that was lost. Each one lost who was a son, a brother, a father, a fiancé, a lover… a man. A man who was a person, a warm flesh and blood human being with their hopes and dreams, men who'd had their whole lives ahead of them to live out, to marry, to raise their own family… but were slaughtered and for what? Never forget him Stuart and do what you can in his memory she'd asked him and in your own small way try to help prevent anything like that ever happening again.

He rose from his desk and crossed the room, picking up the framed picture of Emily, she looked back at him through the thin glass, he touched the glass that separated them, that and nearly a half century of his life. He hoped his efforts would have met with her approval, he'd tried to use the skills and gifts he'd been given to the ends she had set out for him, the pen is mightier than the sword?

He gently placed her picture back alongside Henry's. In accordance with his dutiful interpretation of Emily's wishes, 'Henry' had always accompanied him on his many foreign assignments and had sat on his desk when he had been office based. The little photograph being almost ritually placed on the top of his clothes whenever he packed his case and it had been the first thing out at his hotels. He wasn't a particularly superstitious man, but he knew he would have felt uncomfortable without carrying out his little routine! Henry had been his companion for so long he felt as if he almost knew him!

He replaced the picture inbetween Emily's and another one that he had taken himself, he picked it up and looked at it. It was the one that he had given to Emily the last time he had seen her alive, the last time he had talked to her. She'd had her ninety-third birthday a week or so earlier and as he was home from Uni he'd popped in with a card and his gift. He had been on a hitch-hiking trip around Europe with a pal the year before he went to Uni and they had passed through Northern France. They'd had a bad couple of days, really struggling to get lifts on their way back up to The Channel and it was late on in the day when they eventually got picked up. Their lift was a chap in his late sixties and he had been most enthusiastic about them staying with him and his wife, 'no need for the camping... they could use his son's bunk beds, they were grown up now...'

The old man's wife had been equally friendly although she had at first seemed slightly bemused by the arrival of their unexpected guests! She had fed them in the evening and then again in the morning. After breakfast he had insisted on driving them north to 'a place for them that is good for the getting of a ride to Channel!' Before that though he had been even more insistent that they allowed him to take them to a war grave cemetery. They had both been a bit taken aback, why on earth would they want to visit such an awful place? It was however one of the singular most life changing events of his entire life. The old man had nodded solemnly and with a knowing satisfaction as he'd watched the boy's reaction, to him these boys were a similar age as a great many who forever lay there beneath the row after row of immaculately laid out white crosses that they now beheld in stunned silence, boys he had helped to bury maybe?

"We never forget, never!" he had said, "It is all being looked after so very well, yes?" He had asked, clearly proud that this monument to man's barbarism was even after so many years so wonderfully and lovingly maintained by his fellow countrymen.

Inspired by what he had witnessed, the following summer Stuart had travelled around northern France on his prized possession, his cherry red Triumph 5TA motorbike, he had been a man on a mission. He had carefully quizzed Emily and carried out as much research at home as he could before his trip, trying to improve his chances of success, but anyway he'd fancied making such a trip for ages. His love of motorcycling had never left him, he still felt the same thrill each time he clapped his eyes on his bike as he had done when he was a little lad back in Bristol standing soaking in every detail of grandpa's Banty! There was a pure magic to him in the sensation of flying over the tarmac on two wheels, he still felt close to his grandpa whenever he rode, as if he were riding with him. Then he could never conceive that he would ever trade his two wheels for four! In the end though despite his best efforts to fulfil his mission alone, it had needed the help of a wonderful Frenchman he had met by pure chance on his quest to achieve his aim. His daughter Yvette was lovely too…

Emily's face had lit up when she had pulled off the loose bow of ribbon and un-wrapped the picture. He'd almost had second thoughts as he'd set off to visit her with it, was it too macabre to give her a picture of the grave of her beloved Henry?

She had shed a tear, but had held his hand inbetween her gnarled, arthritic and bony cold hands and thanked him, 'God bless you my lovely boy' she'd said, 'having you in my life has been just as if I had a grandson of my own. I'm so glad you had that temper tantrum outside the tearooms when you did so very long ago!' She'd gone on to say that it was wonderful to know that Henry had been buried properly, with dignity and that there was a marker out there to show that he had lived. 'His name's listed on the monument here in our town too you know?' she'd told him. She said how she had worried in her darker moments that his mortal remains might have been simply lost, or that there may have not been enough left of him to identify… 'it was such a terrible battle he was in, wicked and terrible…'

He'd been a bit taken aback when he'd done the sums during this time and realised that Emily had been already forty-one when Henry had died and he had been in his mid-thirties! He'd somehow imagined them to be childhood sweethearts! When he'd asked her about it she had just smiled, "I waited a long time for the love of my life… and then had such a short time with him…" She'd sighed, but then just smiled as she asked him how he was getting on at University.

Emily had stayed in her house right up until her death. She had been very fortunate in having the money to employ a nurse-cum-housekeeper-cum-companion. She was able to get about around the house right up to the end, which had been sudden when it came, a stroke from which she never regained consciousness.

Stuart had never used the main bedroom of the house after he'd moved in, Emily's own bedchamber. The room she had died in. It had remained more or less as she had left it, once her clothes and personal belongings had been removed. It had only been when Yvette finally came to live with him that they had put the room back into use as their bedroom, with very little change other than a lick of paint and a new mattress on the bed.

For Yvette simply adored the unspoilt Victorian house, retaining as it did virtually all of its original features and furnishings, she would hear none of it when Stuart had weakly protested about them using 'her' room! "Nonsense!!"

She had said, "c'est une belle chambre, one to be used, your Emily she would not want it to be un mausolée…" Yvette was a forceful woman, not to be trifled with, but more particularly in this instance Stuart knew she was right. It was wonderful to hear her laughter echoing around the old house, he was sure Emily would have approved of her, especially as in a way it was due to her that he had met her.

He had so many reasons to be thankful to Emily, her and his alter-ego Joey, between them they had shaped so much of his life, had steered and influenced his course on so many occasions.

He placed the photograph of the stark white cross back onto the mantelpiece next to the ones of Emily and Henry, he wondered if they had been re-united in death after all those lonely years she had spent alone, denied his presence in her life by Mankind's seemingly infinite stupidity? It would be lovely to think so but somehow he doubted it.

He bent down flicking the control to turn on the gas fire. It was getting a bit chilly, it had been many years now since he'd burnt coal on the fire as it had been burned in Emily's time, when he had sat in here with her, in her 'snug' as it was then. He walked over to the window and took one last look out at the garden, the light was fading fast the shadows growing and deepening once more, the end of yet another day.

He drew shut the curtains and was about to return to his chair behind the desk when he heard the front door clunk shut and Yvette call out from the hall as she returned home, "Chérie? C'est moi! Où êtes-tu? His heart lifted as it always did at the sound of her voice and he set off across the room to go and greet her, as he was passing by the glass-fronted bookcase, Joey his old teddy bear caught his eye sat there on the shelf, he could have sworn he'd just winked at him, he looked closely through the glass at the battered and totally inert, stuffed toy, smiled to himself and said simply, "thanks for everything Joey!" "Who are you talking to Chérie?" Asked Yvette who was now stood in the doorway to his study, untying the scarf she had wrapped around her head. Stuart turned and beamed at her, "hi sweetie, talking to my old bear! Here in the bookcase, you know... the damnest thing, I could have sworn he just winked at me!" She raised one of her perfectly shaped eyebrows a little, as she shook her hair loose, "Maybe you 'ave been working too 'ard, or per'aps a leetle drink or two?" She wrapped her arms around his waist and hugged him, he turned his head and planted a big smacker on her lips. "You have no idea my love! The stories I could tell you that I dreamt up about what me and Joey got up to when I was a boy!" She opened the bookcase and ever so carefully lifted the old teddy down from off the shelf, "ah but he is so battered, pauvre vieux Joey! Well Chérie, maybe that's just what you should do, tell those stories?" With that she placed the bear back on his shelf and went off 'to put the kettle on,' she called back as she went "there's a letter come for you there on the 'all table Cherie."

Sat back at his desk an hour or so later Stuart opened up a new file in Word on his computer, it had been a throwaway remark from Yvette but in that moment he had decided that it was exactly what he would do, he had after all earned himself a living his entire working life as a writer, so now he would write a book... a book about his imaginary adventures with Joey when he was a boy! He sat with his hands poised over the keyboard ready to type... what about a title...? His eyes wandered about the room looking for inspiration, they fell upon the letter propped up on his desk that he'd picked up off the hall table on his way back to the study.

He picked the letter up, the postage was franked with a solicitor's stamp, he reached for his letter-opener but just as he was about to slit open the envelope he heard a tapping noise… a sharp tapping sound as of something hard tapping onto glass, he got up from his chair and went over to the window, he pulled the curtain to one side… nothing but the glass and the blackness beyond it greeted him. ***Tap-tap-tap…*** again… it was coming from somewhere inside the room, he looked around… there it was again… ***Tap-tap-tap…*** it was coming from inside the bookcase…

The End…,

A footnote from the author:

A Bear named Canadian Joey was written over a lengthy period of time, probably as long as ten years. It was begun before both 'Clive's Drive' and 'An Ordinary Joe' but not completed till after them.

Most of the chapters up to Joey's arrival in Ursa were written in that first early period, only to remain locked away in a Word document somewhere and copied along with everything else onto successive computers… with maybe an A4 printout I think… lost somewhere!

I hadn't forgotten it but had put it to one side as I'd lost my way rambling around the avenues and boulevards of Ursænia with Joey… Then years later one night whilst marinating in one of my lengthy baths (lengthy in a time-wise not dimension-wise sense) the rest of the story was revealed to me… as if a portal opened-up, or was it that a carefully constructed memory block finally collapsed? ☺

I heard Alan Bennet on the wireless the other day and he was saying in that wonderfully Yorkshire drawl of his that of course what he writes about is from his own life, where else would it come from? How his mother and father's characters, actions and sayings influenced his tales and I'd have to admit (although I hasten to add that I don't compare the merits of my writings with those of Mr.Bennet) that there are a lot of my own experiences wrapped up inbetween my imaginings in the book and tied together with the thread of my lifetime. Where fact and fiction meet, overlap and depart from each other is a moot point, a fate on reflection I fear befalls our memories themselves many times as our minds keep house over the years.

My life underwent a tectonic upheaval in the timeframe of the books lengthy gestation, from when I started it living at *The Farm,* writing smugly in my "study"... then enduring nearly losing my son... through a self-imposed two year sentence served out in a cold and neglected rented bungalow in Chorley... the deaths of both my Mum and then my best friend... then on to my new home in Blackburn... and the end of my marriage... all along the way.

They say as one door closes another one opens? I think the challenge for us is being ready to go on, to go through that new door when it opens... it can be scary to do it, courage can falter, there is familiarity and security, a feeling of safety remaining in our self-made prison cell... even if we make it to the threshold of that new door there can be hesitation... a longing glance back over the shoulder at the world we know, the familiar...

to anyone at that point I would venture to say... lift your eyes up to the sky, spread open your wings and launch yourself off the ledge....

let the wind of life buoy you up as it lifts your wings, experience the richness in the moment... be there in it... be it... it is you... you are it... you are part of everything...

and if this life is really kind to you, reach out your fingertips... and touch theirs...

Skip's website   http://gaiasguardians.webnode.com

Made in the USA
Charleston, SC
22 May 2014